The Iron Palace

A Tangled Spirits Novel

Kate Shanahan

ROAV Press

Paperback ISBN 979-8-9856291-4-9

Ebook ISBN 979-8-9856291-1-8

Cover design by Kelly Carter

*To Mary,
for leaving candy under my pillow
and telling me the fairies did it,
and for our alliance against the boys*

Contents

Recap of Tangled Spirits

The novel you are holding right now takes place two weeks after the end of *Tangled Spirits*. If you haven't read the first book yet, or need a refresher, here's a recap. Please note it contains spoilers. Skip this if you don't want to know how the first book ended.

Tsukuba, Japan, August 2019: while meditating in a power spot on a Japanese mountain with the mysterious stranger Kenji, American college student Mina is drawn into the distant past and into someone else's body.

Hitachi Province, Tsukuba Mountain, 999: desperately lonely after her mother and sister die in an epidemic, aspiring shaman Lady Masako enters the spirit world to contact them. Unable to control her powers, she leaves in a panic but pulls Mina with her.

After a struggle for control and a failed exorcism, the two spirits agree to cooperate long enough to get help from Abe no Seimei, the only person powerful enough to send Mina home.

Seimei assigns Masako to become Empress Sadako's medium. Mina occasionally steals Masako's body to spy for Seimei, and as payback, Masako gives Mina the silent treatment.

They work it out and become friends. After danger, drama, and a death at court, Mina is finally sent home where Kenji is waiting for her. He shows her a copy of a journal Masako wrote about their time together, which his family has preserved and re-copied over the centuries. This journal is called Chronicle of an Imperial Court Medium.

A Note on Pronunciation

Japanese has five vowels pronounced the same way every time. There are no true silent vowels, although the 'u' is often dropped at the end of a word. Pronunciation of each vowel is approximately as follows:

'a' as in 'ah'

'i' as in 'key'

'u' as in 'put'

'e' as in 'get.'

'o' as in 'old'

Adding a line over a vowel (yōkai, Ōe) indicates the vowel is doubled (yo-o-kai, O-o-eh) but remember, even when doubled, it's still 'o' as in old, not ooh as in food.

Japanese words are built up from syllables rather than individual letters. Ka, ki, ku, ke, and ko are the five syllables starting with the 'k' sound. The word kami is pronounced "kah-mee" not "kay-mye." Sei is pronounced "seh-ee", although when said quickly it sounds similar to the English word "say," and so Abe no Seimei sounds like "ah-beh no say-may" to an English-language listener. Suetake is Su-eh-tah-keh. Obake is oh-bah-keh.

If you say each syllable rather than each letter, you will get the hang of it.

I break apart a few words to make it easier for non-Japanese readers to recognize the syllables. For example mono-no-ke instead of mononoke (a classification of negative spirits) or tsuki-mono (any kind of possessing spirits) instead of tsukimono.

Some terms don't have a good English equivalent, so I use the Japanese word instead of an English version, like kami (divine spirits), oni (an ogre-like demon), and other terms for supernatural beings like yōkai and obake (oh-bah-keh.) These words can be singular or plural. So it's one kami, two kami, one oni, two oni, no matter what my spell-checker tries to tell me.

It's customary to italicize non-English words unless the term has become common in English (examples of those would be terms like saké, sushi, and tsunami.) I italicize Japanese words for the first use only, and not at all for titles or place, era, and personal names.

I use the accent in saké to distinguish it from the English word sake.

A glossary is included at the end.

Chapter 1

Sometimes A Shadow Is A Spirit

I pressed my palms tightly together in prayer position and bowed my head. *Please let me be a normal American college student living in Japan.* Which meant hours of studying, an occasional treat of sushi for dinner, and a glass of draft beer when I could afford it. Was that too much to ask?

"Mina, wait!" Kenji gestured to the shrine's purification station. "We haven't rinsed our hands yet."

"Just getting a head start," I said. "I need a *lot* of help."

Kenji didn't laugh, probably because he knew a choconilla twist of hope and dread swirled in my gut at what we'd find here. After all, it was his suggestion we use the Obon holiday to come to Kyoto.

Over the past two weeks I'd searched online for proof that my best friend had ever existed, but found zero hits about a Kamo shrine shaman named Masako. Well, not *my* Masako, anyway. I rummaged through academic research, hoping some professor somewhere had done a deep dive into early eleventh century shrine *miko*. I read everything I could find on the famous diviner Abe no Seimei hoping to find a reference to his only female student. I even went to the tenth page of search results where no one *ever* goes. Even Japanese search terms yielded no relevant results.

So I absolutely had to find Masako's original Chronicle. Kenji's version was dated Chōgen Year 4, the Western year 1031, but it was a copy. Anyone could have written that date on the original. If I could see the date in Masako's handwriting, I'd know she'd lived thirty more years after we were ripped apart. Knowing she'd survived—and thrived—after I left might ease the pain of being torn from the one close friend I'd made since middle school, not to mention the only person I'd ever shared a body with.

Which was why I stared down a long stretch of shadeless gravel on a ridiculously hot and windy day.

The first *torii* gate of the Kamigamo Shrine towered above us to mark our entrance onto sacred ground. White banners lined the path ahead, fluttering prayers with each gust.

"So, where do we start?" I asked. "This place is huge."

"Well," Kenji replied as we walked to the water basin to rinse our hands and mouths. "Masako probably wouldn't have hidden it in the main building. Too many people, even then. I thought we'd start with a small shrine in the forest. It's thought to be haunted, which means fewer people go there."

We walked to the large building where the deity of thunder was enshrined. We prayed to him for success before threading our way through the trees scattered along the path.

"Kenji?"

"Yes?" He was smiling, but not at me. More like he wasn't aware he was doing it, just a gentle curve to his mouth as if the green canopy of the forest, its fragrance of pine and cedar, satisfied his soul.

"How would a book be preserved over centuries? Wouldn't paper disintegrate? It would have to be encased in something waterproof, but technology like that didn't exist then."

"A thousand years is a long time." He hesitated, looking through the trees as if collecting his thoughts. "Traditional Japanese *washi* paper lasts longer than Western paper. There's a book at a temple in Nara from the eighth century. Or perhaps Masako used magic to preserve it."

"She didn't have—" A red flicker interrupted me. I rubbed my eyes in a vain attempt to make the annoying vision disappear.

Bad idea. My eyes burned with mingled sunscreen and sweat. I blinked rapidly, creating tears to wash it out.

"Mina, what's going on?" Kenji sounded a little worried as he handed me a tissue.

"Thanks." I dabbed carefully at the corners of my eyes. "Um, it's just…uh, I'm tired from getting up early to catch the train from Tsukuba." I began to walk again, faster this time. "Anyway, Masako didn't have magic. At least, not the type in fantasy novels. The power of a miko or *onmyōji* came from summoning spirits. Spiritual energy, you might say."

"You don't know what she did after you left. She might have gained new skills. Mina, wait!" Kenji's voice came from a few paces back.

I paused while he caught up.

"I want to ask you something," he said, his dark eyes on mine, earnest and intense.

It was a look I'd seen a few times over the past two weeks, and I never knew how to react. Other than what I couldn't control, of course, like my pulse speeding up.

"You've done that thing a few times now. Turning suddenly like you're looking for something. Muttering to yourself."

He was right, and it wasn't only the weird visions that bothered me. I forgot stuff too, like basic Japanese words I'd learned years ago. Last week I got on the wrong bus and was halfway to Tokyo before I realized what I'd done. And dreaming about

Masako every night. *Help me, Mi-Na,* she'd cry. I'd reach out to save her, but our hands wouldn't quite touch, and she'd slip away. Or we'd be in a car and the brakes would fail. We'd plunge into the river, water closing over our heads as we gasped and choked for air.

I'd hoped Kenji wouldn't notice, but I should have known better. "Are you keeping an eye on me?" I asked with mock indignation.

He didn't laugh. "After what you've been through, how could I not?"

My smile wavered as I struggled to hold tears back. No one else—other than my parents, of course—had ever treated me with such concern. "I keep seeing a red.. well, like a small animal. Like a fox. It's happened a lot in the past two weeks, both in Tsukuba and here." I waved dismissively. "It's just a side effect of *jisa-boke.*"

"Jet lag?" Now his tone was amused. "It's been months since you arrived in Japan, and the train this morning wasn't *that* fast."

"That's the English phrase. As you know, jisa means time difference, and boke means foolishness or dementia. No jets involved. And a thousand years is a whole lot of time change."

"Are you saying time travel made you senile?"

"You laugh, but it's a good description of my life over the past two weeks."

"So, let's see…You see a fox, but you think it's your imagination, so it must be due to jet lag?"

His skeptical tone surprised me. What did *he* think it was? A mental health problem? Well, maybe it was. I'd been through a lot in the last two weeks.

"I have a theory," he said.

"About what? Time travel?"

"Related to that, yes. You saw shape-shifter spirits like *obake* when you were in the past. Perhaps that skill came back with you. You might be seeing a spirit."

That would definitely *not* meet my goal to be normal. "Very funny."

"I'm serious."

A sudden chill raised goosebumps on my arms despite the hot day. "Nope. No way. I don't need to be any weirder than I already am."

"People think you're strange anyway because you keep doing that head-shaking thing. Let me help you."

What could he possibly do? Why did he even care?

Maybe his interest came from a deep sense of responsibility. After all, his ancestors had preserved a copy of Masako's Chronicle for over a thousand years.

Or maybe he liked me. Although if that was the case, he was certainly taking his time to say so.

To be fair, I hadn't made a move on him, either. After spending over a year trapped in another person's body, I didn't want to fall into my old habit of jumping into a relationship too quickly. "You *are* helping me. Finding the original Chronicle will solve all my problems." To forestall further discussion, I pulled a bandana out of my pocket and began dabbing my cheeks and forehead. "You'd think the wind would cool us off, but it doesn't seem to make a difference."

Kenji's half-smile told me he wasn't giving up on his theory, but was willing to postpone it for now.

He gestured to the vermilion gates straddling the trail as it wound uphill. "Those torii lead to the haunted shrine."

An ancient stone marker and a modern white plastic sign marked the start of the path. I examined the marker. "*Futa* is two of something. This *kanji* looks like "*ba*." Isn't *ba* how you count flat things?"

"Yes, very good."

"So this place is called Two Flat Things?"

His mouth twitched in a suppressed smile. *"Futa. Ba."* He enunciated clearly while pointing to each character. *"Hi, me. Hime* means princess."

"So it's called Two Flat Princesses?"

Kenji laughed. "No one knows for sure what it means, although I read that Futaba was a dragon *kami* whose soul is imprisoned here, and that's why it's considered haunted."

He pointed to the next character.

I knew that one. "Inari! The deity of rice and agriculture."

"Yes, and you'll see some fox statues along the way. If you hunt for them, that is. Some are tiny."

"Cool, I love those!" Foxes were Inari's messengers so shrines to Inari often had such statues. Some looked mysterious, some dignified, and some had a mischievous glint in their stone eyes, but all of them had personality.

We walked under the series of torii spaced at equal intervals as the path continued uphill.

It didn't take long to reach the shrine, which nestled comfortably into the hill like an organic part of the surrounding forest. As long as I didn't look to the right where houses were built up to the hillside, I could almost believe I was in a remote area.

The shrine was open on the sides, and wooden struts supported a tin-covered roof. "Hey, Mr. Religion Major, why's the shrine open to the elements?"

"It reflects the original intention of a shrine," Kenji said. "Way back in time, shrines weren't buildings. They were sacred spaces in nature. Buddhism brought temples to Japan, so shrines had to compete by adopting enclosed worship spaces."

"I like this open style better than the Buddhism-infused kind. There's something about temples I don't like, but I don't know what. Maybe they remind me too much of going to mass as a kid."

A green light filtered through lush undergrowth on the hill above the shrine. Tree roots grabbed the hillside where erosion had worn away the ground cover. A wall made of piled rocks looked like one good earthquake would bring it rumbling down the mountain and rolling into the houses below. Stones on the ground appeared to have broken free of the wall, but others were placed here and there as if on purpose.

I stepped under the tin roof and lifted my head to see steep stone steps leading to an altar pressed into the hillside. A faint vibration hummed from the earth, up through my feet and raising the hair on my arms. A sudden, brilliant flash illuminated the figure of a fox sitting on a stone step while thunder rolled in the distance.

I peered upward, blinking with confusion. "I thought I saw a statue, but it must have been a shadow caused by that lightning. Weird."

"Mina, how often has something like that happened to you since you returned to 2019?"

My throat was suddenly dry. I needed to stop telling Kenji about these incidents. "Sometimes a shadow is just a shadow."

He folded his arms. "Sometimes a shadow is a spirit."

"Hey, *I'm* the one who traveled through the spirit world. I think I know the difference. Anyway, why is it so important to you?"

He gave me that look again, the one that made my skin tingle. Did he want to kiss me? Was he waiting for me to kiss him first? We'd spent a lot of time together in the two weeks since I got back. Evenings at the library, coffee shops on the weekends, and the three-hour train ride from Tsukuba to Kyoto. He'd told me about his childhood in Tsukuba, his middle and high school years in Ohio, and the pressure from his grandfather to read and copy Masako's Chronicle, but he never said anything about a girlfriend.

I should just be blunt. *Do you have someone special?*

That wasn't dorky, no, not at all.

"Because, Mina," he said, reaching for my hand, which I was reluctant to give him because it was clammy. But I didn't want to pull away, so I let him hold it. "If you can see spirits, it gives me hope."

"So you're saying if my visions turn out to be shadows and floaters, you'll be hopeless?" I laughed so he'd know I was being flippant.

He nodded with a small smile as if he knew I was trying to hide my discomfort. Another beautiful thing about Kenji: he never judged me.

"Hope that the kami haven't abandoned us," he said. "Human interference with nature, like cell phone towers, radio frequencies, mining, emissions, and industrial pollution like mercury have polluted the kami's pure spaces. This pollution makes the kami uncomfortable so they don't visit us much anymore, if at all."

He might not think I was insane, but I was starting to think he might be. He didn't look crazy, but what did crazy even look like?

He glanced at me sideways. "No rain, no clouds, and yet we had thunder and lightning. These strange things only happen when I'm with you, Mina."

"Lightning can travel from miles away," I said. "It's not *that* strange. Can I have some water?"

He shrugged off his backpack, rummaged through it, and handed me my water bottle.

I'd left my bag, heavy with everything I'd need for a week in Kyoto, in a locker at the station. He'd emptied his pack into the locker to create room for water, mosquito repellent, and sunscreen. He probably had snacks tucked away in it too. He'd pulled out breakfast *onigiri* for us to eat on the train. Like Mary

Poppins, he carried an endless supply of stuff I didn't know I needed until I did.

But no amount of water could take away the ache in my throat. I did my best anyway, nearly draining it. "Here," I said, giving it back to him. "I lightened your load."

Having seen everything in the small space under the roof, we walked toward the wall behind the shrine. Wind gusts bent bamboo stalks and sent paper lanterns swaying, but the sky remained clear.

A blur at the edge of my vision distracted me, so of course my foot hit a rock. "Fu-" I bit my lip. I didn't want to swear in front of a religion major. "Futaba!"

I rotated my foot to make sure I hadn't sprained anything. "It's fine," I replied to Kenji's concerned expression.

I took a tentative step forward but was startled by movement flickering through the green bushes. "There," I whispered. "Look."

He tilted his head, confused.

Stepping up to the wall, I gestured for him to follow. I tilted my chin toward the fox crouched in the dark gap on the other side of the wall, its pointed ears on high alert, ready for flight.

Holding my breath, I risked a glance at Kenji. His puzzled expression told me he didn't see it, but how could he not?

Its bushy orange tail brushed the stone several times as if wiping dust from it, then it bounded up the hill and disappeared.

Suddenly dizzy, I leaned on the wall. "It's gone. This sounds weird, but I think it waited for me. You didn't see it at all? It was sitting right—" I jabbed a finger downward. "There."

"I was looking at that spot and saw nothing." Kenji's voice rose with excitement. "Show me exactly what it did."

The fox's bright orange-red coloring had glowed in the dark

space below us, way too real to be my imagination. "Um, okay. It turned around, and its tail touched the wall."

"It accidentally touched the stone?" He leaned over to examine the area.

"Well, it seemed more like it was on purpose. It brushed the same place three or four times."

"It might be telling you something. Let's search there."

I wanted to tell him that was silly because foxes don't do such things. But I didn't, because, well, what if he was right? "I'm climbing over," I declared. "But it's tight. Not enough room for two."

"Okay, I'll see what I can do here." He crouched down, running his hands over the stones, singing a little tune in Japanese.

Climbing onto the top, I tentatively dangled my feet down the other side. It was only a foot or so to touch the hill on the other side, so I slid down and into the weeds. Pushing aside sasa grass, I sat on the hill with my feet pressed against the wall so I wouldn't slide into it. Following Kenji's actions, minus the song, I leaned forward awkwardly and moved my hands over the stones where the fox's tail had swished. "I feel a little silly, to be honest." One stone jutted out a little. "Oh! This one's loose!" I worked it up and down, then side to side. "But the gaps are filled with moss and dirt. Do you have a pocket knife?"

Of course he did. He flicked it open with a flourish and handed it to me.

"Thanks." The two-inch blade would have to do—anything longer was illegal here.

With a little pressure, it slid between the loose rock and the ones around it. Scraping out the dirt was more challenging, but became easier after I cleared a centimeter or two, giving the knife more room to work.

Even so, the stone barely moved. Kenji watched me through

several rounds of scrape, wiggle, scrape, wipe forehead, scrape, wiggle, scrape.

But I was driven now. The kami had sent a *real* fox to show me where to look. Not a spirit. A living, breathing, tail-waving messenger. Maybe Kenji hadn't seen it because *he* had a vision problem.

"Ha!" I drew the stone block out, set it down by my feet, and peered into the dark hole created by the stone's departure. "I'm going to shine a light in, because, you know. Spiders."

My phone's flashlight lit the space well enough to see an object. "No spiders, but something's in there. A box of some kind." I pulled my hand back. Spots danced across my eyes from heat, excitement, and possibly dehydration. "Hold on, I need a minute."

"What is it? Can I help you?"

"No, two people can't fit here. If I can't get it out, we'll switch places."

After a few calming breaths, I tried again. The rough texture of the box grated my palm while the stone above chafed my knuckles. The space was too tight to allow my fingers to curve around the back end, and tugging on the sides didn't do much. I tried to remove the stone above to create more room to work in, but it didn't budge. "This is a well-made ruin," I muttered.

"Are you sure there's nothing I can do?" Kenji asked, unusually impatient.

I grunted a negative, and put my hand back into the hole, alternating tugging the object and wiggling it.

At last the box shifted, and after a few more rounds of tug and wiggle, it moved forward slightly, came free of the hole, and fell into my hands.

It was unexpectedly heavy, though, and I dropped it. Fortunately, it missed my feet, landing on the ground with a thump and a crack.

Lifting it cautiously, I set it on top of the wall. We bent to look at it from opposite sides and knocked heads. We rubbed our foreheads, chuckling while apologizing.

He bowed. "Please, you first. It's your quest."

It was a stone container, gray with lichen. The lid had cracked loose when it fell, allowing me to push it off. Inside was a green metal box a little smaller than a college notebook. I turned it around, seeking a way to get the cover off, but it appeared to be tightly sealed, without a keyhole or latch. "How are we going to open it?"

Kenji's eyes shone. "May I?" He examined it. "This is very old."

My hands itched to take it back, but I resisted the urge. This wasn't my country, much less my property.

Kenji inserted his pocket knife into the thin, dirty gap between the lid and the box, his hand shaking. The knife slipped. He paused, closed his eyes, and took a deep breath, a calming technique I'd seen Masako use many times. Why was *he* so excited? This mission was all about me. Wasn't it?

He slipped the knife into the crack and twisted gently. The lid creaked over, revealing a sheaf of aged paper inside.

"What is it?" My pulse hammered in my ears. "Is it the Chronicle?"

He bent over as he studied the top sheet, blocking my view. "Ah…" He nodded slightly and moved aside so I could see it.

Even though the ink had faded, the calligraphy was beautiful. Masako's brushwork was never that good, even on her best day.

"That's not… um…" I swallowed hard, trying to get past a huge lump of disappointment in my throat. "It's not her handwriting. Can you read it?"

He wiped sweat from his palms with a tissue before carefully lifting a page from the container. He held it gently with both hands as he read it. The wind had calmed for now, fortunately, because the strong gusts earlier would have torn the fragile paper.

His eyes went from the page to my face and back to the page.

"Well, what does it say?"

"It's, well—it's unbelievable."

I couldn't breathe. "Damn it, Kenji, just tell me!"

"The first line begins—" He lifted his head, his eyes bright with wonder. "To Spirit Mi-Na."

Chapter 2

Connected Across Worlds

My mouth moved, but no sound emerged. I extended a shaking hand.

Kenji didn't give it to me. "It's fragile. It might crumble. And it's in classical Japanese."

"How about you read it to me in English? No, wait! How many pages are there?"

He examined the stack of paper without touching it. "Thirty? More? We shouldn't be handling this without gloves. Our hands are dirty from digging out the box."

I drummed the top of the wall with my fists. "Read it to me now! Please? At least the first page. Come on, you know you want to." My tone was somewhere between wheedling and demanding. "Is it from Masako? Do you think it's a thousand years old? It's not her handwriting, so it must be a copy. But still —it's an old copy. How long do you think it was hidden?"

Kenji let me babble on without responding, his eyes opaque.

"Kenji?" I waved my hand. "Hey, I'm right here, remember?"

He inhaled sharply as if he'd forgotten to breathe. "I'll read this page to you now, and translate the other sheets later. But let's purify our hands first."

Kenji returned the ancient paper to the box and carried it to the ablution basin where we washed our hands in the Shinto method—left hand first, then right hand, then mouth—before sitting on a stone bench under the shrine roof.

After we sat down, he carefully picked up the top sheet, letting it rest on his fingers rather than grasping it, keeping his back to the breeze. "This is a cover page. It says 'To Spirit Mi-Na, from the Kamo Shrine Miko.' Well, it's more formal, but that's what it means." He set it on the inside of the metal lid and took another sheet out using the same careful method. "This one looks like an actual letter."

My heart climbed into my throat.

"It's dated Chōhō 4, the first day of Eighth Month. Eh, Chōhō 4 is—"

"I know!" I jumped in, excited to be able to contribute. "I left in the first month of Chōhō 3, which was 1001. Chōhō 4, Eighth Month, would be a year and a half after that, September or October of 1002."

"Right," he said. "I'll look up the exact date in my chronological table later, but for now we'll say September, 1002. It starts with your name. "Spirit Mi-Na, if you find these letters—" He glanced at me. "Keep in mind I'm reading old Japanese script and translating it into spoken English. I'll need to go slowly, and I might stumble. It'll be better if I take the time to write a translation. Are you sure you don't want to wait?"

As if. "Just the first one, then. Please? And thank you."

He gave me an understanding smile. "I'll do my best."

He took a second to review it before reading it out loud.

"Spirit Mi-Na," he began. "If you find these letters in your world, a thousand years will have passed since I wrote them. It has been more than one year here, and the pain of our separation still haunts me. Not only the agony of your spirit tearing away from mine, but the ache from the loss of my constant companion.

As I watched you depart, I wanted to plead for you to stay, but I kept silent, knowing you must return to your home. Loneliness has consumed me ever since, an emptiness filled only by writing to you. And Mi-Na, this act of writing creates a brazier inside me, a heat and light that flows out of me and into the spirit world. I do not know whether you will ever find these letters, but the spiritual energy generated by writing to you gives me hope the kami connect us across worlds."

Kenji had read slowly, sometimes examining a phrase silently before giving me the translation. I understood why, but I had to restrain myself from urging him to go faster. My friend had written to me—to me!—across millennia. Not a few decades. Not a few hundred years. A thousand-plus years ago, yet here we were, linked by the act of pulling brush against paper.

"When you first possessed me, your intrusiveness and strange ways were disturbing." Kenji paused and glanced at me as if concerned I'd be offended.

I wasn't. My throat ached from withheld tears, but the letter was *so* Masako, I just had to smile. "It's true. I was rude to her. It was quite a culture clash."

"I understand," he said. "I had culture shock when I went to America." He went back to his translating. "But your humor and energy gave me a new dream and a new life. After my mother and sister died, darkness consumed me, but you brought such odd new ideas, such ridiculous stories and visions of your world, life became more interesting. Lord Seimei explained that I had too much yin and Spirit Mi-Na had excess yang. Seimei said this balance between your yang and my yin opened me to powers I never could have gained alone."

Kenji stopped to take a drink of water before continuing.

"Since you left, however, I have not once succeeded in summoning a deity to speak through me. The High Priestess is patient, but I heard her say she needs a proper miko, one who can call the great kami. She said I may have to leave the shrine. Perhaps I need your excessive yang, or perhaps I was only a vessel for your power, and now that you have left, my power has too."

A sob escaped me.

"Is it too much, too soon?" Kenji moved as if to set the page down.

"Don't stop, please." I put my face in my hands, taking a minute to assess my complicated emotions. "It's just—" I lifted my head and gripped the edge of the bench. "I thought she'd be relieved to be rid of me. I learned so much from her, and I'll be better off because of it. But Masako-" I brushed away the tears on my cheeks. "What if she was worse off because of me?"

He raised a quizzical eyebrow. "But she just said you were responsible for her powers, *ne?*"

"But if I'd never possessed her and made her go to the Capital and then left her all alone, she wouldn't be going through this despair."

"She—" He paused as if thinking better of whatever he planned to say. "We can finish this later if you want."

"I need to learn what happened to her, so please go on."

He rested his hand on mine for a comforting second before getting back to reading. "Mi-Na, what became of you when you returned to your world? Did you retain your ability to see spirits? Also, what do others think of your adventure? Have you told your beloved mother? How I envy you, that you have a mother to tell."

"Great, a new reason to feel bad," I said bitterly.

"Not telling your parents about your adventure into the past is understandable," Kenji said. "Spirit possession isn't as accepted in modern-day America as it was in Heian Japan." He carefully set the fragile sheet of paper on top of the others in the box. "That's all that's written on this page. Mina, from what

Masako says here, it sounds like you saw spirits in the past. Excuse me for asking this again, but it's important. Did you bring that ability back with you?"

"No!" My gut reaction startled me. "Sorry. No. At least, I don't think so. Anyway, no one in our world sees obake, so I'd be a freak if I did. Will you read the next page? Please?"

"My voice is hoarse. Let's take this back to my friend's townhouse, and I'll translate the rest tonight. Let's put the stone box back in the wall for now." He began rearranging his backpack. "The metal container will fit in here. I'll translate as much as I can every day, and you can read what I've done every night, or vice versa, depending on what else we do this week."

My muscles tensed with a strange reluctance to let him do that. "Thanks, but *I* want to carry it." I stretched my hand out for it even while wondering why. I trusted Kenji. He'd only ever been kind to me, even giving up his holiday to bring me here.

But one thing had been niggling at the back of my mind since I returned to 2019. "Kenji?" My voice quavered a little.

"Believe me, it will be safer in the backpack." Kenji smiled reassuringly as he set the metal container inside.

I shook my head. "Um, not what I meant. Masako's Chronicle ended with me leaving her. She didn't know—she *couldn't* know—that I returned safely. So even though you knew I'd get there and when I would leave Masako, you had no idea whether I'd return to my body, because it was in the future. The Chronicle mentioned how much danger we were in at times, and how our spirits nearly fused. So why did you put me in that situation when you didn't know if I'd make it safely back here?"

Kenji gazed down as he slowly zipped his pack shut. "At the time," he said thoughtfully, "I only knew your name was Mi-Na, and that you had pale skin and hair. Masako wrote that you showed her a vision of what you looked like. She described your appearance as a hungry ghost with white, stringy hair that was too short."

I touched my dirty-blond ponytail defensively. "Too short for a Heian woman, maybe. Long for Gen Z."

He pulled his hair so it stretched past his shoulder. "I'm Gen Z and my hair's longer than yours."

"Gen Z *woman*," I said. "I didn't mean to sidetrack you from rationalizing. You were saying?"

"Well, Masako said you came from a place with different customs and a different language, which made me a little angry. I mean, I'm *Japanese*. I study Shinto. I pray to the kami. I meditated in that spot many times, but the kami never sent *me* across time. My resentment might have made me a little callous."

"You were envious of me before we met?" I didn't try to hide my surprise. "Bet you aren't envious anymore, knowing what I've been through and how it's affected me."

"I know you better now. You're loyal and sensitive, though you try to hide it. And you look nothing like a hungry ghost. You're much prettier."

"Thanks, but prettier than a ghost isn't a high bar."

He didn't laugh with me, instead setting a hand on mine. "You're beautiful."

When other guys said that, I assumed they were being manipulative. When Kenji said it, it felt like he meant it, so I suppressed my urge to respond with a flippant denial.

"My grandfather taught me to take the Chronicle seriously," he said. "My father thinks the Chronicle is fake. My parents never read it, but when they named me Kenji, my grandfather realized I might be the Ken-Ji mentioned in the Chronicle. He told me all about it before my parents moved us to Ohio for my dad's job. I didn't want to be the person to meet Spirit Mi-Na and initiate her journey into the past. I wanted to study at an American university and live a life *not* predetermined by events of a thousand years ago. I argued with my grandfather about it, but he said I had to consider the ramifications. If I refused to send Mi-Na to the past, what would happen to Masako? Would she have been forced to marry and have children? What benefit did Masako bring to the world because of the power you brought to her? He made me promise to read and copy the book. That's how I knew I'd be your spiritual guide someday."

The roiling in my mind calmed a little. Kenji had a heavy burden placed on him by a journal written a thousand years ago. "Well, it's not like you forced me to go. You guided me through a meditation that, at the most, should have resulted in a calm trance, yet somehow it sent me across the border to the spirit world. I guess that wasn't your fault."

"I have other reasons too," he said. "I'll explain later. It's hot, and we still need to get our things from the station and get to my friend's house." He stood and stretched, which made me realize we'd been sitting on a hard stone bench for some time. "Also, I'll have a late night. I'll be busy translating these letters into English for you." He put his hands at his sides and bowed formally. "Mina-*san*. Please forgive me for the trouble I caused you when I brought you to meditate on Mount Tsukuba."

I stood up and bowed back. "I'm sorry you had to deal with this knowledge your whole life."

He was so sincere, so earnest. I believed him.

But what *were* his other reasons?

Chapter 3

Without You, I Am Nothing

That evening I was too excited to eat much of my favorite convenience-store meal of yakitori from Lawson's. My constant speculation about the letters drove Kenji to finish his dinner quickly and go to his room to translate the next page.

I used the time to re-read Kenji's copy of Masako's Chronicle. He'd copied it from the copy his grandfather had made in the late forties. Each generation updated the language, so it was modern Japanese, which I'd been studying since high school, but calligraphy was harder to read than print. Kenji had helped me over the past two weeks, but without his help I read very slowly.

My phone lay face-down on my desk so I wouldn't be distracted by notifications from my socials, but it called to me.

Minaaa... pick me up. You know you want to. I can translate anything.

No. I needed to practice reading Japanese script.

Still, it might be worth a try.

But that would be cheating.

It'd be faster. Wouldn't you learn more if you read faster?

I shouldn't descend that particular slippery slope.

Slope to what?

The death of my dream of becoming a Japanese literature scholar.

Grabbing the phone before I could change my mind, I stuffed it under my futon. *Get thee behind me, smartphone!*

My eyelids drooped as I grappled with a few more sentences, so I finally set the journal down, put my pajamas on, and slid under my lightweight comforter.

But now that I wasn't struggling to read Japanese, images and memories of the day flashed through my mind one after the other in a rapid-fire progression. The fox brushed its tail against the wall at the exact spot where the box was hidden. That couldn't be a coincidence. *Was* it obake? Was that why Kenji couldn't see it? He couldn't see spirits, and I could? He seemed to think the ability to see obake would be useful, but why? The flashes and blurs irritated me. What if he was right, and they got worse, not better? What if they never went away, even with meds or therapy? At a minimum, people would think I was crazy, even if I knew—and Kenji knew—I was perfectly sane.

I started a "sleep" playlist on my phone, set it at low volume, and made myself empty my mind, a little trick I learned from Masako and her constant meditation.

Wait! Since I didn't have access to her brain anymore, I assumed I wouldn't be able to read classical Japanese. But I remembered things like how to meditate and read hexagrams. If I could read the letters myself, I wouldn't have to wait for Kenji to translate them. And they were *mine,* written to me and hidden for a thousand years. A fox showed me where they were. Not Kenji. *Me.*

A startlingly clear vision of Masako came into my head. Kneeling at her table, sleeves tied back to keep them out of the ink, biting her lip as she thought about what to write.

She missed me as much as I missed her.

"Good night, Masako," I whispered as I drifted into sleep.

A dreamless sleep for a change, because it seemed like only a few minutes later when I woke to the smell of coffee. I checked my phone. *Look at me, sleeping until 10!*

I hadn't woken up at four a.m. with anxiety-related insomnia since I returned from the past. Who knew the cure for anxiety was spending a year in someone else's body? Maybe I should write a self-help book.

Of course, I'd have to list possible side effects. *Spirit possession may cause strange dreams, vertigo, hallucinations, and forgetfulness.*

Kenji sat cross-legged at the table in the living room, reading over what I presumed to be his translation of the letter. "*Ossu*," he said.

"*Ossu*," I replied.

He looked up. "Ossu is kind of a guy's word."

"What's so masculine about asking what's up?" I put my hands on my hips. "I've heard young women use it."

"Just wasn't sure if you knew." He smiled as he dove back into his work.

After preparing a mug of creamy coffee, I sat on a cushion across from him. "This *machiya* feels like the real deal. The *tatami* mat floors, the steep stairs, the garden in the tiny courtyard. How old do you think it is?" Kenji's friend owned this town-house and rented it out, not only to tourists but also to visiting shrine and temple priests. He allowed Kenji to stay here for free when in town.

"From the early 1900's," he replied. "Hiro told me geisha learned to play the shamisen here in the old days."

I took a long sip of coffee, closing my eyes to savor it. Dark roast, very strong. Perfect. The best coffee ever.

When I opened my eyes, Kenji's head was tilted as if puzzling out what I was doing. "Something I got from Masako," I said. "Living in the moment. Thank you for making the coffee. What time did you wake up? It tastes fresh."

"I worked on translation until 3 or 4 this morning, so I got up right before you did."

"Thank you so much for doing that. By the way, it occurred to me I might remember how to read classical Japanese from my time with Masako. Can you hand me the next letter?"

"The paper will crumble if we pass it back and forth. It's better to handle it as little as possible. I'll copy some of it for you to look at."

"I want to read the original."

He sighed while setting his cup on the table. "The *Chronicle* made it clear you and Masako became close, so I know how much this means to you. Trust me on this."

Was he hoarding the letters? Hoping to make a killing in the ancient scroll black market? I looked deep into my mug. Swirls of creamy iridescence floated on the surface, giving depth to the rich brown liquid despite its opacity. Totally Instagrammable. Which gave me an idea.

"Hey, I know! I'll take a picture of each page to read on my phone."

"You know what I believe about cell phones, Mina."

"You said don't use them in sacred places." I made a show of looking around the room, at the ceiling, and over at the kitchen. "I doubt this house qualifies."

He laughed. "You win."

He spread a cotton cloth on the table, lifted a sheet from the metal box with great care, and set it on the fabric. "Try not to touch the paper."

My hands vibrated with anticipation as I leaned on the table, pressing a hand on either side of the cloth for balance as I examined the dull brown paper. The brushwork was legible. My first impression—this wasn't Masako's handwriting—was correct. Someone else wrote this. I made out a few words, but nothing more.

I sat back on my heels. "Well, it looks like I didn't bring that skill back," I said. "*Now* do you believe I don't see obake anymore?"

"Reading is a brain skill. Seeing spirits is a spiritual skill. Not having one doesn't rule out the other."

I dug my phone out of my back pocket and tapped the camera icon. "We might as well get a photo of it. We should take one of every page, right? In case the paper does crumble away."

"Good idea. My phone's usually off so I don't think of taking photos for such practical reasons."

"Kenji, you're an analog dude living in a digital world. Where did you come from? Not modern society, that's for sure."

"I'm postmodern," he said. "You'll get there eventually. Everyone will."

"I can't wait!" I said with fake enthusiasm. "Um, no. I can definitely wait. I have a *lot* of phone-using to do first."

Kenji patted his pockets with mock confusion, then lifted the cushion he'd been sitting on. "Where's my phone?" He looked under the sheaf of papers on the table next, then peered into my coffee mug, making me laugh. "Is it in there?" He sat back and put his hands on his head. "Wah! I can't remember where I put it! Well, I'll find it later." He pushed his latest worksheets over to me. "Here. My translation from last night. Poor Masako. I need to work on the next letter, so I have a suggestion that will feed two birds with one scone."

I smiled at his variation on the usual bird-murdering proverb, and then his other words hit me. "Wait, what? *Poor Masako*? What happened to her?"

"You'll understand when you read it. After you finish it, why don't you go for a walk while I work on the next one? If any of those red flickers appear, stop and concentrate. Try to spot the fox spirit." Kenji carefully put the letter back in the box.

He obviously cared a lot about Masako and what was

happening to her. He also seemed eager to confirm I could see spirits. Why did he care whether I could or not? He told me he liked me. He understood me better than anyone else in this century. But did he care for me *because* of his other interests?

It didn't matter. We were in this together whether he liked me for myself, for my spirit-seeing skills, or for the information I had about the past.

After one last sip of coffee, I picked up the translation and headed up the stairs.

I sat cross-legged on my futon, willing my hands to stop shaking as they held the sheets of paper, half-dreading the emotions the letter might stir. Would reading it bring closure or open a new source of anxiety for me?

Masako was my best friend. More than that, she was my platonic soulmate. She wrote to me across millennia, ensuring these letters would be re-copied over the years, somehow keeping them from being burned in a fire, destroyed in an earthquake, or soaked by rain. The magnitude of her achievement made me dizzy. The words on the page shifted back and forth, converging and diverging.

Her voice rang in my head. *Focus, Mi-Na.*

Taking a deep breath, I closed my eyes and exhaled to a count of six.

When I opened them, I could read.

Eighth Month, Chōhō 4, Kamigamo Shrine

Mi-Na, I have something shocking to tell you. Seimei's rival, the famous diviner Ashiya, asked me to be his student. He sent me a letter, telling me he heard intriguing rumors about my powers. "Seimei is old," he wrote. "Too weak to teach you true *onmyōdō.*"

You may remember the talk about Ashiya among the ladies at court. His powers are nearly as strong as Seimei's. Rumors say it is Ashiya to whom Empress Sadako's brother turned when he wanted to curse the Regent. Lord Korechika knew Lord Seimei would never do such a thing, but Ashiya had no such principles.

Of course, I refused Ashiya's offer. Even if my powers had not disappeared, I would never study with a teacher willing to twist onmyōdō into something evil.

Another shocking event, Mi-Na, and only the second of three I will tell you today. Two months ago our region survived a raging storm. The howling wind tore roofs from palaces, and the common people? You can imagine how their huts were destroyed in huge numbers. And such rain! Even the fine, wide roads of the capital became impassable. It was the worst storm of my lifetime. Well, my life has not been so many years long, but Lord Seimei said he has only experienced a few such storms, and he has many years behind him. We divined this to be an omen sent by the kami to warn us, but we could not ascertain what the threat might be.

The Lord Regent commanded prayers to be said at all temples and shrines in this area, but it did not save Lady Miku, who died suddenly while expecting His Majesty's baby. Do you remember Empress Sadako's sister Miku? She took care of Empress Sadako's children after Her Majesty's sad death. His Majesty fell in love with Miku, and now he has lost her as he did his beloved Sadako. They say Miku's pregnancy somehow caused her death. She was only seventeen or eighteen years old. Perhaps this was the terrible event of which the omen warned us.

And the third event is shameful rather than shocking, I suppose. Despite the High Priestess's faith in my abilities, I have failed to summon kami five times. The most recent attempt was yesterday, and I feel compelled to describe it to you in detail.

This outpouring of my failure to you brings me some measure of peace, for I know you will not judge me. If you were here, you would give me hope and inspiration.

Now, Mi-Na, I will describe my failure yesterday. I executed the Dance perfectly, turning slowly, then faster, whirling, spinning, and moving in perfect rhythm with the shrine priest. He raised and lowered the bells in his hands while I did the same with my fans. And this time, I had not eaten for two days before the Dance, to empty my body as well as my mind, the better to receive the kami.

The summoning failed. The kami ignored me.

I collapsed in despair, pressing my forehead against the cool wooden floor of the shrine's *kagura-den* while smothered laughter came from the shrine attendants observing me. They mocked me, and rightly so. Light footsteps came toward me, and then a gentle tug as someone pulled my fans from under my sleeves. I raised my head, blinking as a ray of sunlight hit my face.

Junior Miko stood above me, lightly brushing dust from the fans. "Does Shrine Miko need assistance from this humble Junior?" she asked. Her excessively polite wording told me she despised me. She resents my assignment as Shrine Miko when she had trained for years for this role.

I shook my head and willed myself to stand, although I could not prevent a slight swaying as I did so.

Why—or perhaps, where—have my powers gone? I summoned you, Mi-Na, pulling you into my world from the future. No one else in living memory had done such a thing, and that gave Lord Seimei confidence he could teach me to become a diviner.

But ever since he sent you home, I have no magic, no power, and no possession by kami. Since you left, Mi-Na, I can do nothing.

Without you, I am nothing.

Yumi—do you remember my faithful attendant?—took my arm. "The priest said you must eat rice and drink water." She guided me out of the courtyard and into one of the inner rooms, holding my arm as carefully as if I were made of paper and might tear. She pointed to a tray heaped with plain but nourishing food.

"I do not want to eat," I told her. "I do not deserve to."

Yumi's gentle brown eyes filled with tears. "You must. The kami would not be pleased if you deny the bounty they have provided."

"This has been my fifth failure at the Dance," I told her. "If I cannot summon the gods, the High Priestess will send me away. Kamo is my home now. I hoped it would be my home forever." I sipped water from the wooden cup in front of me and stared at the bowl of rice, knowing it would taste like ashes in my mouth.

My quiet, simple life at Kamo, my days of meditation and prayer, of divination and understanding the will of the kami—you remember, Mi-Na, how I longed for such a life before I understood what my longing meant. I enjoyed my time in the Empress' court, but poetry games and incense-blending did not satisfy my soul. Stepping onto Kamo's sacred grounds did.

If I am not under the protection of the High Priestess, the Regent would arrange for me to marry. A marriage, no doubt, to one of his warriors, those brutal men who do the killing that noblemen such as Lord Michinaga will not stoop to.

Rather than marry such a man, I will wander the land, begging for alms.

Yumi dabbed at her eyes with her sleeve. "Mi-Na would chide you for not eating. Eat for her sake, for her memory."

I had stopped correcting her when she referred to you as if you were dead. You are not dead because you have not yet been born, but she could not understand such a thing. "Without Mi-Na, I have no power. I need her extra yang energy back."

She disagreed. "She opened you to receive power. She did not take it with her. Lord Seimei would not have allowed it. And perhaps the shrine will need you as a diviner even if you cannot summon the kami."

She was right. I should have thought of such a thing. I have something to offer other than calling the gods to speak through me. Few miko have been trained by the most skilled diviner in the realm. Surely the Saiō-Dai, the High Priestess, can find a use for my skills even if I no longer have spiritual power.

I bowed to Yumi in thanks for her wise words.

Yumi exhaled with relief. She waved toward my rice. "Now, Lady? Will you eat?"

Before I took a bite, a voice called out to say a message had arrived. A young attendant handed a folded paper to Yumi, bowed to me, and left. Yumi held the note out with both hands, her eyes bright in anticipation of what it might say.

I unfolded it with care, examining the paper's light green color and the little flecks of darker green embedded in it, admiring how the calligraphy flowed gracefully down the page.

Yumi leaned forward. "Well?"

"Lady Motoko requests my presence. She has not been well. Her medium and her physician have not found anything wrong. The High Priestess has given leave for me to go to the Imperial Palace."

"A visit to court? It has been so long! We will have to get our robes out of storage. We must both get our teeth blackening renewed."

I smiled at her excitement. "Has it been dull for you here, preparing me for meditation and prayer rather than a poetry competition or book reading?"

Yumi waved her hand in denial, but I knew her too well. She

was my mother's attendant for many years before she became mine.

"I will finish this rice and prepare to leave."

White, soft, and sticky, the rice tasted delicious. I ate it all and drained the cup of water. "Yumi, have you heard any court gossip about Lady Motoko's health?"

She looked down at her hands. "She has always been so lively, almost to a fault. Her health has been excellent, although she has been tired lately. Perhaps she grieves the loss of her sisters. It is said-" She flushed as if embarrassed to share this with me.

I waved impatiently at her to go on.

"It is rumored Lady Motoko's sisters, Empress Sadako and Lady Miku, were cursed. They both died young and unexpectedly. Perhaps Lady Motoko fears the curse might one day cause *her* death. The Regent..."

She stopped, but I knew her thoughts on the matter very well and did not need her to continue.

Lord Michinaga is still Regent, Mi-Na, and his ambition has not changed from when you were here. He must become the grandfather of future emperors. He will not allow any other nobleman's daughter to be named empress, now that Empress Sadako is dead. His daughter Akiko, of course, is Empress. Too young for children now, but that time will come soon. His younger daughter is now nine years old. The Regent will marry her to the Crown Prince when she comes of age, which makes her a rival to Lady Motoko for the future title of Empress.

I told Yumi I did not believe Lord Michinaga would curse the Empress's sisters. "It is sad, but it was simply fate for Empress Sadako and her sister Miku. Let us pray the same sad fate does not await the Royal Consort."

Nonetheless, dread rose within me at what I might find at court.

Chapter 4

Fox Spirit

Poor Masako, indeed. All she ever wanted was to be an imperial shrine miko. She achieved her dream with my help, but it appeared I wrecked that dream when I left her.

Yumi said Empress Sadako's sister Miku died while pregnant with Emperor Ichijō's baby. Masako and I met Miku when we were at court. She was every bit as pretty and sweet as Sadako, so it was no surprise that Emperor Ichijō sought consolation with her after Sadako's death.

I grabbed my phone and searched for Miku and Motoko, finding very little information about either one, other than a brief reference to their deaths in 1002. Motoko was described as dying under mysterious circumstances, and rather horribly.

Masako wrote that she was going to court to meet with Motoko, and her letter was dated 1002. Did she die there with her?

My stomach churned. *Inhale, Mina.*

She couldn't have died then. She must have lived long enough to write at least one more letter because Kenji was translating one now.

Restlessly tapping my fingers on my forehead, I mulled over possible actions. Hovering over Kenji wouldn't get me the English version of the next letter any sooner. More likely it would distract him. Maybe a hike would work off my nervous energy.

Kenji had said our house wasn't far from Mount Daimonji, famous for the mountaintop fire every August 16. During Obon, ancestor spirits came to town for a little family time. Visible from many parts of Kyoto, the flames sent a gentle message to ancestor spirits that, when Obon was over, they needed to leave. *Protect us, don't haunt us.*

I checked my calendar and saw I had a few days before they'd close the mountain for fire prep. I pulled up a map on my phone, touched Start, said goodbye to Kenji—who didn't look up from his translating work—and began to weave my way through city streets to the starting point for the hike.

A group of middle school girls in blue and white uniforms pointed at me, giggling at the weird *gaijin*. I'd dressed for hiking comfort, not fashion. Nothing *kawaii*—cute—about me.

The hiking trail was surprisingly uncrowded for a holiday week. Only an occasional power walker and trail jogger passed me. The path varied between brutally steep log steps and shorter, flatter sections where I could catch my breath. It wasn't quite as sweltering as yesterday but still very hot.

When I reached a plateau with a view, I stopped to rest for a moment.

As my eyes roamed the landscape, a weird sensation of *deja vu* came over me. I waited for a red blur to race along the outer edge of my vision. All the other signs were there. A racing heart. That sense of something terrible about to happen. Shortness of breath.

Duh. Rapid heartbeat and breathing hard were signs of a steep hike up a mountain on a hot day.

But why the dread? Was it fear for Masako's safety laced with guilt for leaving her without power?

I breathed in slowly, tuning out my anxiety by tuning in on nature, and focused my attention on a single tree. Every leaf stood out, edged in light against the sky.

I turned my gaze downward. Each pebble on the trail was distinctly outlined by grains of soil, distinguished by shades of umber, chestnut, and chocolate.

The scent of grilled corn from the vendors far down the mountain made my mouth water.

Perspiration trickled on my forehead as humid air caressed my skin.

I am present. I am in Kyoto. I am in 2019 of the common era, Reiwa One of Emperor Naruhito's reign.

For the first time since I left Masako, that feeling of not being in the right world or the right body was gone.

A reddish blur streaked past my line of sight, startling me out of my peaceful semi-trance. My head jerked around automatically to find it.

And there it was. A fox, crouched in the brush just a few paces away, as still as an Inari statue, but its white throat and orange-red back told me it was real.

The world tilted and spun.

Get a grip, Mina!

Determined to maintain balance, I tightened my core, closed my eyes, inhaled deeply, then reopened them.

The fox was still there, its mouth curved backward almost as if gently smiling, its ears pointed up, alert, but not aggressive.

"Hello?" I said, feeling foolish. "Or, *konnichi wa*? Are you the fox from the Kamo Shrine?" I looked around to reassure myself that no one saw me talking to a wild animal that may or may not have been visible to others. "Thank you for showing me where

Masako's letters were. How did you know they were meant for me?"

It crept closer, swishing its tail in a way I—perhaps too optimistically—interpreted as friendly. I held my breath. Real or not? *Kitsune?* Or kitsune spirit?

I slowly extended my arm, fingers pulled into my palm.

It gazed at me with narrow orange eyes.

I took a quiet step forward, close enough to set my hand on its soft fur. It remained still as if waiting, so I dared a long, steady stroke down its back. A faint buzzing ran from its fur into my hand, up my arm, and straight to my heart like a tiny electric charge.

"Why do I feel this way?" I murmured. "Are you obake? Or a very special fox?"

It perked its ears forward but didn't answer.

Petting a wild fox might give it a false sense of safety around humans. Also, it might have fleas.

I took my hand off.

A strange sense of loss swept through me, and my hand reflexively moved towards it again like I had no say in the matter.

I managed to stop just short of caressing it, however, choosing instead to contemplate its eyes. Orange was a normal color for a fox. It wasn't as wary as one would expect from a wild animal, though. Its reproachful gaze was the opposite of wary, almost as if I shouldn't have taken my hand away.

Well, if that's how you feel…

I set my hand on the fox again, but voices down the trail interrupted our communion. I flicked my eyes for just a second to see a young couple walking up the trail, and in that brief moment, the fox disappeared.

My entire body vibrated, which made no sense. Unless, that

is, I *did* have the useless power to see obake Kenji kept asking me about.

Not only to see obake, but touch them?

Somehow that was weirder and even more insane.

The couple walked past me with a polite greeting, which reminded me to keep hiking up the mountain. I was excited to tell Kenji about the fox, but he'd be disappointed if I climbed all this way and didn't see the place where they'd build the kanji bonfire in a few days.

A little while later, I reached the summit where the bonfire pit was. It was designed to burn in the shape of the character *dai,* meaning large or great. After taking a picture, I wandered to the north view, where the familiar shape of Mount Hiei's peak made me suddenly homesick for Masako. *A thousand years is nothing to a mountain.*

The sweet and savory scent of teriyaki chicken wafted toward me from hikers' bento lunch boxes. My stomach rumbled, and I realized I hadn't packed food. I didn't even bring a water bottle, which I truly regretted.

A man in a Shinto priest's white robe emerged from the little shrine at the top, his lurchy gait drawing my attention because he walked like a zombie from an old cheesy movie. The poor guy probably had hip issues.

He slowly made his way to me and held out a tray of individually wrapped rice crackers.

I was really, really hungry so I reached out to take one. But I pulled my hand back. "Thank you," I said in my politest Japanese. "I didn't bring any water, so I don't dare eat a cracker."

I wanted to ask how he knew I was hungry. That seemed rude, though. Maybe he did this for every gaijin who made it to the top of his mountain.

He smiled at me and gestured down the hill where someone had drawn a design in the dirt. I studied it for a second, thinking it might be a hexagram, but decided it was a hashtag. Maybe he wanted me to post a picture and tag it #daimonji.

I pulled out my phone but the priest stopped me, waving his hands and frowning, so I put it back in my pocket. I examined the drawing again and realized it wasn't a hashtag after all. It was a matrix consisting of five horizontal lines crossing four vertical lines.

An unaccountable chill ran through me. The priest pointed to the drawing and said something, but his words were a little slurred and his Japanese had an old-fashioned quality, like classical Japanese.

"I'm sorry, what did you say?" I asked. "My Japanese is not very good."

This time he scowled, said whatever he said again, only louder, waving the tray so vigorously toward the matrix that several rice crackers slid off.

I crouched to pick them up, muttering an apology for not understanding him, but a loud ringing in my ears distracted me. Surprised and annoyed, I dropped the crackers and pressed my fingertips against my ears. I had my issues, but tinnitus wasn't one of them. Not until today, anyway.

The tone subsided, so I returned to the crackers, which, having fallen to the ground twice, were in no shape to be eaten. I looked up to ask if the priest wanted them back, but he was lurching back to the shrine. He probably decided I was an obnoxious foreigner, although I still didn't understand why he pointed out the symbol in the dirt.

Ah! He thought I drew it and he was telling me to erase it. But I hadn't drawn it, so I was not going off trail to destroy it.

Stuffing the crackers into my pockets to dispose of later, I watched until he was no longer in view. *Funny—that's how I walked when I first took control of Masako's body.*

I hurried back down the mountain, hot and sticky but too

anxious to care. The walk through residential streets to the house seemed to take forever. A prickling at the back of my neck made me turn around a few times to see if the priest was following me, which was silly because the streets were crowded with tourists, salary men and women, and families on vacation. Besides, why would he care? He knew nothing about me.

The house was quiet as I kicked my shoes off and slipped into my house slippers. I grabbed my water bottle and a red bean roll from the kitchen and headed to the other room.

"Kenji?" I didn't want to disturb him but this was important. He'd want to be disturbed by this. "You won't believe what happened!"

He sat where I'd left him at the low table, earbuds in, writing away. I slid onto the cushion across from him.

He pressed the pause button on his earbuds. "You look hot."

"I saw-" What had I seen, exactly? It was most likely a domesticated fox. Nobody saw obake in our world. That's the stuff of light novels and anime, not real life.

"You saw?" he prompted.

"A fox. It might have been the same one we saw yesterday at the shrine. It came up to me and let me pet it."

Kenji did his one-eyebrow lift thing that always made my heart race. "You pet it?"

My cheeks grew hot. "It had soft fur."

He took his earbuds out and set his pen down. "Do you think a fox just happened to be friendly enough to come right up to you and sit there while you touch it?"

"Maybe it's used to tourists feeding it. Sadly, it didn't answer any of my questions. I guess it's too much to expect a talking fox," I said with a weak laugh.

"No wild animal would seek you out and allow you to touch it even if humans fed it. It would annoy you until you gave it food. Besides, who feeds a fox? Squirrels and birds, I understand, but a wild fox?" His tone indicated he was getting excited about this.

I shook my head vehemently. "No way. I can't be that person, the American who played too many Japanese video games and now thinks animal spirits are real."

My inner voice chided me. *Don't be silly, Mina. You know they're real.*

My other inner voice yelled right back. *Be more normal!*

"I know what kind of person you are, Mina," Kenji said softly.

"*Yeah, right,*" both inner voices said skeptically.

"I read Masako's journal long before I met you," he continued. "Which is how I know you were willing to sacrifice your own life to save her. You could have taken over Masako's body and become an onmyōji, but you chose to put your friend first. You're *that* person."

Even if I could push words through the constriction in my throat, I didn't know what to say. I knew I had issues, like avoiding close relationships. I'd always thought if I let people see my true self, they wouldn't like me, so I kept things shallow with classmates and boyfriends alike. "What about the times I stole Masako's body while she was asleep?"

"Not cool, but I understand why you did that. You were trying to survive an impossible situation. What else were you supposed to do? Give up? You'd have been exorcised and who knows where your spirit would have been sent."

Relief washed through me. "Thank you, Kenji. You have no idea what that means to me." I wanted to tell him about the cracker-offering priest, but he started talking before I could go there.

"It's interesting that the fox is red. Inari's messengers are usually portrayed as white. We can do some experiments later to confirm if the fox was truly obake, and to find out if you can see other kinds of spirits too." He waved the translated letter he'd been working on. "Remember how Masako mentioned the diviner, Ashiya? He wanted to become her teacher?"

"Yeah, Seimei's rival."

"She said she didn't want to become his student because she'd heard he performed dark magic. He didn't, though. Other people spread rumors about Ashiya casting curses for Korechika and others."

"What makes you think it was a rumor? The legends say he was a kind of evil twin of Seimei's."

"I've-" He glanced back down at his work. If I didn't know better, I'd say he didn't want to meet my eyes, which was weird, because Kenji was the most eye-meeting Japanese guy I'd ever met.

"Let's keep an open mind about him." He pushed several sheets of paper toward me. "Here's my translation of the next letter." His expression had grown serious. "It's hard to read. I don't mean the vocab. It's, eh, it's dark."

All thoughts of creepy-priest fled as I picked up the pages. "Is Masako in trouble?"

He nodded. "Yes. Read it now and we'll talk about what's happening to her."

It was strange how he used the present tense, but I understood. Masako's letters made it feel like she was here in Kyoto right now.

I started to turn away when a sudden thought struck me. "Uh, Kenji?"

"Yes?"

"I almost hate to ask this, but shouldn't we be looking for the original Chronicle? We'll have time to translate the letters when we're back in Tsukuba, but we can't look for the Chronicle there. You said it would be in Kyoto if it existed anywhere." I bit my lip, hoping he'd give me a good reason *not* to do that.

He pondered my question in silence for a minute, twirling his pen, his eyebrows furrowed with concentration. Then he leaned over the table to pick up the green metal box. "This is more urgent," he said. "Masako is sending you a message across the universe. We should pay attention. She might need us to do something."

Whatever I thought he might say, that wasn't it. Was he a mind-reader? A heart-reader? I was starting to think of it as The Kenji Effect—a ridiculous suggestion that I longed to be right. "How's that even possible? She wrote these a thousand years ago, and they've been copied at least once and hidden for who knows how many decades or centuries."

"I'm not telling you what to do, I'm just giving you my thoughts. If you disagree, we can put this aside and return to Kamigamo Shrine to continue looking for the Chronicle."

"You didn't say anything yesterday about not wanting to go back to Kamo."

"This is your trip. We'll do whatever you think we should do."

I riffled the papers in my hands. If Kenji was right, Masako's letters might tell us where to look for her journal, so we should read them first. On the other hand, they made me feel worse about leaving her, so now I *really* needed to know how much longer she lived. Finding her original manuscript dated with the year 1031 in her handwriting would alleviate my guilt and my fear for her safety. "We could do both, right? Look for the Chronicle after reading all the letters?"

"There are seven of them, but translation will go faster as I get used to the handwriting and vocabulary. I think I'll be done in two or three days. We'll get some indication of what to do next when we read the rest."

"You've been right about everything so far, Kenji-san. Alright. Let's plan on it."

Excited to read the next installment of Masako's life after me, I headed upstairs.

Chapter 5

The Dark Mist

Kenji's translation was six pages long. It would be shorter if it was typed, but Kenji preferred to write by hand rather than use a laptop. He said it felt more accurate that way. His handwriting was better than mine, fortunately. His English was probably better, too.

Eighth Month, Chōhō 4 (September, 1002)

Mi-Na, my brush trembles as I write this next letter to you. Please forgive my disgraceful script, for I do not have enough paper to begin again, and I must tell you of the awful events that have transpired since my last letter. I hope these horrifying memories will flow through my hand and onto the paper, and thus carry away my fear.

When I arrived at the palace, a lady-in-waiting guided me to the Consort's quarters. Lady Motoko sat on a platform, her hair wrapped around her like the silky black fur of a cat, under which pink robes of varying hues were layered. A black cat sat beside her with a pink ribbon around its neck.

"Miko, come in."

I pulled myself along the polished black floor into the room, suppressing a shudder as I slipped through the opening. Why did I feel that sudden sense of dread? The screens were beautifully painted, made of fine wood, perhaps cypress. I noticed nothing about the room to cause my unease.

She gave me a tired smile. "Is it hot outside? You look warm."

"Kamo is cooler than the city. I am no longer accustomed to the heat of the capital."

She waved toward the lady-in-waiting. "Kiyoko, the fan."

The lady-in-waiting raised her head abruptly. "Yes, yes, yes. The fan." She reached into her sleeve and pulled out a fan with a white paper head and a carved bamboo handle. She held it toward me and bowed. "A present from the Royal Consort," she said. She kept her head bowed, so she did not notice the Consort's frown at her rudeness.

Thanking the Consort for her kindness, I gently pulled it from the eccentric young woman.

"Lady Kiyoko is my mother's sister's daughter." The Consort sighed with exasperation. "Her parents raised her without court manners, and I am obliged to rectify that mistake."

Kiyoko had my sympathy. I knew all too well how severely noblewomen at court judged those not raised in the imperial city.

"Miko, I must be honest with you," Lady Motoko continued. "You are not here to diagnose me. I am not ill. My brothers, while not fond of you, appreciate your devotion and loyalty to our late sister, and they recommended you to me. I would like you to become my attendant."

The Consort's statement astonished me. Mi-Na, you know what a poor lady-in-waiting I would be. Despite serving as the Empress's medium, my court manners are not much better than

Lady Kiyoko's. "My life is devoted to the kami," I said. "The High Priestess requires my presence at the Imperial Shrine."

The cat jumped off the dais and stalked away as if annoyed by my answer. Only a cat could commit such a breach of protocol without penalty.

The Consort waved her fan languidly. "His Highness the Crown Prince will be Emperor someday, which means that by serving me, you also serve His Majesty. I will send a note to the Priestess to release you from your duties. If you do not wish to leave your calling, you could serve me as Imperial Miko. Or-" She clapped her hands. "You could study to be an imperial consort physician! You could attend to me in that role. It is not so different from other healing practices such as medium or miko. Well, such physicians are usually of unranked families, and your father is Fifth Rank, so perhaps I have insulted you? It was not my intention."

I wondered if I should consider her offer. If I could not summon the gods, perhaps I could study the art of blood and bone, of humors and herbs.

She brushed her hair away from her face to examine my reaction. "Kiyoko," she said. "Convince her."

Kiyoko's small pink mouth pursed in concern. "With so many deaths in Lady Motoko's family, we are concerned for her well-being. She needs a physician she can trust."

The Consort twisted her sleeves restlessly. "Miko, I need you to protect me. You have until the next solar term to decide."

"You do this humble miko a great honor. I will discuss it with the High Priestess."

A servant set a tray of water and fruit on a low table in front of me.

Lady Motoko gestured to me to eat. "I have no appetite, but you might be thirsty after your journey from Kamo, so please take some water."

I took a polite sip, not wanting to appear rude by refusing, but finding it odd to eat or drink without the Consort joining me.

"My sister Sadako's older daughter, Princess Nagako, spends much of her time with the High Priestess," the Consort said. "Have you seen her at the shrine? She is sweet and so very intelligent."

"Princess Nagako came to the Kamo Shrine to pray last month. She has grown quite tall for eight years. She asked me to read to her from Shonagon's book. She loves to hear about her mother's court."

The Consort covered her eyes with her sleeves, perhaps overwhelmed with emotion at the reminder of her sister's untimely end, and we sat like this in silence until a strange sound interrupted us.

"Kiyoko," Lady Motoko said sharply. "Stop that humming! It is most unpleasant at such a time as this."

Kiyoko bowed several times in succession. "Please forgive me, Lady Consort. I was not aware I was doing it until you mentioned it."

The Consort gave me a forced smile. "Miko, let us speak of something more amusing. The Crown Prince's childhood tutor, Lord Akimitsu—did Shonagon put him in her book? From what I have heard, he would make a good subject for her wit."

I searched my memory for any reference to Akimitsu. "He is the Regent's cousin, is he not? And a member of the Grand Council of State?"

"Yes. It is said Akimitsu was only appointed to such a high post because so many nobles, including his brother, died in the terrible red pox epidemic seven years ago. Before you arrived in the capital, he sent his daughter to become one of His Majesty's consorts. Everyone laughed, saying His Majesty would ignore her, but we were all surprised when he took quite a fancy to her. At that time His Majesty did not yet have a son, so when she announced her pregnancy soon after, her father boasted he would be grandfather to a future emperor. No one liked his proud and vain statements, and no one thought he deserved such an honor. Also, the other consorts were jealous of his daughter's condition. But a very odd thing happened. Akimitsu's daughter went into labor, but only water came out. No baby. Not even blood, despite missing every monthly pollution. She was deeply embarrassed, and she and her father both were ridiculed after that."

I wondered why the Consort was sharing such gossip with me, but Mi-Na, does this sound like something Sei Shonagon would write about? How cruel of them to mock his poor daughter. She must have suffered terribly. Such a horrible, long labor, and then to not bear a child after all, and last, to endure the contempt of others for the very suffering she endured! Our Empress was too kind to allow such gossip in her court. Her sister, it seemed, was not as kind.

I shivered, but not only from this sad tale. That strange unease again filled my chest. I could not breathe for a moment but I could not understand why. The Consort's dais was as it should be. The mats were scattered a bit irregularly, but she was famous for her exuberant character, and was, perhaps, not careful about the tidiness of her room. I examined the screens which separated the room from the gallery. They were covered with colorful paintings of flowers and trees, pretty and cheerful. So what caused my unease?

A chill ran over my arms as I finally understood what my spirit had sensed. "Your Highness, your screens are positioned in an inauspicious direction. We must correct this."

Startled, she glanced at them. "Eh? How strange!"

I trembled with a nameless fear.

"Miko, what is it? You are shaking. Do you have a fever? What is inauspicious about my screens?"

"They create an opening to the *kimon* direction. To the Demon Gate."

We turned to examine the opening through which I had entered the room, and I could not help but cry out. Black smoke filled the gap between the screens.

Lady Motoko looked at me strangely. "What do you see, Miko?"

"Do you not see the black smoke?"

"Smoke? Where?" Lady Motoko sniffed and shook her head. "I don't see smoke. Nor do I smell a fire."

Lady Kiyoko giggled, and I suppressed a desire to slap her. I sniffed the air to determine if an oil lamp had tipped over or the cat had swatted an incense burner. The smoke blocked the opening, almost as if it were solid rather than made of air. I thought it very strange that no one else could see it.

"Miko, leave the screens for now. I will ask servants to move them."

The smoke began to eddy and twist, then slid sinuously through the opening and into the room, becoming a dark mist, moving toward the Consort, curling and thickening into menacing shapes as if supernatural beings existed within it. Moving with intent, but for what purpose? Was it sentient?

A stench filled the room, the same awful stink as a stagnant river when fish die along its banks in the hot summer sun. I waved my sleeves and used my fan to create a breeze, hoping to disperse this sinister mist.

The Consort's forehead creased as she puzzled over my strange movements, while Kiyoko smothered a laugh.

"Do you still not see it?" I waved my fan furiously, my forehead damp with effort even while my skin crawled with fear. "Both of you, wave your fans like so!"

Kiyoko laughed again, but did as instructed, and so did the

Consort, although Motoko's effort was weak, as if she no longer had enough energy to wave a paper fan.

The dark mist now covered the dais. Our efforts made no difference to its presence.

"We must leave the room!"

But my warning came too late. The mist wrapped around the Consort like woodbine around a tree. Her eyes widened in horror as she put her hands to her throat, trying to speak, but all I heard was her sweet voice rasping and choking. She cried out in pain, then bent forward with a moan.

The mist—and the stench—dissipated.

Kiyoko reached Motoko before I could. She pushed the Consort's hair back from her face and screamed. A bright red stain bloomed on the mat. "Help!" Kiyoko cried. "Get the physician! The Consort is ill!"

Lady Motoko vomited again, and again it was blood, not bile. I wished I were already a physician, but I was not, so I began to pray.

Kiyoko turned to me in shock. "Miko, do something! Is she possessed? Exorcise it!"

"I am a miko, not an exorcist!" Pushing Kiyoko out of my way, I put my hands on the Consort's forehead, a practice I learned from you, Mi-Na. Her forehead was not hot with fever. Rather, it was as cold as snow.

Lifting her head with trembling hands, I stared into her eyes, hoping to see the mono-no-ke that possessed her, but her eyes had rolled back and only the white was visible. I laid her on the mat. She convulsed and choked, so I held her head up so she would not suffocate on the blood that continued to drip from her mouth.

Ladies-in-waiting and servants came rushing in, screaming and crying at the horror of the scene. Red flowers blossomed on my white robe, and Kiyoko's hands were stained red. I took paper from my sleeve and wiped the Consort's face. No signs of pox or fever. Why did she vomit blood? Did the dark mist do this? Why had no one else seen it?

The Consort's physician pushed her way through the gathered ladies-in-waiting. Before she reached Lady Motoko's side, the Consort clutched her throat, gasping. Her body jerked forward as if in silent agony, convulsed against the mat, and then lay as still as stone.

The physician put her cheek next to the Consort's mouth. "There is no breath."

The other women began to shriek. "Hush!" I cried out to them. I held my hand against her nose and mouth. The physician was correct. No breath. I sat back, placing the back of my hand to my mouth, feeling the warm, humid air of my exhale.

I breathed.

She did not.

It was my fault, Mi-Na. Why did I not immediately notice the misplacement of the screens? If that is not the job of a miko, what is? I have failed again.

The physician turned to me. "Miko, did the Consort appear to be ill?"

"Well, she told me about recent fatigue. Before she vomited, I saw a dark mist enter through there." With a shaking hand, I gestured to the screens. "The opening to the room is to the northeast. The kimon direction. The direction of the Demon Gate."

The physician covered her mouth in horror. "How could that be? I have never seen the screens arranged this way."

A lady-in-waiting rushed over with a wet cloth. She began to clean the Consort's face, sobbing while she did so. The women were all weeping, kneeling on the floor, one of them with a rosary, most of them reciting sutras.

The physician shifted her attention to Kiyoko. "Has she eaten anything unusual? Or had anything to drink but water?"

Kiyoko shook her head. "I attended to her today, and she ate little, just rice and some persimmon slices. And only water to drink." Her eyelids fluttered. "Is she- is she gone?"

The physician bent her head down again. When she straightened, tears gleamed on her cheeks. "Miko, please begin the process of purification. No one must enter until the servants have cleaned the Princess and the room. We must notify His Majesty, the Lord Regent Michinaga, and the Crown Prince. Lady Motoko is dead."

Chapter 6

Hexagrams

Breathless with anticipation, I flipped the last page over, but it was blank. Growling, I shook the pages with both hands as if that would somehow force more words to appear.

What would cause a person to vomit blood? Ulcers? Cancer? But those wouldn't appear out of nowhere and kill a person, would they? Did Motoko have a contagious disease, and if so, did Masako catch it? Or was she poisoned? If it was murder, was Masako in danger too? After all, she witnessed the whole thing.

Kenji knew I'd read this today. He knew I'd learn Masako witnessed a terrifying and mysterious death. He shouldn't have given it to me until he'd translated what came next.

Don't be so obsessive, Mina. He'd been up until 3 am translating, and he promised to work on it more today.

I had to talk to him about Masako's story and get the next translation, so I headed to his room. His door was closed with a pink sticky note on it. Ignoring the hall slippers by my feet, I skated across the wooden floor in my socks to yank it off.

Kenji had written it in Japanese, but I had no trouble reading his neat script. He'd gone to the *sentō* down the street. Well, he was old-school in many ways, so it figured he'd go to a public bath.

I knocked on his door. No answer, of course, so I slid it open. He wouldn't mind if I read what he'd already translated. After all, he was doing it for me.

His desk was a low table with no drawers to hide things in and nothing on top. No backpack in here, so he must have used it to take his towel with him. The room was nearly empty except for a neatly folded futon and his briefcase.

I'd teased him on the train to Kyoto about how he carried a backpack and a briefcase. "One or the other, Kenji. A backpack is cool. A briefcase is nerdy. Which are you?"

He'd laughed and put on his sunglasses. "A cool nerd."

"*Yappari!*" I liked how it sounded like an English equivalent. *Yep!*

"Your accent's getting better, Mina-san," he said. "If I closed my eyes when you said that, I might think you were a Japanese woman."

"*Uso-tsuki!*" I pretended to swat his arm the way teenage girls did here. "You're lying to get on my good side so I'll take you to the spirit world with me."

His eyes flicked to the window as if hiding a guilty look. I'd have called him out on it, but just then I heard two young women across the aisle whispering. "*Kakkoii,*" I heard them say. They weren't staring at me, the pale foreigner with blond (ish) hair. No, they were talking about Kenji.

Yes, he's a whole snack, but keep your hands off.

I then reprimanded myself for being possessive. Not only was he not mine, but I was absolutely not going into a relationship so soon after the last one. No matter how kind and earnest he was, or that he gave up his vacation to come to Kyoto with me, or how full his lips were, how intense his gaze was when he looked at me…

Stop it, Mina. Such daydreams are not productive.

If the next letter indicated Masako was in danger, Kenji wouldn't have left without saying so.

Or would he? He didn't understand my sense of urgency. Sure, he was thrilled to find a first-hand account of something historical, but it wasn't real to him. It was an account of an event that occurred hundreds of years ago. Interesting, yes. Personal? Not so much.

But it was deeply personal to me. My best friend had just witnessed a possible murder and might very well be in danger herself. More than a friend, she was part of who I was now. Even though we allowed Seimei to rip us apart, bits of her remained in my soul, woven into the fabric of my very existence.

Kenji understood most of what I'd been through, but how could anyone understand *that*?

My throat ached from trying not to scream from frustration, so I went downstairs to get water. As I filled my bottle, I saw papers scattered on the table. Kenji must have left them out for me to read.

I leafed through five or six sheets. Nope, not translations. Drawings? I examined them more closely. Hexagrams? Why'd he have sheets full of hexagrams?

A narrow box rested on the tatami mat next to the table. I lifted it and was surprised at its light weight. It rattled when I shook it, so I opened it.

My jaw dropped. Divination sticks? Kenji was a *diviner*? Why hadn't he told me?

Puzzled, I picked up a hexagram-covered page and examined it. I'd studied divination with Masako, but I-Ching hexagrams meant nothing without knowing the question asked while throwing the sticks, coins, or other divination tools of choice. Also, what was the point of learning divination in a society with the internet and artificial intelligence?

Frowning, I set the paper back down. Glancing over the room, I remembered that the container with Masako's letters lived under the table on a *furoshiki* cloth to protect the mat. He might have put his translation in the same box as the original documents.

Not knowing if Masako's fragile letters were on top, I opened the metal box with caution. I squeaked with excitement to see English words on plain printer paper on top. Carefully rifling through the top layers to ensure I didn't touch the fragile ancient papers underneath, I took out three sheets and folded them to fit in my back pocket.

The front door slid open.

"*Tadaima!* I'm back!"

"*O-kaeri!* Welcome back! How was your bath?"

Kenji entered the room smiling, his hair still damp from his bath, but his face reddened as his eyes traveled over the hexagram-covered papers on the table, the divination box on the floor, the metal one on the furoshiki, and back to me. "What are you doing?"

"Sorry, I didn't mean to—" My face grew hot. "These were just lying on the table. I thought you meant for me to take a look at them." I picked one up. "By the way, what is this? You realize I learned divination with Masako, right?"

He surprised me by grabbing the page, which tore as he did so.

We both stared at it in shock. Tears sprang into my eyes. "Oh, no! I'm so sorry!"

He put it carefully on the other papers and lifted them off the table while avoiding my eyes. "These are personal."

"You left all this out in the open, so I assumed you didn't care if I saw it." It wasn't like I'd read his diary or had gone through his text messages.

He took the divination box. "You're right. I shouldn't have left all this out. I must have been tired."

Not quite ready to forgive him for getting upset but not interested in prolonging an argument, I nodded.

He went upstairs. I heard the door slide shut with a muffled click.

Kenji's latest translation crinkled in my pocket. I forgot to tell him I'd taken it from the metal box.

Didn't matter. Masako wrote these to me. The translation didn't fall into the category of Kenji's personal items.

Taking the papers out, I smoothed them out on the table. Why was Kenji so uncomfortable about the hexagrams? I wasn't some normie who might think divination was weird. Not to brag or anything, but I knew more about it than anyone else in 2019. I spent months listening while the Great Diviner Abe no Seimei tutored Masako in it. Kenji and I could become divination partners.

I'd suggest it when he calmed down. Now I'd seen Kenji's embarrassment, it was a relief, in a way, to learn he was human after all. Nobody could be that perfect *all* the time.

I was a little hurt, though. Why hadn't he told me he was a diviner? Didn't he trust me?

Chapter 7

The Bitter Truth

I leaned against my folded futon, both reluctant and eager to learn what happened after the Royal Consort died a horrible death in front of Masako.

Eighth Month, Chōhō 4 (September, 1002)

Mi-Na, perhaps you can imagine the turmoil and grief within the Palace upon news of the Royal Consort's death. "How can she be dead?" people asked. "She had not been ill." "She was so vivacious, so stylish. This could not have happened so quickly."

Her brothers insisted we wait by her side for three days. "She might wake up," they said. "She would not leave us like this."

The Crown Prince sent poems to her room for us to read aloud as she lay there so still and silent. Her attendants smoothed her hair and read from her favorite anthologies, but tears fell upon sleeves, for we knew she did not hear them. Her spirit had departed.

Rumors swirled that one of the Prince's other consorts poisoned her to remove competition, but I was confident it was not poison. She had not taken one sip nor eaten one bite while with me, and Kiyoko said she barely touched food all day. Without a doubt, an evil spirit had entered the room. It must have been a curse. Why else would a mono-no-ke attack a sweet young woman, beloved consort of an imperial prince and mother to his young children? But if a curse, where did it come from?

I could not ignore how three rivals to Lord Michinaga's daughters for the title of Empress Consort had now been removed. First, Empress Sadako died from a broken heart, although the official reason given was childbirth. Then a few months ago, Sadako's sister Miku, concubine to His Majesty, died while pregnant with his child. And now, Sadako's sister Motoko, who, if she had lived, might have been named Empress when her husband ascended as Emperor.

Mi-Na, you and I believed Michinaga drove Empress Sadako to her death of despair, but surely he had nothing to do with the untimely deaths of her two sisters. Could they have been victims of a curse aimed at someone else?

The Imperial Police sent messengers requesting the Consort's attendants write letters describing what happened. Mine described how screens were positioned so that the only opening to the room was in the northeast direction. Before we could move the screens, a dark mist swirled in the room, but the Consort and her lady-in-waiting did not see it. Soon after, the Consort vomited blood, and the mist disappeared.

The Imperial Police received my letter and sent an officer to examine me further.

He questioned me while I sat behind a screen. "Is it not odd that the Princess passed into the spirit world so soon after calling you into her presence?" he asked.

Horrified at his implication, I protested. "Lady Motoko called me because she was fatigued and nervous, as Lady Kiyoko has verified."

"Miko, everyone in the capital knew about the chaos you created when you summoned a *shikigami* to assist the Empress's labor over a year ago. Perhaps you tried something similarly *helpful?*"

I heard the smirk in his voice, but he continued before I could respond. "Could the Consort's death be due to the chaos behind your magic?"

My face grew warm with embarrassment at his suggestion. "The Royal Astrologer taught me to control my power. I used no magic with the Consort, but as I already described, the opening to the room was in the kimon direction."

"Yes," he said. "The ladies-in-waiting confirmed it. None of them knew who moved the screens to create the opening in that direction, or why. We will ask Lord Seimei and the Saiō-Dai to vouch for your integrity."

The police left me alone after that. Seimei and the High Priestess both confirmed I had no power other than divination and therefore could not have summoned anything to hurt the Consort.

I shed a few tears at the bitter truth of their words, learning in this way that even they, my strongest defenders, recognized my uselessness. Ah, Mi-Na, where are you when I need you most?

Those of us in the room when the Princess died became polluted from our close contact with blood and death, so in addition to mourning, we had to isolate ourselves and conduct purification rituals. Hoping for an answer to what happened in the Consort's room, I prayed continually.

The kami did not respond to my prayers. A heaviness in my soul became a weight that kept me from rising in the morning. After the Consort was taken to be burned, I rode with the other attendants in ox carriages to the river, where I led *harae* purification rituals. We rubbed paper dolls over our faces, arms, clothing, and bodies, and threw them into the river to carry away the *kegare*, the pollution associated with blood and death.

Once it was completed, I returned to Kamo. The harae lightened my spirits a little, and I descended from the carriage to walk through the tree-lined path, breathing in the cedar fragrance of the shrine grounds. The ravens hopped about as if excited I was finally home.

Shrine attendants surrounded me as I walked under the torii, demanding I tell them what happened in the palace. They gasped with horror when I described how the screens were positioned. "Everyone knows that is dangerous!" exclaimed the youngest of them. "Why did you not move them into the proper positioning?"

I bowed my head in shame. "It was a long way to enter the consort's quarters, and I temporarily lost a sense of the room's direction. When I entered, I assumed the entrance faced south, but as Lord Seimei taught me, I retraced my steps in my mind and realized I entered from the northeast."

I told them I did not know why the screens were positioned in that way, or for how long. They had many more questions, but I could only say I had no answers.

I still wonder, Mi-Na—did Kiyoko create the opening to the kimon direction? If so, why?

Chapter 8

Divination Partners

I set the last page down with a heavy heart. Poor Masako, witness to the horrible death of a beautiful noblewoman and interrogated by the imperial police as if it were her fault. What happened to her next? She'd survived long enough to write all these letters, but at what cost?

Those questions might be answered in the next letter. Surely Kenji wouldn't make me wait for the next translation. Surely he knew how much this meant to me. I shouldn't have looked at his stuff, even if it was lying on the table in plain sight. In my pre-time-travel life, I wouldn't have done such a thing, but my ravening hunger to know more about Masako threw off my judgment. I felt like a shadow trying to find its body. Reading her messages made me feel a bit more solid.

Kenji might still be willing to translate the remaining pages for me, but I didn't want him to think his work meant more to me than his friendship. To make a pure, unselfish apology, I had to *not* ask him for more help.

So how *would* I get the remaining letters translated? Masako wrote in classical Japanese, as difficult to translate into modern

Japanese as it would be for me to translate Beowulf from the original Old English. Which would be not at all.

My Japanese lit prof at Michigan specialized in Heian literature. She'd been another reason I changed my major from Engineering to Asian Studies. An emailed photo of one of these old letters might pique her interest enough to assist me.

It was a little too early for dinner and a little late for lunch, so I grabbed my backpack and headed to the coffee shop for coffee, a snack, and some WiFi. Our old-fashioned house was super cool, but the lack of WiFi was odd for a place catering to tourists. Maybe the owner, a shrine priest, believed the internet distracted from spiritual progress.

The welcoming fragrance of freshly ground coffee and a cheery *"Irasshaimase!"* from a server greeted me as I entered. I ordered a cup of Vienna coffee and began crafting an email. I didn't have one of the original letters with me, but I could at least start a request.

The server placed a mug and a piece of green tea cheesecake in front of me. I demolished the cheesecake in no time flat—hiking up a mountain and back will do that—and tackled the fluffy cloud of whipped cream on the coffee.

After those high-priority tasks, I could savor my coffee while reading about Lady Motoko. That led to a rabbit hole of further research about her other sisters. Empress Sadako's death, dryly noted in Wikipedia as "due to childbirth," felt like mere weeks ago. The youngest sister, Miku—short for Mikushigedono, meaning Chief Officer of the Imperial Wardrobe—died in 1002. Lady Motoko, also known as the Shigeisha, aka the Royal Consort, died later the same year. Specifically, she died after vomiting blood over everything, just as Masako described. Further research didn't yield any information about the cause of death for either one.

I finished my coffee before I started the task I'd come here to do, so I reluctantly closed the seven tabs I'd opened and clicked on the email icon.

My professor's email address auto-filled when I typed her first initial, but I let the cursor blink on the subject line for a minute. She might think I was crazy, and even if she believed me, she might insist I turn the papers over to the government or a university to assess their historical and cultural value.

Maybe I shouldn't email her just yet. At least, not until I had a chance to read all the letters first. Kenji would have to help after all.

Someone sat in the chair across from me, startling me into knocking over my coffee mug. "How'd you know I was here?" I asked as I set the mug upright.

"I divined it," Kenji said with a solemn expression.

"Wait, what?"

"*Jōdan.* Just kidding. I saw your empty room, and your backpack was gone, so I guessed you came here to use the internet."

At least I wasn't the only one who looked into other people's rooms when they weren't there. "I'm sorry about looking at your papers."

"*Donmai,* Mina-san. It's my fault for leaving them on the table. You studied divination with Seimei, and I didn't want you to see my feeble attempts at it."

So he'd been embarrassed, not angry. I suppressed a sigh of relief. "Donmai is a new word for me. Does it mean the same as *mondai nai?* No problem?"

He raised his eyebrows and made a wide o-shape with his mouth in mock surprise. "Heh? Don't you speak English?"

"Sorry, no. My native language is American." I furrowed my forehead and pursed my lips in an exaggerated I'm-thinking-so-hard manner. "Hmm... your question tells me donmai is an

English loan word. Doan. Mye. Doan—Mye. Don't? Mind?" Realization dawned on me. "Hey, is it slang for I don't mind?"

He clapped. "*Yatta!* Yes! English, you see?"

"Donmai. I'll remember that one."

"When I first moved to Ohio in the eighth grade," Kenji said, his expression back to his usual thoughtful one. "I'd use a word like that and assume everyone knew it because it originated in English, but of course, with my Japanese accent, no one understood me. I was so embarrassed. I stopped talking to people outside class until high school."

"Oh, Kenji…"

He smiled and waved my sympathy away. "Anyway, I have only two skills: Classical Japanese and American English. You must be so much better at divination than I am. I didn't want you to know about my sad efforts to learn it until I got better."

"Masako had all the divination talent in our relationship. I'm not as skilled at it as you think. Maybe we could practice together? I don't want to forget what I've learned."

Kenji started rummaging through his backpack but paused at my suggestion. "Together? Absolutely!" His excitement made me smile. "It will be so important, Mina, what I'm doing. What *we'll* be doing. The kami-" He stopped.

"Go on," I said breathlessly. "The kami?"

"It's too complicated to explain right now, but yes, it involves the kami. I promise I'll explain everything later. By the way, did you take the letter I translated this morning? The one where Masako writes about the Imperial Police? I couldn't find it anywhere."

My cheeks grew warm. "Yes. I, uh, took it from the box."

He pulled a few pages from his pack and handed them to me with a flourish. "I'd been working on these, too, but somehow they ended up here." He patted the pack.

"Oh, thank you so much," I said as I took them, relieved he wasn't angry about my taking his translation without asking. "Translating takes a lot of time. One of my professors at Michigan might be able to help. I was just working on an email to ask her but-"

His smile disappeared. "Why? Don't you want my help?"

"Well… you're spending so much time helping me. I just wanted-"

"Don't you trust me?"

The coffee churned in my stomach. "Of course I trust you."

He shrugged the backpack back on without looking at me. "I'd rather you didn't tell anyone about the letters for now. See you back at the house."

Startled at his tone, I could only mumble a quick goodbye.

Confused, I deleted the email I'd begun. Maybe he wanted to keep the letters a secret for now so we wouldn't have to turn the letters over to academics or historians. Or maybe he was just annoyed with how much time we were spending together and he needed some alone time.

Closing my laptop, I signaled for a glass of water and examined the translated pages Kenji had just handed to me. These were also dated September 1002, so he was giving me his translations in chronological order. Either he read them through and arranged them first, or they were placed in the box that way. Whichever way, it was helpful.

I gripped the first page with both hands. Masako was trying to tell me something. Did she need my help? Was she asking me to go back to her? She'd written several times that she was nothing without me. Was that a hint or a complaint? Or just venting to the only person who would ever really, truly understand?

We were co-dependent while together, but I'd left her in a

good place, living her best life without having to share it with me. So why did she continue to write? And why did I keep dreaming about her?

Answers to those questions eluded me, but at least I could find out what happened next.

Chapter 9

Outcast

Spirit Mi-Na, Lord Seimei has changed since you left. He is often ill and is too weak to attend the imperial family in person. His sons have taken on many of his duties. His work now is to update and compile his divination practices into a manual to be used by his sons and grandsons with imperial divination responsibilities.

He nodded in response to my bow, his face drawn and pale. "Such a terrible event, Miko. The Crown Prince is distraught. A rumor implies the Crown Prince's consort Seiko had something to do with it, but Seiko is a woman of integrity who is well-loved by the Prince. Why would she do such a thing? She is too intelligent and wise in the ways of the court to think removing Lady Motoko would increase her chance of becoming Empress when the Crown Prince ascends to Emperor. Everyone knows Lord Michinaga will put one of his daughters in that position."

"This was not the work of Lady Seiko," I said. "A dark mist formed and entered the room. After Lady Motoko died, the mist disappeared without a trace. I believe—or rather, I know—an evil spirit entered through the kimon direction. "

He sighed, squeezing his eyes shut as if in pain. "I will

conduct a divination myself. This is too important to leave to less skilled diviners, even if they are my sons. In the meantime, I request your presence at an exorcism. Koretaka's daughter has been unable to leave her mat for three days. Her eyes are open, but blinking and staring wildly, and her legs twitch continuously."

I was astonished to hear that. "Eh? Lord Koretaka's daughter Kiyoko?"

"Do you know her?"

"Lady Kiyoko served Lady Motoko, and was there with me when the Consort died." The vivid memory of that awful day caused a shudder to run through me. "Perhaps a vulnerability from the incident left her open to spirit possession."

Seimei tugged his beard as he does when he is puzzled. "The family exorcist has tried three times to remove the *tsuki-mono* but his efforts have been in vain. Her father wrote to me for assistance, but I am not well. My age is finally catching up with me. I will not die yet, but the next few years will be a great trial. My sons have become quite skilled at yin-yang divination and reading the stars, but because the young lady is—well, a young lady—her father would prefer a miko to be present."

Seimei was not as alarmed as I expected him to be. "Forgive my impudence," I said. "But the malevolence that killed the Consort—could it have attached itself to Kiyoko?"

He lifted his bushy gray eyebrows. "Miko, you may have lost your power to summon the kami, but your wisdom has grown. Perhaps it is similar to how a miko's hearing becomes more acute when she is blind. I will send Akichika as well. He is now a priest at a Fujiwara family shrine. The two of you worked well together previously."

Mi-Na, do you remember Seimei's sweet, awkward grandson? He is married now, so perhaps we can become friends without any of his romantic nonsense interfering.

"Lord Seimei, do you want me there as the medium? My other abilities have left me." I bowed my head in shame.

"You will attend as an observer. A medium will already be there. After the exorcism, report everything to me. I am especially interested in learning the spirit's name." He sighed. "I do not blame you for losing your power, Miko. I sent Mi-Na home exactly when she needed to leave. By the time she left, you had attained the most harmonious balance of yin and yang. Her departure should not have affected you this way."

Encouraged by his words, I raised my head.

"However," he continued, and my heart sank again. "The High Priestess may have to send you away if you do not summon a kami soon. Your divination skills are sufficient for a position in a smaller shrine. Our lessons will end. I must focus on the transition of secrets to my sons."

I stared at my clasped hands. How could I leave Kamo, the home of my heart?

Finally, I gathered the courage to speak. "Your belief in me does me great honor. I will do what is necessary to assist Lady Kiyoko."

I slid backward to exit the room, but he raised a hand to stop me. "Be careful," he said. "And bring extra guards when you go to Lady Kiyoko's residence. You are staying with your uncle?"

"Yes, at his city compound."

"It is not far from there, but be careful. Several young women have disappeared from the capital recently."

"I had not heard that, but I have been in mourning as well as under an abstinence due to the pollution of the Consort's death."

"Those who disappeared have been commoners, so undoubtedly it is the work of bandits replenishing their ranks. Commoners are not diligent about revering their ancestors, and so their ancestors do not become guardians. Even worse, such ancestors might become ghosts or vengeful spirits. Perhaps you know the story of Sugawara no Michizane, a high-ranking offi-cial who died in exile. His vengeful spirit—*onryō*—is said to have killed Emperor Daigo's sons and many others in the government with fires, epidemics, and earthquakes. He most certainly was not a commoner, but I tell you this as an example of the disasters that might strike when ancestors are not venerated properly."

As you know, Mi-Na, onryō epidemics killed my mother and sister, and this odd tale sent a shiver down my spine. "Perhaps Michizane's onyrō sent the dark mist to the Consort's rooms?"

"His Majesty posthumously promoted him to Minister of the Right ten years ago, which appeased his spirit. Other peculiar events have occurred of late. Spirit possessions are on the rise. It did not alarm me at first because these spirits mostly possessed commoners, but Lady Kiyoko is another matter. Her father is a high-ranking official in the imperial administration. Therefore be careful as you move about the city. I see now that anyone might be endangered."

Mi-Na, I am sure you will be pleased to learn Yumi still travels with me everywhere. I informed Seimei she waited for me in the outer room.

Seimei's forehead creased with concern. "If this exorcism does not succeed, I will conduct a divination to learn if some-thing or someone has displeased the kami. You have work to do, and so do I." He waved me away.

Kiyoko lay on her platform, her white robes askew. I surrendered all effort to straighten them, for each time I did, she writhed and twisted the robes around her legs yet again.

I sat on one side of her with a bamboo screen to my back, behind which sat two exorcists and a drummer. One of the exor-cists was Akichika, now a respected priest. The other exorcist was from a local temple. Both were hoarse from hours of chanting. So much incense filled the air that my eyes stung and watered from the smoky fragrance. The drum stopped beating some time ago, and I heard a faint snoring, so I assumed the young drummer had fallen asleep.

Mi-Na, do you remember Natsu, the medium who attended the Empress's labor? She meditated on the other side of the platform, her eyes closed. Natsu and I both wore white robes over red *hakama*. If the patient were conscious, she might be confused about which of us would perform the medium's role today.

My stomach ached to see Kiyoko lying there, her legs twitching and her mouth convulsing. Her eyes remained closed, but her eyelids would flutter rapidly from time to time. Her hair came untied from its ribbon and tangled in and around her robes and arms, strands of it clinging to her damp cheeks, falling over the platform edge, and pooling on the floor as if someone had spilled a ladle of roasted sesame oil.

She startled me by jerking upright. Her eyes rolled back so only the whites were visible. "I will take her with me!" she shouted in words phrased as a man's would be.

I gasped at her odd pitch. The temple priest stopped his chanting. Perhaps he thought the exorcism was working, that the tsuki-mono had been summoned into Natsu's body, ready to be expelled.

"That was not Natsu speaking. It was Kiyoko!" I whispered to him through the screen.

Kiyoko fell backward, as limp as a rag, and hit her head on the wooden edge of the *michōdai*. She cried out in pain, but in her own voice, and began to weep.

Just then Natsu groaned loudly, an eerie sound that caused my skin to prickle. She shouted in a hoarse voice. "I will take her with me!"

Trembling with dread, I had to force my next words through my throat. "That- that was Natsu."

The temple exorcist raised his voice to carry over the screen. "Who are you, Spirit? What do you want?"

Natsu moaned, and her eyes rolled back as Kiyoko's had done. She rose from her seated position, her mouth twisted with anger or pain, and grabbed Kiyoko's arm. Kiyoko screamed and pulled away, turning toward me, her eyes pleading for help.

The exorcist called out again. "What is your name, Spirit? Tell me your name, I command you!"

The medium clenched her teeth, grinding them in rage, and then spat a single word. "Outcast!"

"Outcast, you must live up to your name. I cast you out! Depart, Outcast!"

Natsu sank to the floor in a faint.

All was silent except for Kiyoko's whimpering. I examined her head where it hit the platform. She appeared to be fine except for a bruise.

She grabbed my hand. "Miko, don't leave me! It might return!"

After a reassuring pat on her shoulder, I pulled away. "The medium put herself in danger for you."

Tears sprang to her eyes with my gentle remonstration, and she let go.

Natsu pushed herself up to a kneeling position and then vomited onto the floor. "I am terribly dizzy," she said, holding her head. "What a terrifying spirit."

"Medium," the temple priest called through the screen. "Have you recovered? Did you determine what kind of tsuki-mono that was? It had the voice of a man, did it not? Was it a living spirit? Or a ghost?"

"It was angry." She hugged her arms across her midsection.

"And hungry. For what, I don't know. Hungry for revenge? Retribution? I know nothing more."

"Why would it possess *me*?" Kiyoko wailed.

She was the daughter of a noble at court, young, sweet, and innocent. How could she have wronged someone?

"The demon named itself Outcast," the priest responded. "Perhaps it is the onryō of someone who died in exile. Lady Kiyoko, is your father a judge? Would he have sentenced someone to exile?"

Her lips pursed in thought. "Eh, he is not a judge. He is a minister of the fifth rank, so…" Her voice trailed off as if she did not know what her father did.

"He serves the Lord Regent in the office of administration," I answered for her. "I do not think it is revenge for her father. Lord Seimei said there have been many possessions lately." I realized Akichika had not contributed to the discussion yet. "Shrine Priest, what do you think?"

"Well…" Akichika responded with his usual diffidence. "Lately I have received many requests for exorcisms. Commoners are praying at my shrine in greater numbers. They have said tsuki-mono possessions have become more frequent. Also, they report an increase in kidnappings. While possessions are within my area of expertise, kidnappings are not."

The sound of Akichika's friendly voice made me smile. "Have you sent a letter to Lord Seimei about these events?"

"Well… no. He has been ill. Also, he has been busy with requests from the imperial family and the Lord Regent. I did not want to bother him."

"Aki-" I had to stop myself from using his name. "Shrine Priest, Lord Seimei needs to understand this situation. Perhaps the tsuki-mono are responsible for the kidnappings in addition to spirit possessions. And now-" I gestured to Kiyoko. "It is not only commoners who are affected."

"Lady Masako- ah, Shrine Miko, you speak such wise words. I will send a letter to my grandfather today." He continued in a whisper as if to prevent me from hearing what he had to say next. "Temple Priest, this Shrine Miko is so clever. She used to be possessed by a spirit from the future."

"Yes, yes, it is a famous story." The temple priest's voice was dismissive. "We must inform the young lady's father that the exorcism succeeded. He will be pleased. I wonder why I succeeded this time when I had failed before. Perhaps two of us were required."

"Or perhaps the Miko's presence made the difference."

The rustle of their robes informed me of their departure.

After Natsu refreshed herself with a sip of water, she called a servant to clean up the mess she'd made on the floor and excused herself to leave.

Kiyoko's eyes begged me to stay. I accepted a damp cloth from a servant and gently wiped tears and sweat from Kiyoko's face. "What do you know about the inauspicious placement of the screens in the Consort's room?"

She closed her eyes as if she couldn't bear to look at me.

"Kiyoko, did you move those screens?"

"I didn't realize it would be so terrible." She took a folded green note from her sleeve and handed it to me. "I moved them because of this."

The note contained an elegantly written poem requesting her to move the Consort's screens so the opening to her room faced northeast.

"Who wrote this? Why would they ask you to move the screens?"

She turned onto her side, away from me. "I have been exchanging poems with a young man," she said at last. "He promised it was an auspicious direction for the Consort."

"But all imperial family divinations must go through the Bureau of Divination."

She began to cry, speaking through her tears, pausing to sniffle and wipe her cheeks with her robe sleeve. "What do I know of divination? His poetry and calligraphy were so beautiful that I found it hard not to trust him." She faced me again. "I just wanted to *help* her. She is so tired—I mean, was so tired, and the Prince had not visited her for several weeks. If moving the screens would help her, how could I not do so?"

Such ignorance shocked me. "Do you not understand why the northeast direction is so dangerous? This is common knowledge. It is the kimon direction, which is so named because it is the gate through which evil spirits flow into our world. That is why the Kamo Shrine is placed northeast of the capital, to protect it from such spirits."

She shook her head so violently that strands of hair landed in her mouth. She tugged them out. "No one ever explained that to me, and here in the capital, the diviners tell us a different direction is forbidden every day. It changes constantly. How was I to know that one direction is *always* bad?"

I forced myself to remember that I had not worried about openings to the northeast when I lived in Hitachi Province. "Kiyo, did you recently arrive at court?"

She put her arm over her eyes. "Is it so obvious? My mother died last year, and my father is here, so I came to serve at court and make a good marriage."

I prayed for patience. "Have you ever met this young man in person? When did you first receive a note from him? How does he know you?"

She sat up. "Well…" She began to comb her hair with her fingers, pulling it around from its tangled mess on her back to hang in a waterfall over her right shoulder. "I received a note on lavender paper one day, with a poem describing how he was overwhelmed with love upon seeing my sleeves hanging from my carriage window."

"And did you respond?"

"It was the first note like that I ever received. And so well-written, he must be of noble birth. I wrote him a poorly written poem in return, so I did not expect to hear from him again. But I did, and we exchanged notes nearly every day. I never met him in person, but I understand him, and he understands and loves me." Her hands froze mid-comb. "But I have not received a note from him since the terrible day Lady Motoko died. Not even to ask about my health during the spirit possession." Her mouth trembled. "He did not truly care for me, did he, Miko?"

I exerted utmost control to prevent my face from showing my frustration. She was only seventeen, and not wise in the ways of court noblemen.

She looked at me in terror. "Was it me?" She fell back onto the bed. "Miko, was it my fault? Did I allow a demon in to kill the Consort?"

"Lady Kiyoko, please stop crying. This is urgent. We must learn why and how the young man asked you to move the screens. If he intended to admit a demon into the Consort's room, he must be evil. And I can think of no other reason he would make such a request. Tell me where you sent your notes."

She stopped crying long enough to give me the address. I examined the name and location. "But this is not a residence, is it? Did he wait for your notes there?"

"It was romantic," she murmured. "The servant would bring it to the bridge and place it under a stone. He said his family must not find out."

"Under a stone?" My raised voice caused her to flinch. I inhaled deeply and reminded myself I was seventeen just a few years ago. I signaled to a servant and asked her to ensure the Imperial Police received the information.

I pulled myself away from Kiyoko. I was sure she would sob herself to sleep, but at least it wouldn't be the forever sleep of the Royal Consort.

As you know, Mi-Na, I did something equally foolish when I was younger. Untrained, I traveled to the spirit world and panicked, pulling you into my world. Fortunately, you were not evil, but you *could* have been, so I should not judge Kiyoko for what she had done.

But it *did* seem to be her fault.

Chapter 10

A Positive Spiral

I set Masako's letter on the table with a twinge of anxiety. Kiyoko had admitted to moving the screens for a man she'd never met.

Kiyoko wouldn't have been the first woman to fall for a man sight unseen. In her era, people sometimes fell in love with someone based on their beautiful calligraphy or poetry. A man might fall in love with a woman at a glimpse of her tastefully arranged sleeves from a carriage window or below the screen that hid her face.

Kiyoko was young and naive, and with no mother to advise her, a perfect target for a Heian version of a catfisher.

As Masako said, the unknown admirer *wanted* a demon to enter the room. If not, why ask Kiyoko to move the screens? He could have taken a more traditional route to killing Motoko, like asking Kiyoko to put some secret "special medicine" in the Consort's food.

But while poison might cause someone to die after vomiting blood, nobles had other ways to eliminate rivals, such as Michinaga's slow but successful strategy to deprive Empress Sadako of the Emperor's time and attention. Or they framed people for crimes to have them exiled, as Michinaga did to Empress Sadako's brother.

Could her death have been due to illness? Probably not. Masako seemed certain the sentient dark mist was an evil spirit that killed Motoko.

Why did Outcast possess Kiyoko rather than Masako? They were in the room together when the Consort died.

Maybe I'd given Masako immunity to possession. A vaccine, but for spirits.

That thought made me smile, then frown. If I'd given Masako resistance to spirit possession, even the kami would not possess her. My presence might have been a net negative for her now she was on the verge of expulsion from Kamo.

Meanwhile, I was headed for an honors degree in Asian Studies and then grad school. Life would be good for me, but what had I done to her?

The server placed a check on the table.

"*Dōmo,*" I said automatically as I tucked Kenji's translation into my backpack.

"Your Japanese is very good," the server replied in perfect American English.

Startled, I jerked the pack's zipper and pinched my finger. "Ow! Oh, are you American?"

Her eyes glinted with mischief. "Ow, oh, are you Japanese?" Her throaty laugh reminded me of Masako.

She was around my height and age, but she was buff, like she did weights *and* cardio, very much not like me.

"You know that's not fair," I said. "My Japanese accent isn't as good as your English."

"Sorry," she said, her tone not sorry at all. "I heard you talking with the cute guy who was here earlier. He's Japanese, but you're from the Midwest. I'm good with accents. My dad was assigned to an overseas post in Michigan for a few years."

"Michigan? That's such a coincidence! That's where I'm-"

A manager-looking woman glared at us. "Sato-san!" She gestured to a nearby table where an older couple looked slightly impatient.

"Sorry, gotta go!" She waved as she hurried away. "Stop by again!"

Slipping back into my preoccupation with Masako's situation, I packed up my laptop and papers, left cash with the check, and stepped out the door and into a wall of humidity so thick it was practically solid.

Wandering from alley to side street gave me time to think about what I had or hadn't done to Masako. The heat made breathing difficult, but the mouth-watering fragrance of seasoned grilled corn wafted toward me from a nearby park. I lingered in front of a garden packed with small, twisty bushes and trees and admired the cube-shaped Obon lantern hanging by the front gate before noticing an elderly man lighting a small fire in a clay dish. I watched him for a minute in silence.

When the fire was lit, he smiled at me, nodding to the flames. "O-kaeri, ne?"

Welcome back? How did he know I'd returned to my body two weeks ago? *Oh, that's right.* Fires were lit this time of year to guide ancestor spirits home for Obon.

I bowed. He gave me an approving smile and a nod in return.

After an hour or so of meandering, I returned to the house. I slid the front door open, stepped out of my shoes and onto the tatami mat, and set my backpack down. "Tadaima!" I called, tugging the bottom edge of my shirt to unstick it from my back. *I'm home.*

"O-kaeri!" Kenji called from above me, his greeting an eerie echo of the old man in the alley.

I headed upstairs. Kenji's door was open, and he sat at his desk writing on plain white paper.

"Hey, Kenji, can we talk?"

He put his pen down and gestured to a blue *zabuton*. "Please, have a seat."

When I didn't respond other than to sit cross-legged on the cushion, he lifted one eyebrow in silent inquiry.

Be brave, Mina. Just say it. "I have so many questions, Kenji-san, but first, let me apologize for going through your stuff and for hurting your feelings by asking someone else to translate Masako's letters. I didn't want you to think I was using you." I took a deep breath. "Kenji, I *like* you. I want to spend time with you, but not because you can help me. I like you for *you*."

"Mina-san…"

His serious tone could only mean one thing. *Here it comes. The big letdown.*

"I first read about you in Masako's Chronicle many years ago," he said, "and ever since, I wanted to go back in time the way you did. Because of the Chronicle, my ambition to learn more about the spirit world led me to a decision to become a Shinto priest."

That didn't surprise me—after all, I'd never met anyone who knew more about Shinto than he did—but I hoped he wasn't about to tell me we couldn't have a relationship because he was a priest.

His eyes glinted. "The first time I read it, I appreciated what Masako did for the Empress, and how patient and kind she was to you. I thought you seemed a bit, well, selfish."

He didn't like me because of what Masako wrote? I blinked away tears.

"But when I re-read the Chronicle, I realized how brave you were despite your anxiety. And so funny. Somehow your jokes made it from your American brain into classical Japanese. And you sacrificed yourself to save the Empress. You thought you wouldn't survive the shikigami-monkey possession, but you took it on anyway. I like you, Mina. Not just because you are part of my family's story, and not just because of what you can teach me."

I closed my eyes for a second to hide my excitement. *He likes me!*

"I was upset you asked your professor for help because *I* want to be the one to translate Masako's notes. I want to understand your experience. I want to *know* how it feels live in another person's body. Also, I thought it would connect us spiritually."

That was nerdy and hot at the same time. I wanted to brush Kenji's hair back from his cheeks and see where a kiss would take us. A spiritual connection was all very well, but what about a good old-fashioned physical connection? *That's what I get for crushing on a religion major.*

His lips twisted with suppressed amusement as if he knew exactly what I was thinking, which sent blood rushing to my cheeks. He looked away to give me time to recover before he continued in the same earnest tone. "When you saw those hexagrams, you probably wondered why I didn't tell you I study divination. I didn't want you to think *I* was using *you*. I'm studying onmyōdō, yin-yang divination. Your experience with it, what you learned from Seimei—that all fascinates me." His eyes glowed with that patented Kenji intensity. "I am trying to keep my interest in your *experience* separated from my interest in *you*, but it's difficult."

What a pulse-pounding thing to say. "Kenji, I tried to tell you the same thing in the coffee shop. It looks like we both were afraid the other would think we were using them." My heart raced with excitement. "But we can help each other! I'll tell you everything I learned about divination, and you work on the letters for me."

"Yes. Let's be honest with each other about everything. But, Mina, I understand it feels like a long time since you broke up with Mick, but it's only been two weeks in 2019. I don't want to be your rebound."

Rebound? I'd been stuck in the body of an asexual shaman for over a *year*. I hadn't gone that long without a boyfriend since my junior year of high school.

On the other hand, one thing I'd learned about myself in my time with Masako was that I used my heterosexuality as a defense mechanism. Jumping into a relationship meant I didn't have to invest in friendship. This might be a chance to have both, a boyfriend who was also a true friend. It sounded like that's what he wanted, too.

"You're not a rebound," I said, "but I understand. We should build a friendship first."

He reached across the table and squeezed my hand.

I squeezed back, regretfully changing the subject. "Kenji, about those letters. Reading them connects me to Masako, not as a fond memory, but like she's here in 2019 and we're talking to each other. Well, I suppose it's more like she's texting me. I want to text back to tell her I returned to my world safely. But time only goes one way, and that's forward. So I can't, unless I go back through the spirit world, and I'm not about to do *that* again."

"I've been thinking about that." Kenji closed his eyes and bent his head as if praying. "I've tried *so* many times to cross into the spirit world during meditation, but I've failed every time." He opened his eyes to look into mine. "And then you did it without knowing how to or even wanting to, which means you have an innate ability. No one I've ever talked to about this stuff has done that. So… I was thinking…"

His uncharacteristic hesitation made me nervous.

"Maybe we could go back in time together."

The room began to spin. I pressed my palms against my eyes to make it stop. "No! No effing way!"

I peeked through my fingers to see his expression, but he stared at his hands. I couldn't determine if he was disappointed or was waiting for me to calm down.

"Sorry," I said after the vertigo passed. "That was harsh. I'd love to send a message to Masako, but seriously, you do *not* want to go back in time. You have to leave your body in the present and find a host body in the past. And then, if you possess someone, they could exorcise you, and your spirit would be sent into the void. Or your host could die from battle, disease, or starvation, leaving your spirit homeless. You do *not* want to do that, believe me."

"This is my family's history," he said firmly. "*My* ancestors enabled *your* trip to happen. If it weren't for my ancestor Akichika, Masako's journal wouldn't have been preserved, and I wouldn't have met you on Mount Tsukuba. I've dreamed of this for years. I studied with Shinto experts, learned classical Japanese, and found arcane incantations in my family's archives, but I don't think I can enter the spirit world without your help."

So that was why he didn't want me to think he was using me. Because, in a sense, he *was* using me. "Kenji, you don't understand. From your perspective, I disappeared for a few minutes, but for me, it was a year and a half. It changed me. The world is dimmer even on the brightest day. Part of me is missing while bits of Masako's soul are interwoven with mine. Masako's journal must have seemed like a light novel to you, full of humor and adventure. But it wasn't. I feared for my life. My spirit almost supplanted Masako's in her own body." And… I'd witnessed actual history being made and became friends with one of the most famous writers in Japanese literature. So there was that. But I needed to remain firm on this point. No. Going. Back.

He shrugged his shoulders. "*Jaaa*, I understand."
Finally!

"Masako is in danger from the demon that killed the Crown Princess, and at risk for expulsion from her home at the shrine, but I understand. You can't help her. It wasn't your fault. I'm sure it was a coincidence her powers failed her at the same time you left."

My jaw tightened. "She remained alive long enough to write the Chronicle, not to mention these letters dated 1002."

"We haven't read all of them. Maybe some of these pages are from other people."

"Then let's read them all before we decide anything."

"Don't you miss the adventure? The companionship?"

"Of course! Without Masako's constant presence, I feel like half a person, with no way to know when—or even *if*—I'll ever feel whole again. It's not like the answer's on Web MD, you know? I barely survived, and it wouldn't be fair to Masako to possess her again."

"What if we can find other hosts?"

"It's not so easy. Masako was *in* the spirit world when she pulled me in. So I think any host would either have to be in the spirit world or on the border of it. And the hosts have to be willing to let us possess them. I've had a lot of time to think about the ethics of spirit possession, and rule number one is don't steal someone else's body."

"We could try meditating our way into the spirit world, and maybe we'll find other shamans willing to host us."

"What, like a home exchange? You possess my body and I possess yours?"

"Great concept, Mina-san. Airbnb for bodies! Like hey, I'm not using my body this week, someone else can have it."

"I can see the ad now," I said, trying to keep a straight face. "Strong, healthy body available for short-term spirit possessions."

"Ten percent discount for ten days or more."

"Yes! And rewards for repeat customers, like no cleaning fee with every five possessions. It's a killer app. What should we call it?"

He tapped his fingers on the table and looked off into the distance. "Ehhh…How about spirit dot com? Never mind, it's too much like that American airline. Ah! Got it. SoulBnB!"

"Perfect! Let's buy the domain name before someone steals our idea." I pulled my phone from my back pocket and pretended to search for it. "Aw, it's already taken," I said with a pout.

"What?"

A giggle escaped me at Kenji's expression, which had gone from mock-serious to genuinely surprised. "Just kidding," I said.

"Uso-tsuki!" he said, pitching his voice as high as a girl's and pretending to smack my arm. "Such a liar!"

I couldn't help but laugh out loud, but his fake-teenager expression was so damn cute I had to restrain myself from throwing my arms around him.

"Mina, I have more to tell you."

His serious tone was a cold splash of water on my heated daydreams. *What now?*

"It's important." He hesitated, his eyes traveling over my face as if seeking assurance I could handle what he had to say next. "My research indicates modern technology interferes with the pure spaces of the kami, and because of this pollution, the kami can't descend into our world. The purity of their spaces has been compromised. Contaminated."

The urgency in his voice made me shiver.

"It's all kinds of pollution. Cellular and microwave radio waves, heavy metals. Sound pollution too. Purification at the shrine helps, but it's not enough because those waves go everywhere the kami go."

I opened my mouth, but no words came out, so he continued,

his voice cracking with emotion. "People are essentially good." He cleared his throat. "But without the kami bringing their light and goodness to our world, we're devolving. We're becoming more selfish, and angrier. It's already happening. People think it's because of social media, but social media's a symptom, not a cause."

It made no sense, so why did I believe him? "Most people in the world don't know about the kami," I said. "Much less pay attention to whether they are present in the world. Why does it matter?"

"Do you know the Japanese myth about the catfish who lives underground? When the guardian kami leaves, the catfish tries to escape and its movement causes earthquakes."

"Are you saying that's literally true? Pollution destroys pure spaces, so the guardian leaves, the catfish tries to escape, and Japan has more earthquakes?"

He gave me a faint smile. "The catfish is an allegory for what *will* happen. We've always had earthquakes, but man-made disasters are increasing. The Great East Japan earthquake and tsunami were probably natural, but the Fukushima disaster was a human-created problem. No nuclear plants, no nuclear disaster, right?"

"Let me get this straight. The kami leave because of human-caused pollution, so they can't protect us like they used to. So when disasters happen, they're bigger?"

"It sounds strange, and it's not quite that simple, but for brevity's sake, I'll say yes. In addition to polluted kami spaces, we don't revere our ancestor spirits, or *senzo*, as we call them, as much as we used to. If they are not revered, they can't move on to become guardian kami, which means they won't be able to protect their descendants. They might become vengeful spirits called onryō, or possibly *oni*. You know what oni are, of course."

"Of course! Like ogres or goblins in Western mythology, but supernatural."

He nodded. "Well, the word *oni* originally represented the negative energy that causes illness or death. Without the kami's presence, we have increasingly negative energy in our world, leading to more isolation and loneliness. Do you know how many old people die each year without anyone noticing they're dead until they begin to stink? And the rise in *hikikomori* and *otaku* can also be blamed on negative energy. So much loneliness, even among young people. Like you, Mina."

I wasn't reclusive like *hikikomori,* the term for the growing number of young adults who withdrew from society, nor was I so obsessed with gaming or anime that I couldn't talk to actual people—*otaku*—but I *had* been lonely before I met Masako. "What does this have to do with going back in time?"

His brown eyes darkened as he leaned closer. "If I can enter the spirit world, I'll gain the ability to perceive spirits like you did. But I can't go without you. Together we'll figure out the source of your power, and how much of it you have, and then you help me gain it too."

"You're giving me too much credit, Kenji. How could I possibly have that ability? Me, an ordinary American college student?"

An odd expression flashed across his face. Amusement? Irritation? Probably both.

"I don't know how, but you had enough power to get into the spirit world the first time," he said. "When you came back, you gained spirit-seeing skills, though you refuse to admit it. So if you take me across the border, I'll gain power, and you should gain more since it would be the third time for you. It would be like this." He drew a spiral circling upward in the air. "When we reach the pinnacle," his finger paused above my head, "and we use our divination knowledge, we should be able to create a spiritual buffer to keep tech pollution out of the kami's spaces. Think of it as a positive spiral." His searching gaze reminded me of Seimei. "This is our chance to save the world."

I straightened up with a jerk. Was he insane? I couldn't save the world. I could only watch it deteriorate. Wars. Pollution. Climate change. Active shooters. Racism. No wonder my anxiety dissipated in the past. Sure, my life was in danger—my very soul was in danger—but the constant flow of bad news, the pressure to keep my scholarship and make my parents happy when they weren't going to be happy no matter what I did? None of *that* was in the past.

And yet going to the past showed me how the world today was way better than I used to think. We didn't despise commoners anymore. Smallpox had been eradicated. Measles— or red pox, as they called it then—was back, a bummer since it didn't have to be, but the epidemic in Kyoto in the tenth century killed a huge percentage of the population. In Masako's time, the average lifespan was twenty-eight. Sei Shonagon was a wise old woman at thirty-one. No wonder the young Empress Sadako called her shonagon, or counselor.

Kenji was right about the environment, though, and he'd just offered me an opportunity to *do* something about it instead of my usual slacktivist sharing of posts about climate change as if that was enough.

Instead of resisting my power, I could embrace it. If Kenji had those powers too, maybe we *could* do something. But what? "So, Kenji-san, you want to do this risky thing without knowing *how* it will help the kami?"

He sighed. "There's something else I haven't told you. Remember when we talked about Ashiya?"

"Yes?"

"And I told you that Japanese paper can survive a millennium?"

"Uh-huh," I said uneasily, a little flutter of anxiety in my chest at where he was going with this.

"I found letters on old washi paper, written in classical Japanese, hidden under my family's shrine in Tsukuba. Mina, they were addressed to *me*. From *Ashiya*."

"What? *What*? Are you joking?" He wasn't, but my anxiety was spinning into dread as icy fingers reached into my chest and squeezed. "Why? How would he know you, much less leave messages for you?"

"He said Seimei's *Book of Onmyōdō Secrets* contains spells to protect the kami's spaces, and he'll help me get a copy. He said Seimei's a control freak—well, that's my interpretation—and won't let someone like me have a copy. Ashiya can't be a terrible person if he wants to help me do a good thing, right?"

I bent forward and pressed my hands against my stomach. "No, no, that's not right."

"It's a lot to take in, but if anyone would believe me, it's you. You've been there. You know Seimei. You know how powerful he was."

"Yes, it *is* a lot," I said. "You believe technology threatens the kami's existence, and you alone can save their spaces. Ashiya—the evil sorcerer from gaming—is a good guy who's been misunderstood and vilified by history like a Japanese version of Richard III. But based on my personal experience, he can't be trusted. Nobles would go to him when they needed a curse, not to Seimei. Why would he direct you to find this book? Wouldn't Seimei leave you that information if he wanted you to have it?"

"Maybe he did, and I just haven't found it yet. Ashiya understands what needs to happen. Somehow he knows me and understands how to save the kami's pure spaces. Mina, you said everything that's going to happen has already happened. According to Ashiya's messages, Seimei refused my request for his Book, and only Ashiya can help me. Which means..." he mimed a drum roll. "I've already gone to the past and met him."

Why did I let him draw me into speculation on how we might go back in time? I wanted to move on with my life, finish my study abroad, graduate next year, and figure out what came next, like everyone else in my class. Someday Masako would be a fond and distant memory, like a childhood friend. I *did* want to reassure her I was fine. Her letters broke my heart, but she wrote them over a thousand years ago.

On the other hand, she'd have been miserable if she'd been expelled from the Kamo Shrine and forced to marry or become a wandering shaman. For all I knew, she died soon after writing these letters.

I'd learned a lot from Masako. Like it was okay to be vulnerable with a friend. That shallow relationships weren't as satisfying as deeper ones. That you could see the worst of someone without hating them for it.

A friendship like that should last a lifetime. A *hundred* lifetimes.

Kenji said we were the only ones who could preserve the kami's pure spaces. If he was right, we could help Masako *and* gain enough power to help the kami. My spirit-traveling skills might atrophy if I didn't use them, which meant now was the best time. Also, if Kenji was right—and why wouldn't he be?— the world might devolve past the point of recovery if we waited too long.

I straightened my back. "I'm not saying yes, but let's discuss how it might work. Seimei sent me home from a power spot in Uji, and Uji's a short train ride from Kyoto. Maybe I'll recognize the place. I'm not committing to anything other than that."

Kenji's eyes shone. "I'll divine the most auspicious day and time. We can look at a map of the area and scout what might be the most likely location."

"Before then, Kenji, we should read the rest of the letters because we might find out Masako doesn't need us. I don't buy this idea that Ashiya was misunderstood, but I promise to keep an open mind for now."

He pushed some pages across the table to me, so I settled in to read them. I might be about to make a big mistake, but at least I'd make it with Kenji.

Chapter 11

Disturbing Things

S pirit Mi-Na, you will be pleased to learn that Sei Shonagon visited Kamo today. Our common purpose—to protect Empress Sadako's reputation—brings us together occasionally. She asked me if you had survived your trip home. She seems to think you and I communicate through the spirit world. I informed her that, sadly, we do not. I told her I write to you often and pray that the kami will save my little scribbles for you to find.

Sei was distraught about Lady Motoko. "So much death," she said, rapidly blinking to prevent tears from spoiling her cosmetics. "First our beloved Empress, then her sisters Miku and Motoko, all of them dying tragically while young and beautiful. Other deaths too. Perhaps you have been hidden in this shrine for so long that you have not heard about Lady Izumi's beloved Prince Tametaka. He died a few months ago. Izumi is about your age, Miko, and a member of the imperial family which makes it very sad indeed. Izumi's poetry is beautifully heartbroken. No woman is better equipped to be tragic."

Mi-Na, you always enjoyed Sei's torrent of words. I could hardly keep up with them.

"His Majesty's mother died this year. Well, she was four years older than I, so perhaps it is not tragic, just sad, although rumors abound that someone cursed her. A priest exorcised five or six spirits from her! Can you imagine five possessions at one time? She must have felt quite crowded inside. Well, you know better than I how *that* might feel. Spirit Mi-Na was, perhaps, as intrusive as five spirits of the usual kind. Ah! I must not forget to mention another death: Lord Nobutaka, earlier this year. Do you remember his wife? She writes the Genji tales. Nobutaka was quite old, so perhaps, like His Majesty's mother, it cannot be considered one of the strange events of late. Nobutaka's third wife—they are calling her Murasaki now, after one of her characters—writes more tales now than before her husband died. She should spend a year mourning in solitude, but she continues to write her stories, and everyone at court clamors for more. It is not seemly. Every chapter is more exciting than the last. Everyone loves-" Her voice cracked. "Her tale." Sei looked at me sharply. "Why do your lips move?"

I had been trying not to laugh, but I did not want to tell her that. "Mi-Na would say you are jealous of the Genji author because people prefer her tales to yours."

She sighed. "Ah, the Spirit Mi-Na understood me so well. I miss her."

"I miss her too. I speak to her even knowing she will not answer."

Sei raised her eyebrows, and for once she had nothing to say.

Mi-Na, you will want to know what Sei wore for her visit. Her face paint was expertly applied, and her hair was neatly braided for tucking into her traveling hat. Because it was still summer, her robes were of lighter silk. She wore twelve robe layers, alternating green, orange, and yellow. Her fan was green. I felt dowdy in my white robes but at least I moved lightly and quickly, while she panted merely from walking into the visiting room.

I told her of the strange demon that possessed Lady Kiyoko.

She shuddered. "Everyone in the imperial residence is terrified," she said. "Miko, why do you remain here doing nothing? If the Spirit Mi-Na were here, she would make you go to the Capital to help. If you cannot do that, what *can* you do?"

Tears spilled down my cheek. Sei was right, Mi-Na. I am useless.

"Oh, stop it," Sei said with a wicked little smile. "You are not one of those women who become more beautiful when they weep."

Her comment made me laugh, as she knew it would.

She waved to a box on a table. "Here are the final entries for my book. It is a gift for Princess Nagako. Keep it here until she is of age to take care of it. You may read it but do not make copies for distribution until she is older. My final entries will have everyone exclaiming about my impudence even though they secretly enjoy my wit. Now stop crying and *do* something about this problem in the Capital. Has the High Priestess ordered you to stay here?"

"No, but when Mi-Na left, my power also left. I should have stopped the demon-mist before it attacked Lady Motoko. Mi-Na would have done so."

"Perhaps you need a shock, an earthquake of the soul that will loosen the power trapped under the hard clay of your mundane life. A visit to the Capital might do that, considering the strange occurrences there of late."

"That is what Lord Seimei said. That is why he asked me to attend Kiyoko's exorcism. But I am reluctant to leave the shrine again. Do you really think I should leave?"

She leaned forward in her intensity, strands of white hair

mixing with black against her cheeks. "Perhaps the gods won't speak to you in this sacred place because there is too much competition, too many other holy women here, who, I am sure, have had many more years of training than you."

Her words stung. "Does no one believe I belong here?"

"Miko, you love this place with your whole being. You serve the kami with devotion and sincerity. Hosting Spirit Mi-Na was the beginning of your journey. Sending her away was *not* the end of it. Someday the kami will speak through you again, and you will become as famous as Miko Uchifushi. Our former regent, Lord Kanaie, depended on her for advice. Someday *you* may serve as advisor to a regent—although not to the current one, I hope."

"But Shonagon, I only desire a quiet life at Kamo. If I could summon the kami to send messages to the people, I would be content."

Sei tapped my knee with her fan. "But you cannot summon the kami." *Tap.* "So, you are not content." *Tap.* "Now, what will you do about it? Sit here and cry, or leave this quiet life to do something good? Anyway, I heard a rumor you will not be here long."

My chest grew tight at her words. The High Priestess must have told others how I have failed. I thought I would have more time.

Sei rose to her feet, not noticing—or not caring about—the effect of her words on me. "I have found another husband and will go to his estate, for I am not welcome at court. The Regent dislikes me, and anyone who hosts me risks his displeasure. Miko, heed my words. Bandits will not kidnap an old woman like me, but you are young. Not beautiful, but beauty does not seem to be a requirement. Be careful."

Sei had become more eccentric since the Empress's death, but she meant well. And beauty, like fame, has never been important to me, so I was not offended.

The next day I received the startling news that Lady Kiyoko had disappeared. Lord Seimei summoned me to assist with a divination to learn whether she had been kidnapped or had run off with her mysterious lover.

The journey was downhill, and the ox was young and energetic. The weather has been dry lately, and the habitual sticky mud was firmly packed. Usually, the ox-carriage moved more slowly than a young person walks, but we arrived at the Capital gates before the sun reached its peak.

After I arrived and was escorted to the divination hall, Lord Seimei tossed his bone divination sticks repeatedly while chanting an incantation I did not recognize.

When he completed the required number of throws, he drew the hexagrams and studied them for a minute, then passed his papers to me.

I spread them out and studied their meaning, setting their shapes in my mind, then closed my eyes and sat in a meditation pose. The shapes floated across my eyelids, dancing and reshaping. A flickering light burned against my eyelids, and a face appeared, bright red, with a fierce expression. And... *horns*?

My eyes flicked open in shock. My hand shook as I wrote my findings, making my brushwork scarcely legible. If I was correct, this affected the imperial family.

Seimei accepted my paper when I slid it across the table. He read it silently, then set the paper down. "We must go to the palace immediately," he said.

At the imperial audience hall, I sat behind a curtain stand, but I pushed the curtain aside just enough to allow a glimpse of the Emperor, Regent, noblemen, and warriors seated there. Lord Seimei knelt in front of the Emperor's michōdai. The heavy, cloying scent of musk and cloves from incense-infused robes competed with a late summer breeze floating into the hall from the outer rooms.

My heart pounded loudly in my ears. We had conducted the divination several times to be certain my interpretation was correct. I wanted to be wrong, but I feared I was right.

Seimei bowed low, and after many eloquent expressions of humility, he held up the divination scroll. "Bandits are not responsible for the recent spate of kidnappings." He paused while His Majesty and the Regent leaned forward with great interest. "Oni have taken Lady Kiyoko and the other young women who disappeared from the Capital."

Gasps filled the hall. Faces grew pale.

His Majesty turned to Seimei for answers. "What will appease them?"

"The kami have not seen fit to answer that question, Your Majesty, which tells me the kami did not send them. Therefore we need weapons, not prayers or offerings, to defeat the oni."

A warrior asked for permission to speak. "Your Majesty, even experienced fighters would not be able to defeat a demon so powerful it can kidnap young women without being seen. Can Lord Seimei not fight them with magic?"

The Emperor frowned at him. "You will not fight?"

The warrior spokesman bowed again. "We do not refuse, Your Majesty. As soldiers who have fought enemies of the realm, our loyalty has been proven many times. However, we have never fought oni."

I suppressed a gasp at their rudeness. How would we rescue Kiyoko and the other women if fierce warriors would not go?

Seimei's magic did not extend to fighting demons in open battle.

Emptying my mind of thought, I breathed slowly and closed my eyes, ignoring the murmur of voices in the hall as the men debated what to do.

An image appeared in my mind: the Consort's room; the screens, positioned to create an opening in the kimon direction. Kiyoko had been possessed by a strange spirit called Outcast. And then Kiyoko disappeared.

My eyelids shot up. "Your Majesty, may I speak?"

Mi-Na, you would have laughed at the way the warriors turned to stare at my screen as if an oni hid behind it. Seimei glared at it, however, for my impertinence.

His Majesty smiled at Seimei's expression. "Yes, Miko."

"My divination tells me that a curse widened the Demon Gate which allowed evil spirits to enter the realm, including the demon that killed the Crown Prince's Consort. It is likely the oni who kidnapped the women also came through the opening."

A shocked silence followed my words.

"Your Majesty, I will divine the location of the oni and rescue the young women."

Does my impulsiveness shock you, Mi-Na? I shocked myself a little, but if I am to be expelled from Kamo, my life will be meaningless. Sacrificing my life in the service of His Majesty would give meaning to it once more.

Lord Michinaga spoke first. "Curse? Demon Gate? Lord Seimei, what do you know of this?"

Seimei cleared his throat. "We couldn't divine the true cause of the Consort's death, but it appears connected to the sudden appearance of the oni."

"Royal Astrologer, you have a bright pupil." His Majesty tipped his head toward my screen. "Miko, your courage is admirable." He crossed his arms as he looked down at the row of four warriors kneeling behind Seimei. "She is braver than all of *you*." He looked thoughtful. "Miko, how will you find the oni, and how will you defeat them? Has Lord Seimei taught you such magic? For prayers alone will not work."

Seimei answered for me. "If my health allowed it, I would fight the oni myself. Lady Masako's divination skills are truly remarkable. I will determine the most auspicious day for her to travel, and teach her additional spells."

His Majesty nodded once. "Since you vouch for her, I will accept her offer." He turned back to the warriors. "Go with her. Protect her on her travels, and work together to rescue the poor victims. I will bring my fiercest commander back from the north and send him with you, along with these four warriors. Lord Seimei, please use your divination skills to determine preparations for departure and the most auspicious day to leave."

The four men had the grace to look ashamed as they bowed farewell to the Emperor.

The next day, the High Priestess visited me at Kamo, which pleased me greatly. Do you remember how kind and wise she is? After our purification rituals and offerings to the Great Kami, we broke our fast with boiled millet. She, aunt to the current emperor and sister and daughter of former emperors, deigned to eat millet with me, daughter of a Fifth Rank nobleman.

"Miko," she said. "Your courage is admirable. You appear calm despite the danger."

I seized the opportunity she provided. "Your Highness, a whirlwind of fear swirls within me. The shrine is where I belong, but without the power to summon kami, may I continue to call it home? Seimei believes my abilities will return when I need it most, but the kami have their own will, and can be unpredictable."

"Lady Masako, you have always shown modest and reserved comportment. It was out of character for you to speak in the presence of His Majesty and the Regent. The kami guided your words. I did not make a mistake when I brought you to Kamo as Shrine Miko, but something is missing, something neither Lord Seimei nor I can divine. The kami are telling us this journey is essential to your future."

I bowed. "Thank you for the honor you have shown me, Your Highness. But the men who are to escort me are violent. They will protect me from bandits and outlaws, but will my title and rank be enough to protect me from *them*?"

"His Majesty will instruct them to leave you alone, and we will spread enough rumors about your sacred status to keep them away from you. Their commander, Lord Yorimitsu, is the least likely to be frightened of your spiritual powers, but he will not defy a direct order from His Majesty."

"Thank you, Your Highness."

"Miko, you have been comfortable for too long. This adventure will be good for you."

"If my powers do not come back, and yet somehow I survive, what will happen then?"

She closed her eyes for a moment. "The Regent will arrange a marriage for you. Now, let us pray together before I return to Murasakino."

As you know, Mi-Na, I will not marry anyone, especially not after living a life dedicated to the kami. The Regent's choice of a husband would not be based on how kind a man was, but on what political advantage the Regent would gain from it. Ah, Mi-Na, why did you take my powers with you when you left?

We bowed, washed, and clapped to summon the gods. She prayed for the safety of the Emperor and for the young women who were abducted. I implored the kami to return my powers. I did not question why they took them from me, nor why I must endure a long and dangerous journey to get them back. My faith in Seimei and the High Priestess, as well as my own curiosity and excitement, overcame my fear of leaving.

However, it did not alleviate my fear that I would never return.

Chapter 12

Sushi

I grabbed another plate from the conveyor belt. "This time I'm trying the trio with all my favorites. One piece of regular tuna, one fatty tuna, and one extra fatty tuna. I'll eat from lowest to highest fat, with the richest tasting piece for dessert."

Kenji had suggested a conveyor-sushi restaurant for dinner after I told him how ravenous I was, not having eaten anything other than the roll after my hike and a piece of cheesecake at the coffee shop. The empty feeling in my stomach was now assuaged, so this was my last plate.

Even while scarfing fresh sushi, I couldn't stop thinking about Masako's situation. Fierce warriors hesitated to confront oni, but not Masako. She was about to face spirits so evil they'd killed the Crown Princess and kidnapped young women for some awful purpose. Instead of the peace and closure I'd expected to find in Kyoto, Masako's letters had made me more remorseful, guilty, and anxious than ever about leaving her.

What, if anything, should I do about it? "Masako's Chronicle didn't mention oni or kidnappings in the year after I left, right? My reading ability isn't great, and I want to be sure I didn't miss any references to Motoko's death and what came later."

He finished his mouthful. "The journal only describes the year and a half she spent with you. It doesn't have anything about what happened after you left."

"She's so literal. I mean, *was* so literal." It still hurt to use the past tense. "When I asked her to record our adventure together, I didn't think to ask her to write about her life after me." I took a palate-cleansing sip of beer. "I don't understand why her power disappeared. She said Seimei told her I had too much yang, and she had too much yin. Maybe, without my yang, she still has too much yin?"

"Volunteering to fight demons is a very yang thing to do, so I think she continued to benefit from your extra yang energy after you left. Her missing power is somehow related to your connection to each other. That's why writing to you makes her warm. It's not metaphorical. Her body *literally* heats up when she writes to you. Perhaps that's the source, but she doesn't know it yet."

"Her body grows *warmer* because she's writing to *me*?" Reading Masako's letters warmed my soul, but my body temperature didn't increase.

"Yes, that's how powerful your connection is, how you remain intertwined despite your centuries of separation. You could say it's a kind of magic, or maybe it's a quantum entanglement."

"I've thought about the quantum thing, but how does her action of writing a letter to me a thousand years ago affect me *now*? Quantum entanglement means particles affect each other even when separated by *distance*, but as far as I know, not when separated by *time*. I'd love for all this to be explained by science, but there must be more to it than that. What about the fox?"

Kenji nodded thoughtfully as he pushed his empty plate away. "Do you know the Japanese word *musubi*?"

"Um, isn't it a kind of sushi? A rice ball?"

"That's one of its meanings." He held his palm out so I could see him sketch an invisible kanji on it. "The left radical is the kanji *ito*, meaning thread."

"Yes, I know that one."

"And…" He scratched another character into his palm. "The right radical means auspicious. Together…" He sketched the whole word, which took a few seconds because it had twelve strokes. "They form musubi, which means knotted together. Connected. In Shinto, musubi means the kami's harmonizing, creative power. Both meanings apply to you and Masako. I think the kami created this connection between you, and time cannot destroy something they created."

"I see. Yes, that makes sense. Sort of. Based on your definition, musubi implies entanglement, which brings us back to quantum physics. Have any physicists used spirituality to explain quantum theory?"

He shrugged. "No idea, but probably not. Maybe that'll be my PhD dissertation someday. Anyway, there's something else I want to tell you. A famous legend in Japan fits Masako's description of the disappearing women. Shuten Dōji was an oni king who loved to drink saké. The legend says he kidnapped young women from the capital, and Emperor Ichijō sent five famous warriors to defeat him and rescue the women. No mention of a shrine miko, though."

A vague memory stirred at the back of my mind. "Uh-huh… Yeah, I know that story. My mom bought me an old Japanese movie based on that legend. The English title was *The Demon of Mount Ōe*. I watched it in Japanese with my childhood friend Aya. She understood the Japanese, so I read the English subtitles instead of watching the dubbed version."

"I saw that movie too," Kenji said. "It was made in the sixties. The special effects were lame."

A horrifying idea struck me. "If the legend is based on a historical event, and Masako told us she was part of that event, but isn't mentioned in the legend, do you think she died in the fight with the demon?"

Kenji shrugged. "Records back then didn't include a woman's birth and death dates, or even their names, unless they were imperial family members. We need to find Masako's original journal to confirm she wrote it thirty years after you left. That would tell us she survived."

I stared at my plate without seeing it. "The next letter might tell us what happened on the journey to Mount Ōe."

Kenji murmured something I didn't quite catch, but it sounded reassuring. He finished his beer and exhaled with satisfaction. "*Oishii, ne*? Delicious. This is the best conveyor sushi in Kyoto. It's always fresh. They get their fish from the fish markets every day."

"It's amazing. Thanks for bringing me here." I took another big bite, followed by a sip. "Mmmm... Beer and sushi are a perfect match."

He put a hand on his flat stomach. "*Ippai*. So full. I need a walk."

"I'm full too, but I left the best piece for last. Is it rude to eat the fish but not the rice?"

Kenji said something to the sushi chef, who laughed and responded with a wave. "It's alright this time," he said. "The chef's surprised you ate as much as you did."

I pulled the extra-rich, extra-fatty tuna off the rice and savored its soft, buttery goodness before taking a final swig of beer. "Let's go." I pulled my wallet out of my cargo shorts pocket. "Hey, let me get this. You're doing so much for me."

He nodded his thanks. "My favorite shrine is about a twenty-minute walk from here. Is that too far for you?"

"Lead the way!"

The evening air had lost some of the day's humidity, with a cooling breeze blowing toward us from Mount Hiei. We walked in meditative silence for a while. I quashed an urge to hold his hand, rarely having seen PDAs between couples here, not even younger ones, and we weren't a couple. *Yet.*

Our talk this morning had been on my mind all day. He liked me and I liked him. He wanted to go back in time. I didn't, but that shouldn't be a deal-breaker to prospective couplehood. We'd be back to our normal lives next week and would have lots of opportunities to hang out. Studying together, hiking, coffee, Netflix…

"Are you interested in visiting Seimei's Shrine tomorrow?" Kenji asked. "It was built on the spot where Seimei's residence used to be."

"Oh, cool! I wonder if I'll recognize anything in the area. I visited Seimei's residence quite a few times with Masako."

"Unlikely," Kenji said. "Kyoto was never bombed, but it's changed a lot. Even the Imperial Palace isn't in the same spot as the palace you visited."

"But mountains don't change," I protested. "Except for volcanic eruptions. I saw Mount Hiei on my hike yesterday, and it looked just the same."

He held his hands up in surrender. "You have a stubborn streak, Mina. I suppose it saved your life when you were trying so hard to get home from the past. It'll be interesting to see if you recognize any landmarks."

He pointed out a few sights along our walk. "Nijō Castle is over there. We can visit it later this week if we have time. It was built in the 17th century for the first Edo shogun. When Americans think about ninjas and shoguns, Nijō is the type of castle they envision."

The high stone wall and tree cover above it prevented a glimpse of it. "That's the place with nightingale floors, right? They squeak when someone steps on them to alert the guards to intruders. If we have time, I'd love to go. Let's keep that in mind for later in the week."

We passed yet another Seven-Eleven, which reminded me to hydrate after my day of hiking. "Can we stop and get some water?"

Kenji agreed, and we veered into the refreshingly cool air of the store, crowded with office workers picking up boxed dinners to bring home after work.

"I'd be tempted if I weren't so full," I said. "That chilled soba looks good." I made my way to the cooler with soft drinks.

Kenji followed me. "Isn't Lawson's your favorite store here?"

"Any convenience store in Japan is better than no convenience store in Japan. What should I get? Pocari Sweat? It's so funny it's called that. Who wants to drink sweat?"

"Americans always laugh at that name," Kenji said. "It's not made of sweat, it replaces it, like Gatorade." He picked a bottle from the shelf while I held the cooler door open. "Lime-flavored Ramune is better."

"But you have to carry a glass bottle around," I said. "I'm getting Calpis Water."

Kenji insisted on paying for our drinks since I'd picked up dinner. We drank them while standing outside the store, then dropped our bottles in a nearby recycling bin.

"The shrine we're going to is dedicated to Inari," Kenji said as we continued our walk. "It's not the famous Fushimi Inari Shrine, although you should visit that while we're here. That path has a thousand torii gates."

"Oh, yes, I want to go there too."

"We'll figure out how to fit it in. You might see another fox spirit."

I couldn't quite determine if he was joking. His expression was somber, but his eyes had a devilish glint.

"The kami Inari comes up quite a bit," I mused. "We found

the letters at one of his shrines, and a fox showed me where they were. Now we're going to another Inari shrine."

"Inari is one of the most important deities in Shinto. By the way, you said 'his shrine', but Inari was originally female. It wasn't until Buddhism arrived in Japan that Inari was portrayed as male. Nowadays you'll see pictures of Inari as a goddess and other times as a god."

"So why are *they* so special to you personally?"

He laughed. "English is so.... specific. Japanese is better. We don't have to indicate gender if we don't want to. Back to your question, Inari is an avatar of Izanami."

"Do you think Izanami sent me back in time?"

"I believe she was an active participant in what happened to you, what's happening to Masako, and what I hope will happen to me."

"But why would she?"

He threw me an exasperated glance. "Americans always ask why. Be patient, Mina. Some things can't be explained logically. You have to experience it. Feel the truth of it."

"You sound like Seimei. He always yelled at me for asking why."

Kenji guided me close to a shop window so we didn't block the sidewalk. "I'm sorry. Was I yelling at you? I didn't mean to."

His concern pierced my heart. "No, you didn't yell. Although to be fair, if you had bushy gray eyebrows, a white beard, and a few wrinkles, you'd look just like Seimei."

"Well, that's not exactly flattering, but I'm relieved you're okay with what I said. I'm not used to talking about my spirituality since my grandfather passed away a few years ago. I could talk about Shinto and the kami with other priests or my professors, but I can't talk about travel to the past. It's too far-fetched. My parents don't believe in it. They think the Chronicle is fiction.

I only met you two weeks ago, and I'm still getting used to having someone to talk to about it."

"And *you're* the only one who would ever believe what I went through." I grabbed his hand, no longer caring whether it was culturally appropriate or not.

He pulled me forward into the stream of walkers and cyclists, deftly weaving us through and around without letting go.

As promised, we arrived at a tiny shrine behind a wall in an alley. Even in this small space, two fox statues guarded the entrance. "Why is the fox linked to Inari?" I asked. "Especially when kitsune spirits cause so much trouble?"

His brow furrowed. "Ehhh…Inari's messenger foxes are not the same as mischievous kitsune spirits, but that's a good question. Perhaps it's because Japanese foxes eat wild mice."

I waited to hear the rest, but he just smiled like he wanted me to figure it out.

"Let's see… Inari is the god—I mean goddess—you're right, it's better to have a gender-neutral word, so I'll just say kami—of rice. Is it because mice eat rice, and foxes eat mice? Getting rid of mice improves rice harvests."

"That makes sense," he said approvingly. "Now, let's pray to Inari. Perhaps *they* will answer our requests for clarity."

I was willing to try, but I knew the rice deity wouldn't answer my prayers. I hadn't finished my sushi rice.

Chapter 13

Bikki

The next morning I came downstairs, eager to ask Kenji if we could visit Seimei Shrine, only to find no Kenji and no coffee. Another translation, however, was lying on the table, so after making a strong brew, I sat down with my mug in front of the stack of pages.

I picked up the top sheet, both excited and fearful to read what happened to Masako next.

Eighth Month, Chōhō 4 (September, 1002)

Mi-Na, I have so much to tell you. If you ever find this letter, you will be happy to learn I've become friends with a commoner. You must have thought such a thing would never come to pass. Nor did I. I will tell you the story of my strange journey, and pray that you will find it someday and marvel at how I have changed.

Seimei instructed us to perform a walking meditation to our ancestor-kami shrines before beginning our search for the oni. Yumi accompanied me on her horse, carrying a pack with offerings to the shrine, food for the journey, and so on. However, I had become soft and weak in my years at court, and I stumbled on the path, hurting my ankle. I refused Yumi's offer to ride her horse because I did not want to risk the kami's displeasure with such an interruption to my walking meditation. After instructing me not to move, Yumi rode on to the shrine to seek help.

It began to rain so hard I feared it would wash me down the mountain, so I sat on a large rock, my feet pulled up and my head down. My traveling hat kept the water off my face, but elsewhere I was as wet as a sea bream.

The rain hid the sun, but I knew it had set when trees and mountains became obscured by darkness.

I prayed to the kami for guidance. They answered my prayers when a strange creature appeared before me. An unpleasant odor emanated from beneath its brown covering. I gazed at it in astonishment. Somehow I knew it was not a bandit or a *yōkai*, so I did not fear it.

"You hurt? Need help?" It spoke with a human voice, although the words were difficult to understand.

Mi-Na, can you imagine what it was? A commoner! But not the one I later befriended. No, this one was the worst kind of commoner, the kind which tans leather and is therefore constantly polluted by death. I did not answer, instead covering my nose with my sleeves to escape the sickly sweet scent of wet animal skin.

"Are you a wandering miko?" He stepped closer. "We need a miko in our village." He pointed toward the bottom of the mountain. "No matter. If you are hurt, you should not be out here. Demons and shape-shifting spirits wander these paths at night, many more recently. Come."

I shook my head wordlessly, reluctant to go anywhere with such a creature.

"This polluted one understands," he said humbly. He bowed and turned away.

The rain was so thick I could scarcely see his back. Yumi should have returned by now, but perhaps she, too, feared the demons that might be abroad in the night.

If so, I would sit alone in the rain until morning. But without my powers, what defense did I have against demons? My heart beat rapidly, and suddenly I could not breathe. "I *do* want your help!" I gasped.

"Shelter is a short walk away," he said as he returned to me and handed me his staff. "The path is muddy. If you do not fear my pollution, take my sleeve."

We journeyed slowly up the trail. After some time, we reached a mountain hut. Inside, the rank smell of the man and his animal skins caused me to sit close to the entry despite the rain coming in. My robes and hakama were sodden, and my hair had begun to come undone from its twisted braid, but no warm brazier was lit to dry my clothes. Was this how commoners lived? In the dark, sitting on a dirt floor with no heat?

He unloaded the skins. "Sit on these. Don't worry. They are tanned. The deer has been dead for a long time, and Tusu-kur has blessed them."

"Tusu-kur? What is that?"

"Tusu-kur will help you."

Such an odd name, I thought. "What kind of power does Tusu-kur have that he can heal me?"

"Help you. Perhaps heal, perhaps not. Tusu-kur has magic like an onmyōji or a *yamabushi*, but he is different. Do not fear him, for he is kind."

My paper supply has run low, so I must keep this tale short. Tusu-kur arrived at the hut. If the tanner had not described him to me, I would have screamed in terror, for he looked like no one I had ever seen. His skin, while not as dark as a commoner's, had more red than nobility. His eyes were large and light brown, and nearly round. His beard was long and untrimmed, with wiry gray hair. The hair on his head was also long, an odd mix of gray, red, and brown colors. He wore an unusual cloak made of bark.

He said his people had lived in the realm for a long time, even before the Yamato people. Like a yamabushi, he practices healing arts and divination and wanders through the mountains seeking knowledge. His people use the word *tusu-kur* to mean shaman. He said I should call him Bikki, which means frog in his language. His parents called him Bikki because as a small child, he frequently made a sound like "bik-ki, bik-ki." And when he said that, I had to laugh, for he did sound like a frog.

He sent the tanner to bring a message to the shrine so Yumi would not worry about me. He then rubbed my ankle with a healing paste and bound it with a strip of leather.

Something about his demeanor comforted me. I told him about you, Mi-Na. "When I write to her," I said, "A warm glow shines inside me. It gets stronger the more I write, until sometimes, I think light must shine through my sleeves and into the darkness."

He recommended I continue to write to you. He said the warmth from writing to you comes from my spiritual power, which he said was dormant rather than completely vanished. Mi-Na, my brush is not skillful enough to describe my joy at that news.

I told Bikki of my mission. His people are affected by the demons pouring through the Demon Gate, so he offered to help me.

Bikki stayed outside the hut all night to give me a respectful space to sleep. I thought I would never be able to sleep in my wet *kosode* on animal skin, but I slept better than I had in a long time.

Yumi came to find me the next morning. She had received Bikki's message that I was safe, which was fortunate, for the priest had not found someone willing to rescue me in the storm. She begged my forgiveness for not returning. I forgave her, for what other course did she have?

She was not pleased with me for making friends with a commoner. She tied silk around her face to keep out the odor of tanned skins which she said infected my robes.

I no longer noticed it.

Chapter 14

She's Giving Up

Excited about Masako's new friend, but nervous for her as well—this Bikki might not be who he said he was—I grabbed my phone. He was probably Ainu, one of the indigenous peoples of Japan displaced by the Yamato. A quick internet search for Ainu shaman yielded hits related to games or anime. I lost a few minutes—well, maybe more than a few—reading game descriptions before making myself stop.

After changing my search terms, I found an academic article describing Ainu shamans. Similar in function to onmyōji and miko, they conducted healing rituals and divination using animal bones.

The wooden stairs creaked as Kenji came down them, a sound that sent a thrum of excitement through me. Last night I'd been too alert to sleep, as energized as if I'd had coffee before bed. I'd replayed our conversation over and over, remembering his thoughtful frown and the way his tentative smile told me he wasn't sure how I'd react.

He liked me. He didn't want to use me. He wanted to go back in time. I liked him. I didn't want to use him. I did not want to go back in time. But I did want to help Masako. He said he liked me!

I poured him coffee as a tiny thank-you for his work translating and handed it to him with a cheerful flourish, causing the too-full mug to spill onto the tatami mat. He thanked me with a smile and sipped enough from the top to safely transport it to the table while I wiped up my spill.

"*Ohayō*, Kenji-san. Did you stay up all night?"

"Good morning, Mina-san. I went to bed at 4:30." He took another sip. "I know what you want to ask me. I translated the last letter last night." He cradled his mug, gazing at me somberly. "It's a short one. She's giving up."

"What? That can't be right. I just read her letter about how she looked forward to traveling with Bikki." A sudden thought chilled me. "Did he hurt her?"

"Oh, no, nothing like that. Here." He held out a piece of paper. "Read this."

Eighth Month, Chōhō 4 (September, 1002)

Spirit Mi-Na, I write to you with sorrow. My ancestor spirits did not answer my prayers. My ability to summon the kami did not return. Without it, I may not survive the battle with the oni. Even if the warriors vanquish them, my life in the capital will end. I will be forced into a marriage I do not want, perhaps to bear children I do not want. If I reject such an arrangement, I will be forced to wander from town to town conducting divination for common people.

Mi-Na, if only you could return to me. You would change my fate. You would help me.

Yumi tried to console me, but her efforts were useless.

"I failed His Majesty as well as Lady Kiyoko," I told her. "Both Seimei and the High Priestess believed this journey would restore my powers, but it has not, which means I also failed them."

"Lord Seimei said your powers would return when you need them most. The kami chose you, and they will return to you. Be faithful to them. There is a shrine to the Great Kami Inari not far from here. We can stay the night and pray again."

I agreed. I had nothing to lose by doing so.

We said farewell to the priest of my ancestral shrine and traveled the short distance to the shrine of Ōkami Inari. The priest there said we could have the pilgrim's room for the night. It was a cool evening for Eighth Month, even in the mountains.

Once we completed our ritual purification at the nearby stream, we went to our room to meditate and pray. The priest here, who comes from a noble family, supplied me with paper, brush, and ink. Writing to you, Mi-Na is a form of meditation for me.

As I wrote, I prayed to Inari. And with every brush stroke, a light brightened in my soul, making my skin warm, even hot, so hot beads of dew formed on my cheeks. Such warmth never occurred during the Kagura Dance. Surely it meant the kami were present, so I begged Inari to possess me.

But no. When I finished writing, the light and heat vanished.

Bikki was mistaken. The magic of writing and praying did not bring the kami to me. The warmth that came while writing was not a sign of the gods connecting us across worlds. I do not understand what it is, but it is not that.

I cried myself to sleep.

We will stay another day, and then leave with Bikki to fight the oni. Without special powers, the oni might kill me. If I survive, I do not deserve a life at Kamo and will leave before I am expelled. I will wander as common miko do, from village to village, telling fortunes.

It only took a few minutes to read Masako's letter. "I need water," I mumbled. I put a glass under the tap, staring at it without seeing it until cold water began to run over the top and onto my hand. I took a drink, but choked, unable to get it past a lump in my throat. Water dripped onto my clavicle and slid under my t-shirt in a cold, slow-motion trickle.

Why would she give up on her dream after all I did to help her achieve it? She'd be miserable anywhere else. How could she think of becoming a wandering miko? Without the protection of the imperial family, she'd be abused and misused. Women traveling alone back then were fair game for men who came across them. Yumi wouldn't stay with her. She'd refuse to live among commoners.

Warm hands settled on my shoulders, as reassuring as a weighted blanket.

"I conducted a divination before I went to sleep," Kenji said. "The results tell me that she needs our help."

"Kenji, she's *dead*. She died a thousand years ago."

I must have said 'That was a thousand years ago' twenty times in the past two weeks, but this time it hit me like a blow to the gut. She died long before I was born.

What did it matter whether we went to help her? What was done was done. What had happened had already happened. Masako's fate was decided long ago.

I couldn't bear to look at Kenji's concerned expression, so I stared at the glass of water in my hand instead.

"Mina-" Kenji murmured.

"What?"

"If we travel to the year 1002, she won't be dead."

I set the glass down. "You know how to get to me."

He met my eyes with an open vulnerability that left me

breathless. "I didn't want to tangle my feelings for you with my interest in going to the past, but I can't help it. You're in pain. You deny it, but going back might help you both."

A sudden pang twisted my stomach. I didn't want him to be right. I hadn't recovered from the first trip yet.

But what if Masako needed me? I couldn't abandon her, not after everything we'd been through together. If Kenji inherited even a fraction of Seimei's power, his divination might be correct, and if that were the case, the kami would help us.

My heart pounded. "Let's go to the Seimei Shrine first, and then to Uji. If we find the power spot where Seimei sent me home, we'll know whether it's possible to go back."

As the words left my mouth, I knew they were true.

Chapter 15

Kirihara Spring

Unassuming gray concrete torii gates marked the entrance to the modest shrine tucked into a city neighborhood, half hidden by apartment buildings towering over it.

"This isn't flashy enough. Seimei was the world's most famous onmyōji, and not exactly humble about it. That statue doesn't even look like him. Although…" I examined it for a minute more. "I met him when he was in his seventies, so it's hard to judge."

"I don't think Seimei would be disappointed," Kenji said. "It was a great honor when Emperor Ichijō established it only two years after Seimei's death."

A five-pointed star hung at the top of the first torii gate, and as we walked into the shrine grounds, we saw the same symbol on lanterns and tiles throughout the courtyard and on the building. "It's funny how the pentagram is considered a tool of evil in American horror movies, yet here it's a good symbol that wards off evil. Based on the number of stars here, they must be expecting a *lot* of evil-doers to visit Seimei's shrine."

Kenji laughed. "I never thought about it that way. Did Seimei ever explain what he used it for?"

"Actually, Seimei didn't use a five-pointed star. He used a pentagon. He would draw lines connecting the sides, and he filled in the spaces between the lines with different yin-yang elements, like fire, wood, water, metal, earth, or the five directions—north, south, east, west, and center." I peered at a star. "Hmm… if intersecting lines are added to a pentagon, it becomes a penta*gram*. Okay, now I get why it's his symbol."

We strolled to the middle of the shrine grounds. My hands and cheeks tingled, possibly from the power spot located here. Or maybe it was only excitement at standing on the spot where Seimei had once lived. Nothing looked familiar, though, and power lines and apartment buildings blocked my view of the mountains.

A faint vibration buzzed upward into my feet and legs. A faint echo of Seimei's voice reverberated in my head. *Throw the sticks again. And again. Now, what does it mean?*

"I want to buy a souvenir," I said.

We walked to the case where the public could buy amulets for health, safety, and longevity. I examined a *hachimaki* headband. "Why do you think it has two symbols? Seimei's star and a weirdly big hashtag? Oh, before you answer—I forgot to mention I met a strange Shinto priest on Mount Daimonji. He pointed to a symbol like this that was drawn on the dirt."

"That shape is Ashiya's symbol. Seimei and Ashiya were so different that having their symbols together fosters yin-yang balance, so this kind of hachimaki is worn for double protection."

"So that priest was showing me Ashiya's symbol? Do you think he's another guy who believes Ashiya was misunderstood? Why would he show *me*?"

"Maybe he sensed your spirit had traveled to the past. We can go to Mount Daimonji tomorrow and talk to him about it."

I shivered with a strange reluctance to go back to the creepy priest. "If you think we should…"

I left it at that. If Kenji brought it up again, I'd go. If not, I wouldn't remind him. I paid for the hachimaki but declined the nice shrine wrapper. Instead I folded it into a tiny square and crammed it into a pocket. "People wouldn't wear Ashiya's symbol if he was evil," I said. "So you're right about him."

"The Western concept of evil differs from Eastern, and I could lecture on that all day, but we should head to the station. Do you want to pray first?"

"Pray to *Seimei*? He'd love that, but no thanks."

We hurried to the bus stop and hopped onto a bus that had just arrived, exhaling with relief at the cool air inside. No seats were available, so we hung on to the straps overhead, swaying slightly each time the bus stopped and started. I tried not to bump into the twenty-something guy sitting below me.

Kenji gazed out of the window dreamily.

The little smile on his face concerned me. "Just to be clear," I said. "We're only going to Uji to look for the power spot where Seimei sent me home. That's *all*."

Kenji came back from wherever his thoughts had been. "Agreed. When we find it, I'll divine whether we can enter the spirit world from there."

Passengers jostled past me on their way off the bus so I didn't answer. After it started up again, a seat was available. Kenji waved me to it, but I declined. "Someone else might need it more, and it's only a few stops. But Kenji, even if you get to the spirit world, what makes you think you can go into the past? Masako *pulled* me into her world. I didn't find it on my own. What if we land in a year of famine or war, or during a battle? What would happen if you accidentally possessed an animal or a baby that can't speak yet? You might never return. Doesn't that scare you?"

I kept my voice soft, but even so, the guy below me looked up, startled at my words.

"Gaming," I said with a smile. "Onmyōji."

He turned a little red but gave me a friendly smile in return. "Ah! I like that game." He waved his phone at me.

I was about to ask him where he learned English well enough to eavesdrop, but changed my mind. He might think I wanted to go out with him. I nodded and turned my gaze to the window as if fascinated by the view.

Kenji considered my questions, not paying attention to my sidebar conversation.

His silence warmed me. None of my other boyfriends ever spent a minute pondering my words. None of my other boyfriends made my skin tingle with just a smile.

Not that Kenji was my boyfriend.

Yet.

Kyoto Station was the next stop. Kenji finally answered my questions about spirit possession while we waited in line to buy tickets.

"Remember Seimei's fish analogy?" he asked. "He told you the spirit world is an undersea cave that connects to all other caves. Each cave is a moment in time. You swam into it from our side, and Masako swam into it from her side. She swallowed you like a big fish eats a smaller fish, and you traveled with her back to her world."

I nodded. Seimei's fishy analogy was the only way this whole time-traveling stuff made sense. "I guess our spirits fusing was the spiritual equivalent of digestion."

Kenji chuckled as he purchased our tickets. He handed me a ticket and waved off my offer to reimburse him. "Masako's letter said the Demon Gate connects her time and place to the spirit world," he said as we searched the signboard for our train's location. "It's bigger now, allowing all sorts of spirits to go through.

If we go to the spirit world, we can look for the opening to Masako's time and place. This is where your ability to perceive obake comes in. You'll see spirits crossing through it to get to Masako's world, and we'll follow them."

I shook my head so vigorously my ponytail holder slipped and hair whipped into my eyes. "Oh, no. Not gonna happen," I said as I pulled the hair tie out and redid it. "I am *not* entering the spirit world on the slight chance I can find a specific opening."

Kenji wisely refrained from further discussion on the subject as we hurried to the right platform and found seats on the train.

During the short journey to Uji, I used my phone to research possible power spots. "This website says Ujigami Shrine is the oldest shrine in Japan, built around 1060, a few decades after I left. Hey, this is interesting—it honors an emperor's son who refused to become emperor, saying it wasn't fair to his other brothers. And his brothers said no, *he* was the most qualified. How nice they were back then. But it probably means it isn't the place."

He nodded absently. His eyes were on me while I talked, but he didn't seem to be all there, which, for Kenji, was odd. He was usually one of the best listeners I'd ever met.

I held up my phone. "It says here that Uji is famous for tea. I'll have to bring some back for Keiko and, um, my professors."

I'd spent two whole months in Japan so far, and I'd only made two friends: Kenji and my Japanese conversation partner Keiko. Three if I counted my ex-boyfriend Mick, which I didn't.

Kenji didn't respond, so I stopped talking and tapped a hyperlink to read about a nearby temple. I stared at my phone in shock before bumping Kenji's arm with it. "Look. Byōdō-in temple used to be a villa owned by Michinaga! His son converted it to a temple. Can you believe it?"

"Eh?" Kenji woke from his reverie. "Yes, I knew that.

Murasaki probably visited Michinaga's villa. There's a Tale of Genji Museum near the Ujigami Shrine. Do you have any interest in that?"

"Who needs a museum? I met Murasaki in person."

Just then the loudspeaker announced Uji Station was next. Too excited to wait for the train to come to a complete stop, I stood without grabbing the hanging strap, so of course I pitched forward into Kenji, who had one hand on a strap and the other holding his backpack, which he dropped so he could throw his arm around me. Using the opportunity to keep my face pressed against his chest, I inhaled his unique fragrance of cinnamon and sandalwood.

I straightened as the doors opened. *"Gomen,* or uh, *sumimasen!"* Japanese had many ways to apologize, and I never seemed to pick the right one for the occasion.

He didn't mind. He laughed as he picked his pack up and gestured to the exit. "Let's visit Tachibana Island first," he said as we descended. "It fits your description, and it's near Ujigami Shrine, so if it's not the place, we'll head to Ujigami."

The humidity wasn't as thick as in Kyoto, and the path led along the river, which gave us a slightly cooler breeze. Wooded hills rose above us, scenting the air with cedar. If nothing else came of this trip, the beauty of this moment alone was worth it.

We crossed Uji bridge so I could study the statue of Murasaki Shikibu on the other side. "It doesn't look like her. Her face was thinner, less oval. Her expression is about right, though. Pensive."

"You only met her once, right? What was she like?"

"Well, she had a perplexed expression like she didn't know why she'd been invited to spend time with the Empress. She liked Masako, though."

Kenji started walking toward the island. "Everything you say about your experience in the past makes me jealous. Why can't I do what you did?"

"You're right. It should have been you. I've stopped asking why I was chosen. The kami want what the kami want."

We crossed the Asagiri Bridge, stopping halfway to enjoy the contrast of its red railings with greenery on the opposite river bank.

When we reached the island, I knew immediately it wasn't the right place. "Seimei's island was roundish. This one is more of a rectangle. Also, Byōdō-in is over there," I said as I pointed to the opposite bank. "If that is the actual location of Michinaga's villa, I'd have seen it."

Kenji's face fell with disappointment.

I hated to let him down. "How far is Ujigami Shrine?"

He pointed in the opposite direction of Byōdō-in. "It's just a short walk from here. It's considered a power spot, but not a transformative place because it's not on a mountain or island."

"It's worth taking a look at, right?"

"Yes. Let's walk along the river first to see if you recognize anything. If you don't, we'll head back to Ujigami."

We crossed back over the bridge and turned toward the mountains. Houses and businesses disappeared, and forested mountains rose steeply from the river. Tendrils of morning humidity rose into the air like little ghosts. Traditional wooden houses clung to the hillside above us as we walked along the street.

I glanced over the water as we walked. No tree-covered islands, but if the river had changed course, Seimei's island could be anywhere.

My shoulders slumped. "This is a crazy idea. How could I possibly find a place I spent an hour in a thousand years ago? Also, Ujigami might be crowded."

"It's a short walk, and I promise you'll find it worth a visit."

"Only if we stop to get some green tea ice cream. It's so hot. I need something cold."

"The sweet shops are on the other side of the river. Let's go to the shrine first, then we can treat ourselves to ice cream."

"I see your game. You think if I eat ice cream first, I won't want to go to the shrine after."

He widened his eyes. "What, me? Playing a game? You always tell me I'm so serious."

Lifting my chin, I folded my arms with exaggerated arrogance. "I want ice cream, and I will have ice cream."

He bowed deeply, arms held straight and rigid at his sides. "*Hai, bosu-sama.* You're the boss."

I laughed at his ridiculous phrasing. "Okay, okay, I give up. We'll go to the shrine first."

As we walked up the steps to Uji Shine, Kenji pointed to a sign at the entrance pointing to the right. "Kirihara Spring. We should try that."

"Is that part of this shrine?" My heart beat faster. "Maybe Seimei's island was in a spring rather than a river. This could be it!"

I lurched to the right, but he didn't notice my change of direction, and I bumped into him, knocking us both into the sign. "Sorry! My bad. Let's go this way!"

My excitement drove me to speed up my pace. I'd been lacking in enthusiasm up to now, but adrenaline energized me, and I didn't even care about the pain on my forehead from smacking into the metal sign.

Kenji caught up with me. "It isn't accessible anymore. All that's left is a water fountain. We can explore around that, though. A friend of mine is a priest here. He will vouch for me if we're challenged."

"Do you know every shrine priest in Kyoto Prefecture?"

"Perhaps I do." He grabbed my hand, which surprised me since I'd set a brisk pace.

My sudden stop caused me to whirl around like a game of crack-the-whip.

"Mina-san?"

Laughing, I clutched his hand tightly to keep my balance. "Yes?"

"Ever since I first read Masako's Chronicle, years ago when my grandfather gave me his copy to read, I've known I'd be your spiritual guide. That's one reason I'm a religion major specializing in Shinto." His eyes burned with an intensity that left me speechless. "I'm sorry for the fear and danger you experienced in your journey into the past. Whether your possession of Masako was a divine joke or the kami have a grander scheme, my fate is woven into yours."

Unable to meet his gaze, I looked at the path to the spring. Nothing in my experience had prepared me for someone to state unequivocally that our lives were linked.

A powerful urge to pull away from him swept through me. I was quick to make acquaintances, and just as fast to drop them, afraid to make *real* friends since seventh grade, only allowing myself to develop a true friendship with Masako after spending eighteen months with her. I'd been a terrible guest while she'd been a wonderful host. She hadn't banished my spirit into the void when she could have. She'd undertaken a dangerous journey to get help for me. She'd listened to my 21st-century rants with amusement and allowed most of my culturally inappropriate gaffes to slide over her without insult. She was a truly good person, and I became a better one under her influence.

Was Kenji going to make me a better human? Or was I about to open myself to someone who would hurt me?

I grabbed his other hand. "Kenji-" I didn't know what to say.

We stood still, blocking the narrow path, facing each other, holding hands as if about to say our vows.

He tightened his grip and took a deep breath. "I've always known you would enter my life, but I didn't realize I would be so drawn to you or how my pulse would pound in my wrists when I look at you." He took my left hand and laid my fingers over the artery in his neck. "Feel that."

His pulse felt strong beneath his warm skin, the tempo faster than I expected. A slight sheen of sweat caused my hand to slide to his collarbone. He pressed it there for a second before releasing me.

He had shown me his vulnerability, and now it was my turn. "It matches mine." I took his right hand and laid it over my heart as it drummed loudly in my ears. "See?" My eyes filled with tears. I tried to blink them away, but a few managed to escape.

"Mina-" He tenderly brushed them away. "I understand."

Did he, though? I'd lived in a state of anxiety for years, convinced no one would like me if they knew what I was really like. Friendships and romantic relationships remained superficial by choice.

But except for Masako, no one knew the real me better than Kenji did. I'd done some unsavory things and he liked me anyway. Did I trust him enough to let my guard down completely? If I did, and it turned out he was using me, it would destroy me.

Abruptly letting go of his hands, I turned away. "The spring is this-" I swallowed, cleared my throat, and tried again. "Um, this way, I think.

A wooden hut appeared at the end of the path. "Is that the water fountain? I was expecting, like, a literal drinking fountain."

He caught up with me. "This is it. Kirihara Spring. It's the only one left of seven original springs here. The others dried up a long time ago."

Our voices were normal again, almost as if I'd imagined the moment on the path.

"Does this look familiar at all, Mina?"

What I thought was a hut was a roof over a well. Steps led down into the dark, but I stopped short of entering. "The trees here aren't that old, and it doesn't look familiar, but I have this weird feeling, almost like deja vu. You said six other springs existed here at some point?"

"Yes, seven total."

"Then it could have been any of them, but we have no way to know which. Unless your divination studies include dowsing? You could walk around with a deer bone and see if it bends toward the earth." I laughed so he'd know I was joking. Water dowsing was a completely different kind of divination. Obviously.

He didn't react. "Let's separate to cover more ground. If you detect a pulling sensation in a spot, stop and wait for me."

"Same for you. I'll start on this side and circle that way, and you start there and circle this way."

After a few steps toward the woods, I stopped and closed my eyes. Cicadas had just begun their afternoon humming. A crow called out a hoarse *kaaa.* A slight breeze rustled through the trees.

My fingertips prickled. I stretched my arms out as if feeling for an invisible wall.

"*Mi-Na.*"

My eyes flew open. A fox stared at me as if bored by my obtuseness. "Is this the place?" I asked, feeling only a little bit foolish. "Seimei's power spot?"

No answer. I didn't expect one. Even if it could talk, it probably wouldn't speak English.

"Are you the same fox that showed me the spot where Masako's letters were hidden?"

It gave me a disgusted look and walked away. I followed, because, well, what did I have to lose?

It stopped, swished its tail a few times, and disappeared.

Which, unsurprisingly, took me by surprise. *Real foxes don't disappear like that.*

At the spot where the fox had brushed its tail, I knelt and set my hands against the dirt. A faint buzzing, like a nest of ground bees, tickled my palms. I jerked my hands up. I appreciated bees for everything they do for life on earth, but I did not like to be stung. Did anyone?

Sitting back on my heels, I closed my eyes, emptying my mind of other thoughts.

The buzzing grew louder, accompanied by a mysterious tugging on my legs, almost like the bees had arms reaching up to pull me into their ground hive.

"Did you find anything?"

The sound of Kenji's voice made me gasp.

"Sorry, I didn't mean to startle you, Mina. I didn't find any power spots, so I wondered if you found anything."

"Donmai," I said, happy to use my new vocab word. "Remember how a fox showed me where the box of Masako's letters was?"

"Yes?"

"It showed up again just now. I swear it looked real, Kenji. When I saw obake in the past, they were misty and telepathic. This looked like a regular wild fox. It wanted me to dig here. When I put my hands on the ground, I felt that pulling sensation you mentioned."

"The fox was here?" He was clearly excited. "Where did it go?"

"It, uh, kind of... uh, disappeared into thin air. So, yeah. A spirit fox. Although it wasn't white and only had one tail, not nine like the legends say."

He had the grace not to say *I told you so*. "Does this spot look familiar? Could it be the place where Seimei sent you home?"

"I don't recognize it, but all these trees have grown up since then. And the spring has gone underground. Does that mean it's not a liminal space anymore?"

He shrugged and knelt on the ground. He placed his palms on the dirt, keeping them still for a full minute in silence.

"I don't feel anything," he said at last.

He switched his position to sit cross-legged. "Let's talk through your memory of that place. You were on a small island, right? Which means the spring ran around a higher spot." He waved to the right of the tree. "See how it's slightly higher here? It flowed around this tree at some point. The spring went underground only a few years ago."

An image flashed through my mind. *Masako, sitting on the island in the middle of the stream. Trying to ignore her fear of what would happen, she gazed at the scenery while Seimei prepared his purification rituals.* Through her eyes, from that position, we'd seen the mountainside rise steeply above us.

I lifted my head, but the trees blocked my view of the mountain. Ignoring Kenji's curious stare, I stood up and walked backward until I could see over the treetops.

The hill rose sharply above the trees.

Suddenly dizzy, I closed my eyes.

I've been here before.

Chapter 16

Spiritual DNA

Kenji started digging through the loose, sandy soil, apparently too excited to care about getting his hands dirty. "Something's down here!"

My breath caught in my throat as I ran over. "What? What is it? Bees?"

He was brushing dirt away from an object he'd uncovered. "It looks like a small shrine, probably for family ancestors, but maybe the family moved or forgot about it. The tree has grown around it, and I don't think I can remove it without cutting the roots." He pulled another handful of dirt out. "*Hora!* Look! Another box! And-" He grunted with effort. "The roots aren't trapping this one." He tugged. "Ah, got it." He stood up, a dark brown wooden container in his arms.

My cheeks tingled. "Open it! Please?"

He took way more time than I'd have liked to brush the sandy soil off. "Do you have long fingernails?" he asked. "There's too much dirt in the opening, and I left my pocket knife back in Kyoto."

Fortunately nail-biting wasn't one of my issues. "They aren't super long, but longer than yours."

He handed me the box. It was roughly the size of a laptop in breadth and width but several inches deeper. A slight vibration emanated from it. I ran my fingernails around the opening, then tried to pry the lid up. It moved, but just barely. Not wanting to force it, I tugged gently but it didn't budge.

Kenji reached for it, but I shook my head, hugging it close. I cradled it under one arm and used the other hand to pull. A nail broke but I ignored it to maintain a steady upward pressure. Another nail broke as the lid popped open. "Yatta! I did it!"

A silk pouch lay inside. It didn't look a thousand years old. Another case of caretakers keeping it for years before neglecting it? I gave the box to Kenji and took the pouch out with both hands.

I pulled its flap up and peeked inside. It contained sheets of soft, aged paper. Lifting the top page gingerly, I examined the faded calligraphy. Disappointed I couldn't read it, I handed it to Kenji, taking the box back from him in exchange. "It must be from Masako, right? It's not her handwriting, but it would be a strange coincidence if it wasn't originally from her."

"Eh," he said as his eyes traveled over it. "Yes, it's from Masako. Let's sit down and I'll try to read it. You're good for my translation skills, Mina. I could go professional after this experience."

"No prob, Bob," I said, warmth spreading through my chest. No one else would ever understand me the way Kenji did, and no one else would ever believe what I'd gone through.

Kenji smiled, but in a confused way, like he thought I made a joke but was too polite to ask for an explanation.

Okay, so maybe he didn't *always* get me. "Oh, you didn't watch *Bob The Builder* growing up. It means you're welcome." We needed to get back on track. "Anyway, see how the hillside comes down to this former spring? This is it, the place Seimei sent me home from."

"Excellent! Let's sit near the well so we don't trigger anything in the power spot."

Once settled on a bench, Kenji read the letter silently. I waited, tapping my feet on the ground, jiggling my leg, pulling out my phone, putting it back after Kenji frowned at me. I considered taking up nail-biting but changed my mind when I saw how dirty my hands were.

Finally, he lowered the paper but remained silent, his eyes unfocused.

My impatience got the better of me. "Hey, hey, come on! What's it say?"

He blinked. "Oh. Eh, it's a continuation of Masako's story. Remember the Ainu shaman? He found more paper for her to write on."

I clapped with exhilaration and relief. "Yay! Why do you think Masako put it here instead of with the others? Do you think this was her backup plan in case I didn't find the ones at Kamo?"

His eyes widened with surprise. "Actually, yes. You two must still be connected in some way. I'm thinking out loud here, but could you have exchanged something like spiritual DNA when you two were tangled up?"

"Please don't say that. It's scary to think we're still connected." Scary, but also reassuring. "Is that how she knew I'd come here?"

"She doesn't say. It was written just after her previous letter —it's still dated September, 1002. After you hear this, you'll want to do what you can to help her."

A lack of the one-eyebrow-raising gene prevented my raising a skeptical eyebrow. "Read it to me, please, and I'll see how I feel about that."

"Keep in mind I'm slower when I have to read and translate simultaneously."

I nodded impatiently, so he began.

Eighth Month, Chōhō 4

Mi-Na, I pray you find my letters at Kamo. I will leave this one in a different location to improve the possibility that at least one will fall into your possession. But it does not matter whether you read this or not. It does not matter whether you remember me or not, or even whether you believe I was a dream.

Do not be upset with me for saying such a thing. I say it to console myself because I will never know if you do or do not find my scraps of writing.

When I described to Bikki how I glow with light and heat when I write to Spirit Mi-Na, he said it is a practice I should continue. "It focuses your power like sunlight shining through a drop of dew. I will find more paper for you."

Bikki's magic is different from Seimei's. He conducted a ritual while I wrote, and he made visible something I felt but had not seen. When I write to you, a flame-like thread stretches out from my body through the air and into the darkness.

Bikki said the thread is my power made visible. But where does it go? Does it connect me to you? Or does it link me to the kami?

Bikki instructed me to again pray to Inari Ōkami while writing to Spirit Mi-Na.

I did as he suggested, and this time, Yumi and the priest prayed with me while Bikki performed his ritual. I wrote and prayed, and the thread grew brighter and thicker, from warm to hot, connecting me to the earth and sky. To Inari. To *you*, Mi-Na.

Then, even while I wrote, I entered a dream state. I dreamed you spun a thread that stretched through time, seeking mine, and when our threads connected, they braided together and grew brighter and thicker.

My dream ended and I fell to the mat, no longer aware of the world around me.

When I awoke, Yumi was hovering over me, her eyes filled with concern. She offered me water, which I drank thirstily. The priest told me how I stiffened and spoke in a voice that boomed against the screens. He said Inari Ōkami spoke through me to tell the priest I must journey to Mount Ōe to fight the oni and retrieve the kidnapped women.

I could not suppress my joy at this news, gasping and crying and laughing all at once. Inari had possessed me, even without a Kagura Dance to summon the deity. If you have read my letters, Mi-Na, you understand my relief and gratitude at this news. I thanked Bikki again and again for his wisdom. He was right. My powers had not gone. I only needed to connect to you and Inari at the same time. Bikki's ritual enabled this, but he said he would not be needed in the future, now that it has happened once.

The priest thanked me many times for blessing his shrine with the kami's presence. Yumi gazed at me with wonder in her eyes. I do believe she had given up on me.

News sped through the local village, and within hours, a crowd of commoners had gathered in front, begging for my blessing and asking me to summon other kami or to call the dead to pass messages to loved ones. Of course, I declined their requests. My purpose is to find the oni and rescue the women.

Yumi asked why this possession had not occurred at Kamo. "Perhaps because I prayed to Kami-Nari-Sama, who is enshrined there," I said. "And I did not have Bikki to help me."

My ankle is healed. Bikki's treatment worked so well I suspected he had divine assistance. Onmyōji such as Lord

Seimei can exorcise spirits causing illness or epidemics, but they can not heal an ankle any faster.

The priest provided us with food and water. He wanted me to stay, but I told him I must leave. He begged me to return after I completed my mission.

"If I survive," I told him, "I must return to Lord Seimei and to Kamo."

Bikki divined where to find the warriors, who were on their way to find the oni. He insisted we dress as yamabushi. He left his mulberry bark cloak at the shrine and borrowed a hemp robe from the priest. The priest gave us gray robes and white trousers to disguise ourselves.

Yumi thought it an outrage for a noblewoman to dress as a common mountain monk.

"Bandits have become bold and strong here, stealing the wealth created by mining the mountain," I explained, so she agreed to disguise herself too. The priest said he'd had personal experiences with local bandits and they were not pleasant ones.

Bikki said the noblemen in the capital steal from the mountain people more than bandits do. I never heard of such a thing when I lived in Hitachi Province. Of course, I never spoke to a commoner there, but I prefer to believe my father governed the province fairly, taking no more tax payments than necessary. Of course, temples and shrines need their share too, which, I suppose, does not leave much for the common people.

It was not easy to cover my hair, but Yumi rolled it into a braided bun which fit neatly into a large straw hat. Her hair is not as long as mine, and thinner due to her advanced age, so she did not have quite the same difficulty. I told her that if she was uncomfortable traveling with Bikki, she could wait at the shrine until we returned, but her eyes gleamed as she insisted on coming with me. She desires to serve His Majesty by attending me on this journey, and also, I suspect, she is bored with the quiet life I love so much. This dangerous journey would provide excitement for her.

Bikki replaced his Ainu head covering with a straw hat and rubbed dirt over his face to hide his ruddy skin, but I feared his wiry beard and deep-set eyes would give him away. He said he would keep his head down and his brim low when in the presence of the other men. His Majesty had ordered the warriors to escort me, but they would know nothing about an Ainu shaman. It would be best if Bikki remained disguised thus while with the other men.

I asked Yumi to pretend we were yamabushi even after we met the warriors. I suspected they would not want a woman on their expedition any more than an Ainu, although we would, of course, reveal ourselves when we reached the oni.

We left at sunrise. Yumi and I walked much faster in our yamabushi clothing than in our robes. The hot and humid air was not quite as sticky. The coarse fiber of our yamabushi trousers and shirt itched, but the cut was loose and comfortable.

After the sun passed overhead, Bikki motioned to pause and be silent. We peeked through bushes to see our warriors sitting in a circle and arguing about where to go next. Bikki sank to the ground and crawled forward, keeping his head bowed so they would not view him as an enemy. He called out in a suitably subservient manner.

They jumped to their feet, hands on swords, except for the leader, who pulled his from his belt. He was not taller than the other men, but his demeanor was so fierce, his back so straight, his feet poised for agility, it was clear he must be the commander called Yorimitsu.

He pointed his sword at Bikki. "Are you a bandit or a demon?"

Bikki kept his head down. "I am a holy man. With me are two other yamabushi. We were sent by the kami to whom you prayed." He waved a hand toward Yumi and me, our signal to come forward. "We will guide you to the demon's cave."

Yumi and I would not crawl on the ground like commoners, so we stepped forward with our heads bent in humility.

When they realized Bikki understood their mission, the warriors took their hands away from their swords and bowed, muttering prayers as they did so.

Yorimitsu, however, kept his eyes on us as he sheathed his sword. "The kami sent you to guide us?" He waved impatiently for Bikki to stand up.

Although Bikki's wiry gray hair was well hidden under his hat, his beard was not like the beards of the Yamato people. My heart raced as I waited for Yorimitsu to discover our deception. I felt certain he would resist the presence of two women and an Ainu, even though His Majesty had instructed him to protect me.

Yorimitsu stood with his feet planted wide apart, his arms bent at the elbow and fists resting on his sides, watching closely as Bikki rose from the ground. A rumble of afternoon thunder in the distance caused us to glance at the sky. "Ha!" he shouted, causing Yumi to jump. "Kami-Nari-Sama speaks on your behalf. Guide us, and let's go quickly. We have young women to rescue."

His urgency surprised me. I had heard he enjoyed fighting for its own sake, but he seemed sincere in his desire to save the captives.

Bikki led the way to a nearly invisible path. He used a staff to navigate wild plants along it, keeping his head down as if carefully watching where he stepped, but really to ensure his eyes and beard were less noticeable.

Yumi and I mimicked his walking style, our heads dipped as if scrutinizing the ground for hazards. The others fell in behind us, and the noise of their passage through the shrubs and sasa grass meant any bandits or oni lying in wait for us would be well aware of our location. But perhaps that was for the best. The five warriors sounded like they had twenty men with them.

We strode in single file until the sun crept closer to the mountain's edge. When our pathway fell into shadow, Bikki held up a hand. "We are close," he whispered. "We should camp here for the night. We do not want to attack the oni in the dark. Do not build a fire."

Yorimitsu didn't want to stop, nor did he want to take orders from a mountain monk. He pushed his way forward, brushing rudely against us. Yumi lost her balance and fell with a surprised yelp. I bent to help her, which caused strands of my hair to drift from my hat. Yorimitsu pulled my hat off, and my coiled braid slid down my back.

Shocked, he took a step back. "What is this?" He spun around to Bikki. "What are you?" he shouted as he grabbed Bikki's head covering and threw it onto the ground.

"Oni! Oni! A demon!" the warriors shouted as they saw his long, springy hair.

Yorimitsu turned first to Bikki, then to me, and then, realizing Yumi had cried out in a woman's voice, pushed her hat off with the tip of his sword.

Yumi shrank back in fear. "She is the Imperial Miko," she said, her voice quavering. "His Majesty ordered you to escort her to the demon's lair. You left without her." Her voice grew stronger. "You need her power to defeat the oni."

He examined me as if judging the truth of Yumi's words. He would not know my face, and the other warriors had not seen me behind my screen. After a moment, he grunted and turned his fierce gaze to Bikki. "You are not oni. You are Emishi." He put the point of his sword on Bikki's chest. "Leave us before I kill you."

Mi-Na, perhaps you know what an Emishi is. I did not, but it was clear that Yorimitsu hated them.

"Put your sword down," I said. "He is a diviner like Lord Seimei. He tells the truth. The kami guided him to you."

He did not remove his sword. "Miko, your contact with this dirty commoner has polluted you. Return to Kamo and pray for our success. Fighting is not work a woman should do." He spat at the ground in disgust.

Bikki is brave, Mi-Na. He didn't flinch even though Yorimitsu was one breath away from cutting his throat. "The kami blessed the Miko with their presence. You need her assistance," he said calmly.

"I will kill you for your impudence," Yorimitsu said through gritted teeth. "Miko, take your aged attendant and leave us. Lord Seimei provided the divination for us. What could *you* do that he could not? Useless women. Go!"

My heart pounded loudly in my ears at this outrage, and strength rushed into my body like water through a breached dam. I stood tall and unafraid, stretching my arm toward him. "Brutal warrior! His Majesty assigned *you* to accompany *me*. If *I* return, *you* must return. But I will not! I will find this cave of oni and use my powers to banish them!"

Yorimitsu swung his sword from Bikki to me. "Your rude manners will lead to your death."

Fury kept me from speaking further, and he mistook my silence for fear. "You are useless to us and the Emperor. Go home now. You will not want to watch me kill this imposter. Leave before my men are unable to control themselves at your beauty." He laughed at his jest, and his men did also.

His Majesty protects me, so I knew they would not act upon such a cruel threat, yet anger sluiced through my arms and legs, making them strong and light. I began a Kagura ritual with a low humming chant, sliding a foot toward him when he expected me to run away. His smile froze on his face as I danced slowly forward, raising and lowering my arms, my incantation growing louder.

He was the one who stepped back. The others stood still as if hypnotized. I pulled a piece of white washi paper from my jacket and threw it upward, calling out as it began to fall. "Shikigami, assist me!"

A white fox rose from the ground where the paper had fallen, snarling and baring its teeth. It jumped at Yorimitsu, nipping at his legs, sinking its teeth into his straw leg armor, while the warrior yelled and waved his sword in a futile attempt to kill the animal. It jumped at him, biting and snapping, reflecting my rage, acting my will.

I laughed as power flowed through my limbs and the fox danced with my movements. I gestured forward, and the fox sped around to Yorimitsu's back, leaping to bite his rear, although his armor prevented injury. His fellow warriors ran back and forth, not wanting to harm their commander, but not sure how to remove the fox.

Yorimitsu swung his sword behind his back as if to swat it, but it ran to the front and snapped at his knees and higher, aiming for a man's most vulnerable spot.

Yorimitsu yelled as he brought his sword point-side down on the fox's head—or so he thought. His sword point went through his boot and into his foot. He cried out again, cursing the fox, cursing me, and cursing Bikki.

The fox, unharmed, crouched by my side.

Yumi's voice cut through my rage. "Lady Masako, you must never conjure a shikigami in anger! It will turn against you! Remember? Lord Seimei taught you so!"

Waking from my half-trance, I dropped my arms, drained. "It is the only way I can conjure one, so it must be the kami's will."

Bikki agreed with Yumi, but he agreed with me too. He said

my intentions are what matter most. If I do not have dark thoughts and use my anger only to protect myself and others, it will not turn the shikigami against me.

The fox disappeared and my washi paper floated to the ground. I picked it up and put it back under my jacket.

Yorimitsu clutched his wounded foot, hopping about like a rabbit and as angry as a wasp. Yet after he set his foot down, his expression was calm. "No one told me you had such power, Miko. What do you want? Surely not to travel through this bandit-ridden wilderness with military men. We sleep on the dirt, we travel on foot, and our foe might be too strong for us to defeat."

The shikigami had taken all of my energy, so what I wanted at that moment was to sleep.

I forced myself to stand tall. "I wish to serve His Majesty and the kami, and to defeat the oni and stop these kidnappings and possessions."

"His Majesty knows how fiercely my men fight rebels and bandits, and he also understands they cannot fight supernatural beings with swords or arrows. Miko, I heard you lost your power, so after we prayed to our guardian ancestors, we proceeded to Mount Ōe without you. Today you demonstrated the rumors were false. Both kinds of power will be needed— brute force and spiritual energy."

I held my head high and looked straight at him rather than in my usual respectful manner. (I believe that was your influence, Mi-Na.) "And of course my guide," I said with a nod at Bikki.

Yorimitsu frowned. "I see now he is Ainu. I did not expect someone of his tribe this far to the south. He guided you to us, you said. If he can guide us to the oni, and the two of you use your power in our fight against the demons, he may travel with us."

The other warriors avoided looking at me, but no longer

appeared hostile, so we proceeded to a stream nearby to drink clear cold water. Bikki examined Yorimitsu's foot and saw it was a minor puncture, no longer bleeding.

For our evening meal, we ate rice balls and dried fish. While we ate, Yorimitsu told us his father had been commander-in-chief for the defense of the north against the Emishi people, which is how Yorimitsu developed his renowned fighting skills. He had been raised to view Emishi as rebels against His Majesty's governance.

Mi-Na, you would comment on the Emishi having lived in that area of the realm before the Yamato people did, so they (you would say) have the right to live there peacefully. Perhaps you would be correct, but what's done is done, and now we unite to fight demons who do not care, I suppose, who is Yamato, who is Ainu, and who is Emishi.

But fighting oni is not at all similar to battling humans. My power has returned, but I fear it is not strong enough to send demons back to *Jigoku*. Shikigami will not frighten them. The warriors are fierce but will not be able to conquer supernatural beings. Bikki has only offered to guide us, not to fight the demons themselves. Even if he did join the fight, his strength appears to be divination and healing, not exorcism.

I write this letter before we sleep so that I may have one last communion with you, my friend. I will request a monk to carry it to the nearest village, and send it from there to Seimei to leave for you to find somewhere, should I not return.

Do not fear for me, Mi-Na. Our little band of warriors and shamans may not be strong enough to vanquish demons, but we must try. If we fail, it will not be due to reluctance to forfeit our lives for His Majesty and the realm. Tomorrow we seek the oni's cave.

Chapter 17

Through The Demon Gate

"What? That's how it ends?" I wrapped my arms across my stomach in a vain attempt to ease the ache inside. Masako's power didn't extend to sorcery. She didn't have access to great balls of fire or the ability to turn bandits into harmless frogs. This wasn't some fantasy novel where she'd discover hidden powers that defied the laws of physics.

No. This was real life. Her powers—and presumably Bikki's powers too—were spiritual. Inari seemed to be on her side, but what kind of protection could that deity provide? Inari was the god—or goddess—of rice, not warfare. And, as Masako said, shikigami weren't as useful as you'd think they'd be. Otherwise, Seimei would have sent one to Mount Ōe to fight the oni, which would have saved Masako a trip.

But I was proud of her for conjuring one and relieved that her ability to summon kami assured her return to Kamo, assuming she lived through this oni-battle.

"Kenji, the legend you mentioned, the one you said sounds like what Masako is describing? The warriors were victorious, right? How exactly did they win?"

"Yorimitsu cut Shuten Dōji's head off."

"So they didn't need Masako at all. She seems to think she'll die trying. I wish I could warn her."

"We *can* warn her," he said. "We should go there before it's too late."

"Why *now*? Seimei said the spirit world connects all worlds and all eras, so it wouldn't matter whether we look for that moment now or fifty years from now. It will always be there."

Kenji carefully placed the antique papers back in the box. "Because I'm not *absolutely* sure it works that way. I mean, it makes sense spiritually, and also in a quantum way, but do we want to take the chance it doesn't? We're here, in Uji, at the same place Seimei sent you home from. If we're going to help her, this is the right place to do it. It's the right *time* to do it. The Demon Gate is open. If it closes, we won't be able to find the opening to the specific point in time where Masako is about to fight the oni. You wouldn't want to arrive there when it's too late, do you?"

My hands curled into fists. "Kenji, why are you so keen to do this? You've seen how hard it's been for me these past two weeks, adjusting to life in the modern world. Weird dreams, vertigo, a pain deep inside my body like somebody tore my heart out. Is that what you want?" My voice had risen to a higher pitch but I couldn't stop it. Of *course* I wanted to help Masako. She was my best friend. But she didn't *need* me. The warriors killed the oni and saved the women. The legend said so. "Can't you let me live a normal life?"

Kenji took my right hand—well, fist—and gently massaged it so my fingers relaxed. "From what you've told me of your life, normal means stressing about grades, waking up with anxiety at four in the morning, jumping from relationship to relationship because you don't want to get too attached to anyone-"

"Stop!" Studying divination did *not* make him a fortune-teller. "I'm different now. Once I recover from my trip, I'll be able to lead a better—but still normal—life. What do *you* want? Is it really to help Masako? You don't even know her."

He gave my hand a comforting squeeze. "I believe the goddess Izanami sent you through the spirit world to gain power and to open Masako to hers. Inari is helping Masako, and Inari is an avatar of Izanami. So it's not just what *we* can do to help in the modern world. What if Masako has a role in protecting the kami too?" He increased the pressure on my hand in his excitement. "Remember the positive spiral? When we go through the spirit world twice—going to save Masako and coming back here—we'll gain enough power to be at the top of the spiral. We'll finally be able to *do* something to help the kami remain in our world with their light and positive energy and helping all of us become better humans. Mina, this is our destiny."

I drew my hand out of his and wiggled my fingers as I considered Kenji's grandiose theory. *Japanese goddess of love sends ordinary American college student to the past to save the world as we know it.*

So many things wrong with that headline.

Although it described my lived experience, so there was that. Finding Masako's letters in Uji couldn't be a coincidence. Maybe she sent the fox to me, which would explain why it was red, not white like Inari's messengers. She might need me. Now *that* was a compelling argument. I couldn't deny a request from her when she'd done so much to help me.

Feeling like I was about to jump off a bridge into a rushing river, I took a deep breath. "I doubt I'm part of a deity's grand scheme, but your theory, while a little insane, actually makes sense. Only because of what I've been through, mind you. For Masako's sake, I'm willing to try it. If it works, maybe we'll save the world. If it doesn't work, you'll stop asking about it, right?"

He bowed, not hiding his relief. "Mina, I've known how brave you are since I first read the Chronicle, and now I see your courage in action. We'll return before the sun sets. You won't even be hungry for dinner."

"I doubt that. Time travel and spirit possession burn a *lot* of calories."

We walked back to the tree where we'd found the latest letter. I stumbled, my legs unexpectedly weak from the mixed emotions stirred by our conversation, but possibly from the heat too. I used my forward motion to take a few lunging strides forward and held onto the tree for support.

Kenji knelt and put his head low to the ground. "I hear water running," he said. "This is a power spot. Can you feel it?"

I stepped closer to him. A thrum vibrated upward, tickling my feet and prickling my scalp. "Oh, I feel it, all right. But how will you get the spirit world to open? I don't know how I did it last time."

"You must have had latent power to do it before. You should have even more now from your round trip through the spirit world. You'll open the border and I'll follow you through."

I nodded as if I believed him. And maybe I did. Anyway, if we didn't try, we might never know if it was even possible to go to the spirit world intentionally. And Kenji deserved to know. For so many years he'd known that I went without ever knowing if *he* might one day cross the border.

We washed our hands, faces, mouths, and feet with the pure water from the well, the first step in the *chinkon* meditation ritual. We settled on the grass with crossed legs, put our palms together, and closed our eyes.

I began to swing my elbows back and forth, my body remembering what to do.

Emptying my mind of worrisome thoughts, I focused on sensations and sounds. My hands pressed together, cool and still damp from purification; the gritty soil under me; the faint rushing of water below ground; the barely audible plop of condensation falling from the sides of the well. A breeze ruffled my hair, evaporating sweat from my forehead. The brass bell in the well cover vibrated a slight hum.

A strange absence of birdsong. No insects chirping or buzzing.

The vibration in the ground grew stronger. Gravity pulled at me, insistent I not take its force for granted. I submitted, allowing the earth to embrace me.

The dripping of water grew louder, becoming a drumming, and my heartbeat pounded a matching rhythm. The hum of the bell turned into a ringing like a tuning fork struck once, but growing louder instead of fading away.

A silver bell chimed.

Then complete and utter silence. No water trickling. No breeze rustling through leaves.

I opened my eyes. Gray air surrounded me like a thin fog, but without the dampness. No sensation of dirt under my feet. The trees and grass were grayish green, not the vivid emerald they'd been before.

Water trickled soundlessly on either side of us. The well and its cover were gone.

Relief washed through me. The meditation had worked.

"Kenji?"

His eyes remained closed.

"Kenji! Wake up!"

He blinked. His eyes shifted from me to the gray air around us. He blinked again. "Did the sun set? Or is it raining?" He sounded groggy.

"Did you hear a bell ring? You might have passed out like I did the first time. Wake up before some living spirit drags you into another time or place. Every culture in the physical world has shamans who, at any moment in time, could be sending their spirits here."

He rose to his feet but stood there swaying, overcome with vertigo. He bent down to hold his knees until the dizziness passed. I knew the feeling, that mismatch between what we saw ourselves doing—talking, standing—and what we actually *felt*, which was nothing, really.

I stood as well, stepping toward him but unsure if I should—or could—touch him. We were spirits, not physical bodies, even if our minds couldn't quite grasp that.

"Why is it foggy? Are you sure we're in the spirit world?"

"It might look this way to us because we're *living* spirits. We have living bodies waiting for us. It might look different if we were divine spirits or dead people. But it doesn't matter. We won't be here long. You did it, Kenji. You meditated your way across the border!"

I thought he'd jump for joy, considering how long he'd been trying to get here. Instead, he clapped his hands together, bowed, and murmured what I assumed was a solemn prayer of gratitude to the kami.

After a few seconds, he raised his head. "Let's search for the Demon Gate."

"Wait! We should memorize this location."

Kenji pointed to the stream running on either side of us. "We're standing on a little island."

A vision flashed through my mind of Lord Seimei standing on the other side of the stream, sweating and waving his arms while Masako meditated. "My spirit wandered around in this gray fog before returning to Mount Tsukuba. We need to come back to this *exact* spot in order to return to our bodies at the same time we left."

He pointed to each geographic feature in turn. "Island. Stream. Mountain. Done. Now, let's find the Gate."

"What will it look like?" A few bright spots pulsed through the dim air like stars peeking through clouds. Some were silver, some were white with hints of green or blue . "Do you think those shining places are openings to physical worlds?" I shivered with anticipation, or maybe fear. Probably both.

Kenji's eyes glowed like polished chestnuts in sunlight. "My divination told me to seek a silvery blue opening."

We stepped over the silently running water, feeling neither light nor heavy, like gravity was utterly indifferent to whatever we did. Well, gravity probably wasn't even a thing here, so a lack of it wouldn't result in us floating away any more than lots of it would anchor us to the ground.

I grasped Kenji's hand when we reached the stream bank but dropped it immediately. I didn't want to drag his spirit into my body the way Masako had dragged mine into hers.

He took it back. "We can't risk separation."

It wouldn't be a problem until we returned to our bodies, so I decided not to worry about it. *Note to self: Do not hold Kenji's hand when going home.*

"How will we know which of those shimmering spots is the opening to the right time and place?" I asked.

"It's probably wider than all the others. And Mina, you should have the power to see oni or other spirits going through it."

Kenji had somehow known my useless ability to see obake would come in handy. How *did* he know so much?

But this wasn't the time to delve into it. My heart pounded (and how did that even happen to a disembodied spirit?) as I stared through a glowing silvery-blue circle flickering in the fog. "That one looks larger than the others."

We moved closer, and I noticed how its light rippled occasionally as if it had been disturbed, like a pebble thrown into a still pond. I concentrated on it, and eventually faint outlines became visible just before each disturbance. A red outline, then a blue one, then another red one. "Kenji, I think oni are going through that one."

"Let's head there."

As we advanced towards it, I shifted my vision from staring *at* it to looking *through* it. The silvery shimmer faded to the edges. Colors inside the opening grew brighter—blue at the top, yellow and green below, and a tiny spot of red in the middle.

The colors began to take shape, blurry at first and gradually clear, like I was focusing binoculars. Blue was sky. Yellow— sunlight. A green hill. A stream. Red…trousers?

"Look! Kenji, there's a young woman! Do you see her?"

Kenji shook his head. "No, but keep looking."

"She's wearing red hakama under robes which are…. green… or gray, and maroon. Hair tied in a braid. There's something strange about her, though. Like… an aura? It might be a spirit-glow. It's yellow. It doesn't seem normal." But then again, nothing about this was *normal*.

Kenji shook his head as he peered through the opening. "I still can't see anything but a silver light. The clothing sounds right for the Heian period."

"But it could be two hundred years later or earlier than the year 1002." I did *not* want to go to the wrong place. We'd be in danger of never returning, not to mention failing in our mission to save Masako. "We need more information. Oh. Wait. There's a man on the hill. It looks like he's watching the woman. Big guy, but dressed weirdly. Not like a peasant, not like a noble or warrior either. Gray robe, funny little gray cap, and a kind of backpack. A large sea shell is slung on a rope around his neck. Can't you see it?"

"That description sounds like a yamabushi. They carry conch shells." He closed his eyes for a few seconds, then opened them, examining the scene in front of us with a laser intensity.

I held my virtual breath, crossing my fingers for luck. *As if that would make a difference.*

A faint blue halo shimmered over the yamabushi's head. "Kenji, the man has a glow too. Try to focus on that. Can you see him?"

"Ah- ye-es? Yes! He has a blue shimmer. And the woman—I can see her now! Yes! Yellow above her head. So that's what you call spirit-glow?"

"When I possessed Masako, I'd see a glow like that when someone was possessed or cursed, so I think those two people are possessed."

Kenji fell to his knees, bowing his head.

"What's wrong? Do we need to go home?"

"No, I'm so relieved." He tilted his head to gaze up at me, his expression earnest. "Thank you, Mina. This was a difficult decision for you, but it worked. We have power. We can use it to help our world."

My first impulse was to laugh, but his words were so sincere. Maybe he was right. Surely we could do *something* to help our messed-up planet.

I squinted at the two figures. "We need to find host bodies. We can't do any good as disembodied spirits." Masako had dragged me into her body so it had been her fault when I possessed her. I didn't want to take over an unwilling host. "If those two people are possessed by hostile spirits, or yōkai, maybe we can kick the invaders out and take their places. If the hosts don't want us, we can come back here and make a different plan."

Kenji agreed. "How do we do that from here?"

"Let's propel ourselves forward and push the other spirits out. If it doesn't work, send your spirit back here *immediately*. Otherwise we might become ghosts. Are you okay with that?"

"I don't want to become a ghost, so yes."

"Good. On my count. Ready? *Ichi. Ni. San!*"

We threw ourselves through the opening with as much spiritual energy as we could muster.

I found myself encased in a warm body. The bright sunlight made me squint, while my skin itched from a coarse robe.

An icy hand pressed into my soul and squeezed my heart. An enraged voice rang in my head. *"Get out, intruder!"*

Yōkai! Fear froze my spirit-voice.

"Get out! This is no place for you, strange spirit," the voice said. *"I have taken possession of this body."*

The yōkai pushed at me. I felt myself slipping away, my spirit half in, half out of the host. Forcing myself to overcome my dread, I visualized strong, iron-like hands holding on and pulling myself all the way back in. *"No, you get out!"* I said, using my most commanding tone. *"I don't know what you are, but I'm a living spirit."* I pushed against the hostile force with all of my spiritual energy. *"This is my host now. Go back to the spirit world where you belong!"*

"Who- How- How did —" the hostile spirit sputtered.

Name-dropping might work. *"My teacher was Abe no Seimei! Begone!"*

The yōkai recoiled with horror and revulsion. I gave it one more emphatic push with my imaginary iron hands, and the spirit tumbled out of my host and into… where? Thin air? Back to the spirit world?

No matter. I refused to feel guilty about sending the hostile spirit out. It was clearly not in a healthy relationship with my host.

But now I needed permission to stay. *"Hey, I got rid of the bad spirit for you, you're welcome. Sorry for possessing you so abruptly— although is there a gradual way to do it? Ha, ha—Anyway, I need your help."*

No response.

I knew from previous experience that a possessing spirit uses the host's brain to communicate, allowing the host to understand my words. So why wasn't I getting a reply? *"Hello? Anyone home? I'm a benign spirit. A kami of sorts, you might say. Is it okay if I stay long enough to help a friend out?"*

No answer.

I tried a few more times, with the same result.

Could my host have died just before the hostile spirit's possession? That would be creepy.

No. I refused to believe that. The host had to be in here somewhere.

My neck and shoulders were stiff. I tipped my head from one side to the other and shrugged my shoulders a few times to relieve cramping.

A conch shell banged against my side when I did so.

Uh oh. I examined my hands. Large, calloused, dirty. A man's hands. I turned away to confirm what lay underneath my robes and leggings.

I'd possessed the yamabushi. *Cool, I'm a dude. I can't wait to pee standing up.*

The young woman below gazed up at me. Her aura had shifted from yellow to green. "Mina?" Her high-pitched voice sounded young. "It's Kenji. Is that you?"

I started to call out but changed my mind. There might be other warriors or bandits nearby, so I slid down the hillside instead, a few stones clattering down with me.

The young woman tensed at the noise, watching my progress. She stooped to pick up a rock, in case it wasn't me inside, I guessed.

When I got to the stream, I put my finger to my lips and spoke in a low voice. "Kenji, somehow we ended up in the wrong bodies. Well, assuming the goal was to stay with the same sex. But we never discussed which one to aim for, so apparently,

the kami want us to have a first-person perspective on the opposite one, which sounds like a very Inari thing to do, doesn't it?"

Kenji dropped his rock. "We did it!" His expression of
wonder shifted to confusion, then to amusement. "You're handsome," he said with a weirdly flirtatious laugh. "Although
you're bald under the cap. Nice facial hair, though." He pulled at
his robes, swishing and swaying as if dancing. "These robes are
heavy."

I ran a hand over my beard, marveling at the strangeness of
it. "And you are just-" I struggled to contain a guffaw. "Beautiful. Your hair, on the other hand, is a tangled mess."

We stared at each other in semi-hysterical delight. "Yes, we
did it," I whispered. "We're here, and we managed to possess
two hosts. Wait—is your host in there with you?"

"No. I tried communicating after I forced the yōkai out, but I
didn't hear any response."

"That's good. Not *good*—it's not great the hosts disappeared
—but at least we don't have to share these bodies. It wouldn't be
ethical to take control away from them."

I couldn't stop staring at the young woman in front of me. A
round face, and dirty like she'd been living in a cave or sleeping
on the ground. Or both. Soiled green and maroon robe layers,
tattered at the hems. Thick, black hair in an unraveling braid
falling almost to her ankles. I towered over her, a feeling I'd had
exactly never in my life.

"Based on our clothes, Kenji, I'd say we're in the right time
and place. Masako was traveling with warriors to find the
kidnapping victims, but I'm dressed like a yamabushi, not a
warrior."

I shrugged the backpack off my shoulders and opened the
flap. On top were a few small things—a flask with liquid, some
dried fruit, oil paper—but after I handed those to Kenji, I was
shocked to see a sword nestled inside, surrounded by straw-

padded flaps of what appeared to be armor. "No wonder it's so heavy. Looks like I possessed a warrior disguised as a yamabushi. Maybe he was traveling with Masako but got possessed by the yōkai, which I then kicked out."

"A good theory, Mina. Although it feels weird to call you that. You're so much bigger than I am. Does your host have a name?"

I searched my host's mind for information. "I can't access it, although I'm controlling this body without any trouble. How about you?"

Kenji's movements had been jerky and stiff, a bit zombie-like, reminding me of my first attempt to control Masako's body. My experience must be helping me now because I could move naturally this time.

"A faint echo inside," he said after a minute. "Not a voice. A memory of someone calling her Nariko. But she's not here."

"Well then, Kenji-Nariko—or should I call you Ken-Nari?—let's follow the path over there to look for the oni hideout." I waved to the clothing in the water. "You should bring that in case someone expects Nariko to return with it. She must have dropped it when you pushed the invading spirit out. What is it?"

He lifted it out of the stream and shook it. "A robe." A coarse material, like my robes and leggings. Linen or hemp. Once white, now gray. He held up one sleeve. "A stain. Do you think it's blood?"

I examined the brown-red cuff. "Hmm… It could be. Do you have a cut?"

Kenji's sleeves were tied back, presumably to keep them from getting wet while doing laundry. We examined his host's arms. Slender but muscular. Washing clothes by hand and carrying water from a stream might do that.

"No calluses," I said, "and the skin's not leathery from manual labor and constant exposure to the sun. Your robes are silk, even though they're dirty and tattered. She's not a peasant, then. No pockmarks. That's unusual." Nobles weren't exempt from smallpox and measles, and most people were exposed by her age, which I estimated to be around eighteen or nineteen. "On the back of the left arm, above the elbow. It's a scab, a fresh one."

"In Japanese folktales, oni drink the blood of their human victims and eat their flesh."

I felt sick. "Like vampires?"

"Not really. They didn't have to do it to live. Adding blood to saké was a treat, like a condiment. You know, like ketchup." He twisted his arm to examine the cut. "This scab might be where they drew blood."

That didn't make me feel any better. "So, your host might be one of the victims. The yōkai you expelled might have possessed her to serve the oni, which would explain why she was doing the laundry despite being a noblewoman." My stomach cramped with anxiety. "We have to find Masako before she gets turned into an oni milkshake."

"Yes, let's explore this mountain." Kenji's eyes danced with excitement and anticipation. He'd never done this before, so maybe he didn't quite grasp just how dangerous it was.

He twisted the robe to wring the water out while I repacked the armor. I pulled the conch shell off my shoulder and set it in the pack. I didn't know what it was for, but I probably wouldn't need it.

Chapter 18

Ancestor Spirits

The sun shone high in the sky but not overhead, indicating we'd arrived in late morning or early afternoon. The air was cooler and drier than in Uji. Maple and beech trees lined the path, their leaves mostly green but tinged with red and yellow. We'd left Uji in August, but this felt like September, which is exactly where—or when?—we needed to be.

Kenji started walking up a narrow trail that led steeply uphill from the stream.

"Wait," I said. "We should speak softly, if at all. Bandits gather in mountain areas like this."

"Okay," he whispered.

I was dying to ask how he felt about all this. Was he as disoriented and confused as I was when I first crossed into the past? Our experience this time was completely different. Kenji didn't have to fight to control the body he possessed, and he'd practically begged me to bring him here. He was probably loving every minute.

Catching up with him was easy because he kept stumbling on Nariko's robes, and his legs were shorter than mine. Also, he had the awkward gait of a spirit-possession newbie.

I bent my head to murmur into Nariko's sweet shell-like ears. "Have you ever been to Mount Ōe? Is there any chance you recognize anything?"

"Yes," he murmured back. "I went skiing there once. It seems familiar, but so many mountains look like this. I've got a good feeling about it, though."

"Nariko washed that robe in a stream, and she didn't have food or bags with her, so she must have come from close by."

The path wound steeply uphill, and it didn't take long before sweat dripped down my neck from under my cap, even in the cool mountain air. But soon we reached a plateau and stopped to admire the view while recovering from the steep, fast climb.

Rice fields blanketed a valley far below, and mountains edged the horizon across from us, each peak distinct in the clear sky. I followed the faint shadow of a river to its forever home in a sparkling blue sea.

"Have you noticed how clear the air is?"

Kenji nodded. "It's one thing to *know* how the Industrial Revolution changed the air, it's another to literally *see* the difference."

I opened my mouth to taste the breeze. A faint salty tang, a little bitter from cedar and pine, and just a hint of umami from the decay of leaves fallen early. This was the balance of oxygen, carbon dioxide, and other elements we'd evolved to breathe over millennia, not the unbalanced version created by the invention of the internal combustion engine.

We heard male voices coming towards us, so I flung myself off the path to the right and crouched in the sasa grass behind a large cedar, hoping its trunk would hide my wide shoulders. Kenji bobbed across the trail to hide behind a beech tree on the left.

I peered around the tree to examine the men. They carried thick staffs and wore leggings and knee-length tattered robes. A faint blue glow, visible in the shadow cast by the hillside, outlined each figure. "Kenji!" I whispered. "They're possessed too!"

"They look like bandits," he whispered back. "But why would they be possessed?"

"Because if a spirit wanted to attack someone, a bandit might be a perfect host. Weapons, fighting skills, the whole package."

The men stopped, apparently unable to decide where to go next. They argued for so long that my legs fell asleep and sweat began to drip slowly down my spine. The pack on my back grew heavier and heavier but I didn't dare take it off.

Kenji, still kneeling in the grass, squirmed with his back against the tree that hid him from the bandits. I puzzled over what he was doing until it occurred to me he was trying to scratch a spot where Nariko's long hair irritated his back.

Before I decided what to do next, an eerie, melodic song floated on the breeze. It sounded familiar, like a song I'd heard long ago. It called to me, tugged at me. I wanted to run toward the promise it held, the sweetness of joining in, of becoming one with the invisible singers.

I stood to walk toward it, but my legs, numb from lack of movement, gave way. The jarring impact as I fell to my knees woke me from the spell.

"Hey, Kenji," I murmured. "What's happening?"

He'd stopped wiggling and was now gazing at the hillside, his expression rapt.

"Kenji!" I hissed.

The bandits had dropped their staves and were staring with empty eyes at something in the woods.

"For kami's sake, Kenji, wake up! It's a kind of magic, I think. Don't fall for it!"

He smiled dreamily and began to walk toward… what? What was everyone enthralled by?

Kenji was now out in the open. I stepped cautiously toward him, feeling like I was playing Red Light, Green Light. From my new vantage point, I saw several men lying on the ground, conch shells and packs scattered around them, unmoving.

Two yamabushi walked into the clearing, their hands moving in a complex pattern as they sang. One man was unusually tall with a long, scraggly silver beard, while the other was very short, no beard, and a slight build. Long strands of hair escaped his hat, the only straw hat among them, and framed a round, feminine face.

Adrenaline surged through my body. I tugged Kenji's sleeve urgently.

His only response was an expressionless blink.

"Kenji! It's me, Mina, remember? We possessed these bodies?"

He lifted his arms to see tied-back sleeves and a ragged robe. He picked up his hem to find dirty but dainty feet.

"You possessed a young woman," I reminded him. "Kenji, look at the two yamabushi singing. I think the short one is Masako!"

He inhaled sharply, now fully awake. "What? You spent a year and a half living with her. You don't know if that's her?"

"It's not like she looked at herself much. Mirrors here are metal circles, so it's not super clear. Anyway, the shorter yamabushi moves like her, and her hair is rolled up under her hat. It's her. I might not know her face well, but I know her voice. The tall one must be Bikki."

In my excitement, I forgot to keep my voice low, and the bandits stirred from their enchantment, blinking and murmuring to each other, sleepily examining their empty hands, scratching their heads in confusion. Scowls replaced their stupefaction as they connected their lack of weapons to the singing yamabushi.

I handed my staff to Kenji and reached inside my pack for the sword. The hilt, wrapped in braided black thread, slipped into my hand like it had been waiting for me. "Get ready," I said, sliding it from its plain black scabbard.

The blade curved slightly and was lighter and thinner than I expected. I gripped it with both hands. *Yes, this feels good.* I raised it over my head, reveling in the strength of my broad shoulders.

Kenji's eyes widened with alarm. "Mina?"

"I'm not just in a *man's* body, Kenji. I'm in a *warrior's* body." I stepped in front of him. He was in a woman's body. I needed to protect him. Or her? Well, both.

The bandits picked up their staves from the ground and moved toward the singing monks. The yamabushi stuttered to a stop, clearly dismayed their spell had stopped working.

"Masako!" My deep voice boomed against the hill. She clapped a hand against her mouth and stepped back, edging toward a hole in the hillside as if to disappear into it.

My heart dropped with crushing disappointment. *All this risk I took to help her, and she's horrified I'm here.*

The bandits had spun around at my voice, but instead of being threatened by me and my sword, called for me to join them.

And then it hit me. Masako didn't see *me*. She saw a warrior disguised as a monk who'd been possessed by a hostile spirit.

My heart jumped back into the cavity where it belonged. "Kenji," I whispered. "The spirits we pushed out of these bodies —I think they're friends with the yōkai who possessed those bandits. They seem to think we're on their side."

"Let's surprise them," Kenji said. "Act as if we're on their side, and when we get closer, we fight." He twirled the staff I'd given him, no doubt to show me he wasn't as helpless as he looked.

Nodding curtly, I took a manly stride forward. Kenji tried to do the same but stumbled.

I grabbed his arm. "Those long robes take some getting used to. I'll give you some tips. I got good at it in my previous life here."

He shrugged me off and hitched up his robes, tucking folds into his belt so I could see his little feet. A surge of protectiveness swept over me, but I forced myself to ignore it.

Masako's eyes flicked back and forth between me and the bandits who now surrounded her. She flinched as the leader pushed his staff into her chest, shouting at her in words I didn't understand.

Bikki remained calm. He murmured something to Masako, and the bandit leader turned his wrath to Bikki instead.

My pace increased. As I drew close, one of the other bandits spoke to me. "Warrior, you have a sword, so you fight the tall monk. We'll take care of the small one."

Kenji took that as his cue, swinging his staff down on a bandit with surprising amount of force for his small, feminine frame.

Two other bandits rushed at us, suddenly aware we weren't the spirits they thought we were.

I laughed as I lifted my sword.

Masako gasped. "Suetake! You're back! Thank the kami!"

"Can't. Explain. Now," I said in between blows. A glance told me Kenji used his petite frame to advantage as he spun and walloped his staff against two of the bandits, knocking their hands so hard they dropped their thick sticks.

I slammed my sword against a bandit's wooden staff, cleaving it into two pieces.

Three of the four bandits now had no weapons. They stood, breathing hard, glaring at us with frustration rather than fear, although one of them practically drooled at Kenji-Nariko, a hefty dose of lust mingled with his hatred.

Yuck.

The fourth bandit swung his staff at Bikki, who ducked. He didn't seem to have a weapon, so I leaped forward with my sword raised. We were here to save Masako, and if I had to kill a bandit to do that, so be it.

"Suetake, stop!"

Shocked at Masako's intervention, I ground my teeth as I fought the inertia of a heavy object in motion. My sword stopped just short of the bandit's neck.

"Lord Suetake, this is how it began! You killed a bandit, and its tsuki-mono possessed you. If you kill this one, it will happen again."

I dug the sword point into the bandit's cheek. "Don't move," I said. "I might not kill you, but I could do some damage."

"This isn't my body," he said. "Do what you want to it."

Bruises were forming on my head from a few lucky blows the bandits landed on me, so I knew he'd feel any pain I might inflict. "What do you want with her?" I asked, gesturing to Masako.

The bandit blinked in surprise. "*Her*?" he asked. "That monk tried to exorcise us, but we refuse to leave until our purpose is fulfilled."

"What is your purpose?"

"We are senzo. Ancestor spirits. We possessed these bandits and those living in the cave. Our leader will explain." He pointed his chin to the hole in the mountainside. "He's in there."

"Well? Do we go in there?" I asked Masako. "I, for one, am curious about why these spirits possessed bandits and then fought us."

Masako nodded, although with some uncertainty like she wasn't quite sure who I was or what she agreed to.

I pulled my sword away from the bandit's cheek. Good thing I did, because a rustling near my feet startled me into jerking my sword up, and I might have taken his eye out.

"So they're not dead?" I asked, pointing with my chin to the monks now stirring on the ground. "What happened to them? Did the bandits knock them out? Or did they faint from fear?"

"It was certainly not from fear," Masako said reprovingly.

Her tone made me realize the monks were her warrior comrades in disguise, and she expected me—Suetake—to know better.

"Eh…" Masako hesitated. "We accidentally sent them to sleep with our chant. We didn't mean to."

"Obviously," I said. "If I hadn't come along, you'd have been captured, or worse."

She bowed her thanks. "But Lord Suetake, how did you exorcise the hostile spirit that possessed you?"

I took a deep breath. I had a *lot* to say before we got to whatever fight lay ahead. "Masako, it's Mina." My voice shook slightly. "Spirit Mi-Na. I'm here to help you. I possessed this man's body, but I didn't steal it. I expelled an angry ghost of some kind, but my host isn't responding."

She gazed at me fiercely as if gauging the truth of my words, and then her eyes fixed on a spot just above my head for a long minute.

A radiant smile brightened her face. "Mi-Na, it *is* you! I see your spirit-glow, as dear to me as if it were my sweet sister's."

Letting my breath out with a whoosh of relief, I stooped to give her a big hug, the kind I'd never been able to give her when we shared the same body.

She stepped back to evade me. "Ah! Mi-Na!"

Oops. Not only did I have a man's body, but hugs weren't a thing here. I bowed instead. "Masako, I've missed you *so* much. I was worried about you. I didn't know if I should return to help you or even if I *could* return. But it worked. We found you!"

She returned my bow. "Your man's voice is odd, but I remember your strange manners and words." She lifted her eyes to mine. "I've missed you terribly, and am humbled you took such a great risk for me."

Tears slid down our cheeks as we gazed at each other.

Kenji tugged my sleeve. "Um, Mina?"

"Oh, right," I said as I sniffed and cleared my throat. "Masako, meet Kenji. He possessed this young woman. He's the one who sent me to the spirit world the first time, and he talked me into coming here this time."

Masako tilted her head this way and that, examining Kenji. "Lord Ken-Ji, what is your clan?"

Excited to share the news, I jumped in before Kenji could respond. "Abe clan! Lord Seimei's grandson, your friend Akichika, was Kenji's ancestor, can you believe it? Akichika instructed every generation to copy your journal. Centuries later, Kenji made his copy. That's how he knew I'd show up when I did. It's his fault I came here in the first place. Well, I suppose Akichika is to blame for preserving your Chronicle so Kenji would read it one day. Or was it my fault for asking you to write the Chronicle in the first place?"

Vertigo washed over me at this chicken-or-egg logic. Did *I* create the situation that caused me to travel back in time?

Kenji put his small hand on my arm to keep me steady. His touch sent an electric tingling through me, while the curve of his rosebud lips caused an unfamiliar movement in my groin. Suetake wasn't used to seeing women without fans or a screen, but he liked it. Obviously.

Kenji pressed a sleeve over his mouth and glanced at me flirtatiously. "Lord Mina, is that a persimmon in your pocket, or are you just happy to see me?"

Masako smiled politely. "I do not understand your strange words, Ken-Ji, but thank you for preserving my book and sending Mi-Na to me three years ago. According to Lord Seimei, her presence opened my soul to accept power from the kami. Are you sharing this young woman's body with Lady Nariko?"

Kenji's expression grew serious. "I pushed out a *yōkai* who possessed this body before I did. The host doesn't seem to be in here."

"Lady Nariko is one of the noblewomen who disappeared from the Capital. We," Masako gestured to the warrior-monks, "have been watching this cave to see if the oni had hidden the women here, and when we saw Nariko take the washing to the river, we realized it was, indeed, the right location. Three warriors followed Nariko, but the bandits ambushed them on the way. Suetake killed one, and the *yōkai* jumped to him. The others escaped and returned to this place."

"So this is the oni's den? The oni who kidnapped Nariko, among others?" Being just a few meters away from ogre-like demons didn't scare me, probably thanks to Suetake's warrior instincts.

"We believe so, especially now after learning these bandits had been possessed by hostile spirits. Unfortunately Bikki and I were not successful in our incantation to send the bandits away. Instead, we sent the warriors to sleep. If I cannot even do that simple thing, my abilities are not strong enough to fight the oni, even assisted by five warriors and a wandering shaman. But Mi-Na, it took a long time to send you home. Why did you return?"

"We found your letters at Kamo and Uji describing the danger you were about to face in confronting the oni without having a plan to defeat them. I was so anxious for you."

"Mi-Na, I wrote that letter and sent it with a villager to Kamo just a day ago! The kami have blessed me, indeed. But Mi-Na, I worried about you too. Thank you for facing your fear of returning to my world. You are much braver than before."

I was only a little offended. Masako was right. She'd been the risk-taker as we journeyed to the capital from Hitachi, getting into tippy boats to cross rushing rivers, and stuff like that.

"Lady Masako, has Lord Seimei ever taught you secret spells from his Book of Onmyōdō Secrets?" Kenji asked abruptly. Rudely, in my opinion, but Masako didn't seem to mind.

She did look surprised, though. "You know of Seimei's Book in your world?" she asked. "Lord Seimei guards his secrets closely. He has only ever shared a few rituals with me. He expects my power to be sufficient when it is needed." She glanced at the bandits, who appeared to be listening to our conversation. "When might that be, I wonder?"

She introduced Bikki. "He convinced the warriors to approach the chief oni as peaceful mountain monks. Using this deception, we might learn why and how the oni kidnapped the young women. We hope to appease the oni into releasing the victims."

The warriors were on their feet now, groggy and a little sheepish at having slept through a fight.

"Yorimitsu is the leader," Masako said, nodding at a monk now standing upright with arms folded, glaring at me suspiciously. Four other warriors shifted uneasily from foot to foot.

She did her best to explain to them who I was, but they didn't look any happier. "The Spirit Mi-Na is *benign*," she stressed to set them at ease. "Mi-Na banished the hostile spirit that possessed Suetake when he killed the bandit. Mi-Na will assist us, and after we are victorious, will restore Suetake's spirit, which the hostile spirit seems to have suppressed."

I wasn't convinced I could bring him back, but I didn't argue.

Someone was missing from this merry band. "Masako, where's Yumi?"

"She became ill soon after we met up with the warriors. We escorted her to a temple on this mountain. If we do not return to the temple in three days, the head priest will send monks to find out what happened."

Yorimitsu ordered his warriors to watch over the senzo-possessed bandits. The bandits didn't argue because the warriors, having retrieved their swords from their yamabushi packs, waved them menacingly at their captives.

Masako, Kenji, and I formed a little group for a quick conference. Bikki stood on one side of our little circle and Yorimitsu stood on the other.

Masako described to us what happened since the last letter we'd read. "I believe the oni are deep inside this mountain," she said. "It appears the women they have kidnapped are also there. I suspect the senzo who possessed these bandits are in league with the oni, perhaps by guarding the entrance to this cave."

"You used the term senzo," Kenji said. "Not *shirei*, the spirits of the recently deceased. Senzo spirits are nearly at the stage of becoming kami. Why would such spirits possess bandits and cooperate with demons?"

"Confusing, yes," Masako agreed. "But true. However, I do not know the answer to your question." She emphasized no one should kill a senzo-possessed person, whether a bandit or kidnap victim. An innocent victim would die, and the spirit would possess whoever killed its host.

"Bandits are not innocent," Yorimitsu growled.

She ignored him. "If ancestors are properly venerated, they become divine protector spirits. But if not revered by descendants, senzo might become malevolent."

Kenji tapped my arm. "Mina, remember? That's what I said back home!"

"Then Ken-Ji, you understand the seriousness of what we face," Masako said. "As we approach the oni, remember: Senzo are spirits, which means they can be exorcised from the bodies they have possessed. Oni, however, are physical entities, so the warriors must first cut off the oni's head to release its spirit. Then Bikki and I can send it back through the Demon Gate."

This information was new to me, and I had many questions, but Yorimitsu demanded we go into the cave. His fellow warriors were restless, glaring at Kenji, at the cave, back at Kenji, at me, and holding their swords in a ready stance.

Bikki, to my surprise, agreed with Yorimitsu. "We should not wait to learn what lurks in the cave. Lady Nariko left this place to wash a robe earlier, so kidnapped women must be in there, which means the oni will also be there."

I pulled at Kenji's sleeve. "Since Nariko and Suetake were possessed by senzo, they'll look familiar to those inside the cave. If we go in first, we won't raise any alarms, because whatever is in there will think we're still possessed by senzo."

Kenji's pretty brown eyes sparkled with anticipation. "Agreed. If we run into trouble, use your conch shell to blow the alarm."

"Oh, is that what it's for?" Another mystery solved. Rummaging through my pack, I found it and slung its hemp rope over my shoulder.

Bikki nodded. "Once inside, you two will explain to the senzo that we are humble and peaceful yamabushi, acolytes of the shaman En no Ozunu, and we wish to meet the famous chief of the oni." He frowned at the warriors. "You must put your fighting swords in the packs. Yamabushi only carry striking swords."

Yorimitsu grunted his assent. "The Miko and the Ainu will enter the cave after those two, and the rest of us will follow in the rear. Warriors, put swords in your packs, but place them where you can draw them quickly."

"Draw swords?" Kenji asked. "Didn't Bikki say *peaceful*? And while Mina's host body is a great warrior, I'm in the body of a young woman who lived the soft life of a noblewoman until recently."

"As far as the senzo and the oni understand, Ken-Ji, you are still possessed by a senzo," Masako replied. "Keep them believing that. Negotiate on our behalf, as one of them. Mi-Na," she smiled up at me. "You look strong. Protect Ken-Ji in the fight. Now, let's proceed into the mountain to rescue the poor young women who have been kidnapped."

"I guess you're the brains and I'm the brawn," I murmured to Kenji as we walked to the entrance. "This could be fun."

"Or not," he whispered back.

Chapter 19

A Demon's Cocktail

The packed dirt beneath my feet told me many bodies had walked in and out of this cave. Wood smoke wafted from the inside, seeking an exit. It tickled my throat on its way out and I suppressed a cough. The ceiling grazed my head, but I was the tallest of our group, which meant no one else would have to bend over to get through.

Kenji's robes whispered behind me. I wouldn't blame him if he were a little nervous. Not only was this spirit-possession thing new for him, but he was in the body of a petite young woman with no fighting experience.

The faint light of a fire ahead illuminated an area where the cave widened into a cavern. As we drew closer, I paused to assess the situation.

Kenji bumped into my pack and muttered a few incomprehensible imprecations.

A knot of women stood by the fire, all of them of slight build. Flexing my arms, I enjoyed the sensation of thick muscles along my biceps. Protecting Kenji against tiny women would be easy. My experience living with Masako told me Suetake's muscle memory would allow me to use his sword if it went that far.

I slid a hand back to push aside the flap on my pack. There was no harm in ensuring my sword was within grasping range.

First tapping Kenji to let him know it was time to move forward, I strode toward the group by the fire as if I belonged there, no longer taking care to step quietly.

The women turned with alarm at our footsteps but relaxed when they saw who we were.

A young woman in a tattered green robe stepped forward. "Where have you been?" she asked, her arms folded in a stern, masculine manner. Tangled hair framed a long face and roundish chin. Her silk outer robe, embroidered with gold thread, gleamed in the firelight.

My heart beat faster still, but not from fear. No, from Suetake's male hetero-normative reaction to a pretty young woman.

Kenji stumbled against me again, this time on purpose. "Don't stare, Mina," he muttered.

"What the fu-" I was interrupted by Masako pushing past me.

Hands on hips, I glared at her for not keeping to the plan. And why was I getting pushed around so much? I was a damn warrior, after all.

I hastily changed my pose to a more manly stance of folded arms and legs apart. Although, was that masculine in this culture? So many gender-based things were different here, like how pink and lavender were masculine while red and green were feminine. Maybe standing like this just made me look strange.

As Masako moved in front of me, cries of alarm rang through the group of women.

"Intruder!"

"Stop!"

"Who are you?"

"Lady Kiyoko!" Masako bowed to the young woman I'd been staring at. "Have you been harmed?"

So that was why she rushed ahead. She recognized the Royal Consort's lady-in-waiting.

I nudged Kenji. He nodded to indicate he recognized the name of the noblewoman whose disappearance had sent Masako first to the Emperor and then on this journey.

Lady Kiyoko didn't appear especially happy to be found. Her inquiring gaze moved from Masako to Kenji to me, then back to Masako as if weighing exactly how to respond.

"His Majesty sent me to rescue you." Masako took a step closer to Kiyoko. "Please, come with me, all of you. Quickly. Now, before the oni realize I am here."

Kiyoko didn't stir. "We will not leave until we receive justice."

Masako tipped her head to examine Kiyoko's appearance, then turned her searching gaze to the five or six other women around the fire. "Ah! I see the glow of invading spirits around each of you."

The flickering firelight had camouflaged the tsuki-mono aura, but after Masako's pronouncement, I focused intently and was able to perceive a faint yellow, blue, or green aura above each woman.

I shrugged my backpack from my back to my shoulder in case I needed quick access to my sword. Adrenaline pushed my pulse higher and sent electricity to my extremities. Was it finally time to fight?

Kenji, meanwhile, took a step back.

Good. He understands his limitations.

"Who *are* you, Spirits? Why have you possessed these innocent women?" Masako's rising intonation gave away her anger, although she kept her face expressionless.

Kiyoko frowned. "We are ancestor spirits of clans mistreated by the most powerful nobles of the realm. Our descendants have been dispossessed, banished from their ancestral lands, becoming impoverished and unable to venerate us any longer. That is why I am called Outcast."

Masako gasped. "You are the spirit who possessed Lady Kiyoko in the capital. Why did you possess her again? Begone, Outcast!" She raised her arms as if she were about to cast a spell.

She impressed me with her new sense of authority and confidence. Her letters implied she'd grown weaker and *less* confident. Something had happened to her since her last letter. Was it Bikki's influence or her successful summoning of a deity? Or was it the freedom that came with wearing men's clothing?

"Unh," the Spirit Outcast grunted. "I remember you. It was easy enough to return to this body. We refuse to leave until our descendants have been compensated for our clan's losses."

Masako's shoulders slumped as she lowered her arms.

She'd been bluffing. She was a miko, not an exorcist. She could send them away with her eerie chanting, but they'd leave in the bodies of these poor innocent victims.

I stepped forward. "Excuse me, Masako, but based on your letters, I wondered if Outcast possessed Lady Kiyoko—the first time—after killing the Consort." I glared at Kiyoko. "*Did* you kill Lady Motoko?"

Masako and Outcast both inhaled sharply, perhaps surprised at my blunt manner.

"I most certainly did not," Outcast said defensively. "Kiyoko was vulnerable to possession because she cried all day, every day, about her mistress's death."

"You're saying it was a coincidence? You didn't possess a nobleman? You didn't send poems to Kiyoko to make her fall in love with you? You didn't ask her to create an opening to the kimon direction? You weren't the dark mist that killed the Crown Prince's consort?"

Surprised and angry murmuring came from the group of women as they realized I wasn't one of them.

"Mi-Na!" Masako's alarm at my directness pulled me back from my attack.

Outcast addressed Masako, ignoring me. "Is that strange spirit your companion? Its speech is more vulgar than an oni's."

I opened my mouth to argue but closed it again before I ruined our chance to persuade these spirits to help us.

Masako's only response was a murmur of apology on my behalf.

Outcast, slightly mollified, decided to answer my questions after all. "A curse opened the Demon Gate. *That* is why we are here—we entered through the Gate. We know nothing of a poetry-writing nobleman or a dark mist."

I put my hands up, palms out in a surrender gesture that was probably culturally inappropriate, but whatever. "Fine. For now. Outcast, you are demanding compensation for lost lands. How did you lose them? Who should compensate whom? We can't help if we don't know."

"Yes, tell us, Spirits," Masako said. "Who stole your property?"

"For decades the Fujiwara and Minamoto clans took our lands when we could not pay their high taxes," Outcast-Kiyoko said. "The provincial governor took our rice, and when we had no more rice, they took our young men to work as laborers. Eventually, we became bandits to survive but the Fujiwara private army killed us all. We demand justice for our descendants who live in the villages here, who are near starvation and without recourse. Restitution must be made if you wish us to leave."

"The Regent, Lord Michinaga, will never agree to that," I said.

"And who, exactly, are you?" Kiyoko's pretty face twisted

into an ugly sneer. "What have you done to the senzo who possessed that body?"

"We have as much right to these bodies as you do," I replied. "Which is *none*. But in our case, the hosts aren't here, so we can't just leave. These bodies could die."

Outcast spat, a shocking contrast to his ladylike figure and dress. His spittle landed uncomfortably close to Masako.

She didn't flinch.

"If the Regent does not agree to restitution," Outcast said, "we will possess his young son and bring him here to serve the oni."

"Shape-shifters!" The angry shout came from Yorimitsu, who had led his men into the cave with swords ready.

I spun around. "Yorimitsu, no!"

"Noblewomen would not act this way. They are shape-shifters."

"Leave us, evil warrior," Outcast growled, another eerie contrast with his feminine host.

"Obake, go back to hell!" Yorimitsu pointed his sword at Outcast's—Lady Kiyoko's—heart.

"Stop!" I said. "Yorimitsu, these women are *victims*! You are here to save them. Put your swords down, all of you."

Startled, he turned to me but kept his sword steady. "They appear innocent, but I know better. They are demons."

The other men stood in readiness for Yorimitsu's command to start hacking and hewing their way through the crowd.

Masako stood between Kiyoko and the warriors. "No killing. We must listen to what these women have to say."

"They are not women," Yorimitsu snarled. "They are either obake shape-shifters or oni transformed into women."

"These women are possessed," I said. "Killing them will release the spirits that possess them. The senzo will go on to possess other victims, but you'll have dead women on your hands, and you won't have fixed the problem."

"Why would I believe *you*, Spirit? You might be obake as well." He swung his sword around to point it at me.

Rage flooded through me. *My own comrade?* My heart pounded and my palms, damp with sweat, itched to grab my sword and point it back at him.

Calm down, Suetake. Yorimitsu's angry at me—Spirit Mi-Na—not you.

After taking a few deep breaths to show Suetake who was boss, I raised my hands to show Yorimitsu I had no weapon in them, and also to keep Suetake's warrior reflexes from doing something that would get him killed. "Remember, Lord Yorimitsu, this is the body of a fellow warrior. If you injure me, you hurt Suetake. It's not his fault he's possessed."

Yorimitsu kept his sword up, but its tip lowered as he considered my words. Then he raised it again. "Demons, all of you!"

"Wait!" Masako held out a hand. "I will reveal their spirits to you." She began to chant and wave her arms in a bizarre pattern, creating a swirl of haze from the fire's smoke. "Look."

In front of each of the senzo-possessed women, the outline of a man's face formed in the negative space of the smoke. Kenji's face hovered in front of the young woman he'd possessed. I tried to see my face but my eyes crossed in vain.

Three warriors dropped their swords in shock at the supernatural apparitions. Yorimitsu and one other brave warrior kept theirs raised.

"This does not prove to me they are *not* shape-shifters," Yorimitsu said with a scowl. "If you exorcise them, I will believe you."

Masako, out of breath from her chanting and arm-waving, dropped her arms, bending over to hold her knees like someone who'd just sprinted a long distance.

"She's a miko, not an exorcist," I said.

That brought Yorimitsu's attention back to me. "Spirit, your peculiar face is as hideous as a hungry ghost," he growled.

Startled, Masako straightened, her eyes wide with wonder as she gazed at me. "Mi-Na, I see what you truly look like! Quite pretty, although strange—"

Yorimitsu interrupted the moment by shouting to his men to pick up their swords, including a few references to their cowardice and resemblance to certain farm animals.

The warriors bent to pick up their swords, exclaiming in comical confusion when they couldn't find them. Kenji had unobtrusively gathered the dropped swords while the rest of us were occupied with Masako's spirit-reveal magic.

Kenji handed one to Masako, one to Outcast—although I questioned the wisdom of arming a spirit who wanted vengeance—and kept one for himself. I took Suetake's from my pack.

We hefted them with varying levels of familiarity. Suetake's body had muscle memory from years of sword-fighting. Masako briefly trained with a sword when younger, and Outcast might have been rich enough once to have owned one. Kenji struggled with his.

The remaining women picked up staves and rocks to do their share of fighting.

Yorimitsu barked, which made me jump before realizing it was a contemptuous laugh at the idea we'd defeat him.

The other warriors pulled their yamabushi striking swords from their packs. Those weren't designed for battle, but could do some damage, especially when wielded by experienced fighters.

My entire body felt alive and energized despite the absurd situation of defending ill-mannered tsuki-mono against our allies.

The warriors arranged themselves in a group, swords held

out. Masako, Bikki, Kenji, and I stood with Outcast, our backs to the fire, not exactly an optimum position. One stumble and we'd be roast beef. The women with the stones and firewood sticks stood on the other side.

Outcast stepped away from the fire and closer to Yorimitsu. "Killing these bodies will not kill *us*. Do you have children, Warrior? Do you want me to possess your daughter and give her to the Emishi as their plaything? That will be their revenge for what you have done to them."

"I do not believe you," Yorimitsu said, gripping his hilt tightly. "You are demons, and I will send you back to Jigoku."

Yorimitsu and Outcast stood opposite each other with swords raised. With Outcast in the body of a young woman and Yorimitsu a fighting-fit mature adult, I was pessimistic about Outcast's chances of winning.

I threw my sword onto the ground. It landed with a clang at Yorimitsu's feet.

Kenji moved forward as if to protect me.

I suppressed an urge to push him behind me so *I* could protect *him*. But we didn't need that strange game right now, especially since I could see over his head. "Lord Yorimitsu, the senzo are victims too, wronged by the Fujiwara and Minamoto clans. They want restitution for their descendants."

Yorimitsu scowled, clearly unconvinced.

I turned to Kiyoko. "Senzo, if we solemnly vow to help you, will you leave these poor young women?"

Outcast lowered his sword while keeping a wary eye on Yorimitsu. "We will. But if you do not fulfill your vow, we will return. We will not be as kind to our hosts next time."

Masako set her sword on the ground. "Do not fight each other," she said, massaging her wrist. "We must work together to defeat the oni."

I'd almost forgotten about the oni.

Yorimitsu turned his fierce gaze toward Masako. "How do you know *they* are not oni?"

"Did I not just show you their spirit faces? Mi-Na is correct. We will never defeat the oni if we do not work together."

Yorimitsu finally lowered his sword. His warriors followed suit, and the rest of us exhaled with relief.

"Miko, I have seen your powers at work. I will believe you. How did these invaders get here?" He pointed his sword to the women on the other side of the fire. "What will keep them from making more demands after this one is fulfilled?"

"A curse widened the Demon Gate," Outcast said. "We saw the opening and realized we may never have another chance such as this. We vow to leave after restitution has been made to our descendants."

Kenji dropped his sword too, which clattered as it landed.

Yorimitsu winced at yet another show of disrespect to an experienced weapon.

"Mina, this is our purpose!" Kenji exclaimed. "By helping the senzo in this world, we will learn how to save senzo and kami in our world." He turned to Outcast. "Please tell us who performed a curse so powerful it opened the Demon Gate."

Outcast shook his head. "We only know that the curse led to the death of an innocent member of the imperial family. This death created a dark magic that forced the Gate open, and spirits of all kinds began to flow through it into this world. Senzo, oni, others."

"So Masako was right," I said. "A curse killed Lady Motoko."

One of the warriors stepped forward. "Lord Yorimitsu, this appears to involve the imperial family. Much is at stake if we do not agree to this demand."

Yorimitsu grunted noncommittally.

"Masako, your divination showed the women were kidnapped by oni, right?" I asked.

"Yes," she replied. "But divination is subject to interpretation, and I might have interpreted these senzo as oni."

Outcast shook his head. "Your divination was correct. Oni are entering in tremendous numbers."

I shivered despite standing next to the fire. "Then where are they?"

Yorimitsu jumped in before Outcast could answer. "Even if I agree to represent these claimants to the Minamoto and Fujiwara clan chiefs, the oni will not allow these women to leave."

Outcast had the grace to bow his head in shame. "It is true. We possessed these bodies and walked them from the city to this mountain to provide food and drink for the demons and to cause fear and consternation in the Capital so the great clans would agree to our demands. Lord Oni will not allow these women to walk away."

Masako staggered slightly as if the oni's penchant for cannibalism was news to her. "If this is true..." She trailed off as if the next sentence was too awful to say.

"We have to defeat them," I finished for her.

Masako bowed to Outcast. "We will need your assistance."

"As long as you vow to help us." Outcast waved to his fellow spirits. "We will guide you to the oni's palace within the mountain. Remain disguised as yamabushi. If you say you are acolytes of En no Ozunu, the chief will trust you. En is known in the spirit world as a mystic who did not despise oni."

"And after we defeat them, we must somehow close the Demon Gate," Masako said.

Silence filled the cavern as we pondered how to make that happen.

Bikki came forward, making me jump. I'd forgotten he was there.

"Tusu-kur travel between the oni and the human worlds," he

said. "Tonight I will go to the oni world so we can learn how to close the Gate."

I didn't understand why Bikki would be willing to do such a dangerous thing for the government that oppressed his people, but I'd wait until after this was over to ask him. I wouldn't want to encourage him to have second thoughts about helping us. We needed his experience. Masako was still young, and her training had been unorthodox. Her power had returned, but her level of control was questionable.

Yorimitsu and his warriors huddled to confer, and then Yorimitsu announced they agreed to the senzo's terms. He would support a request to the Minamoto and Fujiwara clans for restitution, but only if certain conditions were met.

"The senzo must support us in the fight against the oni," he declared. "The Tusu-kur must return with a plan to close the Demon Gate. We are warriors, not diviners. We will fight them, but only if you send their evil spirits back to their world when we kill them."

Masako, Bikki, and Outcast agreed to do their part depending on the result of Bikki's trip to the oni world.

Bikki left the cavern to begin his meditation. The warriors stepped away to discuss battle strategy. They didn't invite me. Yorimitsu had made it clear he didn't trust Spirit Mi-Na.

The rest of us remained in the cavern to discuss our next steps.

I was surprised the oni hadn't noticed our presence yet, but Outcast said they drank a lot of saké. "And the chief's palace is through the middle of the mountain. They rely on us—the senzo —to protect this entrance from invaders."

"So that's why you possessed the bandits?" I asked. "These women don't exactly look like fighters."

"Indeed," Outcast said, lifting his—Kiyoko's—thin arms. "We will let Lord Oni know the yamabushi would like to drink with him tomorrow. He is waiting for us now to bring him blood. He likes Nariko's. He doesn't need much. He mixes it with saké."

"Oh, no," Kenji said quickly. "My host already donated." He pointed to the scab above his elbow.

Masako couldn't risk the pollution associated with blood. She might need to call upon the kami for assistance.

I'd donated blood at least once a year since I was eighteen, so I had more experience at it than anyone else. And while the thought of becoming part of a demon's cocktail made me queasy, the sight of blood had never been an issue for me.

Outcast made a small incision in my left arm with the gentle touch of Lady Kiyoko's delicate hands. "It heals rapidly," he explained. "Most of the time, anyway."

He caught it in a saké cup, and since it wasn't a large quantity, it was easy enough to transport without spilling.

When he finished, he handed me a filthy rag to cover up the wound. I declined, pressing my hand against it, and joined Masako and Kenji as they discussed what we would do next.

Chapter 20

Shaman

Bikki staggered into the clearing early the next morning, leaning on his staff like it was the only thing between him and an intimate relationship with the dirt. I jumped up to help him, but he waved me away. He sat on the ground and gratefully accepted a ladle of water from Masako.

We gathered around, some of us still rubbing sleep from our eyes. Kenji had slept well on the hard ground while the warriors took turns on watch.

Masako and I had stayed up talking. Our conversation had been a little awkward at first because the terms of our friendship had changed. The ease of communicating by directed thought wasn't possible, and instead of two young women chatting, it was a male warrior and a female shaman. What level of familiarity was proper? Male versus female pattern of speech? How polite or how humble?

Suetake's brain took care of the problem for me. Whatever I had to say, no matter how American and Mina-like my thoughts were, they came out through his mouth in his fifth-rank nobleman's speech.

At least, Masako said my language was fine, but that might have been her usual good manners.

While the moon rose and fell, as nightingales trilled and tree frogs croaked, we stumbled through the difficult parts. We acknowledged our mutual grief and apologized for the wrongs we committed during our time together. We reconnected spiritually as we discussed her growing talent in conjuring shikigami and my ability to perceive obake in the modern world.

I shared with her Kenji's theory of modern pollution and the disappearing kami, which upset her.

"I'm sorry, I didn't mean to make you cry." I wanted to comfort her, hug her, and wipe her tears away, but that wasn't an option in this male body. Instead, I gave her paper from the bundle Suetake kept inside his robe for quick notes and spur-of-the-moment poems.

"It's not your fault." She dabbed at her nose. "I want to understand your world."

"If it makes you feel better, Kenji thinks the power we gained by traveling here will return with us to 2019. I mean, to the future. We have no idea how, but it's a start."

"When we return to the capital, we'll consult with Lord Seimei. He will understand what you should do."

Her confidence had made me a little more optimistic, but when morning arrived, I was exhausted. "What I wouldn't give for a mug of coffee right now," I mumbled to Kenji.

"Mi-Na!" Masako frowned at me. "Please sit and listen to what Bikki has to say."

She didn't like it when I used words like coffee with no meaning in this world. I wasn't even sure what came out of Suetake's mouth when I said it, but clearly, there was no equivalent for coffee in his brain.

I sympathized with her irritation. Kenji and I shared inside jokes from a world she would never know. "Sorry. Bikki, please tell us everything."

He gave me a tired smile. "The process to enter the oni world required hours of meditation and chanting. I began after sunset, and it was not until just before sunrise that my inner eyes saw the Demon Gate. It constantly shifted colors—silver, gray, blue, and silver again. My body remained anchored in the dark forest, but something tugged at my spirit, vibrating it as if the kami plucked it like a koto string."

"I know that feeling," I couldn't help exclaiming.

He nodded to acknowledge our common experience. "The pull became so strong it drew my spirit out of my body and into the shimmer, which absorbed me and then *pushed* me-" he gestured in a forceful forward motion. "Out of my body, and into the oni world."

Kenji leaned forward eagerly. "What was it like?"

Bikki's expression darkened. "Never have I experienced such a place. A pale red sky, deep red leaves on deeper red trees. The air shivered with spirits drifting from that strange, blood-dark world, floating through the opening through which my spirit had entered this bizarre realm. Hordes of terrifying, hideous oni moved toward the Gate, many with horns on their heads, some with blue skin, some with red, some with many arms and mouths. And eyes—many eyes."

I shivered. "Why do they want to come here? What's in it for them?"

Masako shot me a sharp glance for interrupting, but Kenji nodded as if he'd wondered the same thing, which was all the encouragement I needed to keep going. "Seriously, it's not like they're imprisoned, right? That's *their* world. Why would they want to come to ours?"

Bikki's deeply lined forehead creased still more as he considered how best to answer. He pointed to the incision on my arm.

"The oni enjoy human flesh and blood. It makes them strong. Also, they come for revenge, or the kami might send them here to punish humans when we do not perform sacred rituals."

"Food source, then," I said. "And kami hammer. Please continue."

He took a sip of water first. "The Gate widened and narrowed like clouds torn apart and pushed together in a storm. When oni approached it, the Gate widened, allowing them to pass through. How was that possible? Perhaps the curse that killed the Consort damaged the natural closing of the Gate. We must counteract the curse in order to keep the Gate closed."

Kenji, Masako, and I exchanged a perplexed look. Masako spoke first. "Bikki, none of us know such a ritual. As Tusu-kur, have *you* done such a thing?"

"Ah, no, but I have incantations which might work. First, however, we must return the Mount Ōe demons to their world. The warriors must cut off their heads, then we diviners will push their spirits back through the Gate."

Yorimitsu and his men grunted in agreement. A couple of them appeared a little peaked under their beards at all this supernatural talk, but they enthusiastically patted the backpacks holding their swords.

"But," Bikki continued. "I am the only experienced shaman here, and my power is insufficient for this task. Lady Masako has little experience using hers. Even working together might be insufficient for the strong magic needed."

He didn't look upset enough for such a statement. He had a plan. Otherwise, what were we doing here?

"Mi-Na and Ken-Ji crossed the spirit world, which means they have shamanic power. We will work together—join all of our powers—to banish the oni-spirits and close the Gate."

A confusing swirl of emotions clouded my mind. How could *I* help? I wasn't the one with magic. And neither was Kenji.

I glanced at him, curious if he felt like I did. A bright and confident smile on his face told me self-doubt was *not* one of his issues.

Well, *was* I a shaman? I'd traveled to the spirit world. Twice. I could see obake spirits and senzo auras. Maybe Bikki was right. Maybe I *could* help. My power was weak, but if I could share it with a more powerful shaman like Bikki, we might accomplish something big together.

Everyone was staring at me. "Sorry, was there a question?"

Bikki smiled like he knew what I was thinking. "Mi-Na, have you ever used shamanic power in your world?"

"Uh, no. I didn't know I had any."

Kenji raised a shaved Nariko-eyebrow at me.

"I didn't want to believe I had any," I corrected.

"You found the kimon opening, so you must have power," Bikki said.

"But did my power come from entering the spirit world or did I have an ability to do that in the first place?"

"You could not have entered it from a living body without it, especially because you were not trained," Bikki said. "Once there, you gained more. Ken-Ji, you also left a living body to enter the spirit world. That tells me you are a shaman too. Did you gain additional powers when you did so?"

"I studied divination for years before attempting this trip," Kenji replied. "But I had no power. Mina brought me with her, and I seemed to have gained it by crossing the spirit world. I can see the glow of possessing spirits now. It's not much to offer, but perhaps Mina and I can pool our powers and use them to amplify your efforts."

My doubts came whooshing back. "What if we aren't strong enough? Bikki and Masako are professionals. Kenji and I are amateurs." I looked around our group, desperate for someone to tell me I could do this. The warriors? No. Cutting off an oni's head was all right—their job required slicing off a few heads now and then—but they would leave exorcism-related activities to the diviners.

Kenji had a this-is-what-I've-been-waiting-for-all-my-life smile. *He* believed we could do this. Masako clasped her hands, staring at me expectantly. *She* believed in me. Bikki's expression was grave, his eyes too deep set for me to read, but he'd gone to the oni world, so he should know what he was talking about.

If they all believed I could be a shaman, so should I.

And if we had enough power to close the Demon Gate, we might become a force for good in the modern world.

"It sounds like we have no time to waste," I said. "Tell me what I need to do."

Chapter 21

The Four Guardians

Bikki began to refer to us as the Four Guardians of the Demon Gate. A bit epic-fantasy for my taste, but it sounded better in Japanese. He taught us the chant he and Masako had used on the bandits, changing it slightly to make it stronger and more suitable for four shamans using it at the same time.

First, though, he insisted we purify ourselves with *sakaki* twigs, paper dolls, and water. We needed to transfer unclean spiritual energy into the clean version. No power existed without the kami's blessing and presence, and the kami would not descend to us if we were polluted.

Yorimitsu suggested offering the oni a gift of poisoned saké. Bikki told him they could not be poisoned. "They must have their heads cut off to free their spirits, which we will then send back to their world," he explained.

"Might something *amplify*-" Yorimitsu stumbled over this new word—"the effects of saké? Make it stronger so they remain asleep when we attack? My men are courageous, but supernatural beings do not behave as people do in a battle. Swords, technique, and brute strength do not work against spirits."

Bikki knew of a common herb that might make oni sleepy, so he instructed us to continue practicing our incantations while he gathered some. Yorimitsu sent Kenji into the cave to ask Outcast for an empty barrel.

Before he did that, however, we debated the pros and cons of telling Outcast what we were up to. Our success should lead to Outcast's success, but what if he betrayed us to the chief?

After a spirited debate, we agreed not to tell Outcast about adding sleep-inducing herbs to our gift.

Kenji rolled the barrel outside. Yorimitsu commanded the warriors to pour their remaining saké into it. When they grumbled, Kenji explained it would give the warriors an advantage in the fight by sending the oni to sleep.

They sacrificed their liquid gold willingly after that.

Bikki returned with herbs, mashed them into a paste, and stirred the paste into the barrel.

When the sun was overhead, we took a break to eat some rice balls. I stuffed an entire ball into my mouth just because I could, thanks to Suetake's large jaw. Unfortunately, I choked on it when an extraordinary young man strolled out of the cave.

He was at least eight feet tall. His skin looked like he'd spent a week under a sunlamp, and his hair was cherry red and tangled like he'd never brushed it in his life.

Other than that, he was handsome. Firm chin, big white teeth, huge red irises. He wore a red checkered robe with crimson hakama underneath. He twirled a spiky iron staff as if it weighed nothing, although it was as long as Nariko was tall and thicker than her neck.

I wasn't the only one who choked. Kenji worked at clearing his throat too. Masako froze in place, rice ball halfway to her mouth. The warriors stirred and murmured something unhappy. I didn't blame them. My heart raced, and not just from trying to get rice out of my windpipe.

The stranger walked over to us with an incandescent smile. "Welcome, holy men, followers of En."

Yorimitsu bowed politely. "Greetings, Lord Oni. We are honored by your presence." His voice didn't quaver. His tone was reasonable, his stance dignified. There were things I didn't like about Yorimitsu—his sword at my throat, for one—but I gave him props for courage.

Kenji turned even paler, and Masako's hand—the one still holding the rice ball—was shaking.

"So, what brings you to my humble home?" the chief asked in a chirpy voice.

Yorimitsu put his hands in his sleeves, leaning into the whole mountain-monk aesthetic. "We wander the mountains in search of sacred places. We became lost and sought a place to rest for the night." He waved at the barrel. "A gift for you, Lord, a small thing of no importance, but a token of our respect. Saké from an imperial purveyor in the capital. Suitable for an emperor, one might say."

The tall man's eyes burned red. "*Holy* men, I thank you for your *wholly* satisfying gift. Please drink with me this evening. If you amuse me, I'll let you live. That is not a promise, though. I might eat you. But I might *not* eat you. I haven't decided yet." He roared with laughter, and we forced ourselves to chuckle along. "Lady Nariko will escort you to my palace when the sun falls below the trees. She's beautiful, isn't she? And tasty too! Her blood is some of the most refined I've tasted in this region."

I bit my lip to stop myself from blurting something about Nariko's *terroir* and the micro-climate she grew up in. Bad jokes sprang to my lips when I was scared or in danger, and rarely has that worked out for me.

The oni-man clapped his hands in delight at his own comments—or maybe at the fear in our eyes—and disappeared back into the cave.

We were speechless for a minute, but then a rush of comments and questions flew around our group, most of them at Bikki.

My terroir joke made me wonder if the oni had a sensitive palate. "We should have Kenji eat some of the herbs, and after a bit, draw his blood to put a few drops in the oni's cup. That might disguise the tainted saké's herb taste and odor. If asked, we'll say Nariko's diet affected the taste."

"Mi-Na, excellent!" Masako smiled at me like she couldn't believe I had such a good idea.

Kenji agreed with a resigned shrug. "The last thing we want is for him to take one sip and then kill us for trying to poison him. Poor Nariko. How much blood do you think she has left?"

Bikki gave Kenji a small amount of mitsuba, an herb similar to parsley, which wouldn't make a human sleepy. But oni had their own rules, and we had no choice but to believe Bikki knew what he was doing.

Chapter 22

A Poem About Saké

The sun moved into the western sky all too quickly. I kept checking its position, growing increasingly anxious about the evening's battle. If we didn't have enough power to send the oni-spirits back to their world, they would kill us.

But I wasn't anxious for myself, or even for Kenji. As long as our bodies remained alive in Uji in 2019, our spirits would be too. We might have trouble finding a way home, but if our hosts were killed, at least Kenji and I wouldn't die.

Suetake and Nariko would, though. Suetake was accustomed to danger, and as a warrior, he lived with the risk of dying in battle. Nariko, however, was an innocent victim. If the oni killed her, she'd be gone forever.

I redoubled my efforts to learn the spells.

Just as the sun grazed the tips of the cedar trees, Kenji went into the cave to have Outcast draw some of his now-tainted blood. When he returned, he invited us to Lord Oni's palace in the polite, feminine language suitable for Nariko's rank and gender.

We followed him in our yamabushi gear, but our packs

contained the warriors' swords and armor hidden inside. Two warriors conveyed the barrel of tainted saké between them.

Once inside, Outcast led the way. The rock corridor was dark and twisty, and we had to bend double in a few places to get through. Small oil lamps were placed here and there to light the way. Several senzo-possessed women assumed the rear.

After passing through a cavern, we saw a light ahead too bright to be a lamp, and the air smelled fresh as a soft breeze moved toward us.

We stumbled out of the mountain, blinking in confusion.

I tugged Kenji's sleeve. "Holy kami!"

His little rosebud mouth dropped open at the strange view ahead.

We'd exited the cave and stood at the bottom of a shallow valley, hidden from the world not only by the mountain we'd just exited, but by other hills and ridges that formed a ring around us. The orange aura of the peak in front of us indicated we faced west, and that the sun didn't have much further to go before disappearing for the night.

We had just enough light left to see a traditional Heian palace on the valley floor, with a central hall, two wings, and verandas along the outside. The compound's outer wall appeared to be standard wood.

Not typical, however, were spikes sticking up from the eaves, the blackish-reddish color of the main building's walls and doors, or the azure hue of the roof.

"The Iron Palace," Outcast said.

Iron walls twisted the grace and beauty of a noble residence into something heavy and ominous, the spikes a reminder of the cruel inhabitants within.

"Did Lord Oni force local ironworkers to build it, or did he eat whoever lived here previously?" I couldn't prevent a shudder. "Or eat the iron-workers after they built it?"

Curious to know if Kenji had those morbid thoughts too, I glanced at him. His face—Nariko's face—was pale under smudges and dirt.

Such a sweet young thing. So fragile. *I must protect her.*

My hand reached for my missing sword, and I noticed the other warriors twitching too, their eyes alight with battle fever, their hands jerking toward their packs as if yearning to wield their swords.

I belonged with *them,* not cowering here with victims like Nariko or the sheltered shrine maiden Masako or the ascetic Bikki with his insect-like stick legs. "Leave fighting to us men," I whispered to myself. "Only warriors can defeat His Majesty's enemies."

I strode to Yorimitsu's side.

Startled, he drew away.

"Let's fight," I grunted.

"Suetake." His mouth curled into a wild snarl of a grin. "Welcome back."

"Mi-Na! Over here!"

Masako's urgent appeal shook me out of my trance, and with great effort, I forced myself to leave the warriors and return to the shaman clique.

Kenji's eyes were wide with surprise at my strange behavior.

I didn't blame him. I must have been affected by testosterone surging through my male body in anticipation of battle and at the sight of innocent, weak Nariko.

Focus, Mina, focus. Stick to the job you trained for.

Outcast escorted us to a massive iron door, which stood open as if anticipating our arrival.

Or maybe they always left it open. "It must be hella heavy," I whispered to Kenji. "And who would dare enter an oni's lair uninvited?"

The warriors muttered to each other, no doubt speculating on the reasons and methods for constructing a building made of iron.

Yorimitsu waited by the entrance until everyone else had gone through, including Outcast, the other senzo, and the servants who stood at the door. "The commander wants to ensure the door does not close behind us," Masako said. "If it does, we might not be able to leave, for which of us has the strength to open it?"

The servants—kidnapped victims, no doubt—guided us to the visiting hall.

The main door remained open, so Yorimitsu brought up the rear.

"The oni believe we're peaceful yamabushi," I murmured to Masako. "How can they be so evil and yet so trusting?"

Sconces placed at intervals on the walls illuminated the palace's dark interior. The air inside was stuffy and hot, unlike residences built of wood. I wiped my forehead with my sleeve, while Masako and Kenji used fans to cool off.

Lord Oni greeted us with a friendly bow and gestured to mats on the floor. The four warriors sat in a row across from the chief, and the four shamans sat together next to the warriors.

The senzo-possessed women sat in a line behind the chief. They had their own agenda, and if we served it, they'd help us. If we didn't assist them, they'd find another way to achieve their goals. They didn't care what happened to us. We represented their oppressors. Except for Bikki, of course. His people were even more oppressed than the senzo's clans, who, after all, were Yamato.

The chief motioned with his iron staff for Outcast and Kenji to serve the saké. They dipped a tea-kettle-looking container into our gift barrel and moved around the floor, pouring the divine liquid into shallow green cups resting on trays in front of each guest.

Other people filtered in, mostly women, but young men too. I examined them covertly, as they were not introduced. They were all beautiful, but as I flicked my eyes back and forth, trying not to look shifty, I noticed odd things about each one. A woman's long black hair had strands of green. Another woman's delicate ears were sharply pointed. Several had red irises, and a few had small horns under their long hair. Skins of varying hues including pale red, greenish-white, light blue, and lavender.

Oni, transformed into humans, none of them getting it quite right.

"Let's drink!" Lord Oni boomed. "Saké, saké, I love saké!"

We toasted our host and sipped. The saké was a little cloudy and tinged with green from the mitsuba. It had an odd taste—light, refreshing, a little grassy. Slightly astringent but not bitter. Not bad at all. Maybe I'd suggest mitsuba as a saké flavoring when I got home.

Lord Oni drank his in one gulp and gestured for a refill. "A poem!" he cried. "Who will write a poem about saké?"

My host had been a poet and a scholar, so if pressed, I might be able to dig through Suetake's memory to find a poem.

He pointed to one of the other warriors. "You!"

The man pulled paper from his robe.

"Eh, no. Put that back. Use what I have provided for this illustrious occasion," Lord Oni commanded.

A servant set an inkwell and brush on the table. The inkwell was filled with a red fluid, and the ivory brush was tipped with coarse black hair. The warrior didn't blink at what was obviously human blood, bone, and hair. He held the brush as delicately as if it were the finest rabbit hair, dipped it in the red substance, and artfully wrote his lines.

He sat next to me—I was the last warrior and the start of the diviner group—and I saw he wrote in *onnade*, women's writing based on syllables. Men usually used Chinese characters, so maybe his wife had taught him the benefits of writing cursive.

He blew softly on the paper to dry it, but the red ink was drippier than regular black ink, and it spread over the paper like an omen in a horror movie.

"Read it!" Lord Oni shouted boisterously.

Remaining seated, the warrior bowed and began his recitation.

"No saké as precious
As the one I drink today
With the red-haired lord.
Existence is transient.
Drink now, before it passes.

I nearly choked at his subversive poem. How dare he tell the oni to drink before they die? Was he trying to give us away?

Lord Oni roared his approval. "It passes! Yes! The saké passes, indeed. I must let it pass through me." Laughing, he stood and faced the wall, letting a stream of what had once been saké into a little trough running along the floor. We humans tried not to flinch at such boorish behavior.

Next, he ordered his minions to perform a *dengaku* dance. Several of the weirdly beautiful women and men gathered at the end of the room. Instruments appeared in their hands: a flute, a drum, and something resembling a rain stick. The dancers moved back and forth, swinging their arms and lifting their knees in a stylized version of planting rice.

Lord Oni watched us while we watched the dancers. "This dance is becoming popular with nobles," he mused. "Have you seen such things?"

Yorimitsu nodded. "A marvel, indeed. Let us drink to these dancers. More saké for your chief!"

Lord Oni's eyes flashed red as he lifted his cup, and when

Kenji came around with the kettle, he grabbed it, drank it all, and sent Kenji off for more.

"This wine is good, but it needs a little something. A condiment!"

Outcast went around the table with a cup from which he poured a few drops of Kenji's blood into everyone's cup, turning the saké into an unpleasant reddish-brown color.

"A new flavor for you. Pomegranate!" Lord Oni's minions laughed as if he'd made a hilarious joke. "Drink! Drink!" he insisted. "You will love it! It's made just for holy men!"

I lifted my cup to my mouth and pretended to swallow, but Lord Oni wasn't looking at me. He was observing Yorimitsu, which meant Yorimitsu had to drain his cup. Which he did, smacking his lips and proclaiming it delicious.

Lord Oni laughed like this was the funniest thing he'd heard all day. He clapped his hands, and oni-servants brought trays of food. The fragrance of grilled meat floated through the air. I'd rarely eaten meat in this era, and my mouth watered with antici-pation until I saw the platter held a human leg with the foot still attached. I closed my eyes, breathed in (*one, two, three, four*), and exhaled slowly (*five, six, seven, eight.*) We couldn't allow ourselves to react now. We were too close to battle.

"What's the matter? Aren't you hungry?" Lord Oni asked. "Eat. I will be offended if you do not appreciate my culture. Yamabushi eat very little, and now you have a chance to fill those empty stomachs."

What would the oni do if we failed this test? The tainted liquid needed time to work. We couldn't start fighting now with Lord Oni and his minions fully awake. They were too big and too strong.

"Thank you for your gracious hospitality," Yorimitsu replied. He waved at the platter as if to signify someone needed to serve him. Outcast helpfully used a large knife to cut off a bit.

I looked away quickly, knowing if I saw Yorimitsu eat that meat I might lose whatever I had in my stomach.

He must have passed the test. The chief's booming laugh rang out again. "You enjoyed my rare delicacies! What kind of men are you to eat what a demon provides?"

"We humble monks do not eat meat," Yorimitsu answered, "but you provided this feast in the spirit of hospitality and sympathy, feeding poor ascetics who have become thin and weak, so I overcame my reluctance. In our faith, we do not reject something offered with such solicitude."

The oni chief lifted his cup. "More saké for these mountain monks! If my dainty delights are not to your taste, do not eat more of it. Drink your meal instead!"

Our collective sigh of relief caused a lamp on the floor to flicker.

Lord Oni's eyelids began to close over his red irises and his head nodded to his chest. He forced his eyes open and called for a song, stumbling over his words, but laughing at his mistakes.

One of the women-oni rose from a kneeling position, and in a thin, reedy voice, began a song that reminded me of court music. She moved gently and deliberately in a circle, her arms gesturing widely, singing about living a long life, and how drinking saké would allow that to happen. She gestured to us. *Eat*, she sang. *Eat, and your powers will grow. Eat and drink for a powerful life.*

Masako and Kenji managed to maintain polite smiles while the warriors stared at the singer with fascinated lust. Was I the only one who realized she was telling the other oni *we* were food?

When she finished, she glided toward Yorimitsu. "Holy man, you saw my face. You heard me sing. What else do you want from me?" she purred. "You are the leader of our honored guests. Allow me to show my appreciation for bringing these holy men to our residence."

The other men frowned jealously, but Yorimitsu declined.

She remained still, her head bowed, perhaps assuming her beauty and talent would win him over.

He folded his arms and glared at her.

The rest of us shifted uneasily. Why didn't he speak? Was she going to stay there until he gave in?

Bikki began to chant.

The woman-oni lifted her head, curious about the intrusion of sound into what had been a silent contest of wills. She gasped and shivered as she met Yorimitsu's fierce, unblinking stare. The air around her blurred.

Bikki's chanting grew louder, hypnotic, insistent.

Her true oni form flashed into sight. Blue skin and red eyes, a contemptuous sneer twisting her huge mouth.

She immediately flickered back into human form, but not before the warriors noticed. Expressions of disgust replaced all signs of desire.

Lord Oni's cherry-red skin blurred and shifted to yellow and blue. His face was suddenly covered with multiple eyes. It was just for a breath or two before reverting to his human face, but it was enough. Most of us could not prevent audible gasps at that terrifying, albeit brief, vision of his true self.

"Impressive magic," he said to Bikki. "Come work for me. Your people lived in this land before the Yamato pushed you out. We should be allied against them. Come live in my palace and do my bidding, and I will reward you richly."

Bikki didn't respond other than a bow of thanks.

Lord Oni shrugged. "Give me your answer tomorrow." He turned to the rest of us. "Do not be afraid of my appearance. We demons find humans strange and fearsome at first sight, but I am used to you now. Your appearance amuses me, with your big hats and silly shells." He yawned. "Time to go to my chamber. Holy men, relax and enjoy my beautiful entertainers."

He staggered away, accompanied by a few human women.

Yorimitsu told the remaining oni and senzo that we would sleep on the floor in the hall.

They carried away the empty kettle, the cups, and the mostly untouched leg, and did not return.

Masako turned to me, her eyes shining. "It's time," she whispered.

Chapter 23

Power Cable

The warriors changed out of their yamabushi disguises, putting their armor on and taking fighting swords out of their packs. We Guardians remained in our yamabushi outfits, appropriate for our shaman role.

Outcast led the way to Lord Oni's sleeping chamber. He informed us that oni reverted to their true forms while sleeping. "Lord Oni is as high as the cavern ceiling, so his human size is the only way he fits through the cave entrance. He can't maintain his human form while sleeping, though. The others sleep in their true oni forms too, although none are as tall as their king. The smaller demons usually sleep outside the chamber, but tonight they were so intoxicated, we easily persuaded them to sleep in the chamber."

We arrived at a massive iron door, twenty feet high and ten feet wide. Bikki tried to slide it open, but it didn't budge. He tried pulling on it. Same problem. He turned to Outcast in frustration.

Outcast shook his head. "I have never opened it," he said. "It has always been open. He must not trust you. The door is bolted, and the bolt is also iron, so you will not be able to break through it."

"Should we try knocking?" I asked in a stage whisper. "Attack as they open the door?"

"You underestimate their strength," Outcast replied. "You need the advantage of attacking while they sleep."

Bikki had not stopped examining the door, running his hands over it as if to find a weakness. "Oni-magic created this door. We might be able to dissolve the magic and so dissolve the door."

Masako and Bikki conferred quietly on how to do that. When they finished their discussion, Bikki advised us to stand back. "This might result in an explosion, but don't stand so far back you lose time rushing in."

I'd been reprimanded once for putting my thoughts where they weren't welcome, so I suppressed my urge to ask why a possible explosion was better than knocking.

Bikki and Masako stood tall as they began a chant. Masako started her dance, keeping to a tight circle, her arms gracefully moving up and down. Bikki tossed herbs at the door. They kept their chanting so low it sounded like the hum of bees around flowers.

My skin prickled a warning. Kenji's face perspired as if he were restraining himself from running away. Yorimitsu bared his teeth savagely, the nobleman-warrior now all warrior.

The door shimmered in the flickering light of the oil lamps lining the hall, then dissolved without a sound.

Kenji and I both staggered with relief as Bikki waved us forward into the room.

Lord Oni lay on his back, taking up most of the huge chamber, his bulk a mini-mountain inside the mountain. His hair bristled out from his head, as red and thick and prickly as a barberry bush in autumn. His ugly feet stuck up, each one as tall as Bikki.

The stench of sulfur and rotting meat caught in my throat, and I had to stifle a cough.

Other demons rested around him, all of them in their oni forms. Two or three women napped in seated positions, heads resting against the chamber walls. No aura of spirit possession hovered above them, and since they were sleeping while human, they couldn't be demons. They must be kidnapping victims, forced to serve the oni.

The warriors spread out, protected by helmets, shoulder padding, and leg flaps. No swords lay near the sleeping oni, although a few halberds leaned against the iron walls.

A vision of the human leg on the dinner tray flashed through my mind. Rage and a desire to tear Lord Oni's head from his body propelled me forward.

Kenji grabbed my arm. "Mina!"

I spun toward him with my hand raised. *Just try to stop me.*

Alarmed, he let go. "What are you doing?" he whispered. "You're a shaman, remember? We need you with us."

My fury faded at his words as I realized Suetake's influence was growing on me. "Sorry. I'm fighting my warrior instincts here."

Bikki seemed to understand what I was going through. "Mi-Na, resist your desire to engage in direct battle," he murmured. "We must remain free from pollution. Therefore we will stand close to the door while the warriors fight the oni. After they cut off the head of each one, we will send its spirit through the Gate."

I saw nothing in the chamber ceiling resembling an opening to the Great Beyond. "Um, Bikki? We crossed through the Demon Gate at the stream. How will we send the oni spirits through it from *here*?"

"The whole mountain is within it," he answered. "When we begin the incantations, an opening will become visible."

As softly as we whispered, we still disturbed one of the human servants, who lifted her head as if to cry out.

Masako swiftly crossed the hall and whispered into her ear. The young woman nodded and went to the other two servants to whisper to each in turn.

They rose and came toward us, bowing with pale, tired faces, no doubt anemic from supplying blood to oni. "Can we help?" they asked. "We want to destroy these monsters."

I admired their willingness to get involved, but they'd get in the way. Masako advised them to return to the cavern near the cave entrance to let the other women know the fight was about to begin.

After they left, we assessed the situation. The oni slept on the floor and were many different sizes, shapes, and colors. Blue and red predominated, but a few green arms here and there. Lots of horns, and lots of eyes too, all of which were closed.

The warriors slid silently across the polished wood floor, each targeting an oni to attack. They were instructed to work individually on the minions first, then work together to defeat their chief.

As long as he kept sleeping, that is.

We—the Four Guardians—stood in a line and began our chant.

Without Suetake's anger fueling my bloodlust, dread returned to churn my stomach and squeeze my chest like someone trying to make juice out of me. *Kami, I hate this feeling.*

The dim room brightened as an electrifying surge coursed through me, lighting my veins on fire and sharpening my senses. Suddenly each odor in the room—oni-stench, lamp oil, the remains of incense clinging to Lady Nariko's robes—became distinct. My yamabushi jacket scratched against my arms, the weight of it both intimate and strange. Rats scuttled through the walls as if running away.

A familiar whisper echoed in my head. *"The dread precedes the power."*

I saw everything happening everywhere in the hall as if I had as many eyes as the oni. Masako stood tall, moving slowly in a stately pattern. The warriors were in position, ready to strike when Yorimitsu gave the word. Kenji's round Nariko-face glowed above his dirty robe. Bikki's gray beard gleamed as if lit from within.

Two glowing red filaments curled outward from Masako, swaying and twisting toward me.

My shoulders and arms prickled with energy. My hands spun a pale, silk-like thread of my own.

Masako's threads reached toward mine, and as they connected, began to braid together.

Bikki and Kenji spun threads too, Kenji's fragile like mine, Bikki's bright and thick, twisting together into a red yarn before seeking the strand Masako and I had created.

The two sets of braids twisted together, connecting all four of us.

We chanted in unison, and the chant hummed through the braid. Power drummed in my chest and flowed out through my hands and into the thick red cord.

A glowing, shimmering, silvery-blue light began to shine above us.

The smallest of the oni jumped up as a warrior reached him, shouting, "Traitors!"

The warrior swung his sword downward to cut through its neck.

Dark red mist swirled upward as the demon's body dissolved.

We shifted the incantation, now singing with one voice, arms swinging in a unified pattern.

The oni-spirit fought us, churning as it attempted to form another body.

Our feet slid forward, sideways, backward, forward. Our hands pulled in and then pushed out in unison. The cable unified our four spirits into one soul.

The oni-mist vibrated angrily. In response, our red cable glowed brighter still as we cast the oni-spirit into the shimmering light of the Demon Gate.

The other demons shouted with anger and dismay while the warriors hacked away. As each oni lost his head, its dark mist rippled and seethed while the body dissolved.

We could only trap one at a time in our spiritual net. Our communal energy allowed us to work quickly, but it took four shamans to send one spirit through the Gate, and we couldn't keep up with five warriors cutting off five oni heads. The math just didn't work in our favor.

When a warrior killed an oni before we were ready, the oni-spirit formed a new physical shape. When that happened, the warrior waited until a new head appeared, which he then sliced off again to buy us the time we needed to send it back to its world.

Even tainted saké couldn't keep Lord Oni asleep amid the shrieks and shouts of battle. He stirred, opening his many eyes, taking his time to blearily rub them all before noticing us.

His head grazed the ceiling as he sat up and roared with anger. "I gave you wine and food, and you repay me with lies and disguise! You call oni evil, but demons do not lie. Only humans lie!" He swung his blue arm, as thick as a tree, toward Yorimitsu. The oil lamps flickered with the gust created by his movement, sending horned shadows dancing on the chamber's walls and floor.

The warriors paused, confused, unable to distinguish shadow from demon-mist.

Yorimitsu skipped around the oni's great bulk to reach his head. The demon's multiple eyes turned in every direction to seek the threat, but the warrior crouched low enough for the demon's girth to hide him.

Lord Oni shifted and turned, lifting his giant arms to crush Yorimitsu, but the commander darted out of range as if he had trained all his life for this moment.

Our incantation transitioned to yet another spell, one that would freeze the chief's limbs. Hypnotic, rhythmic, and low, my male voice box growled in harmony with the others. Our red braid of power sent out child-threads which reached toward the oni chief and wrapped around his legs and arms.

Lord Oni raged, his eyes bulging as he struggled to move. He whipped his head back and forth, attempting to catch Yorimitsu with his massive jaw. Yorimitsu darted around him, his teeth bared in a wild, fierce grin, his eyes burning with fury as he sought a vulnerable spot to slash.

A violent urge to fight swept aside my focus. *My comrade needs me. Where's my sword?* I scanned the hall to seek a weapon.

A mistake. My distraction snapped the power cable and weakened the binding threads holding the big oni in place.

His limbs freed from our net, Lord Oni snarled and swung at Yorimitsu, who cursed and jumped behind the demon's back. Lord Oni reached backward with his long arm, and Yorimitsu scrambled toward his giant feet. The other warriors saw what was happening but they couldn't help because they were fighting smaller demons.

Lord Oni snatched Yorimitsu with his huge, ham-like hands, laughing with victory. Yorimitsu's sword clattered to the ground as he struggled to free himself. He glared at me like he knew it was my fault.

I dashed forward, grabbed his sword, and stabbed Lord Oni's feet.

He roared and swatted at me with his other hand like I was an irritating mosquito.

Jumping aside with a swiftness I hadn't known I possessed, I jabbed his foot again.

He shouted and jumped to his feet.

Or rather, he tried to, but his head slammed against the iron ceiling, and the resulting clang reverberated throughout the chamber.

He fell to the floor with a resounding crash.

Yorimitsu pried Lord Oni's fingers apart and slipped out.

I handed him his sword and returned to my place with the diviners. We renewed our incantation, and the red threads strengthened into a strong, bright rope that wrapped around the chief oni again.

He glared at us, his many eyes popping as he strained to move, vowing to kill and eat us all.

Sweat dripped into my eyes as I focused on maintaining the spell. *Yorimitsu, now! Now!*

Either he heard my silent plea or I had more power than I knew. Yorimitsu chose that moment to jump, twist, and bring his sword down on Lord Oni's neck, severing it cleanly in one stroke.

The head rolled to one side, its eyes blinking in surprise.

We waited for the oni's spirit to rise, but instead, the head rose into the air. We watched in shock, our chanting stopped for a moment as it flew toward Yorimitsu.

He whirled around just as the huge demon head descended, jaws open wide enough to crush him like a walnut in a nutcracker.

He jumped aside and the head crashed onto the ground, missing him by a hair.

A roiling rust-brown mist emanated from it but instead of rising, it moved sluggishly along the floor toward Yorimitsu.

We renewed our incantation and called upon the great deities to help us.

Lord Oni's spirit began to drift upwards, but slowly, as if resisting the spell.

A red glow shimmered around Masako, and then Bikki and Kenji too. With my heightened senses, I saw a red aura around my arms and hands, and power ran back and forth along our connected cable, gaining strength with each iteration, the glow outlining each of us growing brighter and wider.

A positive spiral, just as Kenji had described.

With repeated, harmonious thrusts, we pushed the oni king's spirit-mist up and up and up, until at last it melted into the shimmer of the Demon Gate.

The warriors finished the last of their grisly duties. The Gate rippled and shivered as we propelled the final oni-spirits through with a victorious shout.

But we had no time to celebrate or rest.

"It's time to close the Gate." Bikki directed his thoughts through our connected cable.

Masako reached for my left hand while Kenji took my right. Bikki took Masako's left hand and we closed our eyes.

A jolt of energy hit me. Every nerve came alive. My skin hurt and my eyes burned as I gripped my companions' hands, throwing every fiber of my being into our song.

With our heads tipped up, we watched as the Gate became brighter, then hot-white like a lightning flash.

"Kashikomi, kashikomi, mo maosu," we chanted. *We reverently speak this prayer.*

The Gate shrank into a tiny blinding star before pulsing once and blinking out.

Panting from exhaustion, my throat sore from chanting, I let go of Kenji and Masako's hands, and our connecting threads snapped.

"We did it, Mi-Na," Masako said, her eyes tired but bright. "We closed the Gate."

Chapter 24

Someone Else Entirely

I collapsed onto the floor, exhilarated but exhausted. Masako did the same on my left side as did Kenji on my right. The four warriors wordlessly cleaned their swords with scraps of cloth. Bikki remained standing, examining the mess in the chamber. The oni bodies steamed and stank before gradually fading away.

"Apparently oni self-cremate," I croaked.

"No fire was involved," Masako said. "Their bodies dissolved like salt in warm water."

Oh, right. Her sense of humor didn't extend to the supernatural.

"Fortunately," she continued, "their stench does not remain in the air the way water remains salty even after the salt has disappeared."

"Good point. The reek of sweat and stale wine is bad enough."

She sniffed delicately. "Indeed. Perhaps we should seek out a hot spring on our journey to the Capital." She sat up suddenly. "Mi-Na, what happened to you? You broke our connection. Yorimitsu was almost killed."

I put my arm over my eyes. "Uh, Suetake distracted me from the job I was supposed to do. Sorry, everyone."

Bikki had walked over while we were talking. He gave me a sympathetic smile. "Suetake has years of fighting experience," he said. "His body responded as a warrior's would. You are young and unprepared for such things. If you were to do this again, you would know to resist."

Masako sighed. "Mi-Na and Ken-Ji will return to their world. They won't be able to do this again."

Kenji must have heard us because his eyes snapped open. "Our power might not be as strong with only two of us, but I know we can do some good with it."

"I feel different," I said. "Like I'm someone else entirely."

"You *are* someone else, Mi-Na," Masako said. "You are a man."

"What I meant was—"

She smiled mischievously.

"Oh, you're teasing. Well, Masako, you'll be famous as the miko who defeated a terrible demon. Of course, Yorimitsu and the other warriors will too, but if not for you, the demon would have returned with a new body after its head was cut off."

She stood up and brushed dirt off her robe. "I desire neither fame nor glory. The kami returned my power. It is theirs to use as they will. The senzo will see their descendants restored to honor and given resources to revere their ancestors, and those ancestors will, in turn, become guardians of their clans. These young women will soon return to their parents. Nothing else matters."

I forced myself to stand as well, feeling every bit of Suetake's age in creaking knees and aching back. "Yorimitsu deserves credit, of course, but you do too."

"Mi-Na, please, no. I only wish to return to the Kamo Shrine and live in peace, assisting the High Priestess and His Majesty. If

I become known for this, I'll be forced to perform incantations and spells for high-ranking nobles, perhaps for nefarious purposes. If Lord Seimei dies, I might not have enough political support to prevent such a thing. Please do not share my part in this tale."

"What about in a thousand years? Can I tell it then?"

She smiled. "Very well, my stubborn friend. In one thousand years, you may tell this story. Will you return to your world now? You have done what you came here to do."

My fingers still buzzed with residual power. After what we just accomplished, going back to school and living a normal life felt a little anti-climatic. "I think we should wait until we figure out how to neutralize the curse. Or exorcise it, or whatever. Just in case we need to connect our powers again."

"And what does Ken-Ji wish to do?"

He glanced at me for help, but I wanted to hear his opinion, so I shrugged.

"Well, eh..." He gracefully shifted from supine to standing in one fluid motion. No joints cracked. No grunts of middle-aged effort. "I've dreamed about visiting this world ever since my grandfather first showed me the Chronicle," he said in his soft Nariko-voice. "Now that I'm here, I would love to visit Heian-Kyo and meet my ancestors. And Mina, as usual, is right. We don't know who created the curse that opened the Demon Gate and whether the curse might still hurt people. Also, Masako, I knew I'd meet Mina because you wrote about that in the Chronicle, but I didn't know I'd ever get to meet *you*. I'd love to learn more about you."

Masako, clearly uncomfortable with Kenji's admiration, waved at Outcast, who had just entered the chamber and was examining the door-less door frame and the oni-less room with an admiring expression. "We'll tell him what happened," she said.

She and Bikki walked over to Outcast, who was staring at an oily spot on the floor where an oni used to be.

"So," I said. "You longed to meet Masako, and now you have. Is she everything you dreamed she'd be?"

"What?" Kenji furrowed his barely visible eyebrows. The young lady he'd possessed didn't have face paint on, so her eyebrows were shaved but not painted higher up on her forehead as they would have been at court. "Oh. Actually, yes. Everything I'd dreamed. But Mina, you are more. *So* much more than I ever expected." His gaze lingered on me.

My face should be red, but warriors weren't easily embarrassed. Even so, my heart beat faster.

It was time to change the subject. "Fair warning, Kenji. The longer we stay in these bodies, the greater the risk we'll become a permanent part of our hosts, and then we won't be able to go home. It almost happened to me with Masako."

"Well, you lived in her body for more than a year. Staying in this one for a few more days can't hurt, and I'd love to meet Seimei, and Ashiya too. I want to know what he's really like, and why he wants to help me."

Kenji's robes—Nariko's robes—although dirty and tattered, fit her petite frame perfectly, and their layers of light green and maroon were in excellent taste for the season. Her long hair was coming out of its rolled braid, with shorter lengths framing her round face. Her wide-set eyes glinted with Kenji's humor, though.

Drawn by her beauty, I leaned closer. The odor of stale incense and sweat wafted upward from her skin and clothes, triggering an involuntary movement under my monk's robes.

Why did her not-so-pleasant aroma turn me on? Thank the kami for loose-fitting clothing.

A squared plus b squared equals c squared. After I recited the Pythagorean Theorem five times fast, things calmed down.

"All right," I said. "We'll go with Masako to the capital."

"We'll spend a few days there and ask Seimei to get us home."

"That's your plan to get back? He's been very ill. What if he can't help?"

"Then we ask Masako." He was practically giddy at the idea of spending more time with Masako.

Well, so was I. She'd been through so much, yet here she was, all powered up and closing Demon Gates.

Kenji reached out a slim, pale hand. "Mina? Are you okay?"

"What? Oh, yes. Just a lot to think about, you know? The Demon Gate is closed, but the curse might still affect innocent people. Our shaman skill set may be needed to help with that. Let's find out what Masako discussed with Outcast."

The warriors had been keeping their distance. Perhaps they feared our supernatural power. Or maybe they just didn't like us.

Yorimitsu called over to Masako. "Miko, we have a mission yet to complete. We must bring these innocent victims back to their parents. Also, we want Suetake back. Tell your *friend* to leave Suetake's body. Tell the strange spirits to return to their world and leave us alone."

"Lord Yorimitsu," I retorted. "I *want* to give Suetake his body back, but I keep telling you, I'm not sure he's even *here*. If I leave without knowing how to get his spirit back, his body might die, or perhaps be possessed by a more hostile spirit. Who knows how many spirits are wandering the world at any given time seeking hosts? Is that what you want?"

Masako intervened before Yorimitsu drew his sword. "Commander, we will do our best to return Mi-Na to her world and to bring Lord Suetake back to his body. Lord Seimei will advise us on how to do this if we do not find a way before then. Now we must ask the senzo to leave their hosts so we can bring the poor young women home."

Fortunately, the massive iron door at the entrance had been left open, so we walked out of the Iron Palace. The sky above the mountain ridges was dark gray, indicating dawn was about to arrive. Guided by Outcast, we found the tunnel opening and made our way to the senzo cave.

Once there, Yorimitsu informed the senzo of our complete victory over the oni. The few unpossessed women in the cave exclaimed joyfully at the news, while the senzo were neutral.

They did, however, agree to leave their host bodies. "But," Outcast said. "If you don't keep your promise to extract compensation for our descendants, we'll send earthquakes or fires to wreak vengeance upon the capital. And the possessed bandits will remain here at Mount Ōe until they see our descendants revere us once more."

Masako bowed in acknowledgment, then turned to me. "Mina and Kenji, have you decided what you will do?"

I answered for both of us. "We'll go with you to the Capital. Our host spirits don't seem to be in here, and we shouldn't leave these bodies unattended."

"Mina, perhaps we ought to try to find out if our hosts *can* return," Kenji said. "If they can, Masako could try to send our spirits home."

"It is too dangerous, especially with the Demon Gate closed," Masako said adamantly. "The spirit world is unknowably vast. You might lose your way. A journey such as that will require incantations conducted in a sacred location, and I have not been trained to conduct such a ritual."

She was right. She might succeed in sending us out of these bodies, but not necessarily back home. We might end up as disembodied spirits. Even if we made it into the spirit world, we might not find our way home.

Yet I agreed with Kenji. We weren't yōkai. We weren't demons. We were flawed humans who just wanted to do the right thing.

Now that I'd seen Masako, I could get on with my life. I had a thesis to write.

Kenji and I locked eyes. "Let's meditate," we said in unison.

"Jinx!" I said and then regretted it because Masako looked horrified. Jinx must have translated through Suetake's brain as wishing bad luck. "Sorry," I said with a bow. "I didn't mean to call down a curse. I don't know why we say it in our world."

Kenji rolled his eyes. "Not in Japan," he said. "Just you Westerners."

Masako appeared confused but didn't ask for further explanation. She led us to a place near the fire. We sat on a robe and closed our eyes, and Masako began to sing softly.

My breathing slowed and my mouth relaxed. Dream-like visions flitted across my inner vision as I sank into a trance-like meditation. *A woman lies on her side, belt untied, robes fanned out. She smiles with sleepy eyes and slides a green silk sleeve across the mat as if to take my hand. Suetake, don't leave yet, she murmurs. Dawn has not yet arrived.*

A quick switch, the way dreams do. *Stumbling along a dark street, a sour taste in my mouth. The saké had been sweet, the ladles of it generously filled. Fellow students called out Chinese poems, challenging me to finish the last line of each to prove my successful examination result was no accident.*

Another switch. *Armor, a bow, a sword. A dark forest, bandits. Violence, battle. Blood, rage.*

Another switch. *Confusion, vertigo. Falling. Endlessly falling. Trapped, unable to speak.*

Suetake's spirit *was* here, but in a hold, as Seimei called it. In the freezer, as I called it when Seimei did it to me. Unable to speak, unable to direct one's own body to take any action. It was like being in a coma, except I'd been able to hear and see through Masako's ears and eyes when it happened to me, which meant Suetake could hear me and see what I saw, even if I couldn't hear or feel him.

Suetake? I called. *Come back. Please, wake up. I'll leave if you come back.*

My plea went unanswered.

Suetake, come back. Your lover waits for you to return.

No response.

The senzo who'd possessed him before me must have done this, which meant the other senzo did it to their captives as well.

"Mina?" Masako noticed I'd stopped meditating. "Do you sense Suetake?"

"No, but he's in here, I'm sure of it. He's locked down, though, probably by the senzo who possessed him before me. I can't release him. I kicked the senzo out too soon, unfortunately." I shuddered, remembering all too well how it felt to be unable to communicate or make my presence known to my host. "I accessed some of his memories, though. He has a lover. He knows Chinese. He answered a lot of questions in the scholar examination."

Kenji opened his eyes. "Nariko's in a hold, too. She didn't study Chinese, but she's known for her incense-blending skills."

A thought occurred to me. "Masako, could *you* release them?"

"I have not been instructed in such magic. Perhaps Lord Seimei could teach me how to do it when we reach the capital."

Sorry, Suetake, you have to endure possession a little longer. On the plus side, however, Nariko and Suetake shouldn't mind us borrowing their bodies to go to the capital. It was the only way to restore their spirits.

Smoke from the dwindling fire tickled my throat. "Let's get

out of here." I glanced around the empty cave. "Where is everyone?"

"They went outside to prepare for the ritual."

"What ritual?"

"The exorcism of the senzo."

"Aren't they leaving voluntarily?"

Masako put a sleeve over her mouth to hide a smile. "Yes, Mina, but they can't just float away. They need a little push."

Ah, Masako. Still condescending after all this time. I knew a lot about exorcisms, having been exorcised twice. Only one of which was successful, but still. "You're a miko, not an exorcist. Don't you need a drummer, and a medium, and incense, and-"

Masako smothered a laugh. "We would only need a medium if we want to banish them. We only want to pull them out of those bodies."

"Then don't call it an exorcism," I muttered as we walked toward the cave exit.

Daylight made my eyes water, a reminder we'd spent an entire night in the oni's palace. I blinked until my eyes adjusted enough to see the kidnapped women standing together while the warriors stood a few paces away.

I started toward them but stopped, astonished. A pale-pink sea filled the valley below, ringed by the indigo-shadowed mountain range.

Kenji, Masako, and I stared in silence at this unexpected beauty.

"This appears only at sunrise in autumn and spring," Bikki said quietly.

"I bet Lord Oni didn't even appreciate it," I said.

Masako frowned at my flippancy. "No betting," she said.

The warriors turned to see what had stopped us, and for a quiet, communal few minutes, we all watched as the pink hue transitioned to dark red caused by the mountain's shadow, and then, as the sun rose above the ridge, the clouds became a bright blue-white sea filling the entire valley.

All the more beautiful for its short existence.

Suetake? Was that you?

I heard nothing more from him, but he was right. With all the danger and ugliness of the past few days, I needed this reminder.

After we drank our fill of the view, we walked to the knot of women. On the way, I stared down at Kenji, enjoying my height advantage.

"Let me re-braid your hair," I said. "You'll trip on it. You can't handle hair that long."

Kenji pushed away my eager hands. "You're having too much fun with this," he said with mock irritation. He pulled his hair into a long, thick rope and twisted it until it began to curve up. He grabbed a short twig from the ground, pushed it through his bun to hold it, and folded his arms triumphantly.

A few meters away, Yorimitsu glared at us with disgust. He murmured to his warrior buddies. Whatever it was, they agreed with it, and they strode down the hill.

"What was that about?" I asked Masako.

"They don't like you two," she said. "Yorimitsu said you are strange and unnatural. But we do not need them for this."

Masako called the senzo-possessed women over to sit in a circle, directing the few non-possessed women to sit on the sidelines. "Before you leave these bodies, you must release your hosts from the spirit-hold you put them in."

A quiet minute passed as the women closed their eyes and did whatever internal thing they needed to do to free their imprisoned hosts.

Outcast pressed his hands on both sides of his head like he had a migraine. "We must perform the exorcism," he said. "I released my host. Now she is trying to control this body, which

I will not allow. She is screaming at me. What a horrible woman!"

Masako mostly succeeded in not laughing. "We will begin the exorcism now."

Outcast frowned. "If you do not fulfill your commitments, I will return to take vengeance."

Masako nodded gravely. "Understood."

She began to chant, lifting her arms high and moving her feet in tiny, slow circles like a Kagura Dance but without bells or fans. She did have a sakaki twig in each hand, however. She must have kept them in her sleeve for exorcism emergencies.

Her pace picked up and the participants' jaws went slack and their eyes rolled back.

A mist formed around each woman's head. It swirled, then stilled into a blurry outline. The outlines became more solid, forming into male faces.

The faces hovered higher and higher into bright sunlight, becoming harder to see. They shimmered briefly, then disappeared.

Kiyoko—formerly known as Outcast—snapped her jaw shut. She swung her legs around to sit on her knees and bowed, her palms and forehead touching the ground. "Miko, you freed us. A terrible demon trapped me!" She began to cry with great heaving sobs of relief and postponed fear.

The other women did the same. After a few minutes of tears, prayers, and a few sutras, they began to exclaim and shout.

"I could hear everything, but I could not move or speak!" "I could not cry or scream!" "So awful, terrible!" "What did I do in a past life to deserve such a thing?" "It was as if the demon put me in a spell to force me to witness its terrible actions!"

"You are free now," Masako said. "Breathe in, then out, slowly."

The women did as instructed while Masako hummed a

calming melody. Eventually, shouts became murmurs, and then there was silence.

"These were not demons," Masako said. "Senzo possessed you. They were wronged while living, their lands stolen, and their descendants impoverished. They invaded your bodies to demand reparations. We vowed to present their demands to the Regent, and they agreed to release your spirits."

The young women gasped in horror. Several of them began to weep again.

"How do we help?" "Senzo must be honored! This is terrible!" "Senzo should be protectors, not possessors!" "My father will help. He will not want me to be kidnapped again."

Masako bowed to them gratefully. "Your patience is astounding after enduring such a terrible experience. We will journey back to the capital to make this request of the Regent."

They gathered around Masako and bowed. "You saved us." "Please stay with us in the capital." "We will ensure the tale is told to all." "My father will reward you with robes and rice! Your fame will spread throughout the realm!"

Masako flushed. "Please, do not share my part in this story. I only wish to return to Kamo to serve the kami in peace."

"His Majesty must be told!"

"The warriors were brave, but *you* freed us from the senzo."

"Everyone must be told of your power!"

The more Masako protested she didn't want fame or glory, the more they insisted she deserved both. I, too, wanted Masako to get full credit for her role, but I respected her decision to be anonymous.

"Stop," I commanded, using my most manly voice and posture. Startled, the young women turned their eyes from Masako to me, and then bowed their heads, whether from modesty or respect, I couldn't tell.

All the young women, that is, except Kiyoko. She met my gaze.

She's a bold one, looking at a man like that.

Was that Suetake's thought or mine? "The Shrine Miko pleaded with you to refrain from sharing her story. Respect her request," I said authoritatively.

"We will do as you say, Lord."

I tried not to show how much I liked being called lord. I didn't *want* to enjoy the way people listened to me without argument, bowing to me and deferring to my judgment because I happened to inhabit a nobleman's body.

Anyway, it was temporary. No one was going to call me lord in 2019, and 'hey, lady!' didn't have quite the same ring to it.

Kiyoko shuddered. "Even in my trapped state, I could see and hear what Outcast said and heard. I will never, *ever* forget the horrifying vision of the oni eating human flesh. I would rather have been blind. Lord Yorimitsu was brave to speak to Outcast in the manner he did. Was it he who killed Lord Oni?"

"Yorimitsu cut his head off, but we worked together to—"

Kiyoko spun around in a most unladylike way. "Where is Lord Yorimitsu?."

Masako waved to the trail leading down the mountain. "Kiyo-"

Kiyoko gathered up her robes and sped away.

"Was she like that before?" I asked, concerned her mind had become unstable due to her lengthy spirit possession.

"Mi-Na," Masako replied, "your outline glows above Lord Suetake's head. Your eyes are as round as river pebbles. Is that common in your world?" She studied Kenji's aura. "*His* eyes appear to be normal."

"You see more than I do, then. I can't distinguish features. But what does that have to do with Kiyoko?"

She sighed with exaggerated patience. "Mi-Na, have you

already forgotten how possession influences a host? How much you changed me when you possessed my body?"

"Well, you lost your temper more often as time went on and became a little more direct in your speech, which didn't win you any friends among the ladies-in-waiting. And you stood up for yourself more. And, of course, your powers. Lord Seimei said that was my purpose, to open your soul to gain power."

"Yes, that's all true," she said. "The senzo Outcast may have changed Lady Kiyoko by passing along some of his masculine ways, just as you gave me some of the foreign traits you described."

In my world, a woman running after a man to thank him for saving her life wouldn't be seen as odd, but here it bordered on transgressive. She hadn't even taken a fan to cover her face.

Kiyoko wouldn't survive at court with those manners. Spirit possession wouldn't be the problem—many of high rank had been possessed at one time or another—but such masculine behavior in a young noblewoman would be.

Ironically, or perhaps intentionally, Outcast might have turned Kiyoko into an outcast.

Chapter 25

Book Of Secrets

A hollow feeling in my stomach reminded me we hadn't eaten since our rice balls at lunch yesterday, and the young women began to complain about hunger as well. Masako, Kenji, and I rummaged through our packs and found enough rice balls to give everyone a little bit, which made no one happy, but at least they stopped complaining. I told them we'd draw water from the stream where the warriors were waiting for us.

Taking advantage of my muscular body, I offered to take more than my share of bundles. Kenji hefted a pack with a groan and sheepishly asked me if I could take a few items from him.

As we approached the stream, the women began to murmur and shift uneasily, lifting their sleeves to hide their faces from the men. They didn't know Suetake's body hosted a female spirit, but they hadn't shielded themselves from me. Somehow they knew I wasn't the leering type.

Yorimitsu and Kiyoko were chatting while the other men looked on with amused—and bemused—expressions. The women murmured among themselves, glancing sideways at Kiyoko. I couldn't tell if they were criticizing or admiring her boldness in openly talking to a male with her face completely visible.

After drinking water and washing our hands and faces in the stream, we began our trek down the mountain. The cloud lake had dissipated, so we could see the temple complex and village in the valley below.

When we passed the section of the stream where Kenji and I had first crossed into this world, I couldn't help a twinge of anxiety. Closing the Demon Gate kept demons out but also kept us from leaving the way we got here. We were now utterly dependent on Seimei to get us home.

Not long after that, the trail widened into a road. Yorimitsu chose a warrior to walk ahead with him. I kept to the middle to relay messages ahead and behind if needed, and Masako walked with me. Kenji decided he'd be of more use at the end to ensure no women fell behind. Or maybe his feet hurt, and he didn't want me to watch him struggle.

Kiyoko kept pace with me. Grasping her torn and dirty silk robes so she wouldn't trip, her bare feet skimmed over the dirt trail as smoothly as if it were polished wood. Her feet, visible under her raised hems, were callused, probably from going back and forth from the stream to Lord Oni's palace daily.

She chatted briefly with Masako, but after a bit, walked faster to catch up with Yorimitsu. I couldn't hear what he said, but he smiled at her, and then waved back toward us. She bowed her head and slowed her pace so we soon caught up.

Masako glared at her. "You should know better. I grew up in the provinces too, and I would never have addressed a man in such a bold manner."

"But you speak to Suetake with your face exposed."

Masako sighed. "Lord Suetake is not a-"

"And you speak freely to Yorimitsu. I followed your example." A small smile played on her lips. "I was possessed by a male for a long time, and I grew comfortable with a man's manners and way of speaking. We all—" she gestured toward the other women "—acted like men because we *were* men for a while. How could I return to the protocol of court life after this? Yorimitsu is strong and brave, much more so than other nobles. Does he have a wife? Even if he does, being a secondary wife of such a famous and fearless warrior might suit me well."

I tried not to show my dismay at the thought of sweet Kiyoko marrying that arrogant warrior. Masako and I had changed each other, but not so much that she couldn't fit into her own culture. I'd become less selfish, less anxious, and more considerate and compassionate while living with her. She'd become more assertive, more sociable, more likely to do something impulsive.

Would Suetake understand women better after I left? How was Kenji changing Nariko? Would *she* be more masculine? How would that disrupt her life?

Masako shook her head in dismay. "You should not suggest marrying a man like Yorimitsu. He is fearless, yes, but also violent and self-serving. Most noblemen follow the precepts of the Lord Buddha and refuse to kill, but the realm has enemies and *someone* must fight them. Yorimitsu and his fellow commanders are valued for such services, but why marry someone who kills others? Surely you have many other noblemen to select from. You are still young. Take your time and seek your parents' counsel."

Kiyoko set her jaw and stared ahead, refusing to acknowledge the truth of Masako's words.

We stopped by a huge temple compound to pick up Yumi, but the monks had sent her back to Kamo as her illness was beyond their medical capabilities. They offered to put us up for the night, but we had a long way to travel and wanted to get a full day's walk completed before stopping.

Bikki said goodbye after we left the temple. His spiritual

energy had been drained by our power-sharing ritual, and he needed to restore it by meditating in a sacred spot. Anyway, he said, an Ainu shaman wouldn't be welcome in the capital.

We thanked him profusely, and he wished us success in our journey and mission.

We reached a village soon after, where Masako dispatched a message to Kamo to inform the High Priestess and Yumi the young women had been rescued.

Kenji asked for paper and a brush, which perplexed me. "Who are you writing to in *this* world?" I asked. "Who do you know here?"

"I can't explain right now," he said as he folded the note and handed it to the messenger.

"Seimei? Akichika? Why can't you explain?"

"Consider it a backup if we don't obtain what we need from Seimei."

A slight chill ran down my spine at Kenji's vague answer, but I didn't follow up because Masako asked the women, including Kenji-Nariko, to climb into ox-carts for the rest of the journey. These were plain village carts, but no one complained. Everyone wanted to go home.

As a man, I was expected to walk, but I didn't mind. Suetake might have written poetry and studied Chinese, but he was fit for his age. I caught up with Yorimitsu, who'd set a brisk pace at the front of our group.

"Lord Akimitsu blundered through another ceremony," said the warrior next to him. "An idiot, like all nobles who live placidly in the capital and weep about blossoms falling."

Yorimitsu barked a contemptuous laugh. "Those timid fools don't realize they're all the same."

My ears perked. Masako had mentioned Akimitsu in one of her letters. "So..." I said, hoping to be included in their conversation.

Yorimitsu ignored me, turning to his companion to grunt something that made them both laugh.

I tried again. "I'm looking forward to a bowl of soup and a drink. How about you?"

Yorimitsu gave me a cold and glittering glance.

Stand tall, Mina. "What do you plan to say to the Regent about the senzo's demands?"

He stopped with his hand on his sword.

I took a sword-length step back.

"I do not know you, Spirit," he growled. "And I do *not* trust you. Demons kidnapped these women, and their fathers could not protect them. Why? Because most noblemen are useless. Too weak and soft to fight true enemies. They fight each other over silly arguments, but when it comes to battle, they complain they cannot fight in summer because it is hot, and they cannot fight in winter because their hands freeze."

His companion spat. "Weak. Soft." He glowered at me. "Like women."

Yorimitsu grunted his agreement. "Lord Seimei will expel you from that body when we reach the capital. Your part here is finished. We need Lord Suetake's fighting skills back."

I winced at his harsh words. "Believe me, I want to go home, but if I leave before Suetake's spirit is released, his body will die. We'll find a way, but we'll need help to do it."

He took his hand away from his sword and started walking again. "I have decided to marry Lady Kiyoko. She will live with me, not with her parents." He looked off into the distance. "She is very different from my primary wife, who lives with her parents in the capital. Lady Kiyoko would do well as a provincial governor's wife. When I governed Mino and subdued a rebellion, a strong woman by my side would have been helpful."

Yorimitsu was from a noble family, and given the services he provided to the Fujiwaras and the imperial family, he must be wealthy. Her father would certainly agree to the marriage. Her youth wouldn't be an issue. Seventeen was on the young side for a woman of her rank to marry, but it wasn't unheard of.

The most important thing—to me, at least—was that Kiyoko liked him. Maybe the marriage wouldn't be a bad thing.

He wasn't looking for my approval, nor should he seek it from a fellow warrior, so I grunted in response.

* * *

At the end of the third day of traveling, we gazed upon the neat grid of Heian-Kyo, the capital of the realm. Aristocratic residences were easy to identify by their size—one or two city blocks—and huge gardens, many of them with lakes large enough for boating. Lesser officials lived in row housing close to the government center. The imperial palace was the most prominent, with large red buildings surrounding huge courtyards.

I asked our caravan to stop for a bit so I could memorize the sight of the city I'd lived in for a year and a half. Last time I'd been so focused on survival I hadn't paid much attention to the city's architecture and layout.

Kenji exclaimed over each new discovery. "That's where the university is! That's Michinaga's compound!" His excitement made me laugh, but I should have known. This was Kenji's first chance to really learn what Heian-Kyo looked like. Models of the imperial capital existed, but they'd never truly capture the look and vibrancy of a living city.

We pulled up to the city gate just before sunset. Yorimitsu had sent messages ahead to inform the Emperor and the Regent of our mission's success and to inform parents of their daughters' return. Fine ox carriages awaited the young women so they wouldn't have to endure the embarrassment of riding ox-carts into the city.

After transferring the women to carriages with palm-frond covers decorated in colorful patterns, our troop proceeded down Suzaku Avenue.

The wide road should have allowed quick progress, but cheering crowds slowed us down. Apparently tales of Lord Oni's defeat had preceded us.

The warriors strode ahead, ignoring the attention, but the women chattered excitedly as they peeked through their silk curtains.

At the gate to the Imperial Palace, parents claimed their daughters from our entourage to be taken home, given baths and made a fuss over, and handed bundles of silk cloth to the warriors as thanks.

Kiyoko's father sat on a horse next to her carriage and promised us barrels of saké as a token of his gratitude. Nariko's father, however, chastised her for allowing herself to be lured away by a ghost.

We explained she was now possessed by a helpful spirit from the future who wouldn't possess her much longer.

He shouted at her as if that would scare Kenji out. When that didn't work, he decided he didn't want his daughter home after all. Nariko must have done something to anger the kami and he didn't want to risk their displeasure raining down on the rest of his household, so he gave us permission to take her to Lord Seimei. He hoped Seimei would be able to erase the bad luck associated with his daughter's possession.

"Classic victim-blaming," I muttered to Kenji. "Kidnapped, possessed, tapped for blood by oni, only to be rejected by her family. Treat her body well. She deserves it."

Kenji agreed. "I wanted to cry when he yelled at me. I think Nariko heard all that and she's sad. I'll tell her some folktales later to cheer her up. She can't respond, but I think she can hear and see everything."

Yorimitsu and his fellow warriors were invited to give a full report on the trip at the office of imperial administration. Masako asked him not to mention Bikki, Kenji, or Mina if he could do that without lying. He was all too pleased to agree.

"It appears the report will mostly be about the warriors," I said to Kenji. "But that's cool. I'm used to not getting credit for anything here."

We stayed at Masako's uncle's residence that night. We decided not to tell him that Nariko and Suetake were still possessed—her uncle didn't appreciate such things—so I had to stay up half the night drinking with him.

Which, to be honest, was a lot of fun. I tipped back cup after cup with no more effect than a warm, relaxed feeling. An unexpected side effect of this relaxation was tapping more easily into my host's brain to leverage Suetake's vast supply of dirty jokes, Chinese poetry, and gossip.

Even better, no hangover the next day. I slept in, this being the first real night's sleep I'd had in the three days since arriving in this era.

We set out for Lord Seimei's residence in the early afternoon. Seimei lived a few blocks away, but it took an hour to get there due to traffic. Noblewomen rode in ox carriages, noblemen rode on horseback, priests hurried on foot to wherever priests went, and messengers wove their way from one noble compound to another, carrying poems, divinations, and letters.

Townsfolk called back and forth, comparing notes on Yorimitsu's status as the most renowned warrior in the realm, telling each other how he cut off Lord Oni's head single-handedly as the other four warriors demolished his minions.

Masako and Kenji took an ox carriage while I rode. Knowing how much Masako had loved to ride horses back in Hitachi, and how much she disliked being required to ride in the bumpy carriage, I felt sorry for her. Still, it didn't stop me from enjoying my ride on a fine black horse. What might have changed if I possessed a man the first time I came to Heian Japan? Masako accepted my presence because I brought companionship to her lonely life. Would a man have been as accommodating?

Probably not. I inhabited Suetake's body only because his spirit was in a hold. I'd release him if I could, but since I couldn't, I enjoyed having full control of his warrior's body and the masculine privileges that came with it.

As I rode, I inhaled a familiar mixture of odors wafting through the air: horse, ox, and human manure, incense mingled with body sweat, and the appetizing aroma of grilled fish and vegetables.

Nostalgia brought an unexpected lump to my throat. I focused on every detail, trying to cement it in memory, knowing this was my last time here. The rough, ripped clothing of commoners, the irony of homeless people in tents propped up against palace walls, the stolid oxen pulling fine carriages made from fronds or bamboo, decorated with stripes and flower patterns. Occasionally I'd spy the sleeves of a noblewoman's robes through the partially rolled blinds of a carriage. Perhaps she hoped someone like Suetake would take notice of her tasteful selection of colors for the season and write her a poem about it. Suetake would have been good at that. A poet, a nobleman, and an ass-kicking warrior. *What's not to love about that trifecta?*

We finally arrived at Seimei's compound. I dismounted, handed the horse to a groom, and peered through the gate to see the familiar residence looking just as I remembered, with a pond, several buildings, and well-maintained cherry and willow trees placed artfully throughout.

Kenji wore new clothes provided by Nariko's mother: five

robes of alternating layers of dark green and ochre, a green belt, red hakama, and underneath it all, the thin white robe called *kosode*. Biting his plump lower lip with concentration, he gathered his robes with one hand, held a fan in the other, swung his legs around to the back, and slipped out through the back opening. He forgot about his long rope of hair, though. It snagged on the carriage frame, pulling at his scalp painfully as evidenced by his yelp. He ripped it free, but the violent tug and sudden release caused him to fall outward.

Masako caught him before he planted his face in the dirt. Murmurs of disapproval came from the servants just inside the gate. I picked up Kenji's fan and handed it to him with a flourish. The servants grumbled even more at our lack of grace and manners, but I chose to ignore them. "They want a reaction," I whispered to Kenji. "But I won't give them the satisfaction."

"Lord Seimei is expecting us," Masako said to a middle-aged woman in a plain brown robe, who led us to a visiting hall where mats and cushions were laid out on the black wood floor. Masako and Kenji-Nariko kept their veiled hats on to shield their faces from curious apprentices and members of Seimei's family.

Seimei walked into the room, leaning on an apprentice's shoulder. He'd been in his seventies when he sent me home, but his frailty just a year and a half later shocked me. Hollow cheeks and dark circles under his eyes indicated illness. His beard and bushy eyebrows were white now rather than gray. He still had hair on his forehead, though.

I rubbed my smooth head ruefully.

He invited the women to take off their hats as he would be the only male in the room, other than Suetake, who didn't count because he was possessed by a female spirit.

I stuck my tongue out at him when his back was turned.

Not understanding what my strange gesture meant, Masako looked at me askance. I winked at her. She held her sleeve to her nose as if suppressing a sneeze, but I could see she was laughing. That made *me* want to laugh, so I made a point of examining Seimei's stash of scrolls on a nearby table until the urge passed.

Seimei examined Kenji for what felt like a long time. Kenji raised his fan to his face in jerky movements, almost as if he couldn't control it.

Seimei smiled. "A young man's spirit lives inside this young woman, yet her spirit also glows, a faint outline that pulsed stronger just now when her outrage at a man staring at her bare face gave her the energy to push back. Her spirit is restrained but is within." He turned to me. "Suetake's spirit also glows with yours."

"Great!" I said. "So you can release-"

Seimei frowned at me for interrupting. "Ken-Ji," he continued. "It is pleasing that my descendants have continued for forty generations. It appears some of my power has passed to you. Very good, very good." He paused as if deep in thought, then turned toward me. "Mi-Na, sending you back to your world sapped my strength for weeks. Why did you return? Did you not have faith in Lady Masako's ability to save the kidnapped women?"

My cheeks grew hot. "No, Lord Seimei, that's not-" I flinched in anticipation of a slap, remembering what happened last time I contradicted him.

He laughed. "You are not my student now, Mi-Na. And though *you* might be rude, Lord Suetake is a man of strength and character, while I have become weak with age and illness. Say what you will. I will not punish you for it."

I stood tall. "I didn't doubt Masako's ability. Her letters described how her power disappeared when I left." My voice grew soft. "I didn't want to let her down if she needed me to get her powers back."

"So if she hadn't written those letters, or if you hadn't found them, you would not have returned to our world?"

That made me think. "No, I don't think I would have."

He folded his arms and glared at Kenji. "Why did you push Mi-Na to return? Did she not tell you of the danger? My line might end with you, should you die here."

Kenji bowed his head. "Lord Seimei, our world is in danger. The kami are leaving us because we have destroyed the purity of their natural spaces. If we lose the kami, we lose their light and spiritual vibration, and our world will degenerate. To correct this course, I'm studying divination, and if I inherited any power from you, I will use it to help." He lifted his gaze to meet Seimei's. "With apologies to Mina," he nodded toward me. "I pushed her to take me here so I would meet you and learn from you, in addition to gaining the power I saw in Mina."

Seimei's eyes gleamed. "Eh? My worthless grandson Akichika, who can't accurately read a single divination, produced the line that produces *you*? One who aspires to divination?"

Kenji wasn't finished. "To do so, however, I will need your help. Please, Lord, I need you to save your Book of Onmyōdō Secrets for me to find in my world."

Seimei's sharp inhale triggered a coughing fit. When he recovered, his eyes had darkened with suspicion. "If you deserved those spells, your ancestors would have passed them down to you through my sons. Did you come here to steal secrets you do not deserve?"

Kenji glanced at me as if to ask for help, but I shrugged. He'd mentioned several times how much he needed Seimei's Book, but not that he'd ask Seimei for it. Masako's mouth formed an 'o' of surprise as she waited to hear Kenji's response.

He bowed as deeply as possible from his seated position. "Copies exist of your basic rituals for divining gender, finding lost items, and so on, but not of the more potent spells, which are the ones we'll need to protect the kami's spaces. Coming here allowed me to gain spiritual power, yes, but also gives me the chance to ask you to preserve a copy of your Book for me. As far as I know," his eyes flicked to me, "only spirits can travel between worlds, not material things."

I nodded, although I only had my personal experience to go by. But it made sense that only spirits could travel through the spirit world.

"I have one copy," Seimei said, "and I will not make another. If the kami wish you to have it, my descendants will save it for you. If you do not have it, you must not be worthy of it."

Kenji flinched as if struck.

Having been on the receiving end of Seimei's arrogance several times myself, I knew how Kenji felt.

He raised his chin defiantly. "It doesn't exist in my time because your sons—or grandsons—did not preserve it. Perhaps *they* were not worthy of it."

Kenji's spirited defense of his request was admirable, but if he'd asked me for advice on how to get Seimei's cooperation, I'd have told him not to insult Seimei's family.

Seimei gestured to his apprentice, who hurried over to help Seimei stand.

Kenji seemed to realize he'd made a mistake, bowing again before making another plea. "I am deeply sorry for my disrespectful words. But even in this world, we've seen what happens when ancestors are no longer revered. The senzo can't protect their descendants, and they might disappear rather than become guardian kami."

Seimei murmured something to his apprentice while Kenji was talking.

Kenji persisted nonetheless. "Mina and I will use your most

secret incantations to form a spiritual barrier around sacred spaces to protect the kami." He bowed again.

Seimei didn't bow back. "The real battle has yet to be fought," he said to Masako. "The curse-demon that killed Lady Motoko is still in our world, and it will strike the imperial family again if we do not banish it. That is my highest priority. This request of Kenji's is not my concern." He squeezed his eyes shut for a second as if he had a headache. "I am weary. We will discuss how to find and banish the curse-demon later." Seimei shuffled out of the room, leaning on his apprentice.

Kenji dropped his head into his hands.

I opened my mouth to say something reassuring but shut it when I couldn't find the right words.

Masako managed to find some, however. "Lord Seimei never shows anyone that book. It contains spells that might be misused if they fall into the wrong hands. For example, the Spell of Forbidden Magic is designed to defeat death itself. He would never use it, but others might, and at a terrible cost. So he refuses to share it with anyone other than his sons."

A slight queasiness stirred in my gut at her words. All magic was created through spiritual power. What kami would assist with a dark spell like that? It would have to be a demon.

Kenji raised his head. "I don't care about that one. I need a different one, an incantation that will preserve sacred spaces."

Something niggled in the back of my mind. "How do you know one like that is in there?"

"Ah, eh- well, I'll tell you later. Right now I need to use the facilities. It might take a while. You know how it is being a girl. Such a hassle with all these robes to keep out of the way."

Masako gestured to the attendant who waited at the entrance to the room. "Lord Seimei has an indoor space," she said. "Only the highly ranked have such a thing, but it is quite convenient."

While he was gone, Masako and I took the opportunity to

speculate whether Seimei would ever provide a copy of his Book. She didn't think so.

I disagreed. "It's all about the right approach," I argued. "He'll come around if Kenji apologizes for being rude. Again, I mean. Maybe three or four more times."

We discussed the curse-demon and its potential to harm more innocent people. Masako planned to ask Seimei if Kenji could assist with the divination. "He will need practice if he is to use his power in your world," she said.

Before we knew it, an hour had passed. Kenji hadn't returned, so we sent a servant to find him. "Lady Nariko asked for an ox carriage and left the premises," the servant said.

Prickles crept along my hands and arms at this strange news. "I'm sure he's fine," I said to Masako. "He must have a good reason for not telling us where he went."

Chapter 26

Almost Too Easy

We informed Seimei of Kenji's absence after he rose from his nap.

He furrowed his white eyebrows at me. "Why did you allow him to leave?"

Speechless at being blamed, I could only shake my head.

"Did you not tell him of the risks? His spirit becoming a permanent part of Nariko's?"

I forced my jaw to relax. "Oh, he knew."

He called an apprentice over and murmured quiet instructions to him, then turned back to Masako with a resigned sigh. "My students will find out where he went, but for now we must assume he is safe. Our priority today is to divine the source of the curse that killed Lady Motoko. Lady Masako, you will conduct the divination under my supervision."

She bowed. "This miko is unworthy of such honor, Lord, but I will do my utmost to deserve it."

"You deserve this and so much more," I murmured to her as she passed me on the way to the changing room.

Seimei and Masako purified themselves in preparation for

the divination by bathing and chanting. I bathed, too, and was given clean white robes to put on.

After those rituals were completed, we gathered in an inner courtyard. A fire burned in the center, the coals glowing bright red.

I bit my lip with frustration. *Kenji should be here. He'd love to experience this.* Why hadn't he told me where he was going? He was often enigmatic, but it hurt to think he didn't trust me.

Seimei signaled to Masako to begin. She lifted a turtle shell to the sky, chanted a prayer of gratitude, and asked the kami to share their knowledge of the curse. With cloth wrapped around her hand for protection, she pulled an iron stake from the fire, drew it over the shell in a specific pattern, and dunked the shell into cold water. She repeated this pattern until cracks formed in the shell.

It took a long time. I shifted my feet to give them a break, and Seimei frowned at my movement. I glared right back at him, which made him smile for some reason. Maybe he was amused at the contrast between my youthful spirit-glow and Suetake's middle-aged warrior face.

When enough lines formed on the shell, we returned to Seimei's divination room where Masako silently drew hexagrams based on her reading of the cracks.

Next, utterly absorbed and distant, as if in a world of her own, she stared at the series of broken and unbroken lines she'd just written, closed her eyes for a few minutes as if visualizing their meaning, and then wrote her divination on a scroll.

She handed it to Seimei with a deep bow.

He read it and nodded. "I suspected as much." He nodded to me. "Come," he said. "Sit."

I hurried to his low table as he returned the scroll to Masako. "Tell Mi-Na."

She took it with shaking hands.

"Go on," he said. "Explain your divination."

She lifted her eyes to mine. "Ashi-" Her voice cracked. She cleared her throat. "It appears Ashiya cast the spell."

I shook my head. How could Kenji take the side of a diviner who misused his spiritual power to kill people?

"Do you disagree, Mi-Na? Should I conduct the divination again?"

"Oh, no, absolutely not. I have faith in your skills, Masako. I'm just frustrated Kenji left. He needs to hear this."

"Yes, Ken-Ji *should* be here," Seimei said. "He should learn the divination method that Lady Masako has applied so well. If there is any diviner who can save the world, it will be one of my descendants."

I refused to react to his arrogance. "Lord Seimei, did you say Ashiya studied under you? Did you teach him to curse people?"

He glowered at me. "You know better than to ask such a question. Did you learn nothing while I tutored Lady Masako? Ashiya was my brightest pupil, more talented than my sons, but he wanted to use onmyōdō for his own benefit. He begged for my Book of Onmyōdō Secrets. When I would not provide it, he challenged me to a battle for it. When I won, he had to serve me for a year. I threw him out when I caught him trying to steal my book. He disappeared for a while. I heard he studied in China. Perhaps he learned this curse there."

"Why would he curse a member of the imperial family?" I wondered. "Who was harmed by Lady Motoko's death? Other than Motoko herself, of course. Her parents and two of her sisters are already dead, so it wouldn't have been revenge against one of them. The Crown Prince? But he has other consorts. I'm not saying Lady Motoko was expendable, but if the Prince's favorite consort is Lady Seiko, wouldn't *she* be the target of a curse?"

"It might not be a matter of who is *harmed* by Lady Motoko's death," Seimei said. "Perhaps we should ask ourselves who benefits from it? Whoever paid for the curse might have a relative who is a current or future imperial consort, so they're eliminating rivals for the title of empress."

Masako frowned. "It wouldn't be Lord Michinaga, then. His daughter Akiko is already empress. Who else would perceive Lady Motoko as a rival? Who are the other nobles with eligible daughters?"

We were silent for a moment as we considered potential enemies.

"You know what doesn't make sense to me?" I asked. "Empress Akiko would be the rival to target. She might have a son someday. Why eliminate Motoko without also eliminating Akiko?"

"A good question," Seimei replied. "His Majesty has many concubines, but only Empress Sadako provided him with a living son so far. However, two of His Majesty's consorts have become pregnant: The Empress's sister Miku, who died while expecting His Majesty's child, and Lord Akimitsu's daughter Genshi. A strange thing happened with Genshi's pregnancy, which was several years ago. She entered labor in the ninth month, but she did not deliver a baby. She and her father were both ridiculed for that. Genshi has not become pregnant since."

"Why would they laugh at her?" Masako asked. "It wasn't her fault."

"Lord Akimitsu boasted that his future grandson would become emperor, and how Akimitsu would be regent someday. But Akimitsu has neither talent nor intelligence for that role, unlike Lord Michinaga, who has both. Sadly, poor Lady Genshi suffered twice. Her miscarriage, if that's what it was, and the ridicule she endured because of her foolish father."

We processed this information for a few minutes in silence, and then I asked the question I suspected we were all thinking.

"Could *Akimitsu* have asked Ashiya for a curse? But if so, why not curse Michinaga's daughters? They are rivals too, assuming he still thinks his daughter will bear an heir to His Majesty."

Seimei examined the divination scroll as if the answer was written there. "Michinaga outranks him. Akimitsu might be incompetent but he is not stupid. He won't jeopardize what authority he has now by hurting Michinaga's daughters."

I mulled that over. "Wouldn't such terrible treatment of your daughter make you bitter and vengeful? If everyone at court mocked Akimitsu, that might twist him over time. How bullied was so bullied you'd kill innocent people in revenge?" Another thought struck me. "Could the curse have been targeted at Lady Miku? And spilled over to kill Motoko? After all, Miku was pregnant when she died. Masako, in your first letter to me, you mentioned a typhoon. Didn't Miku's death occur right after the typhoon? Maybe the typhoon came from Ashiya performing the curse."

Seimei slowly rubbed the back of his neck. "I am embarrassed to say I did not make that connection. I will re-interpret my divination to see if the typhoon is connected to Lady Miku's death."

If only I had a phone to record Seimei admitting to a mistake. No time to savor the moment, however. "No one said how Miku died?" I asked.

He shrugged. "I did not attend her, and no information was provided. I believed it to be one of the many maladies affecting women."

I winced at his callousness. "We can't bring Miku or Motoko back to life, but if the curse-demon is still around, how do we get rid of it before it kills someone else?"

"I suspect Ashiya twisted a shikigami into a curse-demon, and that demon became the dark mist which killed the Consort. To undo this curse, we will have to summon the curse-demon and then exorcise it. Both the summoning and the exorcising require strength I no longer have. My eldest son has no experience in this type of magic, and he is needed to support the imperial family. We need trusted diviners." He tapped his fingers on the table, thinking.

"What about Bikki?" I asked.

"Bikki? Is there a diviner with such a name?"

Masako's eyes brightened "Yes! The shaman who led us in closing the Demon Gate. He comes from a tribe of people who practice divination and pray to the kami, which they call *kamuy*."

"Ah, indeed. I remember now. Some of you have very little power." He glanced my way. "And some of you more," nodding to Masako. "But none of you have enough, so this Bikki shaman suggested sharing your powers to close the Demon Gate. He must be wise to suggest such a thing." He stroked his beard thoughtfully. "If the four of you combine your powers again... Yes, yes. That might work."

"Lord Seimei, you taught us never to use shikigami for a negative purpose," I said, thinking back to past instructions. "It might turn against us. So why didn't it turn on Ashiya?"

"I can only assume he became too powerful. However, because shikigami are powered by their master's spiritual and life energies, the curse-demon must be draining Ashiya's strength. If we do not destroy it, he will do it. But we cannot wait. He might have another wicked purpose for the curse first."

"If Ashiya used washi paper to summon the shikigami, it should turn back into washi paper when we exorcise it. That seems almost too easy."

Seimei smiled, but not like he was happy. More like he couldn't wait for me to see just how not-easy it would be.

Chapter 27

Lord Akimitsu

Masako sent a message to the village where she first met Bikki, hoping the villagers would be able to locate him. Seimei left to consult his Book of Onmyōdō Secrets to determine which spells would work best to summon and exorcise the curse-demon. He explained that we needed two different rituals requiring two different spells. But before leaving, he ordered servants to bring us something to eat.

I ate rice and dried fruit with nervous energy, pestering every servant and apprentice I saw to ask if they'd heard from Lady Nariko.

"Mi-Na, we can do nothing more about Ken-Ji, but we *can* confront Lord Akimitsu," Masako said. "You are in a man's body, so you should meet with him."

"I agree," I said, "but what if Kenji-"

"We will get word to you if we hear from him," she replied a little too quickly.

Suetake's memories showed me that he and Akimitsu had been drinking buddies at some point. I sent a note to ask Akimitsu to share some saké with me later that evening, and he sent a message back asking me to visit him at his residence.

Seimei prepared me for the meeting by describing Akimitsu's family situation. He was first cousin to the Regent, Lord Michinaga, on his father's side, and his wife was an imperial princess. Akimitsu's position as Minister of the Right was more indicative of those connections than of his ability to govern.

His position on the Grand Council required him to perform ceremonies crucial to the safety and security of the realm. A mistake might result in epidemics, earthquakes, or fires. To avoid errors, Akimitsu wrote himself detailed instructions, yet he often committed serious errors.

So while Akimitsu's position was one of the highest in the Heian government, other nobles and government officials frequently bypassed him in favor of more competent men, an insult not lost on Akimitsu.

To make matters worse, Akimitsu's son Shigeie had joined a monastery the year before. Akimitsu had hoped his son's charisma and good looks would lead to promotions and respect, but Shigeie said he wasn't smart enough for government work, or something to that effect, so he entered isolation with his best friend Narinobu.

"Maybe Akimitsu's son and Narinobu were in love and the monastery was the only way to live together without interference," I suggested.

Seimei pursed his lips. "His son is so handsome and charming that people say he is a model for Shining Genji. Unlike Genji, though, he was never known for flirting with women."

"Which makes my case about why he became a monk," I said dryly. "So Akimitsu's daughter miscarries a potential future emperor, his promising son locks himself away in a monastery, Akimitsu blunders his way through important ceremonies, and everyone ridicules him."

"Correct, Mi-Na," Masako said. "Even commoners enjoy

mocking noblemen, and Akimitsu provides them with much fodder to do so."

That evening I sipped saké with Akimitsu. His receding hairline revealed a large forehead with a permanent frown. He seemed happy to see me, though. He didn't act like someone capable of terrible revenge. He kept my cup full, chatted amiably about this and that person at court, and admired my—Suetake's—role in defeating the oni at Mount Ōe.

"I'm sorry I haven't stopped by to express my condolences..." I trailed off deliberately, hoping he'd fill in the last time he saw me.

He dismissed my apology with a wave. "I am grateful for the poem you sent when my son joined the priesthood. It gave my poor wife some consolation. I have my work, but she only has her poetry and incense-blending to distract her from her grief."

"I am so sorry about what happened to your daughter. I was fighting rebels in Mino at the time."

"Gossips at court say she was never pregnant. They lie. I witnessed her labor. She suffered terribly, yet they mocked her." He closed his eyes as if in pain. "His Majesty spends no time with my daughter. The young Empress Akiko reads poetry to him, and they discuss music and art." He slammed his cup onto the tray. "My daughter is educated and musical. Why does he ignore her?"

I knew why. Michinaga made sure his daughter, Empress Akiko, had the finest of everything: the latest artworks, the best calligraphers, and unusual and rare artifacts aimed at luring the sensitive and artistic young emperor to spend time in her salon. "And how did the death of the Crown Prince's consort affect His Majesty?"

"He grieves." His eyes grew opaque as he muttered something inaudible.

"Excuse me?"

"You know!" His voice had gone from too quiet to much too loud. "My father was chief advisor to the previous Emperor. I was promoted to Minister of the Right seven years ago. One of the highest positions in government. So why do they ridicule my family? Only my son received praise. Handsome and popular, he would have put a stop to the mocking, but he became a monk against my wishes. My wife cried for months."

"Surely it is comforting to know that your son serves Buddha and seeks enlightenment."

He looked around for a servant, but there were none because he'd told everyone to stay away during our conversation. I picked up the ladle and poured more saké into his cup. He drank all of it and held it out again.

"I have one more chance," he said. "My youngest daughter will marry the Crown Prince's son one day."

His eyes wandered around the room as if seeking answers in the walls, and then he hung his head like it weighed too much. "He told me how sweet my revenge would be. He promised help from the kami."

"Um, who promised that?"

His head jerked up. "What?"

"The kami would help with what?"

"Lord Suetake, you make no sense." He stood up, kicking my cup as he did so. "I have business to take care of."

I reached out to pick up the cup, but he set a foot on it before I could do so. "Servants will take care of that," he said shortly.

I froze, unsure of the correct response. *"He's an idiot,"* was all I received from Suetake's brain. *"So treat him like one."*

But he wasn't an idiot. If he lived in 2019, he might have been diagnosed with ADHD or dyslexia earlier in life and learned skills to cope with it. In medieval Japan, his family status and connections got him to a rank and position where his issues were guaranteed to get him in trouble.

I pulled my hand away, rose to my feet, and said farewell.

As I rode back to Seimei's residence, I mulled over what Akimitsu said. He had a dark side, clearly, but how much of his darkness was due to mockery and bullying? In the modern world, he'd get therapy and meds for anxiety and depression. In this world, he had access to demon-conjuring onmyōji.

Specifically, one unofficial onmyōji. My intuition told me Ashiya had persuaded Akimitsu to request a curse.

After I dismounted and entered the courtyard, a servant mentioned a note addressed to Lord Suetake arrived while I was gone.

I exhaled with relief. "From Ken—ah, from Lady Nariko?"

The servant apologized for disappointing me, saying the note came from the Lady of Second Avenue.

I examined the soft, light blue paper, and fragrance rose from it. I held it to my nose and inhaled a pleasant combination of sandalwood and clove.

The scent triggered new memories. *Purple-black silky hair brushed my face as she bent over me, her white under-robe falling off a smooth shoulder. I reach up to untie her belt...*

I most definitely did *not* want to see what happened next. Squeezing my eyes shut didn't stop the vision, so I forced myself to examine the details of the painting on the screen in front of me. *Cranes. This one's flying. That one's standing.*

After the vision faded, I opened the note and a red maple leaf fluttered from it to the floor. I scooped it up before admiring the black brushed calligraphy flowing down the paper. After spending a year at court with Masako, I knew good writing when I saw it. I could read it by tapping into Suetake's brain.

The blazing maples

Will soon be gray
But my sleeves remain crimson
Until I see you again

I showed it to Masako, who was waiting for me in Seimei's divination room. "Crimson sleeves imply tears," she said. "This woman wants Lord Suetake to visit, and it appears she lives on Second Avenue."

"She expects an answer. The note arrived here, so she must have heard Suetake was staying with Seimei."

I didn't want to destroy Suetake's love life, so I had to invent a rational reason to decline her invitation.

A forbidden direction, perhaps? Kami traveled from place to place, and it wasn't wise to cross their paths. Diviners determined which paths were off-limits on any given day, so it was a common excuse for not going somewhere.

I sent a note back to my host's Second Avenue lover to say I couldn't see her for a while because her direction was taboo.

"Well, has anyone heard from Kenji?" I asked when I completed that task. "Or found Lady Nariko?"

Masako's eyes welled with tears. "Nothing," she whispered. "He does not understand how vulnerable he is as a young woman alone in the capital. Women rarely travel without an escort."

Seimei grunted. "Whatever Ken-Ji did, he did it knowingly."

I agreed, but it didn't ease the ache in my heart. Why hadn't he told me where he went? Why hadn't we heard from him?

"Did Akimitsu admit to asking Ashiya to curse Motoko and Miku?" Masako leaned forward, eager to get an update on my visit.

"Not exactly, but he said *someone* told him the kami would help him get revenge. The divination told us Ashiya performed the curse, so I think Ashiya encouraged Akimitsu to pay him for it."

"Yes, I believe such a thing about Ashiya," Seimei said. "I see now I did not pay sufficient attention to the increase in spirit possessions and disappearance of young women which began after the typhoon."

"Because it only affected *commoners*," I reminded him.

He ignored me. "Lord Oni was defeated and the Demon Gate is now closed, but the curse still exists in our world. We must banish it before it can further harm the imperial family. I have determined the correct incantation to exorcise it."

"But what do we do about Ashiya?" I asked. "Do we tell the Regent or His Majesty? What about Akimitsu? Ashiya is the one who called up the curse, but Akimitsu probably paid for it."

Masako had been following the conversation closely. "The Imperial Police could arrest both of them."

"My divination tells me Ashiya was responsible for the curse, but that isn't sufficient to charge him with murder," Seimei said sadly. "We have no evidence at all that Akimitsu was involved, and anyway, a high-ranking official would need to approve the arrest of a nobleman."

Adrenaline surged through my veins and my hand twitched as if reaching for a sword. "Let's fight him!"

Calm down, Suetake.

"On second thought," I said, more calmly this time. "We shouldn't use swords against a man who summons curses. Let's fight fire with fire, as we say in my world, and use our shamanic power against him."

Masako pressed her palms together in prayer mode. "Or ask the kami to punish him?"

Seimei drummed his fingers on the wooden floor for a minute. "Engaging in an onmyōdō battle would be unwise. I am too weak, and even if I weren't, such a battle might harm bystanders. It would be best to bind his magic so he cannot perform more curses. But even a magic-binding spell requires more strength than I have. If you work together as you did on Mount Ōe, you might be able to do that. I will teach you the appropriate spells from my Book. Perhaps Ken-Ji will return in time to join you."

Which reminded me. "Has anyone-"

"No!" Seimei and Masako said together.

"Well, can one of you conduct a divination to find out where he went?"

They exchanged a glance. Seimei lumbered to his feet and gestured for a servant to help him leave.

Masako's eyes showed concern with just a hint of impatience. "Divination requires spiritual strength, Mi-Na. I'm exhausted from the one we did today, and we need to save our energy for fighting Ashiya. I believe we'll receive a message tomorrow."

I hoped we would, but I couldn't shake a queasy feeling about *what* we might hear.

Chapter 28

Yang Hour

Yorimitsu requested Masako's presence at the imperial government compound the next morning to support his presentation of the senzo request to the Regent.

Masako left to support what might be the strangest petition the Regent would ever receive, but one he was likely to consider, considering the senzo threatened to steal his son if he didn't.

She returned with the news that a small amount of rice and land were to be given to the descendants of the senzo, enough for them to stop their banditry and ensure they would revere their ancestors properly, but not so much others would try it as a get-rich-quick scheme.

Bikki arrived soon after, escorted by two nervous city guards. His appearance, so unlike the Yamato people, alarmed them. They didn't want to allow him entry to the capital, but when he dropped Seimei's name, they decided not to risk the Great Diviner's anger. Seimei assured them Bikki was an honored guest, and the guards bowed hastily and left as fast as they could.

Bikki's tusu-kur practices fascinated the Royal Astrologer. The two of them talked and compared notes until the sun began to create shadows in the courtyard.

Masako finally intervened. "Excuse my rudeness," she said. "But when will we conduct the ritual?

"The moon will be full tonight," Seimei said, "signaling the first day of Ninth Month. Nine, as you know, is a yang number. It will rise during Rat, a yang hour associated with north. The next hour, Ox, is a yin hour linked to the northeast, which, of course, is the kimon direction. The harmony of a yang and yin balance will be the border between Rat and Ox, so the ritual to exorcise the demon must begin then."

Bikki mentioned he'd sensed a malevolent presence under the bridge as he entered the city.

"Ah, yes," Seimei said. "I have heard tales of unusual events at that location. Many who cross the river fall ill."

"What happens if we fail? What might the curse do to *us*?" I asked.

He gestured to an apprentice to put his divination tools away. "It killed Lady Motoko. It will not be kinder to you than to her."

Masako shivered, but my warrior's hands itched with anticipation when they should have trembled with fear. Masako was right. I *was* much braver than before, even if some of that courage came from Suetake.

Seimei told us to meet in his divination room after a quick meal so he could teach us the incantations we'd need that night.

We did as instructed. Just as we were getting started, a servant announced a note had arrived.

Seimei held his hand out for it.

"It's addressed to Lord Suetake," the servant said with an apologetic bow.

"Finally!" I took the note eagerly.

The paper had faint writing on one side, and elegant calligraphy on the other. Paper was so expensive it was reused many times, sometimes ending its life as toilet paper or made into hats.

This hadn't gone quite that far yet, but it wasn't the nice new paper used by Suetake's Second Avenue girlfriend.

Masako stepped forward as if to snatch it from my hands. "Is it from Ken-Ji? What does it say?"

The writing was unfamiliar, but I assumed it was Nariko's. I had no trouble reading her calligraphy.

When I finished, I didn't trust my voice. I clutched the paper tightly while I swallowed a few times. "Um, yes, it's from Kenji. He's at Ashiya's residence. He went reluctantly, he says, but had no other option after Seimei refused to preserve a copy of his book for him. He thinks Ashiya will help."

Seimei folded his arms. "*My* descendant did such a foolish thing?" he said. "Does Ken-Ji explain *why* he went to Ashiya for assistance?"

"Well, not in this note, but in our world he found ancient letters describing how the Book of Onmyōdō Secrets contained spells to save the kami's spaces and how only Ashiya would help Kenji find it."

"Why didn't you tell me this before? We had lengthy discussions about Ashiya!" Seimei's anger turned his old man's cheeks a mottled purple.

Because you'd react that way.

I couldn't tell him that, though. "I didn't think it mattered." I stared at the letter in my hand. "Why would Ashiya leave messages for Kenji to find? How would he know who Kenji *was*?"

Seimei leaned heavily on his staff. "Think," he said curtly.

I closed my eyes and swayed as vertigo swept over me at this strange time loop. "Ashiya met Kenji for the first time just the other day, right? But in a year, or ten years, I don't know, but obviously after he met Kenji, he'll write a letter which Kenji will find a thousand years later. The letter says the Book of Secrets has the *only* spell that can save the kami, and that Ashiya will help Kenji obtain the Book. We wouldn't be here now if he hadn't left that message. So what's in it for Ashiya to bring us here? You wouldn't give Ashiya the Book, nor would you give it to Kenji. Ashiya lied about being able to help Kenji get it, right?"

Seimei gave a single sharp nod.

"So he lured Kenji here. He manipulated Kenji's dream of saving the kami to do—what? What does he want Kenji to do?" An invisible vise squeezed my lungs. *Mina, get it together! Inhale slowly. Now exhale to a count of six.*

When I could breathe again, I knew what I had to do. "Get me a horse! I'll ride to Ashiya's to rescue Kenji."

Bikki hadn't said a word yet, examining Seimei's star map with great interest. At my final comment, he turned toward me. "Send a messenger instead. We must practice the incantation to expel the curse-demon. If we make a mistake, it will escape, kill us, and pursue other prey. As Lord Seimei explained, tonight is most auspicious for the exorcism. Masako and I won't be strong enough to complete the task without you. Write to Ken-Ji, and have him meet us on the bridge just before moonrise. Ask him to bring Ashiya."

He was right. I couldn't abandon my fellow Guardians when they needed me.

I called for paper and brush to write a note to Kenji, including the information about Ashiya's role in the curse. Masako approved my note and handed it to Seimei, who called for a servant to deliver it.

With that completed, our instruction began. Seimei reviewed three spells with us. One to summon the demon, one to banish the curse, and a third to bind Ashiya's magic. "These are from my Book," he said, "but I have committed them to memory, as you must do. Do not teach anyone else these rites."

I still didn't understand why he refused to leave a copy of his

Book for Kenji, but I needed to focus on the rituals, so I pushed everything else out of my mind.

After many repetitions, our movements became smooth and natural. I no longer had to stop and think about what to do and when to do it. Our spiritual bond strengthened as we moved in unison, although it didn't feel quite as strong as before. We needed Kenji. We were supposed to be Four Guardians of the Gate, not Three.

Seimei couldn't take Kenji's place in the ritual because the energy required would kill him in his current frail condition, but he watched us enviously.

When we finished the chant for the seventh time, he congratulated us on our quick learning. "You are ready."

Seimei sent a message to Lord Michinaga explaining he needed the bridge to be closed for the night to conduct an exorcism. Michinaga showed his faith in the Royal Astrologer by immediately instructing city guards to ensure no one crossed it.

Seimei said that, due to his frailty, he would ride to the bridge in an ox-carriage. It wouldn't be seemly for Masako to be in the same carriage, so she asked to take his horse.

Bikki and I walked. It felt good to stretch my long legs after sitting so much. My host's body was used to action.

Though the sun had set some time ago, traffic was still heavy. Humble ox carts rumbled along dirt roads. Commoners and merchants thronged the neighborhoods, most walking, some stumbling from drinking saké at stalls lining the streets.

We found Seimei, Masako, and a groom waiting for us when we arrived. The groom took the horse and oxen away so they wouldn't be disturbed by the supernatural presence under the bridge.

Kenji wasn't there yet. *Ashiya better not have hurt him.*

While we waited, Seimei explained how this bridge spanned a bend in the Katsura River, and because of that bend, the sides faced northeast and southwest. The curse-demon was probably attracted to the northeast side to gain strength from the malevolence seeping through the Demon Gate. Closing the Gate didn't make it leak-proof, apparently.

Angry peasants milled about, grumbling about being unable to cross the river, but they fled when guards pointed out Lord Seimei was about to battle a demon. All but two of the guards asked if they could leave as well, and Seimei gave his permission.

The remaining two said they'd stay. "I know why you're here," said one. "This place is cursed. Three people fell into the river today. None died, but all were injured. I've been sick every day since I was assigned here, while poor Jiro…" He waved to the guard next to him. "His wife died last week in childbirth. He asked to be sent to another location, but the captain told him he had to stay. Now he's worried about the baby, which survived the birth but is sickly. I thank the kami and His Majesty you are here. We'll wait over there." He gestured to a spot away from the bridge but close enough to hear us scream.

Seimei expressed his condolences to Jiro, while I gripped the hilt of my sword to keep nausea from reaching my throat. Bikki said nothing.

We stepped onto the bridge. A scuttling sound underneath caused me to freeze with unexpected dread, unable to take another step forward.

Bikki and Seimei continued until they reached the top of the arch. When they leaned over the railing, the scuttling ceased abruptly. *Rats? Or something else that didn't want to be seen?*

Masako waited with me. "Mi-Na? What's wrong?"

I glanced at the eastern horizon. A faint glow behind the mountain ridge told me the moon was rising. "Nothing. Let's go."

We took another few steps up but stopped again at the

rattling sound of an ox-carriage. Exhaling with relief, I turned around.

Seimei and Bikki would be fine without us for a few minutes. They had experience with divination and spirit-banishment. Kenji, Masako, and I had only youth, energy, and a vague spiritual power that we didn't quite understand.

But maybe that was enough to banish a demon and wrap a sorcerer so tightly he'd never cast a curse again.

Chapter 29

———

The Evanescent Shimmer

The curtain at the back of the carriage rippled as a young woman in white robes peeked out.

"Kenji!" I shouted, allowing myself to feel angry now he was back. "Why the fu- why the Futaba did you leave without telling us? We were worried about you."

"I'm so sorry, Mina and Masako, but Ashiya-"

He was interrupted by a horse clopping up to the carriage. A man dismounted, tossing the reins to a groom who'd materialized out of nowhere. He wore yellow hakama under a chestnut-brown robe thickly embroidered with blue mums. His hair was tied in a top knot covered with the usual black cap. He appeared to be in his mid-forties and clean-shaven.

I rubbed my itchy beard. How upset would Suetake be if I shaved it off?

Suetake answered by sending caustic bile to burn my throat.

Okay, okay, I won't shave, I promise.

The stranger focused bright eyes on me. "Lord Suetake? Or should I call you Spirit Mi-Na?"

I bowed, keeping my expression neutral. This must be

Ashiya. *Good.* His presence would allow us to bind his magic tonight.

Ashiya switched his laser-beam focus to Masako. "Miko, come work for me. One day, if you serve me loyally, you might inherit my position. I have no sons to take it over. Imagine the kami doing your bidding rather than the other way around."

Masako's hands were clasped tightly in her sleeves, her lips compressed.

"Well, Miko?" He smirked. "With my tutoring, such skills could be yours someday."

And all for the low, low price of her spiritual integrity. It probably hurt her to breathe the same air as this sociopath, but she had to play nice so Ashiya wouldn't call his demon over to kill us.

"Lord Ashiya, I am not worthy of the honor. I serve Imperial Princess Nobuko, the Saiō-Dai. Any request for my services would have to be approved by her."

"Ask the Saiō-Dai to release you. The loss will be of no significance to the shrine. They will never understand how best to use your abilities. I do."

Kenji, still perched on the carriage platform, nodded vigorously. "He can help. Also, he's the only one who can obtain the Book for me."

"What?" I turned my back to the diviner so he couldn't read my lips. "My letter? Did you read it?" I mouthed.

He shook his head. "What letter?" he mouthed back.

Ashiya slid between us. "Yes, Spirit, I can help you save your world. I am the most powerful onmyōji in the realm, and I'm intrigued by you and Spirit Ken-Ji."

Suetake had a height advantage over Ashiya, so I looked over his head at Kenji. "We need you. All four of us must perform the spell."

"Mina, our priority is saving *our* world, so that's what I'm doing. Also, I didn't practice with you. I'll watch."

I pushed past Ashiya. "Stop screwing around with this man. He's the one who killed Lady Motoko. Come on. I'll help you." I put my hands on his waist. "Upsa daisy!" I lifted him from the platform with ease and set him down gently. Another experience I'd never have in my own body. "Don't listen to that liar. Come this way."

I headed to the river but not before I noticed Ashiya puzzling over my American phrase. I laughed to myself as I envisioned Ashiya using it as a spell in the future.

Masako came with me, and Kenji caught up a few seconds later. "Mina, you're wrong. Ashiya didn't create the curse. He's agreed to help me. He wants me to watch the curse-banishing ritual tonight so I can learn from Seimei, and apply this knowledge someday. He's not Seimei's rival. He's not evil."

It wasn't the time to argue. "For some reason, you didn't get my letter—Ashiya probably destroyed it before you saw it—but I wrote that Masako's divination told us Ashiya called up the curse that killed Lady Motoko." I hesitated, unsure whether to tell him about the plan to bind Ashiya.

Kenji looked up at me with his sweet Nariko eyes. I hated not trusting him, but he'd given me no choice. This obsession with Seimei's Book had skewed his perspective. I muttered something about talking later, and we walked up the bridge together.

When we reached the center, Bikki welcomed Kenji with a warm smile while Seimei greeted him with a frown. I whispered to Seimei that Ashiya had come with Kenji. His faint nod in response told me he understood what that meant for our plans.

Before we began the ritual, Seimei asked if we sensed the demon's presence.

Bikki nodded.

Masako, who had begun to breathe rapidly as soon as she'd

stepped onto the arch, put her hand on her heart. "Yes," she murmured.

Kenji and I shook our heads no.

"Everyone must be able to feel it or the ritual will not work. Close your eyes, put your hands on the railing, and empty your thoughts. Focus only on sensation."

I gripped the railing as if my life depended on it. The wood beneath my fingers felt damp and a little slimy. The river slapped against the pillars below. The wind hissed and whistled under the bridge and over what little exposed skin I had.

A stench of rotten fish filled my nostrils. A metallic taste in my mouth brought the unwanted memory of blood-flavored saké at the oni's palace, and bile rose in my throat. My pulse pounded loudly in my ears. Something—*someone*—was inside me, reaching for my heart. Reaching for my spirit.

I jerked my hands away and snapped my eyes open, shivering as sweat evaporated in the cool breeze.

Bikki was holding Kenji's shoulders as if to keep him from jumping off.

"Hey, are you okay?" I whispered.

He turned around, wiping his mouth with his sleeve. "Uh, sorry. My host body couldn't handle the demon's presence, and her stomach reacted accordingly. But I'm fine. We'll be fine."

"Was that the effect of the curse-demon?"

"Yes," Seimei replied in a softer version of his lecture voice. "It is different from what you might sense with oni, who bring ill luck or ill health but are not utterly evil. Ashiya created the curse-demon from a shikigami. As you know, shikigami are spiritual beings who change bad omens to good ones and help with healing. Ashiya twisted a shikigami's essential goodness into something evil, a terrible action with terrible consequences, as we have seen."

"Lord Seimei," Kenji whispered urgently. "Ashiya didn't summon the curse."

Seimei shook his head with irritation. "Stupid boy," he said. "Open your eyes."

Kenji opened his mouth instead, no doubt to defend himself.

"Stop!" Seimei hissed. "Look!"

I blinked in surprise as the dark sky brightened with white radiance.

"The moon is over the mountains. We must begin," Bikki said.

I looked to the east, and sure enough, the brilliance came from the full moon, huge and luminous against the purple-black ridge of the mountains.

Bikki, Masako, and I moved to our pre-assigned places, facing northeast. Seimei stood behind us to observe. Kenji stood against the railing, watching closely.

Our chanting began, but it took a few minutes to achieve harmony. The moon rose higher, illuminating the bridge. I lifted my arms and legs as if they weighed nothing, the repetitive motions as natural as breathing. Our song strengthened and as our communion returned, creating something new, something better than we'd ever make as individuals. Spiritual energy united us into one powerful being.

A dark mist, barely visible in the moonlight, rose from beneath the northeast end of the bridge and hovered at the edge. Stars shone through it at first, but it thickened as if gathering strength, becoming dense and opaque.

The air was utterly still, yet the mist swirled into eddies, twisting and churning, sliding over the railing. Not floating or drifting, but moving with purpose.

My legs trembled. I faltered, stumbling over the incantation. A glance at Masako's serene expression gave me the courage to continue, and our combined harmony finally brought forth threads of power, stretching outward, twisting and braiding into a thick cord.

The dark mist curled closer. Foggy tendrils emerged and slithered along the planks towards me.

My hands and feet grew icy cold. My fingers stiffened, affecting my ability to form mudras, the gestures required for the ritual. My chest tightened, and I struggled to breathe.

My thread unwound from the braid and began to shrink.

The dread precedes the power.

My breathing calmed, my song strengthened, my thread grew brighter, and the mist receded.

Receded, yes, but it coalesced into a dark and opaque sphere. The bottom bulged downward while the top thinned. Smoky filaments stretched from it, becoming long, wiggly legs.

Eight of them.

I'd seen many strange things in my time here. I'd seen spirits take the form of snakes, foxes, badgers, ravens, and monkeys. But a spider? *That* could be a problem.

Anticipating the usual dizziness from my arachnophobia, I grasped the railing, again as if my life depended on it.

Although this time it probably did. My red thread disappeared.

Seimei murmured something to Kenji, and Kenji sprang into action, smoothly joining the ritual in sync with the other two.

The demon's bulbous body grew larger and darker against the moonlit bridge, and a misty leg again reached toward me. Not toward Masako or Bikki or Kenji. Why *me?* Did it know about my phobia?

It wrapped around my right ankle, burning like frozen iron on bare skin. I flinched and pulled my leg back, which did nothing to loosen its grasp.

It jerked my leg forward, and I lost my grip on the railing.

Game, set, and match to the demon spider.

But I caught myself by throwing my arms outward for balance and using my left leg as an anchor. I stumbled but remained upright, shocked because I was neither dizzy nor scared.

A silent shout echoed through my brain. *Demon spider or demon butterfly, it doesn't matter. Fight back, shaman!*

Suetake? Is that you?

No answer, but it struck me that Suetake didn't have arachnophobia, which meant I didn't either.

Using Suetake's rage, I leaned on my trapped leg and stomped on the demon tendril with my left foot. Nothing happened, so I twisted and turned this way and that to release my ankle, but the spider only wrapped it tighter. My foot tingled as circulation was cut off.

"Mi-Na!" Seimei's urgent whisper caught my attention. "Here!"

I turned to catch the sword he threw at me. *Suetake, this one's for you.*

I swung the sword with ease, bringing it up, over, and down in one fluid motion to slice through the tendril holding my ankle.

The demon pulled back with a hiss. Red eyes appeared in the center of its body, glaring at me with hatred, whipping its many legs angrily back and forth.

Thrilled by my lack of spider-fear, I clenched the sword's hilt, waiting for the right moment.

Masako screamed. While I'd reveled in my Suetake-fueled bravery, the spider had wrapped two of its legs around her, pulling her toward its center.

I darted forward among its other squirming legs, cutting them methodically, somehow knowing where each would appear next.

So this is what it's like to be a warrior. Strength, agility, skill.

But this couldn't *only* be warrior skill. My sharpened senses must be from the new me. The shaman-me.

Masako planted her feet while continuing to chant, pushing at the rope-like legs around her waist, remaining in harmony with Kenji and Bikki despite her horrifying predicament.

For every leg I cut, another one slithered out of the demon's bulbous center. I despaired of making enough progress to sever the body from the legs before it pulled Masako into its darkness. Would it possess her? Eat her? Or dissolve her?

I didn't want to find out.

My slicing and dicing continued as I envisioned routes to get to the demon's body. I jumped over legs that lashed out everywhere.

A sudden opening allowed me to draw close enough to see its eyes burning with a savage intensity that should have petrified me. Instead, a fierce joy drove me forward in a lunge to sink the sword between its eyes.

Momentum pitched me into its dark body, which dissolved with bubbling and hissing and the stink of dead fish.

My head hit the bridge with a bang. Briefly stunned, I lay in the slimy mess for a hot minute.

"Mi-Na, now! Back!" Masako's shout stirred me into action once more. I jumped to my feet and we ran toward the other diviners. We had a narrow window to banish the curse before the demon took on a new shape.

I was about to clasp Kenji's hand when I realized I'd been polluted by the demon's ooze. Seimei stepped forward with a bucket of water and two paper dolls. "The paper is already blessed," he said.

Masako and I washed from head to foot, rubbed the dolls all over our bodies, and then threw them over the railing with a prayer. Seimei said his own prayer and gestured for us to rejoin the others. I grabbed Masako's hand on my left, and

Kenji's on my right, and Bikki took Kenji's hand on his other side.

Power surged from Masako's hands to mine, and from mine to Kenji's. We raised our voices, our words echoing against the river bank.

Now directly overhead, the moon illuminated both the steaming dark circle on the planks and the demon steam rising into the air.

The four of us stepped forward as one. Energy burned like liquid fire from my toes to my fingertips. We lifted our arms as we reached the crescendo of the incantation.

The miasma began to dissipate.

With renewed strength, we moved forward, swinging our connected arms back and bowing our heads while chanting a prayer. With a last forceful push, we raised our arms and our heads.

Moonlight shone through the demon's dark mist like the morning sun burning off fog.

And then it was only moonlight.

I released Kenji and Masako's hands and collapsed, as did they.

I wanted to lie on the cool wooden planks and sleep the night away, right there, on the bridge.

Seimei shuffled over to us.

"Get up! Get up!" The urgency in his whisper bordered on panic, a very un-Seimei-like emotion. "We must conduct the binding while Ashiya is present."

I forced myself to my feet with a groan, then took Masako's hand to pull her up too.

Bikki had no problem rising. His nomadic lifestyle had no doubt hardened him to such exhaustion.

Kenji stood as well, looking between us in confusion.

"We have one more thing to do," I croaked. "Just stay there."

Bikki, Masako, and I began a different spell. We drew strength from it, our fatigue washing away with each movement. Ashiya watched us, his figure outlined by moonlight. He must have walked up to the bridge arch to watch us fight the curse-demon. *His* curse-demon. Why hadn't he stopped us? Maybe he wanted us to do his dirty work and eliminate the demon before it consumed him or turned on him, as twisted shikigami were known to do.

"Ken-Ji?" he called. "What are they doing?"

Kenji shrugged, watching us intently. He knew better than to interrupt.

Ashiya had reached Seimei, and oddly, they bowed to each other.

"Most impressive, Sensei," Ashiya said. "Your pupils have great potential. What is the ritual they are performing now?"

"Ah, only a little spell from my Book. Relax and enjoy it."

Ashiya slouched against the railing, watching us with idle curiosity. "You must admit my skill exceeds yours."

Seimei shrugged noncommittally. "Any diviner of note can twist a shikigami. The question is, why would you?"

Ashiya appeared perplexed by Seimei's calm demeanor. "Not just any diviner has the power to open the Demon Gate. Even you must admit you have never done such a thing."

"I have never attempted it, nor will I. I have a question for you. Your answer will tell me whether you are more powerful than I."

Seimei was distracting Ashiya to improve our chances of successfully binding him. It was working, too. Ashiya's narcissism meant he couldn't leave until Seimei admitted his rival was the best onmyōji in the realm.

"Do you, now?" Ashiya said as if he didn't care either way. "What question is that?"

Seimei looked over the river as if he had no interest in the spell we were casting. "If the great typhoon, Lady Miku's death, and Lady Motoko's death were all connected to the curse that opened the Demon Gate, *that* would be an unprecedented display of onmyōdō skill. *You* have never been that talented."

Ashiya smiled. "That curse demonstrated how my skill exceeds yours, old man. Akimitsu wanted to prevent Miku and Motoko from ever producing a future emperor. I took advantage of his foolishness to send a curse so potent my superiority would never be doubted again."

Instead of replying, Seimei turned to watch us, and Ashiya, irritated with his rival's lack of emotion, walked over to Kenji.

Before Ashiya could pull Kenji away, something about our ritual alarmed him. "What is this spell?"

Seimei shrugged.

Ashiya glared at him and then at us, suddenly alarmed. "Stop that! I demand you stop!"

We ignored him.

He reached into his robe and drew forth a paper cutout. He threw it into the air. "Shikigami, assist your master!"

I almost stopped chanting at the distraction. What would it be? A raven? A dog? *Oh, please let it be a monkey!* I had experience dealing with monkey-spirits.

But I saw nothing so I pushed myself to maintain the incantation. Our power-sharing threads had not yet regenerated after the last ritual. None of us could afford to lose our concentration.

A current in the air, visible only by a few swirling leaves lifted from the bridge, rippled toward me. I shifted to avoid it, but it settled on my shoulders, hugging me in a cold embrace like an invisible straitjacket taken from a freezer. It wrapped around me in a bear hug, pinning my arms to my sides, breaking my connection to the others.

"Help!" I gasped.

Seimei stepped forward to take my place, but he struggled to breathe. His movements grew slower, and he stumbled as if stricken with vertigo.

Masako gave me a quick side glance, her eyes wide with alarm, but she maintained the chant, planning, I hoped, to bind Ashiya's power before I suffocated.

Bikki ignored me as a consummate professional should.

The air-shikigami tightened, allowing me to take only quick, shallow breaths.

Kenji spun toward Ashiya. "Let her go!"

Ashiya shook his head. "If you want to find the Book of Onmyōdō Secrets in your world, you must be patient and work *with* me, not against me. If you don't wish to see this, wait for me at the carriage."

Kenji reached through the shikigami net to take my hand but jerked it back immediately with a cry of pain. "It burned me! What's happening? Seimei, stop him!"

Seimei staggered, clearly too weak for this ritual.

The invisible force tightened even more.

What kind of shikigami was this? A fishing net? *Please, not a shroud.*

"Seimei can't- Two-" I gasped. "Are not-" Short intake in. "Enough guardians. Need Kenji-"

Seimei clutched his chest in mid-chant. He fell with an audible smack of his head against the planks.

Kenji ran to help him.

"Get away!"

Kenji stopped at Ashiya's shout.

"If you want the Book, leave the old man and his useless students. If you want my help saving the kami, leave this place. Now!"

Kenji's eyes went from Ashiya to me to Seimei and back to Ashiya. "Screw the damn Book." He jumped into the ritual as if he'd learned it right along with us, and began to move in unity with Masako and Bikki.

Lady Nariko's clever brain must have learned the spell before I became immobilized.

The shikigami fishing net cut off circulation in my arms. My lips and legs grew numb. Tiny, sharp intakes gave me a little oxygen, barely enough to stay alive, but not enough to prevent vertigo.

"Ken-Ji, I command you to stop," Ashiya called. "Stop or I will kill her."

Don't stop, Kenji. I can last a minute or two more. Bind him now!

A red braided thread now connected Kenji, Masako, and Bikki, and from Bikki, a thread wound toward Ashiya.

Come on, Kenji, it's working! Go, Guardians!

Ashiya moved his hands in a complicated mudra. "If she dies, it will be your fault."

Kenji's thread broke. He raised his hands to his throat making choking sounds. His jaw worked as if trying to call out, but to no avail.

Masako faltered as she gazed at Kenji in horror. Her thread broke too.

Kenji swayed silently, his eyes pleading with me to forgive him. He fell to his knees.

My shikigami-net had loosened while Ashiya was occupied with Kenji. Not enough to move, but enough to speak. "Let him go!"

He ignored me, his focus only on Kenji, who didn't appear to be breathing.

"Stop!" Masako cried. "Let him go, and I will work for you."

Ashiya paused at her interruption but only to laugh. "You *will* work for me someday." Another mudra. Kenji, his face mottling, fell to his knees, then tipped over to fall on the planks.

"Kenji!" My scream sounded weak in my ears. "Nariko! Get up!"

Bikki leaned over the prone figure, his cheek at Nariko's mouth, then placed a hand on either side of her head. She didn't move. His mouth tightened with anger, an emotion I'd never seen him display. He began a different chant, this one in a language I didn't know—maybe Ainu?—and moved his hands over Nariko's face and torso in a complex series of gestures.

Cold fingers of dread tickled my spine. She couldn't be dead. Why would Ashiya kill her? And if she was dead, what would happen to Kenji's spirit?

Ashiya stood breathing hard, watching Bikki closely, his smile victorious.

Bikki's movements were purposeful and directed. He finished his quiet spell with a dramatic gesture, throwing his arms toward Ashiya, his palms out as if pushing something invisible.

The smug sorcerer's smile shifted, became a frown, then a snarl of rage. "Stop-"

His shout was choked off and his eyes widened with horror.

And then a bemused smile crossed his face. He lifted his arms and gazed at his blue sleeves and yellow hakama, and then at me. "Mina?"

My shikigami bonds fell away. I took a few deep breaths to get some sweet night air. "Kenji! Did you possess Ashiya?"

His eyebrows pulled together. "Begone, Spirit!" he growled, but with another eerie shift, his face transformed as he smiled sadly. "Yes, it's me."

"Nariko's dead," Bikki murmured. "I transferred Ken-Ji's spirit into Ashiya's body."

Conflicting emotions—gratitude to Bikki for saving Kenji, grief for poor Nariko, concern for Seimei—silenced my voice.

Masako examined Ashiya. "Ken-Ji, do you have complete control over Ashiya's body?"

"No. We're fighting in here."

Ashiya's face kept changing—mouth twitching, jaw clenching, eyebrows drawing together and spreading apart, evidence of the struggle for control of the two spirits within.

"We need Seimei to freeze Ashiya's spirit to finish the binding." My stomach roiled. "Seimei!" I rushed to his figure, lying motionless on the planks. "Is he-"

"He lives," Bikki said. "But perhaps not for long."

"Masako? Can you do it?"

She stepped forward but hesitated. "I have not had formal training in this."

"You've been on both ends of it, though, and you've seen Seimei do it. I believe in you."

She bowed to me. "I will endeavor to deserve your faith, Mi-Na. Ken-Ji, force Ashiya to look at me, but do not allow him to move after that."

Ashiya resisted. Kenji had to turn his head in small increments, so slowly it hurt to watch, but at last, his eyes locked onto Masako's.

She did it. No chanting, no dancing. Just staring. Just how Seimei did it to me.

"I don't hear Ashiya anymore," Kenji said, "so let's move quickly to complete the binding."

"What about Seimei? Shouldn't we get him medical attention?" I didn't want my friend's teacher to die this way.

Bikki moved back into position. "I understand, Mi-Na, but now that we've begun the binding ritual, we must complete it. Ken-Ji, remain still. The spell will not harm you or Ashiya. It will not take long."

My eyes fell upon Nariko's small, still body. I reached out to touch her, but fell just short, my arm strangely heavy as if weighted down with melancholy. I knelt with my head bowed, vision blurred as I contemplated our failure to protect her.

All living things are fated to die, yet life is beautiful, an evanescent shimmer in a sad world.

Suetake said it for both of us. *Mono no aware.* The beauty of impermanence.

I blinked tears away. "Let's move over there." I pointed to a spot away from Nariko and Seimei.

Masako, Bikki, and I renewed our chanting. Without the distractions of shikigami nets and evil sorcerers, our threads connected, braided, and encased Ashiya's body. Kenji kept still, his eyes trusting and calm as our threads swirled around him.

We completed the binding and rushed to assist Seimei.

Chapter 30

Warrior ·

"What about the Book?"

"I couldn't let-" Kenji stopped as if the next words would hurt too much.

"Me die?" I finished for him. "I'm grateful for that. You could have decided that saving the world justified a few sacrifices. And your reward—or punishment—is to live in Ashiya's body. How's that going, by the way?"

Kenji had changed from Ashiya's flamboyant robes into white hemp as a way to punish Ashiya, who could see the lack of color and feel the scratchy hemp on his skin but couldn't do anything about it.

"I miss Nariko," he said. "Even though she couldn't communicate with me, I saw some of her memories. She was intelligent and quick-witted. Artistic too, with excellent manners and calligraphy. I think people in her circle liked her. Ashiya's completely different. I'm sensing resentment, pride, envy, arrogance—I never felt any of those with her."

"The Kamo Shrine had accepted Nariko as an attendant," Masako said sadly. "Her father had refused to take her back, believing she brought bad luck upon them, although her parents are grieving now. Her father blames Seimei for not protecting her while she was possessed."

We sat on the floor in Seimei's residence, waiting for him to make an appearance. Seimei had recovered consciousness and although weak, had insisted on questioning the four of us about what had transpired.

"If I hadn't gone to Ashiya, she'd still be alive," Kenji said, a comment he'd made many times since last night.

I shook my head vigorously. "Don't ever forget *he* killed Nariko. Not you. Not any of us. And if you hadn't brought Ashiya to the bridge, we couldn't have bound his magic. Who knows who else he might have killed?"

Seimei shuffled into the room accompanied by a young man in onmyōdō robes. He proceeded to launch question after question about our efforts to banish the curse and bind Ashiya's powers. He'd love the modern world with our video cameras and Go-Pros, but since he didn't have that option, his scribe recorded our responses.

Kenji described my unexpected abilities. "The way Mina skipped around the demon, knowing where each leg would appear next, and then get close enough to stab it between the eyes—even a warrior like Suetake wouldn't have that kind of skill. Where did it come from?"

"I've thought a lot about that since last night," I said. "I had a heightened sensitivity and intuition which worked together with Suetake's fighting skills. I think of it as warrior-plus. Suetake's muscle memory plus my shamanic power equals demon conqueror."

Masako had that what-is-Mi-Na-talking-about expression when I used modernisms that didn't translate.

Kenji knew what I meant, however. "Same here. Nariko wasn't a fighter, but she had an excellent memory that allowed me to memorize the magic-binding chant. I've never known what it was like to pick up and apply information so quickly. In our world, Nariko might be considered a genius. I agree with you, Mina. We were able to do what we did last night only because of our interaction with our hosts' memories and skills."

Seimei's eyes gleamed. "Your strange words have given me insight," he said. "The balance between yin and yang is of utmost importance in onmyōdō. A female spirit in a male body creates balance. The same was true for Ken-Ji when he possessed Nariko as a male spirit in a female body. This offers an entirely new area of study."

He interrogated Kenji about Ashiya. Kenji flushed at admitting he had believed everything Ashiya told him, including that Seimei wouldn't share his Book because he didn't want anyone else to be as good at magic as he was, and that Seimei would rather see the Book destroyed than let others have it.

"Why would you believe Ashiya?" I asked. "All the legends say he used dark magic."

"Legends aren't history. After all, they portray Seimei as a good person, and that's not completely true, is it?"

I held my breath, assuming the Great Diviner would smack Kenji for his impertinence.

A grim smile appeared under his beard.

I exhaled. Of *course* Seimei was happy. He just learned he was a legend.

Kenji folded his arms in an un-Kenji-like gesture of defiance. "I found Ashiya's letter in our world, addressed to me. It said the Book of Onmyōdō Secrets was required to save the kami, and only Ashiya could get it for me. Somehow he knew who I was, what I wanted most, and that I would come here to your world. The letter said Seimei would refuse to preserve a copy for me. When Lord Seimei did, in fact, refuse my request, I believed Ashiya must have told the truth about the rest as well."

Seimei grunted, but not in the usual displeased way, more

like he understood, which was all the encouragement Kenji needed.

"No copy exists in 2019—in a thousand years—so it wasn't preserved by your descendants. Do you want the Book to be lost forever?"

Seimei's eyelids drooped with fatigue or resignation or both, perhaps worn down by Kenji's impassioned plea. "Very well. However, several spells in it must not be used. Those are the ones Ashiya wants to learn, but which he must not have. Not because I would rather no one have it if I cannot, and not because I must remain the most powerful onmyōji in the realm, as he told you so falsely. It is to prevent him from using them to extend his own life at a great cost to others. I do not understand your world but I see truth in you. I will study how to preserve the Book for you to find in the future."

Kenji thanked Seimei profusely, bowing from his seated position so many times he looked like a chicken pecking at grain. On his final bow, he dislodged his hat, apologizing for his rudeness as he set it back on his head. "I forgot I'm wearing Ashiya's clothing."

Masako and I smothered our laughter.

Seimei glowered at him. "Use your divination skills to locate the Book's hiding place in your world," he said. "When you find it, read the entire Book, but do not attempt the dark spells. Ever. Do not destroy them, however. Save them in secret, for a day might come when such drastic efforts will be required to balance a new evil force."

I understood why Kenji smiled. He'd finally convinced Seimei to give him what he wanted. But there was a little too much of Ashiya's smirk in it, and I had to suppress a shiver.

I bowed with dignity and only once. My hat remained on my head. "Lord Seimei, you'll be doing the right thing. We'll only use our powers to do good things. Now that's settled, when will you send us home?"

"Your world—and your bodies—will still be there whether you return now or next month," he replied.

"We should return while Bikki is here. He may be needed to help Masako with the ritual." I didn't need to tell Seimei he was too weak to do it. He was the one who'd told us.

He turned to the Ainu shaman. "Perhaps you might remain until the new year? We have much to learn from each other."

Bikki bowed. "You do me too much honor. I will return to the mountains as soon as possible after sending the two spirits home."

"May the kami guide your steps," Seimei said with a resigned nod. "In the next few days, I will teach you the ritual to deliver these spirits to their world."

"Lord Seimei?" I asked tentatively.

"Yes?"

"We gained power when we crossed the spirit world. If that power doesn't go with us to the future, we won't have any use for a Book of Onmyōdō Secrets. Do you think we'll retain this power when we return to our bodies?"

Seimei tapped his fingers together while everyone else leaned forward in anticipation. "Mi-Na, you saw a fox messenger after you returned to your world the last time, which means the small power you gained returned with you. It also implies Inari Ōkami has shown you favor. With such power and Inari's assistance, my spells will be useful to protect the kami's pure spaces."

"Exactly!" Kenji sounded just like a college student, an odd contrast with Ashiya's middle-aged face.

Was that how *I* sounded? College student tone in a fifty-something nobleman's voice? No wonder Yorimitsu didn't trust me. "How, though? We don't want to destroy the world to save it."

Seimei shook his head in a sadder-but-wiser-than-you way. "Your power is too slight to do such a thing, and you won't have the support of these two." He pointed his chin at Masako and Bikki. "Begin by purifying one sacred space at a time. How many polluted spaces can there be?"

"You have *no* idea," I said, trying to be condescending right back at him.

Kenji dug his elbow into my side. "Excuse my rude American friend. What I mean is, she grew up in a different realm and has much to learn."

Seimei stood with a creak and a groan. "Well, if you two have a child together, please send it to me for training at a young age before your world's disagreeable manners and customs ruin it."

I choked on the sip of water I'd been taking.

"Lord Seimei," Kenji said with suppressed laughter. "Mina studies Yamato language and customs, but she has a *long* way to go."

"Ha!" I said, despite agreeing with him.

We all moved into Seimei's divination room, where Seimei stared into my eyes so he could ascertain if Suetake was, in fact, imprisoned in his own body.

His intense gaze tunneled deep into my soul. I wanted to recoil but forced myself to remain still. He released me after what was only a few minutes but felt like hours.

I pressed the heels of my palms against my eyes in a failed attempt to erase the sense that my privacy had been invaded.

"It is similar to the hold I put on Mi-Na while she possessed Masako," Seimei pronounced. "I will be able to release his spirit, but I will wait until I have sent you home so he cannot get in the way of the ritual. The same for Ashiya. I am quite certain he would interfere with your departure if released from his hold."

"Thank the kami!" I exclaimed, my heart lighter than any time since I'd arrived here. I hadn't realized how much I feared my host had been permanently destroyed by the senzo who possessed him before me.

Masako clapped her hands with excitement but Kenji appeared pensive. I suspected he was thinking about poor Nariko.

Bikki was interested in the methodology to imprison and release a person's spirit, so he spent a few minutes chatting with Seimei about it.

After they finished their conference, Seimei reviewed the next steps with us. He would instruct Masako and Bikki in the necessary incantations and exhortations. Kenji and I were to meditate and purify ourselves, abstain from meat (which we hadn't eaten in this world since we arrived, so no sacrifice there), and other polluting activities. He instructed us to pray to our clan's kami for success.

"I don't think the Cooper clan has any ancestral kami," I said to Kenji. "Can I borrow yours?"

"You should pray to Suetake's parents' clans, so either Taira or Urabe. Hirano Shrine is nearby. The Urabe clan reveres the kami enshrined there, Hime Ōkami. She's sometimes referred to as the goddess of productivity."

"Sounds like something I'd worship," I said. "I'll pray to her."

Chapter 31

Those Sweet Rosebud Lips

On the ninth day of the ninth month of the lunar calendar, Seimei and I rode horses to Uji. It was a beautiful fall morning, the sky the deep blue of a dry autumn day. Trees sparkled with melting frost, and maple leaves tinged with red contrasted with green cedars along the way. A north wind brought a chill to the air but I didn't mind, thanks to the warmth of the white diviner's robes and hakama Seimei said we should all wear for the ritual.

The journey took about three hours on horseback. Bikki and Kenji-Ashiya walked, so their journey would take longer. Masako traveled by ox carriage, which meant she'd arrive last.

Uji lay south of the capital, which Seimei said was better for the ritual. "North is a yin direction," he explained. "South is yang. Today is auspicious due to the extra yang energy of double-nines, so I expect it to go well."

Before we left for Uji, but after Seimei had deemed us sufficiently purified, Masako and I had spent hours chatting, sharing everything important about our lives apart.

She promised she would keep writing to me. "These letters will continue to connect us."

She sat there smiling at me, excited about communicating across time. Her laughter pulled her dark eyes into crescents, and her long hair was tied back with a ribbon, except for side bangs cut to frame her cheekbones.

When I possessed her during my first trip, I rarely saw her face, and now I wanted to burn it into my memory.

While I was relieved to have survived a second visit and thrilled Masako would be the one to send me home, I dreaded returning to a world where my friend had not been alive for a millennium. I'd never be dead in her era, but she was already dead in mine.

She put her hand on the wide part of my sleeve. "Is your world so terrible you weep to return to it?"

My pre-grieving shouldn't be her burden. "It's a good thing no one is here to witness your improper behavior, touching a man like this," I teased. I grabbed her arm, partly as a joke, but also because I craved a physical connection. "Masako-"

She pulled away with an awkward smile, uncomfortable with touch. I wanted to give her a hug to last a thousand years, but she'd hate that and it would ruin our goodbye.

"It hasn't been the same, Masako, being in a separate body from you. But seeing you again, watching your skill grow, and knowing you're at home in Kamo—this trip has been the highlight of my life. I'm going to miss you all over again, but if I hadn't come back here, I'd have spent the rest of my life wondering if you survived the trip to Mount Ōe and if your powers ever returned."

Her eyes shone with unspilled tears. "Mina, you have your own powers now. I will never know how you will use them to save the kami's spaces in your world, but I am certain you will. You and Ken-Ji. He seems devoted to the kami, as well as to *you*." She tapped my knee with her fan for emphasis.

My cheeks grew warm. "Oh, I don't know. I'm so ordinary. Why would a guy like him be devoted to me?"

She laughed before realizing I wasn't joking. "*Ordinary*? Your spirit traveled through time twice, *ya wa*! You fought a demon. You gained spiritual power. Is that what *ordinary* means in your world?"

"You have a point," I conceded. "Where I come from, no one but Kenji could understand what I've been through. In your world, such events appear to be *ordinary*."

"Ah, Mi-Na," she sighed. "What miracle produced this friendship?"

"I won't even try to answer that question. Too many mysteries. Oh, that reminds me. I want to find your Chronicle in my world. The original, not the version you'll give Akichika. It's dated—it *will* be dated—about thirty years from now. Since we don't have it, we don't know if you dated it or someone else did. Can you tell me where you hid it?"

She laughed, her voice a little husky with emotion. "After you left, it hurt too much to think about you, so I haven't written it yet. My powers left me and I had no desire to write anything other than letters. Where do you want me to put it? You understand what will happen to the realm in the next thousand years. Fires, earthquakes, tsunamis—and war? Seimei said there will be horrifying wars."

"Yes, all of that and more, but Kyoto—I mean, Heian-Kyo—is never bombed. Sorry, that means it won't be destroyed in the worst of wars. So this area might be a good location. I'd ask you to put it with the letters we found in Uji, but they weren't in your script, so someone else copied them, maybe centuries later, for all I know."

She looked puzzled but promised to consider Uji as well.

Seimei and I arrived at the power spot first, so we allowed

the horses to eat whatever they could find while we waited for the others.

After Bikki, Kenji, and finally Masako appeared, we all followed Seimei through some woods to his little island in Kirihara Spring.

After washing ourselves in the numbingly cold water, Kenji and I sat on the damp dirt of the island. I put my hands over my heart, which thrummed like I was a conduit for a tremor from the earth. My body felt strong and light like it was made of high-tensile steel.

Seimei's outline cut the air around him as if he stood in front of a green screen. The scent of rotting leaves mingled with the fragrance of his incense. Kenji's slow breath rasped slightly in, out, in, out. Cold seeped through my hakama, and the coarse hemp of robes scratched against my skin.

Bikki and Masako started the incantation.

I emptied my mind of everything but their hypnotic singing, the sound of trickling water, the cold, damp sand beneath my robe, and the connection to the earth. Inhaling, exhaling, and counting in unison with Kenji. *Ichi, ni, san, shi,* exhale, *ichi, ni, san, shi,* inhale....

A sense of peace and well-being flooded my soul. The chanting grew muted as if some hand gradually turned down the volume. The ground pulled at me like a lead weight anchoring my body. I was strangely light-headed and pleasantly dizzy, and watched the world spin through closed eyes.

My spirit swung back and forth as if loosening its attachment, and then I drifted slowly away from my body, which remained firmly tethered to the cold ground.

Goodbye, Suetake. Thanks for hosting.

I hesitantly opened my eyes.

The world had dimmed as if storm clouds hid the sun. Bikki

and Masako stood at each end of the little island, waving their arms and moving their legs, but I no longer heard their chanting. Suetake and Ashiya sat between them, unmoving.

Seimei looked up sharply, then bowed his head in farewell.

A dense mist obscured my friends, leaving nothing visible but gray trees, gray land, and gray stream, distinguishable only by varying shades of one color. No gritty dirt under my bare feet, no cool breeze against my skin, no scent of decayed leaves.

The spirit world.

But where was Kenji?

The water ran silently around me, and the mountainside rose above. Kenji had memorized our location. *Island. Stream. Mountain. Done.* This was the right place.

So why wasn't I back in my body? Last time, Seimei had pushed me into 2019. Did Masako and Bikki not have enough power to do that? Did they get me here but no further?

I was halfway home already. Maybe I could finish the journey by adding my power to theirs.

Recalling the incantation Seimei had taught Masako and Bikki—fortunately, he'd let Kenji and I observe—I began the chant and the movements. As I reached outward, my fingertips touched something.

Startled, I pulled away.

Wait! That felt like a person. Grasping blindly through the mist, I touched it again. A hand? I grasped it and pulled with all my spirit-strength.

Kenji stood before me. The real Kenji, with broad shoulders and shoulder-length hair.

I sagged with relief. "Thank the kami! Where were you?"

He held on to my hand as if releasing it would send him back to the world we just left. "I rose from Ashiya's body but something stopped me before reaching the spirit world. I might never have made it if you hadn't grabbed me. I suppose I'd have become disembodied and remained in the past. So, thanks for that."

"Masako and Bikki weren't powerful enough by themselves. They needed at least one more power source, so I added mine. But how do we go from here to our bodies?"

"As you said, Mina, two are not enough. They need amplification. Let's join them."

Still holding hands, we slipped easily into the ritual, even though Masako and Bikki couldn't see or hear us. I saw them as two small, blurred figures moving in unison.

Seimei's outline was distinct, however, as if he were half in the spirit world himself. He looked concerned, as though he knew we were stuck.

Energy radiated out from me and sparked where my hand met Kenji's. Thin gray threads spun out and disappeared into the mist, mine tugging as it twisted with the others into one braid. The other incantations hummed through the cord, so even though I couldn't hear Masako through the air, I knew we sang in harmony.

So this is why we choose liminal spaces. To connect across the border of the spirit world.

With a last forceful push of our arms and the chime of a bell, a glowing spot in the gray mist shimmered blue-green. Kenji and I stepped through it, sending luminous ripples outward. A sound like distant thunder reverberated through our braid, which unwound and dissolved into the mist, which itself disappeared into sunlight, allowing me to see our bodies on the ground above Kirihara Spring.

"We're here!" Kenji stated the obvious, but his relief and joy were forgivable. "Ready?"

We prepared to throw ourselves forward.

"Wait!" I remembered how Masako had pulled me into her body last time. "We shouldn't hold hands as we enter our bodies."

We dropped our hands.

"Now!" *This time I need to land in the right body.*

I opened my eyes, blinking in the bright sunlight, feeling beads of sweat trickling down my hot cheeks.

Kenji sat across from me, both of us still in our original meditation position.

I collapsed backward onto the ground with equal parts relief and exhaustion.

He did the same, then raised a hand slowly as if it weighed much more than expected. "High five?"

I struggled to raise my own but managed to give him a weak clap.

We lay for a few minutes. My eyelids drifted down and I allowed them to close, but the bright sun interfered with taking a real nap. Putting my hand between the sun and my eyes, I noted the time on my watch. Not quite two o'clock. I mentally patted myself on the back. Returning so soon after we left meant we'd found the right opening.

"You were right, Ken. Back before dinner. Long before. Hungry, though." I was too tired for full sentences. Surely Kenji wouldn't mind me calling him Ken. His American high school buddies must have called him that.

"Me too, Mi."

I turned my head to see if he was being sarcastic, but he had his eyes closed and a contented smile on his face.

The ground was oddly comfortable. I'd done a fair amount of sleeping on the ground in Suetake's body. Maybe that made the difference.

My eyes closed again, but an ominous squeezing in my

calves foretold an oncoming cramp. *Time for a full-body stretch.* I extended my arms as far from my head as possible while pressing my toes in the opposite direction. *Weird. I feel taller.*

I sat up with a jerk, worried I'd landed in the wrong body after all. I looked myself over again and sighed with relief. Short legs, thin arms, small feet. Khaki shorts. Blue short-sleeved shirt. Yep, all mine.

Kenji too, same full lips and wide cheekbones. His eyes were still closed, so I allowed my gaze to linger. I leaned closer. And closer, driven by an urge I didn't understand.

Nariko's face flickered like an overlay on his.

Ahhh…Those sweet, rosebud lips.

I straightened abruptly. That was too weird.

"Kenji?"

"Eh?"

"Do you feel… I don't know. Different?"

He brushed his wavy hair out of his eyes in a Nariko-like gesture. "I'm tired."

"I'm tired too, but I feel stronger, like I could fight with a sword if I had to."

His gaze moved over me.

Blood moved into my cheeks at his examination, a very Mina reaction.

He winced and choked off a yelp.

"Am I that bad?" I said with an awkward laugh.

"I, uh, I saw something, sort of an image, or a memory or something, shimmering over your lower face. I hate to say it, but-"

I rubbed my chin. "What, is my face dirty?"

"I saw a beard."

"What? That's crazy."

We stared at each other, and it happened again. The flicker of Nariko's rosebud lips. *Beautiful.*

My fingers twitched, aching to hold a pen. No, a brush. And ink. And handmade paper. I longed to write a poem about those lips.

Another urge swept through me, and this time, I leaned into it. I bent over, put a hand on either side of his face, and kissed him.

He kissed back, his mouth as soft as I'd imagined, tasting faintly of cinnamon.

I jerked away with a gasp of pain as my lips began to burn like I'd pressed them against a live wire. "I'm sorry! I don't know what came over me. And why did that hurt?"

Kenji ran his hand over his lips. "Strange. Don't get me wrong—I'd love to do that again—but my lips feel singed like there were sparks. Real ones, not metaphorical ones."

"Me too!" I sat back on my heels in relief. "Something odd is happening, something that didn't happen last time. I think we've retained some traits from our hosts."

"I agree. I want to giggle."

I was feeling a bit giddy myself. "Let's move away from the power spot. That might be what caused the burning sensation. Anyway, I'm sure Suetake and Nariko's traits will disappear after a while. It might be like picking up an accent when you live in another region. Hopefully, you didn't inherit any of Ashiya's traits."

"I only possessed him for a few days, so that's not likely. Although if I brought back any of *his* power, I'd be cool with that." He must have seen my horrified expression. "Jōdan, Mina. It was a joke. I agree with you. Remember what I said about spiritual DNA? I don't know how else to describe it other than we each still have bits of our host embedded in our spirits. Perhaps Suetake retained some of yours."

"Poor Suetake. I hope I didn't ruin his life." I stood and brushed dirt and grass from my shorts, humming a little tune, my heart singing along with it. I'd possessed a man and fought a demon, and now I'd kissed Kenji, something I wanted to do since I met him on Mount Tsukuba two weeks ago. And he liked it.

No wonder I couldn't stop smiling as we walked a few steps away from the power spot.

A sudden thought jolted me out of euphoria. "Do you have any idea why Ashiya left a message for you? He must have left those messages *after* we put the binding spell on him. He didn't know who you were before that. Why would he want us there after what we did to him?"

His eyes glowed as he gazed down at me. "Let's talk about it later. No rush, right?"

"I guess so. But how will we find Seimei's Book? And how do we purify the kami's spaces?"

He pulled my scrunchie from my ponytail in an unexpectedly intimate gesture, and my hair cascaded onto my shoulders. "It was about to fall out," he said, pressing the tie into my palm, moving closer to me as he did so. "Why worry about that now? We traveled through the spirit world and back. We did amazing things together. Let's appreciate the moment." His voice had grown soft and his eyes more intense as he leaned in for a kiss.

An exhilarating, spark-free minute later, he drew back.

"We should leave now," I said, my heart pounding all over again. "I never got my ice cream."

"Ah, Mina?" Kenji murmured, pointing to the path leading to Uji Shrine.

"What?" I peered through the shadowed trail.

A red fox watched us with great interest, its tail twitching impatiently.

My breath caught. Obake. No real fox would sit there waiting for us. "Wait- *you* can see that?"

"Yes! Do you understand what this means? Should we follow it? See what it's going to show you next?"

If Kenji could also see nature spirits, what else could we do together? "Um, first of all, show *us* next. Second of all—yes, to both."

The fox headed uphill.

So did we.

Acknowledgments

I'm a fast writer and a slow editor. Feedback allows me to edit faster and makes me a better writer. Critiques from fellow historical fiction writers in the History Quill coaching program contributed quite a bit to this, so thanks to all of you and to The History Quill for connecting us.

My editor, Kahina Necaise, provided helpful and abundant input into both story and character development.

I am grateful to my Japan Writers Circle and First Tuesday Writers for encouragement and moral support along the journey of the past two years, and for keeping me accountable to get done what I'd said I'd do.

Members of the Tarpon Springs Writers and Authors Guild cheer each other on, celebrate each other's writing and publishing accomplishments, and provide advice and lessons learned, so thanks, y'all!

I found Dr. Noriko Tsunoda Reider's essays inspirational. I think of her as the "guru of Japanese demon lore" because most of what I found on the subject was either written by her or her work was cited in other academic essays on the subject. I re-read her work often, always finding something new to mull over. I highly recommend her work for anyone interested in Japanese folklore.

Thanks again to Dr. Aileen Gatten, an affiliate of the Center for Japanese Studies at the University of Michigan. She supplied me with so much information to improve my knowledge of Heian Japan (clothing, religion, architecture—so *much*!) for my first novel that I saved it all and referred to it often while writing and editing this novel. Thank you again, Aileen!

Many thanks to Heather Brooke for surveying nonbinary and transgender young people so I could better understand how to approach the gender reversal for Mina and Kenji. Big thanks to Xavier Rose and the other individuals who requested to not be named, for their honest and brave responses to my questions about gender identity. I took their advice to heart on the best way to approach Mina and Kenji's temporary possession of opposite-gender hosts.

My early readers provided feedback to make the story stronger: Amanda Mickelson, Erin Shanahan, Evelyn Presley, Anne Whitfield, and Kermit Whitfield; beta readers Lisa MacDonald, Evelyn Presley, Joyce Morgan, and Kermit Whitfield, and proofreaders Joyce Morgan and Kermit Whitfield.

I'm grateful to Anne for her insightful feedback, and to Riley for always liking my posts.

Kermit's support, encouragement, and suggestions allowed me to keep moving forward with this book when it would have been so easy to stop after the first one.

I wish I could thank Vee Shanahan in person for her encouragement and enthusiasm for my work, but she passed away in April 2024, so I can only tell *you*, dear reader, that she was the first and best fan an author could hope for, as mothers often are.

Historical Notes

When I began to outline the plot of this novel, I was quite sure that Murasaki Shikibu, the real-life writer of *The Tale of Genji*, would be a primary character, but the story took a different turn when I discovered some intriguing historical incidents that practically begged to be part of the plot. Read on if you wish to learn what they were.

Empress Sadako, who appeared in *Tangled Spirits*, died at twenty-four in the year 1001, apparently in childbirth, but possibly of heartbreak. Her younger sister, whose name and birth year are not recorded in history, but was known as Mikushigedono, died in 1002 while pregnant with Emperor Ichijō's child. It's thought she was around seventeen years old at the time, and the cause of her death is unknown. I call her Lady Miku for brevity.

A third sister, Motoko, consort to the Crown Prince (the future Emperor Sanjō) died in mysterious circumstances at the age of twenty-two in the year 1002 shortly after Miku's death.

Lord Akimitsu was rumored to have asked Ashiya Dōman to put a curse on Lord Michinaga. This curse was blamed for the deaths of two of Michinaga's daughters in the early 1020s. I decided that if Akimitsu paid Ashiya for a curse once, it wasn't much of a stretch to have him do it twice and link it to the mysterious deaths of Sadako's sisters.

Lord Akimitsu's daughter Genshi, another concubine of Emperor Ichijō, reportedly went into labor in 997 but did not deliver a baby. Whether it was a miscarriage or a false pregnancy is not clear, but it was noted in *A Tale of Flowering Fortunes* that this poor young woman was mocked for it. Genshi is also pronounced Motoko, but to avoid confusing her with Lady Motoko, I used the on-yomi pronunciation.

The legend of the demon of Mount Ōe (also known as Shuten Dōji) is one of Japan's most famous folktales. It's legend, not actual history, but many of the characters in it were historical figures. The original version of the tale takes place during Emperor Ichijō's reign, which was from 986 to 1011. In that version, Seimei divines that Shuten Dōji lives on Mount Ōe. Minamoto no Yorimitsu, also known as Raikō, was a real-life military commander. In the legend, he was the one who led the fight to save the young women from the demon. The four warriors who went with him are known in folklore as the Four Heavenly Kings. Suetake was one of those warriors.

I invented the Four Guardians of the Demon Gate—name, role, and powers. I also invented the story element of senzo (ancestor spirits) possessing the young women.

Onmyōji, or diviners, used their skills in astrology, calendar-making, and yin-yang rituals to determine auspicious and inauspicious directions, whether omens were good or bad, and to dispel bad luck. The most powerful of these onmyōji was Abe no Seimei, who lived from 921-1005 CE.

Ashiya Dōman is famous as a rival to Seimei, but no historical record of him seems to exist, so he might be more legend than historical.

I refer to Lord Michinaga as "the Regent" throughout. Michinaga held various Japanese titles, and not all of them were regent, but that is the role he performed in the period of this story, so that is the English language term that I used.

Miko were female shamans whose duties included summoning deities or spirits of the dead. They are not exorcists, although they might function as mediums. "Wandering miko" (*aruki miko*) would travel from village to village, and because blind girls were often sent out to train as miko, many wandering miko were blind, but it wasn't a job requirement. Masako's training by Seimei is unorthodox, as is her assignment at Kamo, because she didn't train to become a miko from a young age.

Female physicians existed in this era specifically to treat female members of the imperial family.

The imperial police force, called Kebiishi in Japanese, was established in the year 810, and over the next few decades became a true law enforcement organization with the power to investigate, try, and convict.

Noblewomen were taught to read and write so literacy rates, at least in this elite class, were extremely high compared to the rest of the world in this period.

It was not common to address someone by their given name, but that makes for difficult reading, so I use both given names and titles for frequently recurring characters while keeping to the convention of using only position or title for lesser characters.

The Yamato, the Ainu, and the Emishi are indigenous peoples of the Japanese archipelago. Over time the Yamato became the most dominant ethnicity in Japan, due in part to suppression and forced assimilation of other ethnicities over centuries. My Ainu character Bikki is fictional, but his bark cloak, his title Tusukur (shaman), and reference to the kamuy (kami) are not.

I use the terms yang and yin rather than the Japanese equivalents *on* and *myō* (as in onmyōji) because those words are more familiar to English-speaking readers.

As with *Tangled Spirits,* the fantasy elements of spirit possession, shikigami conjuring, and the summoning and exorcism of spirits are based on beliefs of the Heian era and Japanese folklore.

Time travel is not part of this belief system, but my readings on Shinto beliefs, shamanism, and spirit possession inspired the method of time travel.

Kenji's strange idea that cellular waves cause pollution of the kami's pure spaces is not an element of Shinto. It's Kenji's personal belief (in other words, it's fiction.)

Read on for a list of historical characters.

Several books and articles provided me with insight into this period of Japanese history. Please visit my website kvshanahan.com to see titles, descriptions, and links as well as blog posts that go into more detail about some of these interesting details of history. If you are interested in learning more about the traditional Japanese calendar, including era names, months, and time, you will find more information on my website.

Historical Characters

Names written with Chinese characters have several pronunciations. I chose to use the Japanese pronunciation (kun-yomi). In history and legends, names are often given using the pronunciation based on the Chinese origin of the word (on-yomi.) For example, Yorimitsu is also known as Raikō, and Motoko is also known as Genshi.

Akichika: Abe clan, Seimei's grandson.

Akiko (Empress Shōshi): Fujiwara clan, Michinaga's daughter. Empress from 1000 to 1011.

Akimitsu: Fujiwara clan, cousin to Michinaga. Attained various high-level government positions over time including Minister of the Right and Minister of the Left. His daughter Genshi (Motoko) was a concubine of Emperor Ichijō's. His son Shigeie was a Captain of the Palace Guards but became a monk while still a young man.

Ashiya (Ashiya Dōman): Not much factual information about him exists, but he appears in many folktales as a famous magician and counterpart to Seimei.

Ichijō: Emperor of Japan from 986-1011 CE.

Michinaga: Fujiwara clan, functioned in the role of regent between 996 and 1017, although his actual titles changed during that time.

Michitaka: Fujiwara clan, regent after his father Kaneie died, older brother to Michinaga.

Michizane: Sugawara clan, a 9th-century scholar, nobleman, and high-ranking government official who was unfairly demoted and exiled. His vengeful spirit (onryō) was blamed for any number of disasters and tragedies until the problem was solved by posthumously restoring his titles.

Miku (Mikushigedono): Fujiwara clan, Michitaka's daughter. Her real name is unknown, so she is referred to by her title, which means "chief officer of the imperial wardrobe." She took charge of her sister Sadako's three children after Sadako died, and it wasn't long before she became Emperor Ichijō's concubine, in part, it is thought, because she reminded him so much of Sadako.

Motoko (Genshi, also known as the Shigeisha): Fujiwara clan, Michitaka's daughter. Consort from 995 to 1002 to Crown Prince Iyasada (the future Emperor Sanjō.)

Murasaki Shikibu (Nobutaka's wife): Author of the Tale of Genji, considered to be the world's first full-length novel. Lady-in-waiting to Empress Akiko.

Nobuko (Imperial Princess Senshi): Saiō-dai (High Priestess) of the Kamo Shrine for 57 years, daughter of former Emperor Murakami, cousin to Emperor Ichijō, Fujiwara clan on her mother's side.

Sadako (Empress Teishi): Fujiwara clan, daughter of former regent Michitaka, empress from 990 to 1001.

Sei Shonagon: Kiyohara clan, birth name unknown, lady-in-waiting to Empress Sadako, author of *The Pillow Book*.

Seimei: Abe clan, Head of the Bureau of Computation, famous for his divination skills. Folktales have him conjuring shikigami and conducting other magic. He was well respected in his own time, and a shrine was built in his honor in 1007, just two years after he died. It's been rebuilt since, but you can visit it in Kyoto today.

Suetake: Urabe and Taira clans, a military commander who served Yorimitsu, and is known in legends as one of the Four Heavenly Kings who assisted Yorimitsu in defeating Shuten Dōji.

Yorimitsu (Raikō): Minamoto clan, a nobleman and warrior, a close advisor to Michinaga, and governor of several provinces. He was known for suppressing rebellions and bandits. In legend, he is the leader of the group of warriors who defeat Shuten Dōji.

Glossary

Ainu: Indigenous people of Japan, related to the earliest (Jōmon) people

Chinkon: A form of Shinto meditation

Da yo: You know! A phrase of emphasis

Dengaku: A form of traditional dance, originally as a prayer for a good rice harvest

Donmai: Slang made from the English words "I don't mind"

Emishi: Indigenous people of Japan, also called Ezo or Ebishi.

Furoshiki: A cloth used for wrapping

Gaijin: Foreigner

Gomen: Pardon me

Hai: Yes

Hachimaki: A Japanese headband

Hakama: Wide-legged trousers worn under robes by both women and men

Harae: Purification

Hora: Look!

Ichi. Ni. San: One. Two. Three

Ito: Thread or silk

Inari: The deity of rice and agriculture

Ippai: I'm full

Irasshaimase: Welcome, please come in

Jaaa: Well…

Jigoku: Buddhist version of hell

Jisa-boke: Jet lag, time difference lag

Jōdan: Joke

Kagura: A traditional religious dance to summon deities

Kakkoii: Handsome, cool

Kami: Divine spirits, deities

Kamuy: Ainu word for kami, meaning deities

Kanji: Chinese characters used in Japanese writing

Kawaii: Cute

Kimon: The name for the north-east direction, translated as "demon gate"

Kitsune: Fox, also a fox-spirit

Konnichi wa: Hello

Machiya: An old-style Kyoto townhouse

Michōdai: Platform or dais for sleeping and sitting

Miko: A female shaman

Mondai nai: No problem

Mono no aware: an awareness of the beauty in the impermanence of things

Musubi: The creating power of the kami; also a rice ball

O-kaeri: Welcome home

Obake: Animal spirits, shape-shifters

Ohayō: Good morning

Oishii: Delicious

Oni: An ogre-like demon that can transform into human shape

Onmyōdō: Yin-yang divination

Onmyōji: A yin-yang diviner

Onigiri: A type of rice ball, usually with a filling inside

Ossu: Slang for Ohayo gozaimasu, good morning, also means "what's up?"

San, Sama: Honorific (Mr., Mrs., Ms.)

Sentō: A traditional public bath

Senzo: Ancestor spirits who are one step from becoming kami

Shikigami: Spirits conjured to assist a shaman

Shirei: Spirits of the recently deceased

Sumimasen: I'm sorry, excuse me

Tadaima: I'm home!

Tatami: Straw mat covering for floors

Tsuki-mono: Possessing spirits of any kind

Tusu-kur: Ainu word for shaman

Uso-tsuki: Liar, fibber

Washi paper: A soft, handmade paper

Yamabushi: Wandering ascetics, also called "mountain monks"

Yamato: Yamato province, also the name for the dominant people of the region

Yappari: Sure thing!

Yatta: We/You/I did it! Yay!

Ya wa: Heian expression of emphasis

Yōkai: Spirits, ghosts, monsters

Yūrei: Ghost

Zabuton: A flat cushion made for sitting on the floor

About the Author

Kate Shanahan received her MA in Asian Studies from the University of Michigan, taught English in Sapporo, Japan, and enjoyed a long career with a Japanese company in Ohio as a human resources manager, ethics officer, and new model project leader, among other roles. *The Iron Palace* is her second novel.

If you enjoyed this book, please consider writing a review on your favorite book website. Reviews are helpful for both authors and readers, and even a sentence or two can make a big difference.

Please visit Kate's website at kvshanahan.com to sign up for email updates. You can also find a list of book club questions, blog posts about Japanese history and folklore, and a bibliography of resources that informed the research behind Kate's novels.

Also by Kate Shanahan

Tangled Spirits: A Novel

Journey to tenth-century Japan in this captivating tale of magic, imperial intrigue, and a friendship that spans a thousand years.

The ultimate study-abroad. When an American college student is thrown into the body of a tenth-century Japanese noblewoman, they must work together to navigate political and spiritual forces in a race against time.